The Kissing Garden
'A perfect escapist cocktail for summertime romantics'
Mail on Sunday

Love Song
'A perfect example of the new, darker romantic fiction . . . a true 24-carat love story'
Sunday Times

The Blue Note
'Will satisfy all of Bingham's fans'
Sunday Mirror

The Nightingale Sings
'A novel rich in dramatic surprises . . . will have you frantically turning the pages'
Daily Mail

To Hear a Nightingale
'A story to make you laugh and cry'
Woman

The Business
'A compulsive, intriguing and perceptive read'
Sunday Express

In Sunshine Or In Shadow
'Superbly written . . . A romantic novel that is romantic in the true sense of the word'
Daily Mail

Stardust
'A long, absorbing read, perfect for holidays'
Sunday Express

Nanny
'Charlotte Bingham's spellbinding saga is required reading'
Cosmopolitan

Grand Affair
'Extremely popular . . . her books sell and sell'
Daily Mail

Debutantes
'A big, wallowy, delicious read'
The Times

Also by Charlotte Bingham:
CORONET AMONG THE WEEDS
LUCINDA
CORONET AMONG THE GRASS
BELGRAVIA
COUNTRY LIFE
AT HOME
BY INVITATION
TO HEAR A NIGHTINGALE
THE BUSINESS
IN SUNSHINE OR IN SHADOW
STARDUST
NANNY
CHANGE OF HEART
DEBUTANTES
THE NIGHTINGALE SINGS
GRAND AFFAIR
LOVE SONG
THE KISSING GARDEN
THE LOVE KNOT
THE BLUE NOTE

Novels with Terence Brady:
VICTORIA
VICTORIA AND COMPANY
ROSE'S STORY
YES HONESTLY

Television Drama Series with Terence Brady:
TAKE THREE GIRLS
UPSTAIRS DOWNSTAIRS
THOMAS AND SARAH
NANNY
FOREVER GREEN

Television Comedy Series with Terence Brady:
NO HONESTLY
YES HONESTLY
PIG IN THE MIDDLE
OH MADELINE! (USA)
FATHER MATTHEW'S DAUGHTER

Television Plays with Terence Brady:
MAKING THE PLAY
SUCH A SMALL WORD
ONE OF THE FAMILY

Films with Terence Brady:
LOVE WITH A PERFECT STRANGER
MAGIC MOMENTS

Stage Plays with Terence Brady:
I WISH I WISH
THE SHELL SEEKERS
(adaptation from the novel by Rosamunde Pilcher)

THE SEASON

Charlotte Bingham

BANTAM BOOKS

LONDON · NEW YORK · TORONTO · SYDNEY · AUCKLAND

THE SEASON
A BANTAM BOOK: 0553 812750

Simultaneously published in Great Britain by Doubleday, a division of Transworld Publishers

PRINTING HISTORY
Doubleday edition published 2001
Bantam Books edition published 2001

1 3 5 7 9 10 8 6 4 2

Set in 11/13 pt Palatino
by Phoenix Typesetting, Ilkley, West Yorkshire

Bantam Books are published by Transworld Publishers,
61–63 Uxbridge Road, London W5 5SA,
a division of The Random House Group Ltd,
in Australia by Random House Australia (Pty) Ltd,
20 Alfred Street, Milsons Point, Sydney, NSW 2061, Australia,
in New Zealand by Random House New Zealand Ltd,
18 Poland Road, Glenfield, Auckland 10, New Zealand
and in South Africa by Random House (Pty) Ltd,
Endulini, 5a Jubilee Road, Parktown 2193, South Africa.

Printed and bound in Great Britain by
Cox & Wyman Ltd, Reading, Berkshire

SPRING 1913

'The world's great age begins anew,
The golden years return . . .'

Shelley

Prologue

There was so much to be done now that their daughters had turned seventeen, but rich though the two women might be, they knew that there was only one place to meet, and that was London, although journeying from their country estates, even in the new age of the motor car, was still long and tiresome, and involved many stops. Of course they were both aware that this new London was not the London of their youth, which meant that as the portmanteaux were dusted down by their footmen, and the family trustees diplomatically warned of the expenses that might lie ahead, they individually sighed and looked back to that gaily giddy time now remembered with such affection – the year of their own first London Season.

That had been the real time, naturally; now could not be the same. They had already resigned themselves to that idea – that the present was not, could never be, as brilliant and as beautiful as the past. There was too much trouble abroad, too many disasters that seemed to threaten, too much talk of liberation everywhere – not to mention the hideous new fashion of the 'V-neck' or 'pneumonia blouse', as the small opening to the front of ladies' tops had been recently dubbed. Doctors and vicars might declaim against it, but, as the ladies well knew, if women liked a fashion, it stayed.

No, it was sad, but true, that unlike the past the present had a habit of being full of tedious troubles. Happily of course there was still a king on the throne – a more sober individual than their beloved King Edward, but still a king and still Emperor of India, even if he did lack his father's love of wine, women and food. For despite the scandals of his many mistresses, King Edward VII had been a very popular fellow. The reason for this was that he had really enjoyed being king, and his people had known it. And he had been popular not just in England, but also in France, forging a new and cordial relationship with the French, who dearly loved a man who appreciated the good things of this world.

Not that any of this really mattered to the two ladies advancing on the capital in their great, old-fashioned carriages with their husbands' coats of arms emblazoned on the side. Their thoughts were not with politics, but with their young. Mrs Pankhurst and her suffragettes might have followers being force-fed in prisons all over the land, but these ladies had other more pressing problems on their minds. All they were concerned with was that their children were of an age to be married, and it was up to their mothers to find them suitable partners.

Never an easy task at the best of times, nowadays the battles fought in ballrooms had become more intense than ever, for the fact was that blue-blooded Englishmen everywhere had not dreamed of English roses for some long while, but of American heiresses;

and while their girls might be from rich backgrounds, while they might have blood as blue as any ducal heir, they could never begin to compete with the mother of an heiress prepared to lavish thousands on a wardrobe from the House of Worth, priceless jewels and stables full of thoroughbred horses.

And yet, it had to be done, for without a husband a young girl was still merely a cast-off from last year's fashions, to be hidden away in some country house somewhere, an anxious sort of figure, always a little too willing to help with the young, or fill in for governesses, the desperate expression in her sad eyes a reminder of her failure to attract a husband.

So there was one thing of which these mothers were quite certain, whatever Mrs Pankhurst and the suffragettes might have to say on the matter: a lonely life lived between the servants and the drawing room was not going to be their daughters' fate. However difficult or plain, their daughters had to find husbands, and soon, before the girls' bloom wore off, before they reached twenty-one, unmarried and unwanted, or worse, they gathered for themselves a 'reputation', or caused a scandal.

PART ONE

The Agreement

It would be too good to be true if they had found that she was dead, but the truth was that she was no more dead than they were. In fact, she was very much alive, and what was worse, ready to do battle.

'Dear heavens, I had thought that the Countess – well, that she would be at least retired to respectability by now, particularly after that dreadful incident when that Yorkshire fellow who sponsored dear May through her Season – what was his name, Forrester – when he so humiliated her. You would have thought she would have called it curtains after that, really you would.'

Emily O'Connor stared at Portia Childhays. They had both only, but only, just arrived in London. As they tasted the deliciously fresh ices set before them, they smiled appreciatively at each other from under their new modish hats, knowing that each was experiencing that particular contentment that comes from having been intimate friends when they were young and skittish.

They also had the satisfaction of knowing that

as the ices grew lower in the tall, crystal glasses, the covers at the London addresses at which they were staying were even now being thrown off the old-fashioned furniture, and the ancestors and the mirrors in the ballrooms and the saloons were being dusted furiously by excited servants. The new London Season was opening, battle was about to commence.

'Oh, I don't think that women like the Countess of Evesham ever retire, do they, Emily? Besides, London would not be the same without them, would it? Indeed not. As a matter of fact, it is so long since I was in London, dearest,' Portia exclaimed, 'I had almost thought never to see it, or indeed her, again.'

'It's a wonder that you're here at all, considering your adventuring, Lady Childhays, ma'am,' Emily teased, waving her long-handled, Italianate spoon with gay Irish abandon at her old friend. 'How long did your voyage in the *Belvedere* take you, and to where? Tell me, dearest, do, for I know it will make hunting with the Galway Blazers sound terribly tame. I must hear. Was the China Sea rougher than the Channel, and did you find a new kind of dog like Lady Brassey and her famous black pugs?'

'We took somewhat the same route as Lady Brassey on our voyage, but we made better time for the good reason that *Belvedere III* is as fast as any vessel built, and in any sea, I may tell you.' Portia stopped, shaking her head suddenly. 'But at any rate, enough of that. My days of travel are now over, and we must face the future.'

Discretion forbade Emily to remark on what she already knew, namely that the long and at times perilous voyage in the *Belvedere III* had been undertaken by the present Lady Childhays with the sole purpose of recovering from the loss of her husband some two years previously.

'Yes, dearest, of course. Even so, you must allow your old friend to be impressed by your intrepid undertaking.'

Portia shook her head again. 'Don't be impressed, Emily, please, dearest. Believe me, there is only one reason for travel and discomfort, for cutting oneself off from everything that one knows and loves, and that is sorrow. There were times when, selfishly, as the *Belvedere* seemed to become like a matchbox bobbing on those wild waves, when the sea grew so high above us that it might as well have been the Himalayas and we just pygmies standing beneath it – there were times when had I not had my family with me I might have just slipped into the sea and ended it all, such was my unhappiness.'

Emily was silent, herself now feeling not so much selfish as positively ashamed, for the truth was that she had been glad to come to London from Ireland, at last, for the Season, leaving her husband, Rory, and their Irish estates behind her. Indeed, it had been more than a pleasure – it had been a positive relief.

'What a blessing you have always been such a superb sailor, my dear Portia. Your brilliance at the helm must have finally worked the miracle. How you must have thanked God for such a gift as you have with a boat. Myself I hate the sea, but I envy you your skill.'

'It was the saving of me, Emily, it truly was.'

There was a short silence and then Portia remarked, a little over-brightly, 'Well, dearest, to change the subject to something more cheerful. Tell me, how is your dear Mr O'Connor?'

She dabbed delicately at her small, perfectly shaped mouth and fixed her large grey eyes on Emily's green ones with her usual direct interest. She had never met her friend's husband, but knew him to have been a stalwart in the swerving fortunes of Emily's family, stepping in to buy Glendarvan House and their estates in Ireland just when the family were themselves threatened with eviction, something more usual among tenants than landlords.

'My dear, Mr O'Connor is at present as well as can be expected considering his hunting accident. Apart from that inconvenience, I believe he is, yes, in the best of health,' Emily replied briskly. 'He has, I am happy to say, over the last years improved our estates beyond measure, but unhappily he is involving himself with country house politics. He has joined the Celtic Club, much encouraged by our American friends across the ocean, and is busy inciting madness, as if there is not enough abroad already.'

'Oh, so the two of you are presently not in agreement?'

'No, we are not, for it seems that despite my family's having lived four hundred years in Ireland I am not now Irish. It seems that he is *native* Irish, and that I am not! Such balderdash, such tosh, dearest, you must agree!'

Portia stared at her friend, her head slightly on one side. Emily had always been hot-headed, as she would be, given her russet-coloured hair, but now that this same hair was silky white – a beautiful contrast to her green eyes as it happened – it was somehow surprising to hear her still so full of vim and brimming over with the same sense of indignation.

'Still the same old Lady Angry Heart,' Portia murmured affectionately. 'Lord Childhays and myself could hardly agree about anything other than that the sky was blue, or that it was raining, but we always enjoyed ourselves so much in the disagreeing, if you understand me?'

'No doubt of it, dearest,' Emily concurred, nodding her head rapidly so that her fashionably low-set hat appeared to be agreeing with Portia even more violently than its owner. 'Husband and wife need never be of the same opinion. Isn't that why I am over here with my dearest Edith, rather than over there with him, draped around some damp old pianoforte listening to his Irish friends caterwauling on about the Celtic twilight, while the candles gutter and the wind whistles and all the horses in the stables go unshod?'

Emily's eyes glittered with mockery and she raised her gloved hands to shoulder level and spread them out dramatically, just missing a busy waiter bustling past her as she mimicked her husband's Celtic friends.

'Oooh, but Lady Emily, surely you must believe in the Celtic past, *shur-allee*? Ooh, but you must know, Lady Emily, we are reviving the true history of *Eirann* – we shall all soon be speaking in the Gaelic at dinner, mark my words. Lah-di-dah, lah-di-dah, I say to them. You and your mincing theatricals. What good will that do when it comes to feeding all those poor little Irish babies under the Spanish Arch in Galway city? Humph, and humph again, says I!' Emily squinted humorously at Portia as the feathers at the front of her head nodded in complete agreement with their wearer.

There was a short silence during which Portia reflected on what Emily had said, and diplomatically allowed time for her friend to calm down. Any more imitations of the Celtic Revivalists and, Portia felt, Mr Gunter's famous strawberry ices, being carried past them so hectically by the busy waiters, would undoubtedly be in jeopardy.

'And now to our young,' she stated, thinking that since Emily was in England she might feel it appropriate to leave her indignation on the other side of the Irish Sea. 'You have your darling Edith to launch on Society, and I have my dearest Phyllis. I suppose they must meet?'

Emily's feet, well concealed under the table, and shod in new and expensive shoes, nevertheless shifted a little at this. Her daughter Edith must of course meet Portia's daughter Phyllis. They had not known each other at all while growing up, Edith being confined for her whole childhood to the Glendarvan estates in the West of Ireland, and Phyllis being brought up between her Childhays' homes in Sussex, London, Leicestershire and Italy.

'I dare say they will take to each other?'

Emily looked at Portia, doubt in her eyes, her heart sinking. If Portia had found Emily wild in her youth what would she, if you please, find Edith? Edith was the wildest of the wild, being half O'Connor and half Persse, and wholly devilish. There was no other word for it, she was unacceptably wild.

'I am sure they will take to each other,' Portia agreed, while her heart too sank as she thought of her elder daughter, Phyllis. Such a hoyden. Not at all restrained, wild and mischievous, and, when not wild or mischievous, *odd* – all characteristics for which Portia's family, the Tradescants, were, alas, somewhat famously known.

'Dearest.' Emily leaned over the table and touched Portia's arm with her gloved hand. 'I have to confess that I am not at all confident of my Edith's having the necessary social graces to take her through a London Season – Ireland, you know. We are more informal, our butler rarely out of his outdoor clothes. I really think she will have to be consigned to the Lodge and Lady Devenish for at least a month before she can be taken to even an At Home.'

Portia heaved an inward sigh of relief. Thank heavens for Emily O'Connor's honesty, for her kindness, for her ability to say what was what.

'Do you know, Emily, ever since you snatched at the bridle of my bolting horse, all those years ago in Rotten Row, I have thanked God for your friendship. The truth is . . .' Portia paused and sighed. 'The truth is I returned from my voyage on *Belvedere III* to discover my Phyllis gone – how can I say – from wayward to – well – feral is the only way I can put it. She bicycles around our estate in a pair of those dreadful old bicycling bloomers that fast young women made so fashionable some years ago. You can imagine what that does to the gardeners. I should *never* have travelled as I did. But she would not come with me on *Belvedere III*, as her younger sister and brothers did. *They* came along for the adventure, but *she*, being the eldest, elected to stay at home with her dog and her governess. I should *never* have gone! I say that to myself every night after I have said my prayers. My only excuse for going was that my grief was inconsolable. In desperation, while I was still on the high seas I had her sent, with my Aunt Tattie, to darling Childie's Italian estate near Florence, but she was back soon enough, unchanged by Art, unchanged in every way. Only Aunt Tattie was transformed, and is now become a Papist, would you believe?' Portia laughed suddenly at the irony, only to find it was Emily's turn to sigh.

'Ah me, my dearest friend, and here was I hoping that Phyllis would be a good influence on my Edith. I was sure you would, without any doubt, have produced a daughter of quiet good manners and composure.' There was a pause, as their ices were delicately masticated, and then: '*Feral*, you say?'

'Quite, quite feral.'

'Oh, my dear, that is the very word to describe Edith. She will suck on straws and whistle in front of the servants as soon as beat the band. As to her courtesy, it is non-existent. She reminds me of . . . how shall I put it? She reminds me of the scandalous Lady Caroline Lamb of Lord Byron fame, with a little touch of Queen Boadicea.'

'Then it is to Lady Devenish that they must both go, and at once.'

Emily nodded in agreement with her old friend's pronouncement, but remembering how she herself had made Lady Devenish's life a misery she felt her heart sink.

Portia half rose, such was her eagerness to go back to her London house and put into motion their plan, and then she remembered.

'But May. We have not spoken of our darling May.'

Emily too sank back in her seat. 'Nor we have, Portia dearest. And she must be on both our minds, since she has only sons, and no daughters.'

They both nodded. A silence followed. May was now the Duchess of Wokingham. A former chorus girl and protégée of Herbert Forrester, a rich Yorkshireman, she was as good as she was beautiful, and having been brought up in a convent had more common sense than both of them put together.

'Have you seen May since the birth of her sons?'

Emily shook her head. She had seen no-one except the followers of her husband's hunt, since only the most intrepid of country house guests ever hot-footed it to Ireland, and then only for the sport.

'I have seen her, although, I must admit, infrequently of late. She has been the delight of her husband and his family.' Portia smiled wryly. 'Edward, my bachelor brother, is continually holding up May and her household as being everything that an English family should be.'

'But your son is as fine as anyone's, surely?'

'Yes, Tristram is a good boy. There at least I have comfort. But my younger girl, Arabella . . . oh, Emily, she is such a handful, and behind her little Blakey, so dreamy and already so eccentric, so very Tradescant, so like his Uncle Lampard.'

Emily nodded, but a little impatiently. 'We must stop wallowing in self-pity, or we will not last the week, let alone the Season. It is most important, dearest, that we do not find ourselves, how shall I say – *up against each other* in the coming months?'

Portia stared blankly at Emily for a second.

'I am saying, dearest,' Emily touched her friend on the arm with one gloved hand, 'May has a handsome son, a future duke, and likely to be the catch of the Season. Which of *our* daughters will take his eye?'

Portia coloured slightly. Emily had always been more direct than herself, but to state their positions quite so clearly was, to Portia at least, embarrassing.

After a few seconds she smiled. 'Poor George Cordrey, I almost feel sorry for him. The handsome son of a duke, he really has no chance against all these girls, does he?'

'Not a hope.'

'The Countess of Evesham will have laid her plans already, as we said at the start. She will be hoping that her American gel will catch the young Marquis's eye. Have you heard whether or not the Countess's American protégée is a *beauty*?'

'Dearest . . .' Emily paused, before pronouncing, 'It is a rule of society that every woman worth several millions *must* be a beauty.'

'Ah yes, of course.'

'First things first. The girls must meet Lady Devenish, and each other of course, as we did.'

Inwardly both women sighed. If only Phyllis and Edith would behave themselves. If only Lady Devenish could convert them to civilisation. If only they would be, as their mothers now remembered themselves, and so clearly, two perfect cygnets just waiting to turn into a perfect pair of graceful swans.

'So, it is done. We are agreed.' Portia looked solemnly across at Emily before summoning her maid to pay the bill. 'Either Phyllis must capture the Marquis, or Edith. Whatever happens he must not be snaffled by the Countess for her protégée. But we must be realistic, dearest. The American gels have quite captured Society over the last twenty years. And to be fair they *are* beautiful. The Duchess of Marlborough . . . all of them who have succeeded are beautiful.'

'We must just trust to Lady Devenish to work a miracle on Phyllis and Edith.'

They both smiled, but despite the smiles, and despite any agreement that they might make, neither of them felt hopeful that either Phyllis or Edith would have a single chance of capturing a future duke.

'And yet,' Emily said, laughing, suddenly knowing how they were both thinking, 'if Lady Devenish could work something of a miracle with me, Portia dearest, surely she could do the same with our two?'

'You were beautiful,' Portia stated loyally, both of them knowing that Emily had hardly entered a ballroom before every young man within a mile was scrambling to write his name in her dance card.

'And you were both pretty and personable. Your Childie fell in love with you at first sight. I remember you writing to tell me that was what he told you. That he saw you at Medlar House, at your Aunt Augustine's At Home, and knew at once that you were for him.'

'And that despite Aunt Tattie's wearing her favourite old hat with the dead bird on the front!'

Portia started to laugh and there was a small pause as both their eyes softened, remembering. Portia's husband Lord Childhays had been one of those people who had the habit of *softening* people just by his presence, and before he had even uttered a word.

'Well, now, we must put our best feet forward, into the future. No more looking back to the golden days.'

Their eyes met and for a second Emily could appreciate the determination in her friend's eyes, knowing that what she saw in them was only a reflection of how she herself was feeling. Between them, they must ensure that one of their daughters married May's son, if only to thwart the Countess of Evesham.

Past Participants

The subject of so much conversation between Emily O'Connor and Portia Childhays, Daisy stared at her face in her silver-backed hand mirror, and sighed, for her, quite deeply. Just for a tiny second she had a perfectly horrid feeling that she was not just feeling but looking her age. She said as much to Jenkins when the maid brought her ladyship her usual cup of early morning chocolate in a small eighteenth-century cup decorated with ribbons of turquoise and tiny flowers – flowers so small that it was only when a person truly stared into them, as Daisy was intent on doing, that they revealed themselves to be made up of as many as six different colours.

Daisy closed her eyes momentarily. It was too awful to think of all those poor people ruining their eyes to paint those flowers, and then, doubtless, not getting paid a single little *sou* for what they had so painstakingly accomplished. But then she remembered that since the china cup was foreign the people concerned would not have been English, so she stopped concerning herself with them.

She was sure she was looking older. She put her silver mirror back on the side table beside her bed, and called to her maid.

'Jenkins!'

Jenkins was busy stoking the fire that must always burn in my lady's bedroom. Daisy could see the maid through the fine old silk curtains that draped her bed at each corner. She had not turned at being called, so Daisy threw a book at her back. Well, not exactly at her back, to the side of her. At which noise Jenkins at last turned.

'My lady wants me,' she stated.

'Yes, Jenkins, of course, uvverwise why on earth should I haff frown a book at you, for heaven's sake? Of *course* I want you. People such as myself, Jenkins, do not go round frowing books at people for no good reason, believe me. It is just not done.'

'And what is it my lady wants?'

'Come here, Jenkins. No, *here*! That's right. Now, tell me, and you must be truthful, do I look older van I should, Jenkins? Now, do I?'

Jenkins narrowed her eyes at her mistress.

'My lady asked me this yesterday—'

'Well of course I asked you vis yesterday, Jenkins, and now I am asking you vis again. Do I look older van I should, given that everyone says I am looking so young? They have said it so often of late that I now fink I really must be looking older, or they would not keep saying how young I look.'

'As old as your tongue and a little bit older than your teeth, my lady.'

'Jenkins, vis is not a time for levity and awkwardness. You know how very much I dislike people who will insist on going round saying fings that uvver people have said. Vis is a time for calming me at an anxious moment. A time for calming her ladyship, not exciting her, Jenkins.'

'Yes, my lady.'

Jenkins moved away, continuing her routines, as she always did, with her usual deliberate calm, ignoring her mistress.

As Daisy watched the bath tub in front of the fire at the other end of the room being filled with perfectly warmed water she stared once more at Jenkins's back. She had always disliked Jenkins, who had been her maid for well over – well, a long, long time at any rate, and she knew, instinctively, that Jenkins disliked her, but that they were stuck with each other. There was no other expression for it, vulgar though it might be. No-one could dress Daisy's hair the way that Jenkins could dress Daisy's hair, no-one could lay out her clothes so perfectly, no-one else, worst of all, even knew exactly where Daisy's jewellery was kept – quite apart from when to put it out. No-one else would handle jewels the way that Daisy liked to have her jewels handled, with care, with reverence, with the sort of awe that Daisy expected of a maid. And yet, for all this, Daisy was perfectly aware of exactly why Jenkins stayed with her, and it was certainly not for love.

'Jenkins . . .'

'Yes, my lady?' Jenkins leaned over the bed,

smelling slightly of smoke from the fire and slightly of very strong tea, and her now whiskery face stared into Daisy's still remarkably unlined and beautiful visage.

'You have not answered my question, Jenkins,' Daisy demanded as if Jenkins was a doctor with a doubt about her prognosis. 'Well? What do you say in answer to my question, please?'

'My lady looks younger than ever,' Jenkins pronounced. 'My lady looks as young as my lady looked last Season. There are no new lines,' she added emphatically.

'There *are* some new lines, Jenkins, but you are not prepared to see them, vat is what I think. There *is* one new line here, underneath the curls at the top of my forehead. I know there is.'

'No, my lady, that is just where the hair stops.'

Jenkins turned away, satisfied, as Daisy took up her cup of chocolate once more.

Daisy realised that Jenkins was lying, of course, but nevertheless it was reassuring. She knew that if there was some frightful change in her face Jenkins would, in the end, take great satisfaction in telling Daisy about it. Jenkins had her nasty side, of which Daisy was only too aware, and for which she was oddly grateful. Half an inch on my lady's waist and my lady knew all about it from Jenkins. Still, she must be thankful, for in many ways it was Jenkins's being so very beastly that kept Daisy up to her mark.

'So, vat is vat. And vat being so, Jenkins, you may now lead me to my bath.'

The bath was laid out in the old-fashioned way in front of the bedroom fire. Daisy still insisted on this, and Jenkins too. They were neither of them prepared to change in any way at all. The fashion for installing marble bathrooms all over London and country houses was not one of which either of them could approve, for, apart from anything else, it would mean that Jenkins would have less work with which to fill her day, and that would never do.

Daisy stepped into her bath, sat down, and watched with some interest, as she always did, the perfectly warmed water rise to exactly the right height around her body. It was annoying, but it was a truth, Jenkins was, like Daisy, a perfectionist. She liked everything to be quite, quite perfect, as Daisy did. It was probably the reason why she was still in service. She would never have found perfection in marriage, certainly not to a member of her own class, and she would never have known perfection in motherhood. No, Daisy knew, she had really done Jenkins a great service. Although she was also aware that this was not the only reason why the woman was still happy to be Daisy's maid.

'Jenkins.'

Daisy lifted up her leg for Jenkins to soap.

'Jenkins, you know my samovar?'

'Yes, my lady.'

'I have told Ogilvy, my lawyer, that it is to be yours. I have made a – what is it called now?'

'A codicil, my lady?'

Inside herself Daisy purred with the perfection

of the moment. Jenkins's whiskery face turning to her, Jenkins's eyes narrowed with the knowledge of what was to come to her when Daisy ascended (she would not go in any other way, naturally) to heaven.

'Oh, how clever you are, Jenkins. Vat is right. A *codicil*. Vat is what I have made. So you are not only to get ve gold Russian box, ve Sèvres coffee cups and ve large ruby ring, but also, Jenkins, ve *samovar*. Will vat make you happy, Jenkins, do you fink? Will vat make you happy?'

'Oh yes, my lady. Most happy. And more than that, it means I will have something to remember you by.'

'How *very* touching, Jenkins. Very touching indeed, and what is more, when you retire, which I hope is not so soon, you are to have ve use of one of ve cottages on ve estate for your lifetime. Vat will suit you, won't it Jenkins?'

'Yes, my lady.'

Jenkins sponged off the second leg and hurried over to the wooden towel horse to fetch a large coroneted bath towel. As she did so, Daisy leaned back in the steam, her hair dampening. Nowadays she almost dreaded the moment when she was laced into her corset, when her hair was tonged back into its curly style, and she had to step into her high-heeled shoes and once more become 'Daisy Lanford', as she was still known, despite being the Countess of Evesham. She had to keep going, she knew that. And yet, sometimes, just occasionally, it was hard.

She allowed herself a few seconds' indulgence in self-pity, and then she quickly turned her thoughts to her newest of new protégées, Sarah Hartley Lambert, the heiress from New York, whose ambitious mother had set her eyes on her daughter's acquiring a titled husband at the end of a short London Season.

She would have to get rid of the mother, as soon as was conceivably possible, or poor Miss Hartley Lambert would have no chance at all. But how to remove the mother when she was so fantastically rich? The fantastically rich were very difficult to influence, as Daisy knew to her cost. Even the old king, *her* dearest Kingy, could have his funny ways on a bad day, suddenly becoming stubborn over the silliest things.

Daisy's mind began to work towards this end, so deeply and so fast that by the time Jenkins was urging her to breathe in, more and more and more, until Daisy's waist returned to a painful twenty-five inches (so ghastly after one was used to what had seemed to be going to be the forever and eternal *eighteens*) she was able to all but ignore the pain of it, so intent was she on making a plan of campaign.

Perhaps it was because she herself had not had a daughter that she was able to take such an overt and particular interest in the launching of other people's daughters upon the London Season, or perhaps it gave her a more substantial reason to follow the usual routines that Society demanded. Or perhaps, nowadays, to be perfectly candid, she just liked to be *paid* to introduce johnny-come-latelys to the right people. It made the fact that they were often so unreasonably dull more bearable.

Not that she was not still quite rich, but no-one was ever rich *enough*, particularly when it came to the fripperies of life. She still dearly loved to expend money on Dresden figures and new parasols and other nonsense, and the knowledge that some debutante's entrée had paid for these, that she was, in effect, getting them free, made their purchase a great deal more enjoyable.

And of course, more than that, she felt a duty to keep up the old style, as it had been when the old king was alive. There was so much that was deplorable nowadays, so much that put you off life, like that silly suffragette killing herself by throwing herself under the present King's horse at the Derby – such a nonsensical way of going on when all she had to be was charming. If only Mrs Pankhurst had come to Daisy, the whole Women's Movement would have been over in a day. They would have got the vote in a tiny little minute, and in a much more enjoyable fashion too. But there, some women must like to suffer, otherwise they would not go on as they did. Daisy herself was intent on trying to teach the younger generation how to get their own way with style.

As Jenkins slipped the first of her cambric lace underpinnings over her head, Daisy realised that she was ready for the fray. She knew it as Jenkins pulled up her stockings and clipped the tops smartly into their rubber suspenders. She knew it as the first part of her dress was being prepared for her, as the second part was presented to her, as each and every garment was coming towards her, held out on sticks. Oh yes, of a sudden, Daisy knew that, undoubtedly, she was ready for another London Season.

Unlike Daisy, Sarah Hartley Lambert was not beautiful. Sarah knew this. She had to know it; after all, it was, alas, quite obvious. Her mother had told her many, many times when she was growing up that she was not beautiful, and that she was too tall. She knew this to be a fact, in the same way that the British Empire was a fact, and she had never thought to doubt her mother's word about either her beauty or her height.

To make up for this unfortunate fact she had therefore decided, many years before, to *pretend* that she was beautiful. By pretending she had hoped to bring about what nature had not bequeathed to her at birth.

She could at least try to walk as a beauty should walk, she could at least try to sing as a beauty might sing, she could at least try to waltz as a beauty might waltz, and, more important, amuse as well as any married woman might seek to amuse. This had been her ambition, and to date she had worked as hard as any European girl to achieve it.

What Sarah knew she could never acquire was the English girl's general air of faded acceptance. Being an American she had not been squashed from an early age, she had not been told that as a female she 'simply did not count'. She was Sarah Hartley Lambert from New York, and knew that being an only daughter and heiress counted for a great deal.

She stared at herself in the long mirror. London had come as a shock to her after Paris. Paris was so beautiful, all the boulevards smart and clean, their private hotel so very well run, and Mr Worth's salon, although filled with the newest of the new as far as couture fashion was concerned, still able to extend the proper reverential awe towards Sarah and her mother.

After Paris and its elegance, London seemed so small somehow, everything so near to everything else, and everyone so serious. They did not laugh or glitter as the people she had met in France had laughed, seeming somehow to glint with a kind of steely intelligence and warm appreciation of everything that was beautiful and stylish. The English accepted everything, whether it was money, the trappings of grandeur, motor cars, or horses to pull your carriage, in a calm manner, and if they did appreciate them as well as accept them, it was, alas, in silence.

And oh the terrifying nature of an English silence!

Sarah had, only the day before, been presented to her chaperon for the Season, the famous Countess of Evesham, an old but still stunningly beautiful woman. Brilliantly elegant, she had looked Sarah up and down, in silence, as if she was an object not a person. And when Sarah had walked across to shake her hand, as she would do in New York, or Paris, the Countess had not offered her hand but stared at Sarah, in silence, and from her, in that same silence, to Sarah's mother, before eventually saying in a clipped tone, 'I fink we should see *dear* Miss Hartley Lambert make us a courtesy, do you not agree, Mrs Hartley Lambert? I fink we must, if you do not mind? I fink a courtesy is what will be expected to a countess.'

At which Sarah's mother, who did not frighten easily, had said in a strangled voice, 'Curtsy, dear, for the Countess, you know, *curtsy*.'

Of course Sarah had curtsied, quite elegantly as a matter of fact, while blushing furiously at the realisation that she had, in a matter of seconds, already put not just one foot but several feet wrong. After the curtsy the Countess had inspected her.

She had actually walked round her one way, reversed, and walked back round her again, and in the heavy silence Sarah had heard her high-heeled shoes on the polished wooden floors making the least little sound, as if her ladyship had learned to walk permanently on the balls of her feet and never, ever allowed her heels to make an unbecoming noise.

'She is too tall, Mrs Hartley Lambert. You at least must know vis already, surely?'

Poor Mama, she had turned horribly pale at that, so much so that Sarah had quite feared for her. Mama was always so dearly vulnerable when it came to any mention of her only daughter's great height.

'Her poor late papa was also tall.'

'Englishmen do not, as a rule, enjoy gels as tall as vis one is. They fink tall gels make them feel, and indeed look, small. Englishmen do not like feeling and looking small. And there is anuvver fing. So many of the aristocracy have only married each uvver over the last few hundred years with the result that they have stayed really quite small. So I am very afraid vat Miss Hartley er Lambert will be just too tall for many of our small aristocrats.'

Daisy had stared across accusingly at Mrs Hartley Lambert after this pronouncement, as if the poor woman, with all her millions, could have perhaps done something about Sarah's height earlier in her development, and having patently failed must now take the entire blame if the girl did not have her dance card filled up and could not be found partners who came up to her shoulder, let alone matched her great height.

'But Countess, I mean, we have been to Paris, we have bought all our dresses for Ascot, for everything, debutante's white ball gowns for Sarah; all those things that you told us we might be going to need, we have bought them all.'

'Yes, but I did not know ven what I know now, namely vat Miss Hartley Lambert was going to prove to be such a very tall gel. You did not let me know vis fact, and now I do know it . . .' Daisy gave an imperceptible shrug of her shoulders. 'Now I do know vis, I don't really understand what I am expected to do, Mrs Hartley Lambert.'

Mrs Hartley Lambert's already paling complexion had threatened to turn quite as white as the frothing lace on the front of her blouse.

'She cannot of course be allowed to carry on as previous 'Merican gels have carried on, Mrs Hartley Lambert. We want no *Daisy Miller* type jokes about our protégée in ve newspapers and fashionable journals, now, do we?' Both Hartley Lamberts having looked blank at this reference to a heroine of a fashionable novel Daisy added, 'Well never mind what I mean, but we don't, believe me. But d'you see, if we are not very careful it might take several seasons to find the right match, and that might be tarsome, would you not say, Mrs Hartley Lambert, quite tarsome? I mean, if a gel takes too long to become engaged I always fink it is a little like a racehorse not selling straight away. She can acquire a reputation long before she reaches the racecourse – I mean the altar. There does not have to be anything wrong with her either, vat is my point. She, like ve horse that does not sell, can be simply a victim of rumour, people supposing that there is something wrong when there just is not. Just some sort of setback, however small, and there we are, saddled with what everyone around town assumes is some sort of damaged goods. It is an unfortunate fact. I have seen it time and time again. Vat is why we, in England, like to shift our debutantes, Mrs Hartley Lambert, to save them from innuendo. It is by far ve best thing, believe me.'

Mrs Hartley Lambert found it just a little

confusing to follow the Countess, yet she was quite determined, nevertheless, that she must do so. The Countess and she did after all share a common language, although 'common' was not a word that either of them would have wished to use. They *had* to find a way to understand each other. Mrs Hartley Lambert was determined on it. And now of course the very mention of 'damaged goods' had put Sarah's mother into a really quite dreadful fluff. After all, 'damaged goods' meant the same either side of the Atlantic.

She reddened heartily, and she fanned herself, forcibly, but still she could find nothing to say. Of a sudden the very idea that her darling Sarah might have innuendo surrounding her name was so awful that Mrs Hartley Lambert's corsets felt too tight, and the room a great deal too hot.

'If I may say so, Mrs Hartley Lambert,' Daisy continued, ruthlessly, 'I suggest Miss Hartley Lambert will really benefit from some weeks, perhaps just a fortnight, spent with a relative of my husband's, a Lady Devenish. She will, as it were, mould Sarah into ve right silhouette, make her less *outrée*, less artlessly 'Merican, without of course taking away her character. Give her some polish, if you understand me? Sarah has charm, natural charm, but now she needs patina. Lady Devenish will give her patina, although of course she cannot, alas, make her any shorter.'

'By all means, by all means then, give her a patina, or two patinas, or three, whatever is necessary. But what a pity that Lady Devenish will not be able to help with the height. Are there no tall Englishmen? In America we always thought that Englishmen were tall. They have a reputation for tallness in America. Are you quite sure she could not suggest some sort of shorter shoe perhaps?'

Daisy had shaken her head sadly. 'No, alas. Had Sarah of course had an *English* nanny of the old school, as I did, she would *never* have grown so tall. In England our nannies like to starve the female children who are in their care on the nursery floor.'

'Never say so!'

'Oh yes, Mrs Hartley Lambert. Every week they are measured against their brothers, and if, most unfortunately, they are found to be growing at the same rate as their brothers the nannies at once put gin into their milk. Gin is a known cure for height, do you see? And quite effective I believe. My own nanny kept me to just the right height, and so I haff much to be grateful to her for, as you may imagine.'

Sarah would never forget the silence that had followed this statement. And whereas she knew that her mama had not been able to follow words such as '*outrée*' she certainly would have understood 'gin' as well as the next mother. Indeed, at the mere mention of it she had gasped, quite loudly, as a matter of fact.

'Gin? Your girls are fed gin as babies by their *nurses*?'

'Oh, yes,' the Countess had agreed affably, seating herself as suddenly and gracefully as a floating feather on a nearby sofa and inviting Sarah to do the same by tapping lightly on a cushion nearby. 'Oh yes, the nannies in England have always relied on gin, Mrs Hartley Lambert! And a little whiff of gas to put us to *sleepies*. Oh, there is no stopping them with their old fashioned remedies. And I must say, by and large, it has helped to keep our gels admirably small – and therefore admirably marriageable. The boys of course are *quite* different. The nannies know that they must be fed up, so that they can join the army and be tall enough to be shot at for the sake of family pride.'

At this poor Sarah, while managing, somehow, to keep her eyes demurely downcast, had been forced to bite her lip to keep the bubble of laughter which threatened to burst out of her under control.

'My, my, I must confess myself a little shocked.'

'Yes, well you would be, Mrs Hartley Lambert, and I dare say you would far rather be back in New York all tidied up and cosy, with your daughter beautifully and safely married to some scion of a great English house, which is why we must be quite direct with each other at this moment.'

'But this Lady Devenish, she will not I hope attempt to feed my Sarah gin, will she?'

'Bless you, no! My gracious heavens, far too late for that. No, this should have been done when your Sarah was a tiny little baby. Vat is what I am trying to *tell* you, Mrs Hartley Lambert.'

'In which case I am really rather glad she was raised in America, Countess.'

'No, exactly, quite. No. My husband's relative is all that she should be, I must tell you. I must tell you vat she will not even allow a punch bowl in the dining room, so now you know exactly what I mean about Lady Devenish's propriety, *n'est-ce pas*?'

'Yes, of course.'

Mrs Hartley Lambert did at least know that punch was a *fast* drink given to girls by young men who wanted them to behave as it was often rumoured the maids did on their days off, so it followed that if this Lady Devenish would not hold with a punch bowl in her house then she must, when all was said and done, be on the side of the angels after all.

'So I will see to it that Lady Devenish is immediately instructed to take Miss Hartley Lambert as soon as possible.'

'Which is?'

'Tomorrow. But remember Lady Devenish can do everything about all things, except, alas, the poor gel's height.'

And so tomorrow had arrived and found Sarah as she was now, waiting for her mother's motor car to arrive, and for her luggage boxes to be put up behind. For the chauffeur and the footman to fuss around and for mother and daughter to settle back, rugs on their knees, and trust that they would not have to change to the car following on behind before they reached their destination. For although there were motor cars all over London,

Sarah's mother, in common with all her generation, would not trust herself to only one, feeling as Queen Victoria apparently had, that the motor car was unreliable at best, and noisy and dirty at worst.

Reaching Ascot from London did not really require a stop, but stop they did for some considerable time while chauffeurs and footmen washed the wheels of the motor cars and polished them off with rags and dusters, much as they might have washed down the legs of their horses a few years before.

'We must begin as we mean to go on, dear. That is, impressively,' Mrs Hartley Lambert told her daughter, as they sipped tea from picnic-set silver mugs as the chauffeurs busied themselves.

'Yes, Mama, of course.'

Sarah was very, very sure that this was not going to be necessary, for common sense told her, if not her mama, that if this relation of the Countess of Evesham took charge of girls it would not be in return for nothing, which meant that she was being paid, which meant in turn that really they did not need to impress her. But it was useless to tell Mama this.

Sarah knew that her darling mother was not as sure of herself as she pretended, despite being such a very rich woman and having all the trappings that accompanied great wealth. Faced with such people as the Countess of Evesham, she seemed to diminish, showing herself to be what she really was, just a very nice woman who wanted the best for her daughter. Seeing her trying to follow sophisticated English talk had made Sarah want to take her outside the drawing room door and hug her and say, *'Come on, Mama, let's just go home to 'Merica, as the Countess calls it, and curl up with a good book!'*

Lady Devenish's house was just outside Ascot, conveniently opposite the racecourse and modestly fashionable. She had, over the past years, had any number of successes with debutantes, and although there were some who nowadays made fun of her custom of making the girls in her charge laugh in time with the piano, so they could sally forth into Society with a 'tuneful laugh' as the saying goes, none of the husbands or relatives, nor even the servants of those same now married girls would laugh at her methods. For if there was one thing that betrayed a woman's background more than another it was, as everyone would agree, a vulgar laugh. A girl should laugh beautifully, tunefully, and without reminding anyone of a horse or a donkey neighing in the stable.

This afternoon she was reassuringly dressed in palest dove grey. This was particularly appealing to Mrs Hartley Lambert for ever since her interview with the Countess of Evesham the poor woman had become contused with confusions, some of them so bad that her maid had to bring her a tisane in the middle of the night, and rub her back with camphor cloths while burning lavender wafted over her bed.

But all these worries took a back seat once she had seen the taste, elegance and near Quaker-like appearance of the decorative Lady Devenish. Grey silk with an embroidered pelisse in the same colour, palest blue beneath, and pearls of course. It was all very old-fashioned, but so reassuring, so beautifully reassuring that all fears of perhaps leaving her darling Sarah with a gorgon who would either gas her or fill her water glass surreptitiously with gin fled for ever.

'You will take care of yourself, dear, will you not?'

Sarah hugged her mama, quite tightly. 'Of course.'

'And if there is anything of which you cannot approve or feel that I would not, you must send to me at once, you promise?'

Sarah nodded, determined to be brave. They had never been parted for more than a day or so before. Her relationship with her mother had always been loving and close.

'Lady Devenish is waiting for me, Mama. I must go.'

Sarah stepped up once more into the carriage and kissed her mama again. She was not to worry, and Sarah in her turn would try to do everything that Lady Devenish asked of her and more. By the end of the fortnight 'you will find me a changed and better person, you'll see'.

'You could never be better, dear. Such is my love for you, you could never please me more than you do. You have always been my delight.'

Sarah stepped down, the chauffeur touched his cap and the motor car moved off, turning in the short carriage drive with some difficulty before accelerating smartly off into the main highway, and so back to London.

'Come, my dear Miss Hartley Lambert, and meet the other two. They are just arrived. I am sure you will all get along famously.'

For some reason that Sarah now could not imagine, she had thought to have Lady Devenish and her instructions to herself, and so it was with some sense of nervous expectancy mixed with dread that she realised she was to share her deportment classes, her laughing practice, her Court courtesy rehearsals and her lessons at the piano with other girls.

'Miss de Nugent, may I introduce Miss Hartley Lambert to you, and Miss Hartley Lambert, may I introduce Miss O'Connor? I had the honour of teaching both their mothers their Court courtesies, and indeed Miss O'Connor's mother was one of my protégées during her first and only Season in London. Alas, she had to curtail her stay in England and return to Ireland where she happily married Mr O'Connor and has helped to run his splendid Irish estates. And Phyllis de Nugent's mother, Lady Childhays, is an old acquaintance through her aunt, Miss Tatiana Tradescant.'

Lady Devenish sighed with some satisfaction, as well she might. Despite Lloyd George's being shot at by maddened suffragettes, despite all the predictions of the newspapers, upper class girls would always need to be married, and there would therefore, she was sure, always be a need for a Season, and hence a need for Lady Devenish and her niceties.

'So, now we are all together and all intent on improvement, *n'est-ce pas*? You will grow to appreciate during your fortnight with me that all the people we talk about are known to each other. We are very tightly knit. The patrician class in England has been meeting each other during the social Season for hundreds of years. The custom has come down through the centuries, enabling members of the aristocracy, old and new, to get to know each other, in really rather a magical way, in the ballroom, or on the racecourse, safely and beautifully.'

Lady Devenish paused.

'In fact, now I come to think of it, you could say that the aristocracy is surrounded by a magic circle. It cannot be seen, but it is there. It surrounds its members with the light of its magic. Sometimes the magic circle includes new people, and sometimes it rejects old ones, people who go too far, but by and large the circle remains around the same families and the same names, giving stability to the countryside and a sense of continuity to the nation.'

All during Lady Devenish's speech Edith, Phyllis and Sarah were surreptitiously examining each other. None of them was in the least bit interested in the magic circle that Lady Devenish was so fervently advocating, and of course there were good reasons for this.

First of all Edith and Phyllis both came from aristocratic backgrounds, and there is no-one less interested in their heritage, or more desirous of throwing it over, than a young person from a patrician background. And Sarah was already far too aware of *not* being a member of the magic circle, and so naturally any mention of it filled her with a sort of dull fear. For Sarah to hear Lady Devenish talk was like knowing about beautiful music that everyone else could hear, but she could not because it was being played in the next room.

'You are very, very up to the minute, are you not?' Edith announced, staring at Sarah's blouse with its tiny suggestion of a vee at the top. Just enough to suggest fashion without being too daring, Mrs Hartley Lambert had thought.

'Yes, I know,' Sarah agreed, suddenly feeling even more awkward under the intent gaze of her two fellow pupils. 'Mama took me to Paris first, you know. We Americans do so love Paris.'

'Paris, my dear!'

Phyllis raised her eyes to heaven and made a little movement with her hand as if it was a fan. 'Paris for one's clothes, how too, too, don'tcher know? And to think that we poor little English gels have only Chester, or Bath, or London for our clothes, whereas you were taken to Paris!'

'I do admit,' Sarah agreed, reddening, 'that I must look a little too fashionable. That is not right in England before you are married, is it?'

'It is not right in Ireland either,' Edith told her, tartly, and she turned and bossed her eyes at Phyllis.

'I have tried to tell mama, but you know how it is with mamas. They do not really want to listen to their daughters, do they?'

'Our mothers would not buy us clothes like yours if they were commanded by the King himself,' Phyllis told the now thoroughly discomfited Sarah. 'They would not want us to stand out, do you see? It is not done in England, to stand out. Just not done.'

'Yes, but even so we shall all be able to be friends, do you not think?' Sarah asked them a little ingenuously. 'I mean, you will not be put off me by my darling mama's taste, will you?'

'Of course not.' Phyllis looked so innocent that Sarah knew her to be lying, and Edith looked of a sudden so disinterested that Sarah realised at once that any thought of friendship was going to be an impossibility.

'It is silly for girls such as ourselves, I always think, to be rivals. After all, Society, going to balls, attending Ascot, is not life, is it?' Sarah continued, knowing all the time, her heart sinking, that she was sounding more and more silly and desperate, and worse, lacking in any kind of pride.

'Gracious, of course not. We will all be such friends, just you wait and see.'

Phyllis and Edith looked at each other, and then at Sarah, and laughed. Sarah's heart sank to an even greater depth as she realised that, although she too was laughing, they were laughing not with her but at her, so much so that her first day at the Lodge with Lady Devenish was one that Sarah would always remember with horror for the rest of her life. Indeed if she was ill, or out of sorts, she would only have to think back to that particular time for any passing discomfort to fade in significance in comparison.

Edith was the ringleader, of course. She had mischievous green eyes and dark hair, and although she had an elegant figure she walked everywhere, as Lady Devenish remarked at once, as if she was kicking aside an over-long hunting skirt.

Edith had only to look at Phyllis while Sarah was practising laughing to scales played by Lady Devenish for them both to start laughing too, but it was not the kind of pretty or elegant laughter which Lady Devenish was aiming to teach them all. Theirs was the suppressed giggling of the schoolroom, yet when Sarah, red-faced and uncertain, on hearing the noise they were making, turned from the piano, it was only to discover that they had faces as solemn as if they had just listened to an organ recital in church.

Sarah sensed that although Edith was roundly Irish in her tones, and already giving Lady Devenish twin fits, it was Phyllis of whom she should be most afraid. She was decidedly what was known in American as a 'goer'. She did not know her limitations either. She would pull a face to make Edith laugh at just the moment when Lady Devenish turned from sinking into an amazing and difficult Court courtesy and so her guide and mentor would catch sight of her mocking expression, although she always carried on as if she had not, of course.

None of them shared bedrooms or even bathrooms, for the Lodge was many-bedroomed and had endless corridors down which could be found yet more washrooms, and yet every time Sarah passed one of their doors they would be together, laughing and talking.

Sarah longed to join in, but if she made some remark, or began a conversation, they would either turn their backs or pretend not to hear that she had spoken. It was shameless and it was wretched-making, but Sarah knew herself to be made of as stern a stuff as they, and so she determined to brazen it out. She would out-laugh, out-sing, out-dance and out-ride both of them. It was the only possible way to escape her increasingly desperate situation.

Lady Devenish did not of course supervise the riding lessons, except at a distance. They were conducted by an old ex-cavalry officer, who dearly loved to begin every lesson with 'my dear young ladies in horse', while Lady Devenish, merely chaperoning them, would dart in and out of the school every now and then supervising the manner in which they should mount and dismount, receive assistance from a gentleman, tuck their riding skirts, and set their hats and whips.

Sarah often thought during that fortnight that it would all have been lovely had the other two been prepared to be friends, but they were not, and so, after the first few days, when she realised that they were determined to ostracise her, Sarah became equally determined to ignore them. She was not prepared to crawl to them for their friendship, far from it. In fact, she now realised that she was quite determined to outwit them at their own game.

And so it transpired that as Edith wobbled down into her Court courtesy, Sarah would catch Lady Devenish's eye and sigh, and shrug her shoulders, very slightly, and Lady Devenish, perhaps guessing what was up, would also sigh and make Edith try again, which she would do, with equally poor results.

Phyllis on the other hand was undoubtedly musical. There was no point in trying to upset her piano playing or her ability to laugh in tune with Lady Devenish's scales, for musically Phyllis reigned supreme. This was only as it should be, for, as Lady Devenish later told Sarah, Phyllis being (on her mother's side) a Tradescant, it would be a miracle had she been tone deaf.

'The Tradescants used to give whole operas in the gardens of their house in summer and in the great barn in winter, but of course Phyllis is not wholly Tradescant. She is half de Nugent, and although Lord Childhays, her father, is no longer with us, I fear that she has inherited a great deal of the de Nugent *hauteur*. It is very difficult for her. Two such fascinating parents, and yet she herself is not, and not likely to be, a peerless example of English maidenhood.'

'But surely that is why she is with you, Lady Devenish? Why we are all with you?'

'Oh yes, indeed, Miss Hartley Lambert, but I cannot do anything about her familial characteristics. Her poor mother, Lady Childhays, did warn me, of course, when she came here to talk to me, as did Miss O'Connor's mother. Both were of the opinion that they had produced daughters who were bound to bring disgrace on their families in some way or another during the Season. They had few hopes of them, I am afraid. Whereas your own mother is all too proud of you.'

Sarah and Lady Devenish were seated by the fire. It was not particularly late in the evening, but the other two girls had gone to bed early, as they did most evenings, to laugh at the day's doings, and most especially, Sarah felt sure, at herself and Lady Devenish, whom they had already nicknamed 'Lady Devilish'.

'I feel so ashamed for their mothers, and yet I must struggle on. Did you notice, Miss Hartley Lambert, how Edith whistled today as she was mounting her hack, and Phyllis kept winking and smiling at the stables lads like some common little hoyden? I mean, after nearly a week here, still whistling as if she was a stable boy, and not a young lady about to make her court appearance before her king. And you know the King! And Queen Mary! They are sticklers. Utter, utter sticklers. Not that the darling late king was not a stickler too, in his own little way, but he liked to enjoy himself in between, and King George does not like to enjoy himself so much. As is often the case with a second son, King George is not at all the same as his father. More serious, wouldn't you say?'

Sarah did not know the King, but she did not like to say so, so she said instead, 'Would you say then, Lady Devenish, that His Majesty is very exacting?'

'Exacting? His Majesty is famed for noticing the wrong placing of just a medal. To be reprimanded by His Majesty is to be courting social disaster, *always*. One reprimand and a young lady can find herself without any prospects whatsoever of a good match. It is far worse than even being seen without one's maid, or some such. By the way, your maid is very well trained, my dear. I do compliment you. It is very difficult in England to find a maid as well trained as yours.'

'Corkie? How kind of you to say so, Lady Devenish. She started off as my nursemaid, and now she is my maid. She is as devoted as anyone would wish, perhaps more so,' Sarah confessed, smiling. 'Dear Corkie, I could not do without her if I tried, not for an instant.'

'I tell you what may help you unquestionably, if my maid were to instruct your maid, it would assist you in every way, Miss Hartley Lambert. You would be surprised how often a good maid with a sound knowledge can haul you out of potential trouble. Many is the time when Buckler has remembered what I had long ago forgotten, or might have forgotten. In the morning, I will tell her to pay particular attention to your Corkie. That at least I can do. What I cannot do is to change the attitudes of Miss O'Connor and Miss de Nugent towards you, Miss Hartley Lambert. It is, alas, just not possible.'

'Will your Buckler help the other maids too?'

'If the gels do not ask me personally, I am afraid not. That is how it is with certain people. And so if they wonder why they are struggling, or being buffeted too hard by circumstances during the Season, they will only have themselves to thank.'

Sarah held out her hand impulsively, and placed it on Lady Devenish's arm.

'Please, allow Buckler to instruct their maids too. Imagine if they have not the right gloves, or if their maid left their fans behind as the carriages were leaving for Court. There are a thousand ways that this could happen, and a thousand ways they might be found wanting.'

Lady Devenish nodded briskly.

'Very well.' She stopped by the door as Sarah curtsied to her. 'You are a very nice girl, Miss Hartley Lambert. I have high hopes for you. You are generous and kind, and thoughtful of others. You deserve a great deal. You certainly do not deserve less than I intend you should get.' She paused. 'There is no question that we must work together on the other two. My mind has been made up by your generosity of spirit as much as anything else. After all,' she went on, thinking back to the past, 'Lady Emily, the mother of Miss O'Connor, was just such a handful as she is.' She closed the door suddenly and came back into the room. 'She once, if you please, slid down the banisters of this house.'

'I cannot believe this . . .'

'She did, she slid down the banisters, and it was some time before she stopped whistling and talking Irish too, I do remember that. Well, well, there is hope yet. We finally became the very best of friends and today you could not find a greater lady, for all that she is Irish.'

'I cannot believe what you have just told me.'

'It happens to be true. Petticoats flying, down the banisters she slid – the servants, you can imagine! But, aside from that, I have a notion that we may conquer these two. What we shall do is unite, Miss Hartley Lambert. We shall unite together against them. And that will be at least a step towards making order out of some kind of chaos.'

Sarah nodded, smiling. 'I shall do whatever you wish, Lady Devenish, you have my word on it.'

Lady Devenish opened the door again, and then stopped. 'Oh dear.'

Sarah looked across at her questioningly.

'Yes, my dear, *oh dear*. Either the maids were listening to our conversation, or they were.'

It seemed that it had been Edith and Phyllis listening in on their conversation, for the following morning they appeared at their first lesson in the drawing room with grimly determined expressions, as if they had decided to be a team and really concentrate on Lady Devenish's lessons rather than lark about as they had been previously intent on doing.

'Very well, now that we are gathered here, in our little circle, I will ask you all to imagine that I am the King and Queen. This is your last chance to rehearse before me, and I will not tolerate anything less than perfection. We have, after all, rehearsed and rehearsed, with really rather varying results, I am sorry to say, so now imagine please that you are being brought in behind your presenters to make your obeisance to Their Majesties. One, two, three.'

Lady Devenish clapped her hands together lightly and nodded at Edith to begin. She never usually opened her class in such a cold manner, but perhaps there was now, on her part, an intention to shock the two recalcitrant young ladies in her charge into some kind of immediate discipline.

Edith, blushing furiously, for she had paid not the slightest heed to her previous lessons, stepped forward and, to the sound of the regular clapping of Lady Devenish's hands, advanced towards her.

'One, two, three, one, two, three. And down we go, Miss O'Connor, right down, right down – and up, one, two, three, we come, and back we go.'

Edith trod back, her hand held out with her imaginary fan and train, but she did not step away from Her Imaginary Majesty to the sound of Lady Devenish's hand beating out the time, she stepped back to the sound of a long and tuneful peal of Lady Devenish's genuine and uninvited laughter.

'Oh dear, oh dear, Miss O'Connor, what amusement you are going to provide for everyone at the Court. So amusing. You will become famous overnight, however temporary your fame – for believe me fame based on scandal is extraordinarily fleeting, although the persons involved rarely see it as that.'

Edith, now roundly red, and feeling that even her toes might be blushing, looked questioningly towards the King's representative.

'What amusement in particular am I providing, Lady Devenish?'

Lady Devenish's grey eyes were steely with enjoyment.

'You have your dress caught up, Miss O'Connor. Your underpinnings are showing.'

Edith turned and looked behind, and even though she knew that this was only make-believe she found that she was almost fainting under the embarrassment of her own belief in the possibility of such a moment.

'I have no such thing!' She turned back to Lady Devenish, the expression on her face changing to fury.

'Oh but you have, Miss O'Connor, for have I not been telling you *all week* that you are to mind your train and the back of your dress? And have you not been ignoring me all these days? And have I not known that you were ignoring me? And am I not now enjoying your discomfiture as much as you have been enjoying mine? You, Miss O'Connor, are a dolt. And because you are a dolt, you have just joined the ranks of the most famous failures at Court. Congratulations. Now – Miss de Nugent, step forward please.'

Smiling, composed, and thoroughly at ease with the situation Lady Devenish clapped her hands once more, and quite smartly too.

At this Phyllis stepped forward, trying not to show that she was just a little cowed by Edith's experience. To the sound of the brisk clapping of Lady Devenish's hands she began her routine. One, two, three, one, two, three, and down into the full Court courtesy, and slowly up, and back, one, two, three, one, two, three. She had listened so little, practised so little, that she wobbled down and seconds later wobbled up again.

Again Lady Devenish burst into peals of laughter, laughter that was, if anything, more hearty than before, at which Phyllis promptly stamped her foot.

'What? What is it *this* time?' she demanded, fury written all over her face, her blue eyes coldly staring at Lady Devenish. 'This is all just make-believe, and your laughter foolish.'

Lady Devenish snatched a fan from the top of the piano. It was a beautiful ivory fan, large, and strongly made, painted with wonderful scenes of Court life in previous centuries. She smacked her own hand with it, and there was no doubt in anyone's mind for whom the fan might really be intended, had not Lady Devenish been at heart both gentle and kind.

'So this is make-believe is it, Miss de Nugent? I doubt it very much. Do you not know why I was laughing? I am vastly afraid that you do not. I was laughing because you stepped back without waiting for the Court pages to adjust your train, you stepped back before even turning to see if the little wretches had done their duties, so what in *real* life would you have done if you conducted yourself in such a manner? *You would have tripped,* Miss de Nugent! That is what you would have done. You would have fallen in front of Their Majesties and the whole court, thus doubtless affording them their first laugh of the day. No, that is not make-believe, Miss de Nugent, that is the truth. That is the truth of what will happen to you if you do not do as you are told by me at your Court lessons. You will be the laughing stock of the Season. But, perhaps, that is what you wish, Miss de Nugent?'

Phyllis went to say something, but found, as she inevitably must, that there was nothing *to* say, and so stayed silent.

'Oh dear, Miss de Nugent, nothing more to add to your mockery of the make-believe, as you call it, that we are going through here? Nothing more to say?'

'No, Lady Devenish.'

'I am sorry, did I hear you make your apology?'

There was a long silence.

'I am waiting, Miss de Nugent.'

Yet another silence, during which Lady

Devenish fixed her eyes in assumed boredom on something outside the floor-length windows at the other end of her drawing room.

'I am sorry, Lady Devenish.'

'And for what are you sorry, Miss de Nugent?'

'For making fun and larking about.'

'Better, but not good.' She stared from Edith to Phyllis and back again. 'You, both, to me, are the "know betters",' she told them, smiling, for it was surely her turn to smile? 'Every now and then we do have a "know better" here, and sometimes they leave me just that – no better. And sometimes, always, as a matter of fact, the "know betters" come to me much later in the Season, utterly destroyed, because they have made solecism after social solecism. But by then of course there is nothing I can do, believe me, nothing. It is too *late*. Sometimes they have made themselves a laughing stock. Sometimes the "know betters" are just so foolish that they destroy their reputations within seconds of their coming out, and there is nothing to be done but to return to the Shires, or Scotland, or Ireland, and become old maids. That is their lot, and more than likely always will be. Or they might pick up an elderly husband, or a widower, much later in life, in which case they become glorified housekeepers with nothing to reward their efforts except a roof over their heads. That is the fate of the "know betters".'

Lady Devenish's colour was now heightened in a quite pretty way, for the truth was that she was really rather enjoying herself.

'So, there it is. You two, Miss de Nugent and Miss O'Connor, you will remain standing – both of you, and in Court position, eyes down, holding your ostrich-plume fans, while I take Miss Hartley Lambert through her courtesy. You will now note, please, that an American gel is already able to cope with train and fan, remembers to pause and check on the pages before stepping away from Their Majesties, and can laugh to the sound of my scales on the piano, and mount and dismount gracefully. She walks without whistling and looking as if she was wearing riding boots instead of shoes, and altogether conducts herself in a better manner, after only one week, than you two are capable of at this moment. Miss Hartley Lambert, step forward, please.'

In high dudgeon the 'know betters' watched from under their eyelashes as Sarah stepped forward and executed the perfect Court courtesy, sinking into the most elegant obeisance, remembering to look for the pages, and then, having finished that lesson, turned to the piano and played and laughed exactly in tune with each note before rising and pirouetting as gracefully as any dove.

Lady Devenish watched her, thrilling to her grace and elegance. No matter that she was tall, she was truly marvellous to watch, and took the eye in everything that she did.

But that night as she wished her good night she could see in poor Sarah's eyes that the 'know betters', although they might be newly concentrating on the finesses that they now realised were going to be necessary to them if they were going to get through their first London Season without a hitch, were still not able to like or embrace Sarah in their company in any way at all.

It was hurtful and puzzling, but it was, nevertheless, a fact.

As Lady Devenish turned out her bedside light she thought that both Edith O'Connor and Phyllis de Nugent were hard and cruel, for it seemed to her that it must be because Sarah was American that they so delighted in ignoring her at every turn. And then it came to her, in the darkness, and she quickly put on her bedside light again, and sat up and leaned back against her mountain of cushions and pillows.

Of course! It was nothing to do with poor Sarah Hartley Lambert's being American, or an heiress, but everything to do with Sarah's patroness for the Season's being Daisy. The two girls must surely have taken sides with their mothers against the Countess's protégée. The past had come galloping into the present, as it nearly always did, in some form or another.

'Oh, how foolish I am,' Lady Devenish told the photograph of her late husband on her bedside table. 'How very, very foolish. And really, if I am so foolish I should make this my very, very last Season. Imagine not thinking of this before. Imagine not realising what a clash it was bound to be – the history being such, Daisy having been so triumphantly embarrassed by their dear friend

May Wokingham's Mr Forrester. Oh dear, oh dear, is it not always the way! The past will not lie down, but insists on popping up when not wanted or sent for.'

She put out her light again, and sank down against her pillows once more. What was history was history, and really, no-one could be blamed for taking arms against Daisy and the sea of troubles that she constantly created. She was, and always would be, a typhoon, a volcano waiting to erupt. Like a gun in St James's Park, Daisy needed only a touch, and she would explode into terrible, noisy life.

Every Season it had been the same. Always some scandal to be hidden, some new devious plan to be carried out.

'The past is the past, is the past,' Lady Devenish murmured to herself into her top pillow as she hugged its soft beribboned lawn surface to her face, 'but the past, as we all know, will *never* go away.'

She thought she really ought to warn Sarah Hartley Lambert against the Countess and her doings, but then, knowing that Daisy, since the fall in land values and other misfortunes, would be sure to be being paid, and quite substantially, by the Hartley Lamberts for entrées and other such favours, she realised that to do so would be to create an impossible situation.

Finally, she sighed, and putting on her bedside light again she took her husband's picture from the table and spoke to it once more.

'I am afraid, darling, this is going to be our last Season. It is not that I am too old, but they are all too young. The motor car is everywhere, people are dancing dances that you would never believe and no-one is content with just going to balls, they have to go to *costume* balls. They cannot be just decorous and charming any more, and frankly I am too tired to go on. I would look ridiculous in a hobble skirt, and I like going about in a carriage and horses, not a motor car, so I am going to take us both off to a villa in Florence where we can be quite quiet, and friends will visit. It will be so much better to be ageing in a gentle way. No more debutantes, no more Seasons, from now on the most exciting thing to which I wish to look forward is a glass of wine in the shade, and you beside me in my heart.'

After which she switched off the light yet again and fell into that particularly contented sleep which is brought about by coming to terms with both the past and the present and welding them together to make a settled picture of the future.

The Name of the Month

May was her name, and May was the month when she knew that she must, most reluctantly, obey her husband's request to leave him and their beloved castle and proceed to London, where their town house was already prepared and waiting for her.

'But *you* never bother to come to London until the very last moment.'

The Duke of Wokingham smiled across the luncheon table at his duchess. She was a charming, beautiful woman, and he, in unison with everyone around him, their servants, and the people who worked on the farm, in the stables, in the laundry, in the town, adored her. May had what his mother would call 'the common touch'.

'My dearest of dears,' John replied, 'you must, alas, prance and dance attendance on the London Season or you will never be able to pick the most suitable gel for our eldest and very beloved son.'

'But *George* has no interest in debutantes at this moment. He is far more interested in his gun and his fishing rod.'

'All the more reason, my dearest, all the more reason.'

The Duke rose in his chair, and as he passed his wife, because they were nearly alone – only three footmen present – he tickled her lightly on the cheek.

She in turn touched the tips of her fingers to her lips and blew a kiss up to him. And so John walked happily away, leaving his wife, as always, to arrange everything that he wished, and some of what she wished too.

Leaving the luncheon table shortly after him May passed out into the great hall, pausing in front of the portrait by Lavery of herself and the Duke, George their eldest son and John, always known as 'Boy', their second son, and the family dogs. It now seemed to May that her life had passed all too quickly since the painting of their portrait, and yet there had been a time when it had passed all too slowly.

For the fact was the first months of her marriage to John, then Marquis of Cordrey, had not passed but *crept* by – each dull day following the other with an inexorability which reminded her of the days that she had known as a child at her convent school, days of Lent and fasting and penance, and church, church and more church.

Indeed so slowly had those first months of her marriage passed that she realised, now she looked back down the years, despite her so-great love for John there had been moments when she very nearly wished that she had never met him, let alone married him.

No, if she had her life again, she would not go back to that particular time, not for anything in the whole world.

May's marriage to the future Duke of Wokingham had thrilled everyone alike. Of course it had thrilled May too, until she had returned home from her honeymoon.

Cordrey Castle, near the city of York, outwardly a magnificent statement of power, remodelled in the eighteenth century by John van Petersen, was to all intents and purposes a brilliant palace for any returning bride to begin to think of as her marital home.

Indeed, to May, born on the wrong side of the blanket but now seated in the back of an open carriage and waving as graciously as she knew how to the crowds of tenants on the side of the road, it seemed as if her life had truly turned to fairy tale.

And, as the young couple's flower-bedecked carriage was pulled by eight strong tenants under the archway of the great, grand house and into the courtyard, she *could* only thank God for her good fortune. A handsome young husband with a brilliant future in politics, marriage into a family with an ancient history, sixty indoor servants, twenty gardeners, luxuries beyond the expectations of any normal human being – they were all more than anyone from her supremely un-patrician background could have ever hoped or indeed longed for.

That sunny summer morning May was wearing what at the time was the most fashionable of summer clothing. Palest blue picked out her high collar, her waistband, her large hat most beautifully set upon her long neck with its blonde, blonde hair. The sun caught at the tip of the parasol held over her head, and the light, English summer breeze swayed only slightly the fringes of the Chinese silk shawl at the back of her carriage seat. She was a great beauty, and never more so than that morning. Indeed, the tenants' wives would never ever forget the sight of May, the future Duchess of Wokingham, returning to Cordrey Castle from her month-long honeymoon. What, they must have wondered, as they stared at the apparition that was May Cordrey, what could it possibly be like to be her, to be born beautiful but poor, only to have married into a great and wealthy family?

At dinner every night, they knew very well she would be wearing jewels worth thousands upon thousands, and she would never have to do more than turn her head and a footman would be at her elbow. She would be required to go to the opening of Parliament each year wearing upon her blonde hair both a coronet and the family tiara, not to mention a diamond necklace worth a king's ransom. What would they, in their small, tied cottages with their authoritarian husbands, their too many children, and their daily tasks of washing and cooking, ironing and baking – what would they not have done to swap places with May, the new Marchioness of Cordrey?

But as they all turned back towards their homes, towards the work load waiting for them, towards their husbands and their too many children, one of the more sage among them was heard to remark, 'Poor little scrap, wait until she comes up against Her Grace.'

Happily perhaps as her carriage was pulled by strong men and true into the castle courtyard May did not hear the old woman's remark, any more than the woman herself, sincerely wishing the young future duchess every happiness, would ever come to know just how true her statement was going to prove to be.

Of course May had met her mother-in-law before the marriage, and of course she had realised that she was being looked over, and had felt nervous. But with the union's receiving the approval of no less a personage than the Prince of Wales, she had not thought that there really was so very much cause to worry. The then heir to the English throne had always appreciated a beautiful young woman, and His Royal Highness had certainly appreciated May, even going to the trouble of congratulating John Cordrey on his choice of bride and saying, in an aside to his godson, 'Well done, Johnny, well done!'

And May *was* something for which to be congratulated, for the young May was beautiful beyond the dreams of man.

But she was not just beautiful, she was virtuous, and kind, and that, naturally, added to her beauty. She loved people, and had the sweetest ways with them. She loved to talk to ordinary folk, because she knew herself to be one of them. Everyone could see that having the 'common touch' meant that she would make the best kind of duchess. Everyone, that was, except the then Duchess of Wokingham, her mother-in-law, who had remained a silenced witness to the whole courtship of her only son to a former actress.

May would never forget her first sight of the Duchess at home, standing at the top of the great, grand staircase that led down to the great, grand gilded reception rooms that seemed to mock the smallness of human beings.

On seeing May standing beside her young husband, who himself had stiffened at the sight of his mother, Her Grace had made a sound that was something between a 'humph' and a 'huh'.

'So you are arrived.'

Naturally the flurry of footmen, the housekeeper outside, the butler inside, the Duke waiting in the library, had already pointed to this.

May had dropped into a deep Court courtesy, not because she had been told to do so by her young husband, but because she knew, instinctively from her days in the theatre, that it was the right thing to do, to exaggerate her curtsy to her new mother-in-law in a way that would say to everyone present: *This young woman is acknowledging the fact that her parents-in-law are, in their own way, monarchs. They are monarchs of all that they survey. They are the King and Queen of this particular part of England.*

'Much good did it do her,' Watt, the young Marchioness's newly appointed maid at the castle had commented wryly, and as she said it, to a circle of admiring younger women, she raised her eyes to heaven. 'You know how it is with Her Grace. Let's face it, I'm not a native of these parts, but havin' watched her these last ten years, the deeper the curtsy the more she treats you like you're lickspittle. However. For God's sake and her own, let us just get down on our knees and hope that the Marchioness will soon be delivered of a son and heir, and that way she'll have the hold on the Duchess, rather than the other way round, eh?'

The pattern of life at Cordrey Castle was more like that of a small township rather than of a normal household. And so now Watt, having given her opinion on the matter and seeing the housekeeper advancing towards her, moved off into a large gathering of other domestic servants, much as an illegal salesman on the corner of a crowded city street on seeing a policeman might quickly move off and disappear into the crowd.

Watt might be praying 'for God's sake and our own' for a son and heir to the great house to be born to the Marchioness, but the young Marchioness herself, wildly in love with her husband though she might be, had no joyous news to announce to his family as yet.

Weeks crawled by, and as what sometimes seemed to be endless and tedious meals were served at horribly regular intervals in the great dining room with its Italianate painted ceiling, its church-like atmosphere and its rich dishes, May felt more and more desperate. She might be getting plumper from the regularity of the fare, but not, alas, for any other reason.

Perhaps her underyling disconcertion at the distancing that she sensed between herself and her new family had frozen those parts of her that were meant to be fecund, but there was no doubting the fact that she was not pregnant. Even she, ignorant of so much though she still was, knew that she was expected to become pregnant and produce an heir within as short a space of time as possible. It was her duty, and, while John was nothing short of a saint as far as she was concerned, it was not a matter he could discuss with her. He just was not that sort of man.

There was however someone to whom May knew that she could talk. A man of the world, of common stock like herself, someone who would understand her sense of isolation, her sense of being adrift and quite unable to cope with her new circumstances. For, despite the jewels, the evening clothes – the silk and satin and lace dinner gowns, the sometimes as many as seven changes of clothes a day – the curtsying and the bowing, despite all the sophistication and the comfort, the reality of her life was that, at that precise moment, May was deeply unhappy. And the only person to whom she could talk about her sense of unease was her dear former patron, Herbert Forrester.

After both the disasters and the final triumphs of their social adventuring in London, the Forresters had returned to York in a spirit of great thankfulness. Their daughter, Louisa, had recovered her speech, May, their protégée had married a marquis, and they had effectively avenged an early social humiliation brought about by the ever mischievous Daisy.

'I reckon we've 'ad enough adventuring in the wild seas of the social Season to last us until the next century,' was how Jane Forrester had put it, as she settled down to a seat in front of the fire in their beautiful house on the outskirts of York.

Jane would not add much more, knowing as she did that their 'adventuring' had all been due to her desire to improve their social position. But now she had no wish to continue to do so, any more than she wanted to see May, who was now safely married to a future duke.

Having learned the hard way that achieving social success was not as easy as just having the money to buy the trappings of the upper classes, Jane had decided that she would look no further than Yorkshire for a husband for their daughter. As far as she was concerned York, with its ancient history and its beautiful buildings, was the height, width and breadth of all that a person should ever wish for in this world. And quite enough for folk such as herself and Herbert, or Louisa, for that matter.

Furthermore, now that Louisa was married, and already in a happy condition, the future had indeed brightened, and her mother was certain that the miseries of the past could be put firmly behind them. She herself had no wish ever again to go through all the social sufferings that she had endured before, nor had she any wish to see her Louisa again in such an emotional state as to lose all power of speech, or Herbert humiliated by so-called fashionable folk who were, in reality, no better than themselves.

Unsurprising, therefore, that when Herbert announced at breakfast one dark, cold and rainy northern day that May, now the Marchioness of Cordrey, was coming to see them, Jane nodded to the maids to go out of the room, and then took him to task for even contemplating such an idea.

'Just think what it will do to Louisa, apart from anything else, Herbert – and in her condition too – if she sees our May, albeit she is now Lady Cordrey. Gracious, it might bring on bad memories, after all that happened to us in London, and in her delicate state. And as for myself, for all that you had your revenge on the Countess of Evesham, I have no desire to see the poor girl ever again.'

'Now, Jane, that is not like you.'

'No, I will have my say, Herbert. It was nice to see May married, I admit that, and watching all the famous and fashionable folk at the wedding was fascinating, to a certain extent. And I might add that for a daughter of a woman like May's poor mother – for the daughter of that poor Ruby – it has to also be said that May has done well for herself. She has done more than haul herself up by her boot straps, she has positively leaped the social barriers. But even so, it would be quite uncalled for for her to come here. She may be going to be a duchess one day, but she is still the daughter of poor Ruby who was' – Jane leaned forward and lowered her voice even further – 'who was a *floozy*, Herbert, for all that she was a childhood friend of yours.'

'Ruby was a lady to all of us who knew her, and when Ruby was dying, Jane, she left her beautiful young daughter to my care. I hope that, one way and another, I have done my duty by our May, because as you know – well, you know, Ruby was *Ruby*.'

But his wife paid no attention to Herbert's burst of sentimentality. Her eyes were already running anxiously round the room, and she was trying to imagine how lacklustre the future Duchess of Wokingham might now find their simple dining room with its mahogany furniture and mock Gobelin tapestries. Everything in their house would, she thought, seem paltry and impoverished after the grandeurs of Cordrey Castle.

'Anyway, Herbert. I have no idea why she would want to come here. It's not as if we became particularly close to her, and she and Louisa, for instance, were not friends. And now never likely to be, such is the social divide between them. I mean, a future duchess, what would she want with coming here?'

'She wants to come here because she is still Ruby's daughter. Ruby, my oldest friend, whose life I saved as a boy, remember? And May, my Ruby's daughter, can come here or anywhere else as far as I am concerned, Jane. Not because she is a marchioness or likely to be a duchess, but because she is Ruby's daughter.'

'Herbert.' Jane eyed her husband as severely as she could. 'Herbert. I do not wish to entertain the Marchioness of Cordrey, or any other member of the aristocracy, here, or at any other place where we might be living. I do not like the aristocracy, and frankly, Herbert, they do not like us. We are best kept apart, now and for ever.'

Inwardly Herbert sighed.

Jane had never really recovered from the social slights that they had both suffered after leaving York for London with the sole intention of launching Louise into Society, and probably never would.

It was obvious to him now that Jane was going to be extraordinarily stubborn about this issue of May's coming to see them. And although he would like to stand up to her, for all sorts of reasons, he was not, in view of Louisa's interesting condition, prepared to do so. Besides, in some ways Jane was right. In some ways it *might* be a bad thing if Jane saw May, and bad memories came flooding back. He had no wish for that. He only wished the *status quo* of their lives to be maintained, their domestic contentment to continue as it had been.

But, on the other hand, his darling old Ruby, the true love of his life, was always somewhere in his heart, and the knowledge that her daughter might be needing help was enough for Herbert.

'Don't worry, love, I'll send to tell May I'll see her at my office.'

'Not your London office—'

'No, love, of course not. Now don't fret. I expect she's in trouble with her pin money and daren't tell her husband, or some such. Was ever so with bored aristocratic ladies in large draughty castles, as far as I can gather. They have nothing else to do, except play at cards when their mothers-in-law aren't looking, or follow the hunt in their carriages, or lose their pin money on betting.'

Two days later the office boy, blushing to the roots of his already fiery red hair, announced, 'The Marchioness of Cordrey, sir,' and having stepped back to allow May into the grand office with its new plush rugs and its vast gilded pictures of religious reformers and rich industrialists, promptly backed out and away from the said Marchioness and into the secretary carrying a tray of tea.

May closed the door diplomatically on the confusion, smiling and pulling a little face.

'Poor lad, I should have said "Mrs Cordrey", shouldn't I?'

Herbert took her small, gloved hands in his, and kissed her on both cheeks, as a father might do.

'Look, love, no matter what you say to young

Tom out there, he would still back into the tea tray. He never sees beautiful women here, only the secretaries, and you know my policy – no point in appointing a beautiful woman as your secretary if she'll be gone down the aisle and married and left her job before you can say warp or weave. There are no beauties here. No, love, it's your beauty that's caused the confusion, not your title, believe me. And don't you look beautiful.'

He turned her round so that she walked away from him and back, knowing what her role at that moment must be. The afternoon dress underneath her fur-trimmed coat was made up of what must be a thousand pleats, and her hat and muff were of matching fur. She was the height of elegance and fashion. Her hat was vast, as fashion that year dictated, so that Herbert had been forced to duck underneath it to kiss her, which had made them both smile.

'Oh, but you do look like your mother when you smile as you did just then. You looked just like my poor dear Ruby.'

May sat down, and as she did so Herbert noted with approval her little button boots, and her dark parasol, but he also noticed how tightly her gloved hands were holding the top of the parasol, as if it were a railing to which she was clinging.

Herbert retreated behind his desk, quite prepared for monetary disaster, and after lighting a cigar from his thermidor, to which – May having been an actress – he knew she would not object, he waited for her to speak.

'My dear, dear patron, I have come to see you to beg for your help in a matter about which, in all honesty, I had hoped to speak to your wife. But I really have to talk to someone, and there is, in truth, no-one else. And it is not something about which one could possibly write to anyone. Besides, there are the servants, and we all know how letters can be intercepted, and the servants profit quite dreadfully from the information in them. In many ways, really, I feel myself to be a prisoner in my mother-in-law's house. Yet I know it is probably asking too much to beg of you yet another favour?'

'My dear, I am like a godfather to you. Your mother was the love of my life. I saved her from drowning when she was a little girl and she in return, in so many ways, saved mine. One time, May, I was wretched about so much, so wretched that I actually contemplated suicide – you didn't know that, did you? But it's true, and Ruby, your dear mother, she set me on the right road again. She had, in my view, that seldom found but often mentioned attribute – a heart of gold.'

'I wish I had known her.'

May had blushed on hearing such intimate details of Herbert Forrester's life, which was ridiculous, she suddenly thought, considering that she had come to him, in this particular instance, to discuss just such intimate details of her own life with him.

'You would have loved her. Now, tell me, May love, how may I help you?'

'You can't help me, but you could listen, and

perhaps *that* would help me more than anything. You see, I should not have come to you if I had anyone else to whom I could turn, but the truth is I have no-one, and so, my dear patron, I am very much afraid that it has to be you.'

Herbert leaned on his free hand and smiled, waiting to hear the story of some dreadful gambling debt, or some tale of being drawn into a game that had meant the hocking of her diamond ring, or the borrowing of some large sum from her maid until such time as she had been able to come and see Herbert.

'I cannot become *enceinte*,' she murmured, as discreetly as she knew how. 'I am a disaster. I am a pure failure.'

Herbert did not know exactly what '*enceinte*' meant but he knew enough to know what it *must* mean, and he now blushed scarlet. Women in his social milieu would never discuss such things in front of a man. But May was desperate, and also now a member of the aristocracy, and they, he knew, having most of them grown up in the stables, discussed these things all the time, albeit they discussed them in French.

Women, mares and whelping hounds, it was all the same to the aristocracy. The eternal search for the best breeding in everything preoccupied the patrician classes, as well it might considering what was usually involved: thousands of acres, jewels, titles, and not least positions in Society.

'I cannot face yet another month of coming down to family meals and everyone staring at me as if I were an empty jewel case, or – or – or a barren thoroughbred mare of which they had high hopes. Oh, the silences at those meals, and those cold eyes pretending not to be fixing themselves on your barren waist! It is torture, and when I say torture, I mean it.'

Herbert, whose heart was less flinty than his business reputation, came round to May's side of the desk and sat down on a chair opposite her.

'You poor child,' he said sympathetically. 'You poor, poor child, it is most likely that you are getting yourself into such a state about this as to make it impossible for you to get into any other state, if you will see what I am saying? If you freeze up you cannot warm up, and if you cannot warm up there will be no truly excellent result.'

'I should so love to go away, to be freed from all those silent family meals, from all the gossip among the servants as the weeks drag on and I am still not carrying a *petit quelque chose*. But I have married into the Duke of Wokingham's family and they do not go away, it seems, ever, from their family estates. If they do up sticks and go somewhere else, it is always to another family estate, and again, we would all go together. John would never think of being separated from his family, or they from him.'

Herbert frowned over his cigar smoke and stared for a good few seconds at May after this.

'You know what your trouble is, May, my love? You're living no better than poor people live. You're living over the mother-in-law's shop, and in the father-in-law's house, no different from poor people. Gracious heavens, that always leads to trouble. The problems I have seen from just that around these parts is too terrible to want to remember. No matter how big the rooms, how many the servants, when families all live together in a heap you're still in their house and no different from a poor person. Well, well, well. And after that grand wedding, and all the presents and the pomp, that's how you end up, no better than my poor kitchen maid, and even she's just moved out from under her mother-in-law's feet, thanks to my obtaining a loan for her to buy a four up four down for herself and the man of her choice. You know what this is, May?'

'No.' May shook her head absently, still reeling from the idea that she might be living no better than Herbert Forrester's maid of all work, still absorbing the idea that for all that she had married a duke's son, she was as badly off as a skivvy.

The problem was, it was true. She *was* living no better than some poor young couple who had to share their living with their in-laws. For all the gold decorations, for all the myriad servants, it was still her mother-in-law seated at the table eyeing her severely twice and sometimes three times a day.

Of a sudden, which was unusual for May, she felt terribly sorry for herself. She very well might have burst into tears had she not known that it would embarrass Mr Forrester, and send any new thoughts he might have on what she could do about her unhappy position, her miserable state, flying out of the window.

'Yes, May love, you're no better off than a skivvy. Someone in your position should have their own house, be their own mistress, have some independence. No wonder that – well, no wonder that nothing's been happening to you. How could it? Nothing worse than the feeling that something is not happening, and what's more, that everyone knows it. I know, because Mrs Forrester suffered very much in that way, and although we have been blessed beyond our hopes with our darling daughter, she was a long time coming for just such reasons. They shouldn't have lumped you under one roof, however big the roof, with your husband's relations all swarming around you, and doubtless endless guests at the weekend, all being told the same thing: *No news yet, you know*. Oh dear, I see it all now.'

'So what shall I do, do you think?'

Herbert rose from his chair and started to walk about.

'What should you do? Mmm, that is a very good question, now. What should you do?'

Herbert took a turn about the room.

'In my view you should do nothing until you hear from me. I will send for you as soon as possible when I have made a plan that will signal some kind of escape for you, and your husband, of course. I mean – you can be honest with me, May – you do still love him, I mean I take it you still love him I suppose?'

'With all my heart.'

'In that case, there has to be a solution ready and available and even – nearby.'

Herbert smiled broadly. He did so love to help people.

The next morning found Jane Forrester at breakfast as usual with her husband, but with some estate agent's details on the plate in front of her instead of the usual bacon and eggs and fried bread, which she still so enjoyed.

On seeing the details Jane paled, as well she might, for the last time they changed residences they had bought one of the Countess of Evesham's houses, and the result had been not just unhappiness but calamity, of the kind where if the memory comes to you in the middle of the night, you pull the pillow over your head and groan loudly, as the agony of your ridiculousness comes back to you with a force that is all too real, and all too painful.

'What is this, Herbert my love? Are we moving somewhere smaller and you have not thought to tell me? Or is it that your business has not prospered as it should, and so we are to be forced to go back to our roots and live in a far less grand manner? Because if this is so, then I think you should have apprised me of the situation before this, really I do, Herbert, love.'

Herbert laughed, affably, but not so much as would set poor Jane's already very fragile nerves jangling, and turn the look in her eyes to one of a woman at the end of her tether.

'Why no, Jane, no. No, love, by no means – I say again, absolutely not. No, this is for you and me to look over for poor May Cordrey, our future Duchess of Wokingham. I have not confided in you until now, because I hate to worry you when it might not be necessary, but I need a woman's eye on this. I must find May a house to live in.'

'I don't understand. May is to be the Duchess of Wokingham, and she has no *house* to live in, Herbert? I am amazed. No, I am bowled over, but not in a nice way. I am speechless, except I am not. Worst of all I am not shocked. That is the worst, for I know that the aristocracy can be the meanest folk of all. I have heard tell of it and now it seems I am proved all too correct. May, a future Duchess, has no roof over her head!'

Jane leaned back in her chair and closed her eyes and flapped her linen napkin, not coroneted as she knew that May's would be, but quite plainly embroidered with the initial F. It was too appalling, what happened to folk in this life. And yet at the same time a warm and quite delicious feeling of enjoyment in the distress of others started to steal over her, for, being the mother of a daughter herself, it was, after all, just a little fascinating to hear that May, who had married so well, must be worse off, in every respect, than her own dear Louisa who had married a young gentleman of a much lower station in life.

'My dear, you have not heard me correctly. May has all too big a roof over her head. Recall, my love, just how immense is Cordrey Castle, and just how many servants there are, and how many bedrooms, and how many saloons, or reception rooms, as we poorer folk call them. How many the stables can house, just how vast is the roof – why, I hear there is three miles of roofing. Recall all this, and you can see that our dear, dear May is not without housing, nor indeed likely to be. No, what May is without is a *home*.'

Jane opened her mouth to say something and stopped just as suddenly. Seconds later the thought arrived, slowly, bit by bit, as to how it must be for May Cordrey living in that vast palace that was Cordrey Castle. It must be dreadfully lonely.

'Oh, I see, love, I see.' Jane was nothing if not tender-hearted, as Herbert well knew. 'Oh, I do see. Of course, poor May, it must be like living – well, like living abroad. Among foreigners. Always hoping to understand but not quite being able to. Catching a word here or there, and then – nothing.'

'That is exactly what it is like, Jane. The aristocracy, let us face it, are not like other people. The aristocracy are like foreigners to the rest of us. And they *do* have their own private language, as I understand it. And if you don't do as they do, but do as normal folk do, well, then they go out of their way not to speak to you, which they do not do anyway – speak, that is – not even in their own homes. They are people of few words, and I know that to be true, for, as *you* know, I had an aunt who was a housekeeper to a Lady Southwold.'

Herbert stood up, pushing his finished breakfast aside and leaving his chair out, which always rather annoyed Jane, despite the fact that they did have four indoor maids, because her late mother had always said, at least twice a week, '*A gentleman always pushes his chair in and closes the toilet seat.*'

'I knew you would see how the land lay, Jane. I knew straight away. So, let's do as we can and as we should, and try to find young May a nice little home to which she and her husband can come and enjoy themselves, quite away from anyone else, the way young people always have, and please God, always will.'

The house they were going to see was in that part of York where the housing was cheaper, and some of it dated back so far that the origins of the sites were said to date from Viking days. Not that Jane Forrester would have liked to have thought of that; she had no great interest in history beyond the previous twenty years and looked at houses with the same eye she brought to clothes for her wardrobe – was it something she truly wanted?

Besides, as soon as you delved into the history of a place, it always seemed to her that it became sinister. There was always some nosy historian happy to point out that there had been a plague pit nearby, or a hospital for contagious diseases, or some poor woman had been found dreadfully strangled in the back garden in Elizabethan times.

No, Jane was not for history. Comfort, yes, but not history.

'Oh, look, Herbert, do!' Jane pushed open the front door. 'Look how marvellous it all is. So bijou and so neat, dear. Really, it is too marvellous for words. I would quite like to live here myself, it is so delightful.'

Herbert turned and looked at his wife. He really did not know what to say. After all this time, all the effort he had expended becoming a successful man, here was Jane declaring that she would be just as happy as any other woman living in a four-bedroomed house in the lower part of York, and on the unfashionable side too. What a thing! There was no understanding women, of that he was quite, quite sure.

'Well, if all goes well, dear, we could move here after May and her husband have benefited from the loan of it. I can see to it, if that is what you wish?' he teased.

Jane turned at that. 'Every woman delights in such things, Herbert, you know that. Playing at housekeeping again, and you with your feet on the fender in front of the flickering flames, knocking out your pipe in the hearth and ash down your waistcoat, and no maids to offend.'

Jane sighed suddenly. It was always delightful to look back to the early days, but would it be so delightful, in truth, to go back to them? Perhaps not. At all events they would soon see if young May benefited from such an experience, coming from a castle and footmen and heaven only knew what. She would soon see all right.

But first must come the test.

'Herbert. What is it you want me to do, my love? I mean, what is the purpose of our coming here?'

Jane's eyes drifted out towards their new carriage which was waiting outside with its team of four matching greys. Herbert dearly loved luxury and ostentation, which well he should, considering that he came from poverty.

'The purpose of our coming here, Jane love, is for you to assess just what is needed to furnish this place and bring it up to muster for a future duke and his wife to use as a love nest.'

Just at first Jane felt that lovely warm rush of emotion that comes when a person realises that they are to be given a free hand to decorate an empty place. Her mind's eye travelled quickly over the chintzes and the furnishings, the cretonne and the fittings, the oak furniture – oak was always so nice and welcoming in small places – and she could see just how she could make number two Stilley Street quite perfect for a young couple, and, it has to be said, not entirely different from her own dear little first marital home.

'Oh, dear Herbert, no, I really must *not* take on the furnishing of this little house. That would be quite wrong, in every way, really it would. No, the person who should furnish this, if she is to think of it as *home,* is our dear May herself. There is nothing like furnishing your first home, as every married woman will tell you. It is a moment so personal and tender, Herbert, that no other woman should have a hand in it. And Herbert love, when all is said and done, if you think about it – she has so much to learn, and much better if she learns it for *herself*. No point in us teaching her our taste; the Lord knows that will not stand her in good stead when it comes to being a duchess. She must decorate this place for herself, and all alone. It's only right.'

At first Herbert thought this a pity, but after a few seconds he conceded that after all was said and done, Jane probably had a point. It was probably best to let the young get on with it, make their own mistakes.

The subject of the Forresters' earnest discussions was hanging about doing nothing very much after breakfast the following day, which was the fate of women who were neither sporting nor social. She had no liking for talking scandal or gossip in some upstairs sitting room, but neither did she wish to be outside, on such a rainy day, taking a picnic luncheon to some hut set out for the men shooting on the moors, so instead she was hanging about the morning room waiting for letters to arrive, and particularly a letter from York.

As soon as May saw it she realised that it was the one letter for which she was really yearning. The longed-for letter from Herbert Forrester. She opened it as quickly as possible, almost snatching it from the silver salver that the footman was holding out to her, and hastily slitting the envelope with a small silver paper knife.

The paper knife was much set about with coronets and crests, so much so that it seemed to May, before she had even opened the letter, that it was almost as if the letter itself did not belong to her, despite its being addressed to her. It was as if the very design of the paper knife was so extraordinarily anxious to remind May of the immense importance of the Wokingham dukedom, of its grandeur, it was as if the letter and its contents were already owned by the Cordreys.

My dear May,

I have found just the place for your intended assignations with your beloved. It is small, but pretty, and Mrs Forrester is quite willing to do it up to your taste. (She herself has very good taste nowadays.) And she will come and see you there, as I will. Let me know, as soon as you can, when you can visit?

I remain, as always, your devoted foster father,

Herbert Forrester

May quickly replaced the letter and threw it on the fire. Unfortunately the footman, as they did at perfectly timed intervals at Cordrey Castle, opened the morning room door just as she had dropped Herbert's missive upon the logs. But May had not appeared on the London stage for nothing.

'Thank you,' she said calmly, and she took

another log from the footman's hands, and without a word deposited it on top of her half-burnt letter. 'I do so love to handle wood, you know. My grandfather was a carpenter,' she added suddenly and ingenuously, to the open astonishment of the young man in his country livery.

It was not until he had left and she had checked that there was nothing left of the letter beyond a few cinders that May sat down at the gold-inlaid French writing desk and started to pen a reply.

'May I take that t' post for you, my lady?'

One of the servants had stepped forward and curtsied deeply as May left the morning room.

'No, thank you. I dearly love a morning walk, even in the rain. So refreshing, so good for the complexion.'

She started to cross the vast hallway to the main outer doors, tucking her reply to Herbert Forrester inside her fur muff, because the Yorkshire weather, although it was still only autumn, was not just wet, it was already cold too. Determinedly opening up her umbrella for herself, but followed by her maid, May set off on the four-mile walk to the post box that was situated beyond the outer wall of the estate.

The doors having been shut behind her ladyship, two of the footmen swung down to the lower part of the house, chatting as they went.

'Where did thou learn to open a letter like that, eh?' the taller one asked in some admiration of the other.

'Used to be assistant to a magician. It's like Father says about women, it's easy when thou knowst how!'

'I never would have known thou'd had it open and put it back, not when I handed it to her.'

'Ah, it's easy. A little piece of wire, a few fine wiggles and hey presto!'

'Thou must teach me.'

They both laughed, preparing to join the rest of the servants in the hall for their midday meal.

'I wonder what's going to 'appen when t'cat gets out of t'bag and they finds out what's goin' on?'

'Blooming mayhem I should think.'

More laughter from the two young men, until at last they fairly sprang into the large, light-filled room which served as a dining room to all the servants. Everything below stairs at Cordrey was conducted in imitation of their masters, down to the upper servants' retiring to their own private dining room for the final half-hour of the meal.

'Roast mutton for dinner. Ee, but the smell of it would fair melt t'tongue in t'mouth, wouldn't it?'

May had agreed to meet the Forresters at Stilley Street, and when she saw how sweet and charming the house was, how small and delightfully old, eighteenth-century and engagingly pretty, all in all, just how a house should be, she was more than pleased, she was delighted.

'You will help me with the furnishings, though, won't you, Mrs Forrester? I have no taste to speak of, and I really do need help.'

Jane Forrester opened her mouth to say 'Very kind of you, May, love, but no, it's something you should really do for yourself', but seeing the look in her husband's eyes she closed her mouth again, and nodded.

It was always difficult to deny young people anything, and particularly young May, who had, when all was said and done, been abandoned in a convent by her mother, and left to get on with life as best she might. Jane shuddered to think of what might have happened to her had not Herbert come along and rescued her. She might have become a nun!

There was no denying, though, that after their humiliation they had wanted to revenge themselves on the Countess, and May had been something of a pawn in their elaborate plans, now that Jane came to think about it. So really she *should* continue to help May, for if it had not been for Herbert's paying for the girl to have a London Season, May would never have met a future duke, and therefore, in a way, she would never have been as unhappy as she undoubtedly was now. In other words some people might say it was the Forresters' fault the poor young girl was so miserable.

'Of course I will help you, May love. How delightful it will be, I am sure, to work on this little house together.'

And it was delightful, and May's taste – hardly formed as whose is who has only been married a few months – was developed by Jane, who had nothing more in mind than to make the place as homely and as comfortable as possible.

'We won't be wanting no gold leaf and fol de rol here, our May,' she kept saying as they went from cheap shopping to cheap shopping, both of them being as penny-conscious as curates when it came to what they must both have known might turn out to be both an extravagance and a failure.

The house set on four floors would have appealed as being exceedingly commodious to anyone but a future duchess. However, to May – although only at Cordrey Castle for what could not have been more than seven or eight months – number two Stilley Street now seemed to be a positive doll's house after the great echoing rooms of the castle. So tiny and so neat that her heart quite turned over in the excitement of thinking about it when her thoughts dwelt on it at night. And of course it was all the better for being a secret, so that she was able to hug its reality to her before reluctantly turning down the gaslight and waiting for her husband to join her in their vast, cold, gold-decorated four poster bed with all its old red eighteenth-century silk furnishings which could be closed quite cosily, but in reality never were.

May dreamed well into the night, long after her husband had made love to her in the dark. She dreamed of the wallpaper patterns – the Chinese patterns that she did so love most particularly – of the oak chairs and table that she and Jane Forrester had found for the tiny dining room. Of the deal table in the first of the two kitchens, and the flight of steps that led down to the cellars beneath the pavement, and to the rooms set aside, now, for the maid of all work.

Even that phrase 'maid of all work' seemed personal and exciting to May after so many months of not being allowed to so much as put a log on the fire for herself. Putting on her old convent school apron and getting down on her hands and knees to lay some worn old carpet that she and Jane Forrester had found in the attics seemed more wonderful than anything of which she could dream. And hammering it all down with the aid of tacks and heavy old hammers – not to mention the help of the old coachman from the Forrester stables, whose feelings, it seemed, had been considerably ruffled by Herbert's driving the team to Stilley Street himself.

'He still can't get used to Herbert's wanting to take the reins, you know, and I for one don't blame him. But, as Herbert says, if the motor car comes to be a reality, which friends at his club swear it will, there will be no more coachmen driving him or anybody else – the men will all want to take the wheel themselves.'

May looked out of the newly washed windows onto the street outside. She did not count the time passing now that she was at Stilley Street, the way she counted it when she was seated with her tapestry at the castle, but thinking of the old Forrester coachman it fairly caught at her heart to imagine him washing down rubbery black tyres instead of glistening horse's legs.

'Oh, well,' she said, turning back to Jane. 'Let's hope the motor car does not catch on. After all, horses are so much more beautiful, aren't they?'

Jane sighed. 'I only hope you're right, our May,' she agreed. 'I really do not want my Herbert buying one, but you know men. Well, you probably don't, as yet, you're too young. But when you are older you'll find that they are inclined to go for what is newest, in every way. I must say I sometimes find myself praying that the wretched combustion engine will go away, I do really.'

'I suppose at least motor cars, as John says, can't suddenly bolt—'

'Don't you believe it, May love. Motor cars if they come into being will set about killing folk left, right and centre, really they will.'

May's eyes widened. It did not seem possible, but she also felt a twinge of fear, for she knew that John would be the first to want a motor car, even though the Duke, old as he was, would not like change of any sort. The clocks in his bedroom still stayed unwound at five o'clock for some reason she could not remember, but she thought that it had something to do with the battle of Waterloo, or was it the charge of the Light Brigade?

'Well, May love, we're right finished now, so the rest is up to you.'

Jane looked around at the cheerful little sitting room, at the many bright touches, and the fire ready to have a taper put to it, or one of the spills they had made for the lighting of it. It was indeed a love nest, but would it, she suddenly wondered, suit a future duke?

The Duchess looked at her maid. She trusted her more than most, but not so much that she would trust her with her life, or any of that nonsense.

'I have heard what you said, Brimpton, and I have understood your intentions, which I must presume to be good. Now, if you will, please send Lady Cordrey to me, here, in my sitting room, but without her maid – without Watt.'

Half an hour later, May, who had no idea why she had been sent for, followed the grim-faced Brimpton down the old faded strip of carpet until, eventually, they reached the Duchess's private quarters. As she followed the maid into the sitting room, with its cheerful fire and its feminine fittings, ornaments of shepherdesses, blue velvet chairs, and many other features reminiscent of the era of Madame de Pompadour, May realised that her heart was beating so fast that it might well have been a speeding motor car of the kind of which the duke would so definitely disapprove.

She curtsied. Her mother-in-law nodded, briefly, her eyes travelling from the rising figure of her daughter-in-law to a chair, after which a slight movement of the head indicated that May should be seated.

May sat down, an elegant, slender figure, even to the Duchess's eyes, and beautifully dressed in a tailored coat and skirt with a high-collared blouse, and shoes buttoned neatly to the side.

'There is no news, as yet, for myself and the Duke?'

'No, Duchess.' May blushed, turning such a high colour that it seemed to her that even her toes inside their perfectly fitting shoes were scarlet.

'That is a pity. But there is no need to panic, you know.'

May stared hard at the carpet in front of her shoes. It was old, and she knew that a previous duchess, some hundred or so years before, bored to ribbons of the bad weather and being confined for weeks to the castle had, on a whim, supervised her servants while they painted it its present all too bright blue, thereby blotting out all the patterns, all the graceful swirls, all the decorations that had been so carefully hand-stitched into it by the Persians who had made it.

'These things take time.' The Duchess picked up a piece of paper and started to make a spill, looking at it absently as if it had no reality, but was merely something to aid the conversation. 'John was not born for many, many months.' She nodded again, and May, taking it for a nod of dismissal, stood up, curtsied again, and made thankfully for the door. But there was something more to come, and May realised that she had perhaps been a little previous when the Duchess spoke again, forcing May to turn back.

'Just remember there is no privacy here at Castle Cordrey, my dear. Everything you do or say is seen, overhead, or noted. Living here is really more like being in the middle of a small town than a house. In time you will get used to it, but until then, take my advice and – note it well.'

May almost fell into the corridor outside. She suddenly knew, without any doubt at all, that somehow or other the Duchess had come to know of her letter from Herbert Forrester. May could not have said how she knew, she just did – women's second sight, or intuition, whatever it was. Someone had told her mother-in-law of Herbert's plan for buying a small house, or love nest, for her, which meant, if it were indeed so, that there was no time to waste at all.

May hurried off down the corridor, and within minutes was being helped by her maid into her third change of clothes that day. It would not be very surprising if her mother-in-law had been told about her plan. Anyone could have told her. Perhaps even the lawyer who had handled the purchase of Stilley Street.

'My fur muff please, Watt, and hurry.'

She turned at her bedroom door and smiled warmly at the maid. 'And Watt?'

'Yes, my lady?'

'I have no use for you this afternoon, so you may stay here at the castle. I wish to be quite alone. There must be some mending, and if there is not you may have the afternoon off.'

'But my lady, Her Grace will not hear of you going anywhere alone. My instructions are quite explicit.'

'I am going to find my husband, Watt. Not even Her Grace would see a need to take my maid to find my husband, would she, surely?'

Watt hesitated. Part of her was quite willing to have the afternoon off, and the other part of her, the part that was in the pay of the Duchess, was in dread of missing something that she should be reporting back to her employer.

'Very well, my lady. If you are just going to meet your husband, for a walk or some such?'

'I am.' May shot out of the door.

'John!' Outside she fairly pounced on the young Marquis as he emerged from the stables, a small terrier at his heels. 'John, as soon as maybe, you must come with me. I have a surprise for you, my dearest.'

John stared at his young, beautiful wife, the word 'surprise' engendering none in either his eyes or his face. May registered this, then thought: *Oh, the agony of it. The eternal frustrating agony of the slowness of the male reaction to surprises. First the thought reaching the brain, then the suspicion that if it is a surprise it is bound to be a nasty one, and then, at last, and thank goodness, the* well, all right *look coming into the eyes as he is finally persuaded that he will* allow *himself to be surprised.*

'I must change if we are to go into York, dearest.'

'Well, if you must you must, my darling, but do hurry, if you will.'

May waited downstairs while John was changed by his valet, and Watt, spying on him, was satisfied to note that he did indeed join his wife in his street clothes, some half an hour after her ladyship had left her own bedroom.

They were halfway across the great hall, hundreds of feet by hundreds of feet – exactly how many had never really interested May, only that it was desperately large and draughty – when John stopped and pulled May back.

'If you have a surprise, so have I! A new team of greys, and I am going to drive them myself in the new carriage. We will fairly race along.'

It was only a matter of a handful of miles to Stilley Street from the Castle, which meant that May could enjoy the journey. When they arrived at last she realised that any longer would have been too long.

'Where are we?'

Naturally, the arrival of such a smart turnout was drawing a great deal of attention, and the groom had not climbed down from the box, nor May out of the new carriage, before there was much pulling back of curtains at many windows, not to mention gatherings of small boys who stared and ran away, only to run back again, this time with a friend, and stare for a while longer.

'We are in Stilley Street. I told you, John. Stilley Street.'

'Yes, but why are we here?'

May turned the key in the door, her face lit up with the joy of her own surprise, and the fun of the moment, her hair blown into clusters of curls, and her cheeks pink with the effects of the drive in the open carriage.

'We are here' – she pushed open the door and

pulled John after her, shutting the door firmly behind them both – 'for one reason, and one reason alone.' John stared down at her, his expression suddenly both serious and wondering, looking quite the small boy. 'We are here, John, to make love and be properly married, all alone, just the two of us, no-one else!'

He stared at her for a further few seconds. 'But this is not our house, May dearest. We should surely—'

'No, it's not our house, it's *my* house, given to me by my old friend Herbert Forrester as a late wedding present, and I have brought you here for that single reason: to make love.'

'But May dearest, it is the afternoon. We make love at night, don't we?'

Inwardly May sighed, but outwardly she smiled, and pulled her young husband up the stairs behind her.

'Not any more we don't, John. Not any more, dearest one!'

After that, afternoon after afternoon, and in the most ingenious manner, with no comments to each other, and everything done by looks and signals, the two of them were able to slip away and escape to Stilley Street, where May was able, afternoon after afternoon, to demonstrate her domestic and other skills to her young husband.

And of course John, being a young aristocrat brought up in a cosy nursery with a loving Yorkshire nanny, was transported back to the happy years of his childhood, as with feet up on the sitting room fender, and a plate full of slightly burnt tea cakes, May read to him, or sewed the first of what they both hoped were many small garments for their much longed-for baby.

And so the time progressed, but so also did Watt's reports to the Duchess, for May had, unfortunately, become all too skilled at losing her maid of an afternoon, and the maid, not seeing that the young Marquis was also absent, his valet being all too often after luncheon quite the worse for wear, was naturally forced to make her young mistress's frequent absences from the castle known to the Duchess.

'Thank you, Watt.'

The Duchess always gave the maid some small token for her troubles. Today it was a thin, old gold and turquoise bracelet. She did not believe in giving money. It was too little for knowing so much.

Later that evening, she sent for her son. The Duchess did not ever ask for anyone, she always 'sent for' someone.

John, reluctant to leave the company of his wife in their private apartments, nevertheless went immediately.

His mother was a very good-looking woman. Every time he saw her John appreciated her looks, and her refinement, her air of having been sculpted, not to be put in the Long Gallery along with the other statues, but to stay, still, and perfect, in her life, exactly as she was. Even her cheek or her hand, if he touched them, would, he knew, be as cold as marble. When he was with his mother he could never imagine something quite as human as a baby emerging from her. Indeed, it seemed quite impossible.

'John. I am afraid I have sorry news for you.'

'Really, Mama?'

'Yes, John, sorry news indeed.'

John's eyes roved around the room in which they were seated. Mentally he counted how many of his mother's pugs were present, but finding every one of them not only present but also alive he put aside the idea that one of them must have died. Coming to the conclusion therefore that the 'sorry news' must be the death of an old servant, or some relative, or an old friend, he waited in some dread.

'As you know, John, when you married May, I was in some trepidation, although I said nothing to your father. It was not just that she had been an actress, she was not used to our ways. Women like May are not like us. They just do not have the breeding, they do not understand our way of life. And no sooner are they married than they turn back to being how they were before.'

John, who now loved his wife more, if anything, than ever before – and when he thought about the fun that they had enjoyed at Stilley Street these past months he realised it was with good reason – now felt his expression changing from anxiety to amazement. What was his mama talking about, if anything?

'My wife is both beautiful and virtuous, Mama, and I am more than happy with her. I am ecstatic, particularly at this moment, in fact, most particularly.'

'That is you all over, John dearest.' The Duchess put out a thin, cold hand and touched her son on his warm one. 'You cannot see anything but good in anyone. You were ever like that, and always will be, for, for some reason that we cannot know, you have been blessed with a golden nature. But other people, I am sorry to say, take a terrible advantage of good men like yourself, John. I am dreadfully afraid that your poor young wife might be one of them.'

John Cordrey's mouth fell open, and he went to say something, but, not being able to quite assemble his appalled thoughts and form words, for a second or two he just stared at his mother in utter silence, until, finally, one word burst from him. 'Balderdash!'

It was of course quite shocking to swear in that way in front of his mother, but he was past caring. His darling May was everything to John and, as far as he was concerned, if May was not there, if anything happened to May, he had really rather not go on living.

'I am sorry to say it is nothing of the sort, my dearest son.'

The Duchess was full of aplomb. She knew and

trusted her servants to be telling the truth. It would not pay them, after all, to do anything else. And the fact that her dearly beloved son had been fooled by an ex-actress was just too bad. Something would have to be done to get rid of her, and soon. Divorce being unthinkable, they would just have to come up with a way of setting the marriage aside for some technical reason.

'May and I have never been happier, Mama. In fact, we are so happy that we have some good news for you and Papa, news for which you have been waiting. May is to give birth next year. We were hoping to save the news until your birthday, but, since you sent for me, now must be the time I tell you. May not virtuous? Who has been telling you such hogie-pogie? One of the servants has been spying again, I suppose. Well, servants are as servants must be, particularly if you are in charge of them, Mama! You should not grease their palms the way you do, it makes for temptation, I always think.'

But the Duchess would not be swayed by what she saw as her son's petulance. 'This – *expectation* – cannot be acknowledged as yours, must not be acknowledged as yours. Lady Cordrey has been seen escaping from the castle almost every afternoon for what are now known to be secret trysts. A letter was intercepted, in which that patron of hers has promised to give her a "love nest". I think that was the phrase that was used, or some other such vulgarity.'

'The secret trysts were with her husband,

Mama.' If the situation had not been so emotional, and if he had not been so angry, John could have laughed out loud at the expression on his mother's face as he said this. 'That is the truth.' It was his mother's turn to stare at him as he went on. 'May, because she was having trouble conceiving *un petit quelque chose*, and because we are always so overlooked here, instead conceived the *idea* that we could have our own little love nest: a proper home such as normal people enjoy. That was her plan, and Forrester went along with it, because he always has her best interests at the centre of his generous heart. He knew that if he bought May and me a little home of our own he would be freeing us from the stuffy atmosphere of the castle, and allowing us time to ourselves, as all young couples must have, Mama. And how right he was and, as you now know, a happy outcome has resulted. So, Mama, far from wishing to be rid of my actress wife, I have found that she is indeed a pearl among women, a rare flower, a person of honesty, and, what is more important, wise beyond her years. So, Mama, on hearing this news, perhaps it is time you discovered the same thing?'

After which speech John kissed his mother on her smooth, cold, white cheek, bowed to her, and left her still seated, the fire dying in the grate, her pugs snoring, and her daughter-in-law the winner in the first, and he profoundly hoped the last, battle with his mother.

* * *

But all that was long, long ago, and nowadays May even missed the old Duchess, having discovered, as the young must always do, that she had, in so many ways, been all too right about all too many things.

Not that May could ever bring herself to spy on her children, or keep their servants in her private pay – she was just not that kind of person – but she did understand that she had to be always on her toes, always aware of what was going on, or, worse, what might be going to happen.

Everything in a house as large as the castle was a matter of import. If one mouse was allowed to breed, then a whole attic of invaluable inheritance might be destroyed in one winter. If one maid was made pregnant and it went unnoticed, there might be an outbreak of immoral behaviour among the lower servants. If a butler was found to be drinking far too much (all butlers drank – they would not stay if their employers did not turn a blind eye to this), then this over-indulgence might spread to the footmen. It was a matter of constant vigilance, at all times, of that there was no doubt.

And there was no doubt at all either that now she was the chatelaine of Cordrey Castle May looked back in gratitude to her mother-in-law's stern disciplines, to her deep appreciation of order, to her belief that what was done today made sense of what happened in the future. In time, and now that time did not seem as far away as it once had, in time her son George would be bringing home *his* wife, and it would be May's turn to show her how things had to be done, not by words, but by example.

With this in mind, May made a note on the little gold pad that accompanied her from boudoir to breakfast table, and from breakfast table to dinner table, to ask John to take her to Stilley Street. There they could be young once more, or make believe that they were, until George brought home a wife, when the little house would, she hoped, come into its own once more and greet a new generation of lovers.

Sea Breezes

Occasionally when Edith O'Connor stood on the corner of a London street, waiting for her maid to catch her up – Minnie was *so* slow, her feet being afflicted with arthritis – she would try to imagine that the slight breeze and the light rain that were coming towards her, making her bend beneath her umbrella in order to keep her hat from running off down the street, were the wind and the spray from the Atlantic Ocean driving towards her on some windy day in Galway city.

Coming to England from Ireland had been a shock, not just because she had to leave behind the younger children, not just because she missed her dogs and her horses, but because in England she felt so alien, and above all so Irish. At home, in Ireland, at Glendarvan, she felt English in comparison say to Minnie, but in England now she felt as Irish as Minnie. Indeed, she felt as though they were not mistress and maid at all, but compatriots in a foreign land.

And of course it was not just the younger children and the animals that she missed, she dearly missed the lilt of Irish voices, particularly of an afternoon when they all went walking or riding and would be forever stopping and talking with anyone and everybody. And too she missed the ever open doors of the cottages with the babble of sound coming from inside as you rode past; and the sound of laughter, too. And she missed the humour of the people, for despite the agonies of the previous fifty years Ireland was as full of humour still, as England, it seemed to Edith, was full of snobbery.

Great heavens, she even missed Papa's strangely dressed friends always arriving at all hours to discuss some matter of moment, or to read their poetry at him, or to do something strange like try out a spell on one of Mama's hens, or send a book from the library to Galway and back. There was always something supernatural, or a sporting event, or some new personality of the day to talk about, always something happening at Glendarvan, never, ever, a dull moment, such as now, in London, with the constant sway of people passing who never stopped and smiled at you, never turned their heads, unless a carriage passed them by with some swanky coat of arms on the door, or some newly attired lady of easy virtue swept by with horses waving yellow plumes pulling her carriage, or something vulgar of that nature.

It seemed to Edith now, in her self-pitying mood, that England was a cold place, and that although there was less rain, and less poverty, there was also less gaiety and less happiness. And undoubtedly the fact that English doors were always shut was something to do with the state of their hearts, for in England no-one danced because it was fun and for the sheer joy of the moment. She could never imagine a day in England like the one at Glendarvan when Papa had let a band of beggars and musicians into the hall because a storm was blowing, and they played an air so irresistible that all the servants, not to mention Papa and Mama and their friends, stopped doing whatever they were doing and got together to dance; and drink was taken and everyone danced all the faster because of it. In England they only danced to make eyes at each other and then to marry each other for financial reasons. Whereas in Ireland the doors were always open, and people called on each other and offered hospitality at all times, and they did not give you queer looks when you gave your name as 'O'Connor'. And more than that they *talked*.

It was that perhaps more than anything that Edith was missing in England, for all that she was being chaperoned by her own mother. She missed the endless flow of chatter, the constant sound of the servants talking, the sounds of voices singing and laughing in the stables. She even missed the sound of her parents arguing, but more than all that – she missed the laughter. Gracious heavens! The English, until they came to Ireland, were so *serious*. They rarely laughed and hardly smiled, her papa had warned her.

And that was the main person that Edith missed – her papa. He was always so kind and so happy, and this despite his never being able to ride or hunt ever again, and having to have special chairs to cope with his terrible back injury. Papa loved life so much that Edith knew he would never, ever let such a trifling thing as pain get him down. Any more than he would listen to Mama about not asking his strange poetical friends to Glendarvan. Mama was dreadfully put out by *Mr O*'s strange friends. She particularly objected to their dematerialising and then materialising again somewhere else. She said it was 'importunate' and 'irresponsible' and worse – a bad example to the servants.

Edith did not really have much of an idea what all that meant, and cared less for that matter, but she did understand that dematerialising was not something that 'nice' people did, although she had a feeling that quite soon – very, very soon – she herself would be only too happy to dematerialise from some London ballroom, or from the presence of Their Majesties on the morning of her own presentation. The truth was that Edith had less than a thread's interest in the opposite sex. She truly only liked dogs and horses, and was quite sure that she could favourably swap any young man's company for that of their groom and his friends in the stables at Glendarvan, for all that nowadays the old man never seemed to remember to put in his teeth to have his tea.

'What is going to *happen* to me, Minnie,' she asked her maid – her mother's maid, really – as they now both bent their heads against the impact of the rain that was coming down harder and faster.

'What do you mean, Miss Edith, *happen*? Why, you're going to get married the same as every other young girl, that's what you're going to do.'

'Yes, but Minnie, who to? Or as Lady Devenish would say *to whom*? The fact is, and there's no denying it, Minnie, the fact is that I am a hoyden and only fitted for the life of the stables in Ireland, and although I care not two hoots for Lady Devenish, the awful fact is I certainly know when a person *is* speaking the truth, and she was, Minnie, she was, she was speaking the truth when she said that I would never get further than the tack room in the stables of a country house. I have no more chance of surviving in an English ballroom than I do of driving a coach and four through a hunting gate. I begged and begged Mama before we came here to have me thrown to the wolves in Dublin – just a quick curtsy to the Viceroy and I'd have been home to the stables before you could say powder on your nose, so I would. But no, Mama wanted me "done" here so that she could leave Ireland, and order dresses that we know we shouldn't afford, and generally enjoy herself without Papa tagging along and bringing all his poetical people with him.'

'Lady Emily is doing what she thinks best, and that is all there is to it, Miss Edith,' Minnie told her, putting on her most squashing face. 'Your mother has been a gorgeous mother to you, and your brothers and sisters, and I will have no word said against her. For all that what you say is true, it does not stop her being head and shoulders above most women, nearly all women, in my opinion, God bless her. Why, the local people speak of her as of a saint beatified. Wasn't it your mama who caught the scarlatina for herself in trying to save the O'Gradys' grandson's life? And didn't he survive because of her, and haven't they said a thousand novenas in Glendarvan for her ever since? And wasn't she the one who would take the priest up to the nursery for you all to be christened the second time in order to please Nanny, Nanny being a Catholic woman in a Protestant house? And indeed because of that you would not know that any of you were Protestant, thank the Lord so, because of her and her natural sweet ways.'

Edith nodded, her eyes now drifting towards the Park, and towards the host of horses and carriages, and the brilliance of the turn-outs that were passing them, albeit miles ahead. She knew that the O'Connor fortunes could never run to a brilliant horse for her in England, or a beautifully cut riding habit from Busvines, but that did not stop a girl from dreaming, did it?

'If you had behaved yourself better at Lady Devenish's house you could have made friends with that rich American heiress and she could have loaned you one of her thoroughbred horses. That would have been a start anyway, Miss Edith. But you always did know better, didn't you? Ever since you were knee high to a grasshopper, you knew better all right. I used to say that to your poor nanny, but she never could see anything but good in you, the Lord have mercy on her.'

'But Nanny's still alive, Minnie.'

'All the more reason for needing God's blessing,' Minnie stated piously. 'It's God's mercy that we need after we have been gathered, not His blessing. The Lord save us all, but the English are so pagan nowadays that if you mention the Almighty below stairs, or cross yourself or say grace before your meal, sure they all stare at you! It's a terrible thing to be as godless as the English, with no bottom to their souls except money.'

'Ah come on, Minnie, now, we are not going to say that we Irish do not like money, are we?' Edith started to laugh as they turned the corner into the Park and Minnie's cloak and cape flew out and up over the umbrella. 'We Irish not like money? We like it as well as the next person, don't we?' She pulled down Minnie's cloak straightening it out again before handing the gamp back to her, and they continued with their walk, both of them grateful for the smell of the rain coming at them from across from the grass and the trees of the Park.

'Well, I'm not saying that I would not be grateful for a bag of gold sovereigns if I came across them on this walk,' Minnie conceded. 'The difference being that if I found it—'

'You would say a novena of thanks to Almighty God, and an Englishwoman would forget to, so – is that right, Minnie?'

'I would do more than that. I would go on a

pilgrimage to St Patrick's holy shrine.'

'It would be a long walk for you, I am thinking. The only shrine you will find in London, Minnie, I'm afraid, is to Prince Albert.'

'And he was not the saint he was cracked up to be, by all that I hear tell – over fond of the bedroom, which is why the poor Queen had so many childer.'

'Why, Minnie, this is fast talk indeed from one as holy as you.'

Minnie blushed furiously, because it was true. She would never normally speak as she just had to Miss Edith, but being away from all her friends below stairs she missed the other servants, the friendliness of the chats and the talks and the innumerable innuendoes, the marvels of the gossiping over tea, the soda bread and the home-made butters and jams of the kitchens at Glendarvan. She missed it all, for all that she did agree with her mistress that Miss Edith had to come to London for a husband if she was to have any sort of chance, the young men in Ireland being wild and woolly and not up to much when it came down to providing for a wife.

'If I have fallen into bad conversations in front of you, Miss Edith, forgive me.'

'You have no such thing.' Edith squeezed Minnie's arm. 'It's all right, I knew about the Prince of Wales at the Curragh and all those things from Papa. He never has paid much attention to whom he is talking, a son or a daughter, and to tell you the truth, when I see other girls of my age, their innocence and their ignorance, I am, it has to be said, quite grateful. For if there is one thing I know, it is that if your own dear father has always had the habit of honesty, you know where you stand in life. And I am a plain Jane, as he says, but I have a good wit on me on my day, and Papa has always said you spend more time talking to a woman than you do staring at her nose, so I must not worry about looks.'

'You are not plain so, sure you're just not a beauty. But beauties can be all trouble, especially when age comes upon them, and when there is nothing but a mirror to tell you who you are you turn into a poor sad sack of a sort of a creature, I always say.'

And so on and on their talk went, as it always did, until eventually maid and mistress turned once more for 'home', or more particularly Medlar House, where Edith and her mother were now staying, it having been long ago arranged that Edith was to be introduced to London Society with the help of Lady Medlar.

Edith's spirits sank lower and lower the nearer their steps brought them to the grand entrance to Medlar House, with its massive arch, and its court-yard with its steps leading up to the great doors, everything proclaiming to the visitor that they were approaching not just the doors of an aristocrat, but a seat of power. These were the doors of a person-ality of the day who could, and did, make and break not just reputations and individuals, but political parties.

Power was what London Society was about, and that was why the London Season, for all its apparent fripperies, was so important to so many. The London Season was all about luring the men with the money away from their country estates and bringing them to London. It was about laying before those same men, and their heirs, not just the flower of upper class girlhood, but also political possibilities, ideologies, causes, ambitions, that might perhaps change much that was good, and much that was bad. That was what the London Season at the height of the British Empire was all about, and that was what Medlar House from its entrance gates onwards declared. It declared grandeur, it declared importance, it declared influence.

'Abandon hope all ye who enter here,' Edith murmured as she and Minnie turned under the arch, and their feet started to tread across the stone setts of the interior courtyard and so towards the great doors with their enormous panels which would be opened by the flunkeys, their town liveries declaring them to be in the service of the Medlars, in effect a small private army that stood between the old family and the populace that walked past their doors in nearby Piccadilly. 'ABANDON ALL HOPE!' Edith raised her voice.

'Shushy, shushy, will you now, Miss Edith, one of the footmen will hear you and tell.'

Edith squeezed Minnie's arm and then quickly let it go, for in England no-one seemed to like their servants as much as the Irish did. It just was not done to treat them as anything except *lah-di-dah* and *don'tcher know*.

Or as Edith's youngest sister Valencia always put it, as *nose-in-the-air, crook-your-little-finger, how-h'are-you-today-my-ladeah and hawfully-well-thank-you-but-ahctually-couldn't-care-a-damnty-about-youah-folk*.

Except the way Valencia said it was always very, very quick, almost a party piece. But that was Valencia. She never did like anything to go by without making a meal of it. Edith put away the thought of her youngest sister, ethereal, pretty as a flower and the most lovely of all of them, but with such frail health that leaving her had torn at Edith's heart.

'Bring me back a big hat from England, Edie, oh do!' she had pleaded.

'Course, darling, and anything else I can get my greedy hands on too.'

They had parted with laughter and kisses, and many promises to bring back the earth if not the sea too, and Edith had walked towards the waiting coach with Minnie a yard behind her, whistling softly to keep away the wretchedness of the moment. Valencia's kisses and her rounded childish arms had caught at her eldest sister's heart in such a way as to make even the memory of it now just too painful. Indeed, Edith had been hoping that, with the help of Phyllis de Nugent, she would have been sent smartly back from Lady Devenish's house to Ireland, and straight away. But it had not been that easy, simply because nothing is as easy as you hope, she had always found. Except riding over the gorse on a wild pony on a sunny day with a light summer breeze blowing, and the wild flowers in the hedges making patches of colour that would stay locked in your memory long after you fell asleep in your bed with the sound of the sea in the distance, and the warmth and the cool of Irish linen sheets to cover you.

Once again Edith headed up the wide shallow stairs of Medlar House. It had to be faced, whether she liked it or not, there would be no going home until she had fairly frightened the ballroom bare of likely husbands, and even Lady Devenish had given up all hope for her. If she was to ever see Ireland again, or watch Valencia opening up a big box with a great plumed hat in it, she would have to prove that no man would want her, and given her looks that surely would not be difficult?

She strode ahead, up the second flight of stairs, ignoring the great mêlée of people in the saloon on the first floor, who were there for something or someone whom they could use to their own benefit, in the hope of aggrandisement, or of enrichment.

'Lady Medlar does not have guests to her house,' she remarked, *sotto voce*, to Minnie as they went on up the stairs to the bedrooms above, 'she has *petitioners*. All wanting something! From her. Or, in the old days, via her from King Edward, who used to love her, they say. But then the old king loved everyone didn't he?'

'Shush, Miss Edith,' said Minnie for the second time. 'We don't want to offend her ladyship, not with us hardly having arrived here.'

'Oh, so it's all right once we've been here a month or two, is it, Minnie?' Safely outside Edith's bedroom door now they started to laugh.

'You're a caution!'

Portia paused at the turning of the street, and wondered at where she had found herself, for it was a very different street from any she would normally walk down, a street she knew few of her acquaintance would find themselves in, albeit she was not so foolish as not to be still accompanied by her personal maid, the ever faithful Evie.

'Lordy, Miss Portia – I mean my lady – what are we *doin'* 'ere, eh?' Evie shivered. Her eyes ran round the shabby doorways and the general air of fading gentility, and a look of fear came into her eyes, the kind of fear that sharp reminders of former days of poverty can bring into the eyes of those who have known what it is like to go hungry for half the week. Nowadays Evie was used only to the grand life, and the feeling of ease which associating with wealth can sometimes bring in its wake, when all the doors seem newly painted, and gold leaf and silk fabrics and beautiful objects abound.

There was certainly no beauty in this street. There was nothing of new quality, and what there was of old quality had to struggle to show itself, so that doors and window frames that had once been properly joined were starting to split, and brass knockers that had been made to resound heavily against good-quality wood were now darkened to black, and the doors to which they were attached forlorn and peeling. Evie would have dearly liked to ask her mistress what exactly they were both doing in such a street, but Lady Childhays – or Miss Portia, as Evie knew her – was not a person to communicate with her maid, no matter how long Evie had been in her service.

Of course she talked to her – Evie would not have stayed with a mistress who did not confide in her, for that, after all, was what maids were for. Maids did not just dress you and bath you, they were a shoulder on which to lean. A person to confide in as they dressed you, as they bathed you. In every way a maid was there to listen to you.

But Lady Childhays, as Evie well knew, had the artless, or artful, habit of communicating to Evie, or anyone else, everything about herself except that which truly mattered. Therefore Evie would know of all her mistress's worries about Miss Phyllis, about her dismay at having a daughter who had become feral to a degree that was almost distressing, but nothing at all about why they had, of a London afternoon, taken a hackney of all things, and driven off to such a shabby address, an address which Miss Portia had written down in a little beaten gold notebook – her *aide memoire*, as she called it.

Portia stopped. 'Ah, yes, here we are.'

'Where are we, Miss Portia?'

'Here.' Portia had said *here* very flatly. Even she could hear how flat her *here* was. 'Yes, this is it.' She nodded her head at Evie, as if Evie was cognisant of where they were, and why.

'Where are we, Miss Portia?'

Portia liked the way Evie still called her, in private, 'Miss Portia' but never more than at that moment. She did not want Evie's clear voice ringing out with a *Lady Childhays* in a place like this. It would be enough to bring around every pickpocket and thief in the neighbourhood.

She glanced nervously towards the hackney carriage, and having reassured herself that it was still waiting, she nodded at Evie to follow her, and the two women walked up the short flight of steps to the doorway of the shabby house to which Portia had directed the driver of the hackney to bring them, Evie tightly gripping the old silver handle of Portia's black umbrella, ready, in her own mind at least, for anything.

The old Georgian door swung open all too easily, and ahead of them stood a short flight of stairs, uncarpeted, and now barely painted. The sides of the stairs proclaimed that they had once been painted brown, and then old white, but inevitably each had flaked off in places to reveal the original wood.

'Wait for me here, Evie.'

As Portia nodded, her maid's grasp on her mistress's handsome old gamp tightened.

'I can poke whoever's eyes out with this, Miss Portia, don't you ever worry yourself about that.'

Portia nodded. It was true. An umbrella was a very useful weapon, and many a redoubtable woman had found it to be so, from its carved wooden or silver head to its heavy silk body and the steel tip at the end.

'I will not be long, I hope.'

'And so do I hope, and more than that, I pray for it, Miss Portia.'

Portia mounted the stairs, hardly believing that she had found herself in such a place. The smell of damp, the feeling of a building not properly lived in, was overwhelming. She wished that she had not come. She hoped against hope that the person she was meant to be visiting would turn out not to have given her the right address, that it was all a great mistake, and that when they did come face to face it would be at quite another address, with a gay interior filled with firelight and pretty things, and the sound of servants cooking and laughing together in the basement, and that the lamp over the door would be shining, and polished bright, and the first floor drawing room redolent of all pretty first floor drawing rooms at all good addresses all over London – a little over-crowded, a little too curtained and with slightly too much chintz and silk.

But it was not to be. The person for whom she was looking was there, and he was slumped in a dirty armchair, and his face was scarlet from the cold of the room, and his eyes were as red as any man's will become who has been drinking far too much for far too long. Portia stared for some seconds at the man she had loved as a young girl and thought of so often since.

'Richard. It's me – Portia.'

The eyes stared blearily up at her. 'So sorry, cannot get up. I am not quite myself, do you see, madam, just not myself?'

Portia's heart, already overburdened with the sadness of her widowhood, now experienced a piercing dart of pain of a quite different kind. It did not seem possible that Richard, handsome Richard Ward who had done everything that could have been required of him for both king and country, and had married his childhood sweetheart, the beautiful Miss Cecil, of impeccable lineage – that her Richard of such dear memory should have come to this, a slouched wreck of a man in a derelict building.

'Richard.' Portia knelt down in front of his chair, despite the awful dust on the filthy floor. 'I am – I am Portia Tradescant, that was. I married Lord Childhays, but you knew me as Portia Tradescant. I heard that you were a little down on your luck from your cousin Selina Ward, Richard, and so here I am. To help you – to help you get better, my dear. To help you recover your proper personality.'

'How do you do, my dear. Very nice, I am sure.' The love of her youth smiled vaguely down at her, and then stood up, swaying and holding out a hand to Portia, who also stood up, but did not take the hand, which was pointing in somewhat the wrong direction.

'I don't suppose you remember me, Richard, but we used to sail together in the dear old days at Bannerwick—'

Portia stopped suddenly, realising that she sounded ludicrous. How could a man in such a state and after so much time possibly either understand or remember her? And so, in a matter of seconds, possibly from having grown up with a number of eccentric relations, Portia immediately resolved that she could and must deal with her old friend's very evident predicament, and with this in mind went quickly back down to the hall to collect Evie.

'We have to take this gentleman back to Miss Tradescant's house, and send for a doctor. He is not at all well, Evie, not at all the thing, as you will see for yourself, but I think we can manage him between the two of us. We are not after all made of fine sewing cotton, are we?'

But as soon as Evie saw him she rolled her eyes at Portia and their urgent conversation, conducted in low voices, continued.

'I sees what you mean, Miss Portia. Not at all the thing, is 'e? No, more like parted from his senses some two bottles ago, I'd say, if you was asking me. Who is 'e anyways, when 'e's at home, may I ask?'

''E's – *he* is – er, Admiral Ward, Evie. Well, Vice Admiral really, but I cannot be bothered with that bit. An old friend of my family. The Tradescants and the Wards knew each other quite well, in the old days. The Wards holidayed near our house, and we all sailed. You might not remember. It was a long time ago.'

'Course I remember! Well I never, Miss Portia, Master Ward, of all people. This is Master Ward?' Evie pointed at poor Richard as if he was a prime exhibit at the Victoria and Albert Museum. 'Well I never! And him the talk of the neighbourhood and everyone sweet on him, so handsome, and so clever, and in the Navy and all, and decorated too, I believe. Come to this!'

She stared in some disgust at the middle-aged man now seated back in his chair.

'There is no need to go too far, Evie. He has only drunk too much, as so many gentlemen do.'

Portia was attempting a diplomatically low tone, but her maid would not adopt the same discreet note. Indeed so deep was her disgust at seeing a former friend of her mistress in such a state that she actually seemed to raise her voice.

'He's not just drunk, my lady. He is perfidiously intoxicated.'

Inwardly Portia raised her eyes to heaven. A part of her admired her darling old maid's long term determination to educate herself by learning a new word every day, but another part of her wished that Evie would keep her verbal experiments for her day off.

'Well, so be it, Evie. Perfidiously intoxicated or hopelessly drunk, either way we have to try to get him downstairs to the hackney carriage.'

'I will remain . . .' interrupted the object of their

mutual concern at this point, 'I will remain here. You all go on without me.'

He said this so many times in the next few minutes as the two women dithered about him that it was all Portia could do not to beg him to keep quiet until they were safely away to Aunt Tattie's house.

Happily Evie, being quite used to dealing below stairs with drunken butlers and footmen and the like, took no more notice of his interruptions than if he were a canary in a cage singing too loudly and too long.

'Well, but, Miss Portia, we can't do this on our own, really we can't. If there is one thing I know it is that a dead drunk man can be as much of a dead weight as a corpse, if not more so, and that is as much a fact as the fact that the Vice Admiral here is as pixilated as any common sailor on his shore leave.'

'In that case you had better fetch the hackney driver,' Portia told her, immediately seeing the truth in what Evie was hissing at her.

'The driver won't leave his cab in a neighbourhood like what this is, Miss Portia. Lord, they'd rather have their arms cut off of them than that. It's the 'orse, you see. Someone'll pick it out of the shafts and run off with it sooner than you can say disruptive, and that will be that.'

'In that case, you hold the horse, and I'll help the driver.'

Vice Admiral or no Vice Admiral, Richard

Ward might as well have been any drunken sailor, as Evie had so caustically observed, and as Portia and the reluctant hackney driver discovered when they took an arm each and helped him down the uncarpeted stairs, and then thankfully out into the street, and up into the hackney cab.

'You know what I'm now looking forward to, Miss Portia?'

Portia shook her head, thankful for the veiling hiding her feelings of impatience from her maid. Nevertheless she waited, expecting to hear that Evie was looking forward to a nice cup of cocoa.

'I am looking forward,' said Evie, panting from the effort of trying to keep the esteemed Vice Admiral somewhere near his seat, clutching on to one part of his body while Portia clutched on to another and all the while their victim switched between partial consciousness to low talk of an embarrassingly male nature, 'I am looking forward to Miss Tradescant's face when she sees what we've brought home to her.'

Portia half closed her eyes, despite the protection of her veil. As always Evie was completely right. Aunt Tattie would doubtless take one look at Richard Ward weaving about her drawing room and ring a bell for her butler and have him taken out and put in a home for derelicts. For 'bohemic' though Aunt Tattie might be, a longtime and very ardent supporter of the Arts and Crafts Movement, and a very recent convert to Rome, she would never be able to tolerate such a smelly trampy sort of person in her house, and who could blame her?

Tradescant House, the London home of Miss Tatiana Tradescant, although only round the corner from Piccadilly, despite having its own private ballroom was a great deal less grand than Medlar House, where Emily and Edith O'Connor were staying for the duration of the London Season. As it happened this was something that greatly appealed to Portia, more particularly, strangely enough, since her widowhood. She had no wish to return to the Childhays town house at this moment in her life, and frankly she did not think it worth the expense to open it up for Phyllis's London Season. As far as Portia could be objective about her daughter – always a difficult stance for a mother to take – she could not see Phyllis being the toast of her Season, any more than she could see her being swept off her feet by May's son, a future duke.

No, Phyllis was Phyllis, and while she was a brilliant horsewoman and was kind to animals and children, she was so awkward, so difficult, so contrary to the poem after which she had been so fondly named by her parents, that it would be a miracle if she married at all. In fact so difficult, so contrary, so awkward was she that it occurred to Portia that she might be the perfect person to deal with Richard Ward. After all, it often took a particularly brilliant rider to understand a particularly awkward horse, so it might be that it would take someone like Phyllis, so hoydenish and so determined to stand on the outside of everyone, to bring Richard Ward to his senses, in every way.

Portia tucked away this thought, as she so often did. She frequently had small thoughts upon which she sometimes acted, and sometimes did not. It was in this, as in so many other ways, that she missed her husband so much. He had always been so wise. Older than herself by some years, more experienced in every way as he was, she had always found that she could go to him with her problems and he would set her on the right path to doing or saying the proper thing. It was for this reason that she sometimes found herself praying to him, up above the skies, begging him to send down some good old common sense and plant it into her poor head.

As she looked up the stairs to Aunt Tattie's drawing room, and tried to prepare herself to witness the shock that she must be bringing home to her beloved relative, Portia wondered, albeit very briefly, what exactly her darling late husband, the wholly perfect Childie, *would* have done in her circumstances. Would he have brought the less than admirable Vice Admiral home? A few minutes later Aunt Tattie's expression of amazement told her niece all.

No, was the short answer, her dear Childie would never have brought Richard Ward, Admiral or Vice Admiral, home. He would have dealt with him in a proper place of restitution. He would never have brought this tall, still slim but red-faced inebriate home draped across his wife, her maid and a hackney cab driver. Childie never did have much time for such impetuosity.

'Dearest,' Aunt Tattie managed to say, speaking in a low, shocked tone. 'Is this a friend of yours? Because if so I think he seems a little – a trifle, let us say – unwell, to say the least.'

'He is a friend of both of us, Aunt Tattie. An old acquaintance from childhood days at Bannerwick, I am sorry to tell you.'

Aunt Tattie's expression, one of permanently heightened sanctity since her recent conversion to Rome, assumed a puzzled air.

'To both of us, dearest?'

'Yes, Aunt Tattie. This is Richard Ward. Do you remember, I used to go sailing with him at Bannerwick, in the old days?'

'My dear!' Aunt Tattie's expression quickly changed from heightened mysticism to one of all too human amazement. 'Never say so, dearest! This is Richard Ward? Whatever has happened to bring him to this pretty pass?'

At that moment Richard Ward, once more slumped and smiling vaguely, if amiably, was to be seen staring into the middle distance, the stupefaction on his face really only too evident.

Portia lowered her voice, and drew Aunt Tattie down the lower half of her drawing room towards the windows.

'It is since the tragedy, apparently, of losing his wife and daughter last year. The *Titanic*, you know.'

There was a long shocked silence. The disaster of the *Titanic*, of a ship so splendid that it had been boasted that it had been unsinkable, was still a stark and terrifying reality in everyone's minds. Hardly a family that they knew had remained unaffected by it.

'Dearest!' Aunt Tattie's hand went to the crucifix around her neck and she sighed. 'How too terrible.'

'Yes, it was too terrible, for as I understood it from his cousin, Selina, he had made a present of the voyage to his wife and only daughter, and they were both lost, Aunt Tattie. Both of them! Can you imagine? One moment they were a family and the next there was just him, all alone in a dark, desolated world.'

Portia was silent for a second, momentarily turning back to look over her shoulder at her own recent past and the loss in her own life. But she at least had been left with her children to sustain her in her grief.

Aunt Tattie's eyes softened as she stared at Richard Ward. 'How can we ever understand the pain of human grief except through God's eyes?'

'I know, darling. So you do see? Why he became so very – er – unwell as a result, Aunt Tattie? He is vastly unwell most of the time, I understand. Which being so, I wonder if we could take him to one of the upstairs rooms and lay him down?'

The two women stared at the slumped figure, his long legs stretched out in front of him, and then back at each other.

'We have to do something, dearest. When my brother, your Uncle Lampard, is prostrate like this, we usually find it best to drape the top half and let the legs take care of themselves.'

Aunt Tattie rang the bell for her butler, and between him and the hall boy, with Portia following on, they managed, somehow or another, to help the still rambling Vice Admiral up the stairs to a bedroom, where the butler and one of the footmen had no hesitation in locking him in. Meanwhile Aunt Tattie had retreated back to her drawing room, much as a general might retreat from the battlefield to his tent.

Once she had seen her old friend into the room, closely attended by the male servants, Portia came downstairs and told her aunt, 'he is not at all himself. But how providential that I should meet his cousin at Medlar House and she should tell me of his plight. Is it not providential?'

Aunt Tattie nodded, her stitching staying unsewn on her lap, the expression in her eyes changing from bewilderment to that of a person who wants to believe that helping a soul in distress is admirable but at the same time is fighting the very real idea that he may be going to be a great deal more of a nuisance than even the most intensely Christian person would desire.

'His cousin said that he came to this pass because he did not look after himself sufficiently, after – after the disaster, and the result is that he contracted a fever that affected his brain, apparently,' Portia repeated a little hopelessly.

Aunt Tattie started to twist the new amber-beaded rosary at her waist around her fingers, much as in the old days, before her conversion to Rome, Portia remembered that she had used to twist her Arts and Crafts necklaces around her long neck. Sometimes the necklace was twisted so tight that, as a child, Portia would become convinced that Aunt Tattie was going to leave herself without any breath at all, or that she would pass out from the pressure of the tightly wound necklace.

'Oh, dear. Then is he not just an inebriate but also – how can I say – insane, dearest? For if that is so, would it not be better if he was taken to a place for lunatics and such like?'

'We have locked him into his room, until morning, when the doctor could visit. That would be the best thing, would it not?'

Aunt Tattie raised her eyes to heaven, her lips moving, and was silent for a few seconds. It occurred to Portia that, unlike the clasping of beads, this was a new way of expressing her aunt-like emotions, giving her beloved relative a look all too reminiscent of a painting of some medieval saint. But happily for Richard Ward her decision turned out to be saintlike, and therefore entirely in keeping with her appearance.

'Very well, dearest, let him be locked up until a physician can pronounce on him. But after that it might be better if we found him somewhere more suitable.'

Portia nodded. It might indeed, she agreed to

herself, silently. On the other hand, she thought next, where?

'Or,' Aunt Tattie added, hope suddenly using a stronger tone for the first time since Portia had arrived back with Richard, 'dearest, being a sailor boy, he might decide to go to sea again, might he not?'

The look of hope in her eyes was most touching, whereas the look in Portia's eyes was one of confusion. Admittedly there had been times in her life when she had longed to see Richard Ward again, but not, *never* like this.

Phyllis, fresh from Lady Devenish's critical hands, and only newly arrived back from her ladyship's Ascot house, had no idea of the latest arrival at Tradescant House until her mother passed her in the upstairs corridor the following morning. Portia, wearing a grey silk skirt and half skirt – she was determined to remain in demi-mourning for her husband – together with an embroidered waistcoat complemented by a large-sleeved white blouse and a cameo brooch, was hurrying ahead of the doctor, a comfortingly unfashionable sight in her old if classical clothes, or so it seemed to Phyllis.

'There is never a good time to call a doctor out, is there?' Portia had asked of the solemn-faced gentleman when he was shown into her aunt's drawing room, and judging from the frosty look in his eyes which was his reply it seemed that the doctor could only agree with her.

'Doctor Bentley, dearest. He is here to see our new house guest, Vice Admiral Ward, who is not at all well,' Portia murmured as she passed Phyllis in the upstairs corridor, to allay any fears that she might have had when she saw their granite-faced visitor.

Phyllis had no idea why the doctor had been called, and as it happened cared less. She hated London so much that she would have been quite happy if Portia had told her that the doctor had been called for her, and that they must all return straight away to the country.

'Who *is* Vice Admiral Ward,' she demanded a few minutes later of her mother's maid. 'And why is he staying with Great-aunt *Tattie*?'

'The Vice Admiral is unwell, miss, and on no account must you go in there. He is not to be disturbed, not nohow, not by no-one. That is how it is, and no argufying, please.'

Phyllis walked round in front of Evie, who was busy ironing some of Phyllis's underpinnings in the small sewing room off her bedroom reserved for such niceties. To attract the maid's deliberately averted gaze Phyllis frowned at the garment the older woman was holding in her hand, and said, 'Uh – look, there's a crease there!' which had the desired effect of sending Evie hurrying back to the ironing board, and giving Phyllis an added purchase on the conversation.

'He may be unwell, Evie, but who *is* he?'

Evie frowned at the petticoat she was holding and her face assumed its most vague expression.

'He's an old friend of your mother's family, Miss Phyllis. He and your mother, as I remember it, used to go sailing together when they were young, and that. His family kept a house nearby, and they sailed together. Your mother always was a great sailor, not that you would know much about it, you having stayed at home with me rather than going off on a long and exciting voyage with her and the other children.'

But Phyllis was not really listening. Instead, she sidled out of the sewing room and walked down the corridor. She could not say why – it was probably because she was bored – but she truly had an impish desire to see this 'Vice Admiral Ward' for herself. Hearing her mother and the doctor's ebbing voices, she quickly stared over the banisters. A look at their heads below her, going further and further away, told her that the Vice Admiral must be all alone now.

It never occurred to her, because Phyllis was not blessed with an imagination, that the Vice Admiral, or whatever he was, might be truly ill with something horribly catching. Not even when she felt the handle of his bedroom door, turning it slowly one way and then slowly the other, only to find that the key had been on her side all the time. She had always found adventure and daring, most particularly doing things that she should not, to be intoxicating, ever since she was quite tiny. Apart from anything else it was always such fun to see how much attention was paid to the truly wicked – much more than to the vaguely good.

She turned the key in its lock. It made a reluctant, and finally quite a sharp click. She paused. Again she turned the door handle, and pushed open the large, old polished mahogany door. It went heavily and slowly across the thick carpet, inch by little inch in her cautious hand, until eventually Phyllis's head followed its direction and she could see into the room from where she stood beside it.

In front of her was a group of chairs, set about quite invitingly, two of which perhaps had only just been vacated by the doctor and her mother. Phyllis, who had large grey eyes, just like her mother, and a slender figure, just like her mother, and hair that although it was much lighter in colour than her mother's was nevertheless of the same texture, stared at the last, still seated, occupant of the casually arranged furniture. He was a tall man. To Phyllis of course he was an old man, perhaps forty. His hair was swept back in a rather old-fashioned way, and he had a beard, which gave him the look of some old tar, like those Phyllis had used to see when walking with her papa along the harbour-side when they were going to and from their much beloved family yacht.

Bold as brass Phyllis remained standing by the door until eventually, slowly, and quite obviously reluctantly, perhaps awakened by the sound of that first click of the key turning in the lock, the tall man slouched in the chair turned and stared up at this latest arrival in his dressing room.

'Hallo.' Phyllis shifted a little from foot to foot, knowing very well that she could be ruined for ever for just entering a gentleman's rooms on her own. But then that was what made it so particularly fascinating to be there, the knowledge that it was so daring, so wicked, so completely wrong.

'Who are you? Whoever you are! Get out!'

It seemed that the occupant of the chair was perfectly aware of the rules too, for he was frowning at her. No, he was positively scowling at her, but Phyllis, who always boasted that she was not frightened of anyone or anything, held her ground.

'I know who you are,' she told him in her determinedly truculent way. 'You're someone who used to go sailing with—'

But that was as far as she got, because of a sudden he sprang to his feet and started to lunge at her with a strange wiping gesture, as if he thought she was a ghost, or some sort of manifestation, and was wishing her a million miles away from him.

This was too much, even for Phyllis, and she darted quickly out of the room again. Having locked the door once more, she leaned against the outside wall half laughing and half gasping at her own audacity. No sooner had she calmed herself a little than she heard her mother's familiar quick, light step on the staircase leading up to the upper bedrooms, so she darted off once more towards the sewing room to find Evie still ironing and talking to herself.

'I will say for your mother that she never does pass up an opportunity to help another. A true Christian is your mother, Miss Phyllis, even if she does take it into her head to sail halfway round the world with her children and her dogs at a moment's notice, leaving me to look after you – what is such an 'andful that most people would rather catch a bolting horse one-handed than chaperon you for more than two minutes flat, Miss Phyllis, and that's a fact, so it is. That is a fact.'

Evie finished the garment that she had been ironing and held it up in front of her to inspect it. In the silence of that moment Phyllis decided on distraction as being the better part of valour.

'Learned any more new words today, Evie?'

Phyllis looked up at the maid from under her fringe of curly blond hair. It always stopped Evie to be asked to name her 'word' for that day. Phyllis glanced slyly across at her, encouraging the maid with her most entrancing smile, knowing that the maid would not be able to resist her bait.

'Pedagogue.' Evie sighed with satisfaction, spelling out the word after she had named it. 'It means someone who is a teacher,' she added.

Phyllis nodded, although she had not known this herself.

'That is a good one,' she said encouragingly, adding, 'I did go to see the Vice Admiral just now, as a matter of fact, Evie. I cannot tell a lie to you, because you have always been such a friend to me. I went to see the Vice Admiral, or whatever he is called.'

Evie went white. 'You never!' She darted round the other side of the ironing board and shook Phyllis hard and suddenly. 'You never!'

'No, of course not!' Phyllis backed away, laughing.

'Oh, Miss Phyllis, you are enough to give a person a twin fit, really you are. I just hopes that you does your courtesies and all that at Buckingham Palliss, and then gets on with it, and hops up the aisle with some unsuspecting young man what will never know until it's too late what 'e's lettin' 'imself in for, that's what I hopes for you. And for me too now I comes to think of it. Because as sure as eggs is eggs, Miss Phyllis, I have had more'n enough of you these last seventeen years, and that's the truth. You are not what I would call a good gel, you really are not. You like to make unhappiness where there is none. Now sit down and stay sitting till I gets you into your walking clothes, and then good riddance to you until it's time to go downstairs and out into the park.'

'Sorry, Evie. I just feel so cooped up here in London, just like one of Mama's prize hens.'

'Hens! You're a beautiful girl, Miss Phyllis. You're more beautiful than your mother was, I'll say that for you, and you can ride better than a man, but if you ask me, honest, I would say that you make more trouble than a—'

'Bolting horse – I know, so you keep telling me, Evie. But – I just feel so cooped up here.'

'The very idea of teasing your Evie with that

about visiting Vice Admiral Ward. I dunno.'

Phyllis bit the side of her thumb. So what if she had seen some old lunatic in his dressing room? It was hardly like murdering someone, was it? Besides, he had not been in a state to do more than stagger to his feet and then fall back into his chair waving his arms helplessly at something she could not see.

'As a matter of fact I did go to see the Vice Admiral,' she reiterated, sulkily, but half to herself, knowing that Evie was not really listening. 'And he's as mad as May butter and as dull as a dead seagull.'

She sighed suddenly, longing for the sea, longing to be small again, standing beside her father in his yachting clothes and holding his hand, and the whole world seeming to sparkle with the light on the water, and the gentle sound of the waves when they went below.

But her father was dead, and she was in London, and sometimes it seemed to her that she would never see the sea again, and certainly she would never see her father again in this life.

Of a sudden, and for no reason she could think of, she made up her mind to go to see the Vice Admiral again, unbeknownst to Evie, or anyone. It would be fun to go into the room again, and daring herself to do something would alleviate her boredom. And this time, this time she would not run away, she would stand her ground, and see what happened. Whatever did occur it would have to be yards more fascinating than sitting around waiting to be undressed and then dressed again to go for a walk in the Park.

Downstairs Portia was trying to explain to her aunt something of Richard's precarious state of health.

'He has just the same problem as Uncle Lampard, Aunt Tattie, and we all know what that is. There is nothing *congenitally* wrong with him. Dr Bentley examined him, and he has pronounced him physically perfectly fit, but mentally unfit for anything except staying where he is, and being given large doses of strong tea to get him through the first few weeks. Strong, strong tea, when the urge to – you know – is upon him.'

Aunt Tattie nodded. 'Your Uncle Lampard, before he retired to the seaside, always swallowed black treacle. He swore that killed the urge.'

'Black treacle? Well – that is interesting.'

'Yes, black treacle.' There was a small pause, and then, 'You know he never speaks to me now – now that I have gone over to Rome? He will not communicate either by the telephone or by letter unless completely necessary. Lampard is cross with me. You know he has quite disowned me?'

'I had heard.'

'We always were spiritually miles apart, dearest, as you know, but now we are even further apart. He thinks it is unpatriotic to belong to anything but – well, you know how people think of Rome and the Papists, dearest. Papists are all meant to be spies and things, usually disguised as nuns, and working against England, when in truth it is just the oldest religion of this country. Really, dearest, quite the oldest religion.'

'No, surely that would be the Druids, Aunt Tattie—'

'The oldest Christian religion, that is. The old English way of worshipping which made people perfectly happy, really. And the monasteries and the abbeys were the hospitals and full of quite good people, not just wicked monks making Benedictine as is so fondly supposed by so many.'

Portia nodded again. She had never been particularly religious. As a matter of fact she really rather took God for granted. Even now, despite Childie's being taken from her, she still saw God as the beloved creator of the most beautiful parts of the world, and the devil as the cause of all the evil parts. But she nevertheless drew the line when it came to becoming too admiring of any one religion. Aunt Tattie's recent conversion in Italy, while obviously suiting her beloved relative, would not suit Portia, any more than a fervent following of the Arts and Crafts movement had suited her when she was growing up as a child at Bannerwick.

'You are just not a joiner,' Childie would say, when Portia occasionally touched on such matters with him. 'That's why you like sailing. You are alone with the sea and the seagulls and that is all. The wind and the sun, the waves and the sky, and the boat, are enough for you.'

And it was true. They were enough, or at least they had been until Childie had been gathered, and then suddenly even they were as empty as a child's hand trying to hold the sea in its palm.

'I think I had better go and check on Richard again, Aunt Tattie. He might be more himself now. It is over twelve hours, after all, since we brought him home. It might be time to start giving him tea, or black treacle, or some such.'

Aunt Tattie shook her head. 'I should not do any such thing, if I were you, Portia.' She gave her niece a sudden piercing look. 'In my experience locked doors are better kept just as they are, locked.'

But of course Portia would not believe her. Watching her sidling out of the room a few minutes later on some pretext or another, Aunt Tattie shook her head, and raised her eyes to heaven. No good would come of it, of that she was quite, quite sure. She twisted the amber rosary around her waist, tighter and tighter. It was immensely comforting, although she could not have said why.

On with the Dance

Now that she was fully prepared, her wardrobes bulging with the new Season's costumes for every occasion, Daisy, Countess of Evesham, was once more as full of youthful energy as if it was her own coming out that she was engaged upon. Of course it was not her own coming out but the launch of yet another American debutante with an anxious mama somewhere in the vanguard, her eyes firmly set on her daughter's acquiring a title.

Daisy gazed at her best and oldest friend soulfully across the short piece of carpet that separated them. Unlike the rest of the world her friend had always been *such* a friend, always so complimentary, so anxious to please. But even her greatest friend, it seemed, was turning against her. Refusing to pay her compliments, not troubling to try to reflect Daisy's beauty, only telling her over and over again, sometimes as much as twenty times a day, the terrible news that no amount of ear blocking or eye shutting would now delay, namely that Daisy was at last – to her own and her best friend Mrs Looking Glass's astonishment – *older*.

'Jenkins,' Daisy demanded suddenly of her maid, 'do you fink it is time we changed Mrs Looking Glass? She really does not seem quite as good as she used to be, somehow.'

Jenkins stood behind her mistress and they both stared at Daisy's best friend, her silver-backed cheval mirror tilted at just the angle to take in the whole of Daisy, down to her tiny elegant feet.

'I'd say this mirror is as good as it always was, my lady, and that cannot be said of all of us, can it?'

The maid walked off, and as she did so Daisy poked out a small, pink tongue at the older woman's back. Jenkins always had been such a downright pill. Despite the extreme disparity in their circumstances, nowadays Daisy actually suspected her of being jealous of her mistress, which was preposterous of course, because jealousy should really be confined, in Daisy's view, to equals. It was surely quite enough that Daisy had kept Jenkins in a fashion that would never have been available to her in any other sphere, but now, if you please, needs must be that Jenkins took ruthless advantage of Daisy's increasing age and girth, refusing to pay her compliments however much they might be needed, which they most definitely were.

Daisy lay down on her bed so that Jenkins could pull on her stockings. She stared at the heavy swirls of plasterwork that decorated her bedroom ceiling, which seemed miles above her bed, and thought about her plans for the Season.

Of course, the one good thing about poor Sarah Hartley Lambert was that she was no stunner, so Daisy would not be entirely eclipsed by this season's protégée. Although admittedly Sarah Hartley Lambert's face was really very pleasant, and she had magnificent eyes of a lovely blue, she was, happily for Daisy, far, far too tall to ever be described as a beauty. No-one would ever, Daisy guaranteed, stand on chairs to see Sarah Hartley Lambert when she passed by in a ballroom or at a soirée, as people had so often been known to do when Daisy had passed in years gone by longing to catch sight of her *en plein beauté*.

And even now, of a late afternoon when the light was kindly and the fire lit, there were still people who became quite spellbound by Daisy's presence, mesmerised by the brilliance of her looks, by her famous profile, by the delicacy of her features, by her voice, by her laugh that could, at will, climb up and down the scales as tunefully as an opera singer's soprano. It was a strange fact, but it was a fact, that beauty in a human being was as fascinating as a famous building, most particularly, for some reason, in the female form. Cleopatra, Helen of Troy, Daisy Lanford, were more famously fascinating to people in general than inventors or explorers.

And of course Daisy knew that she was just such a beauty, and, happily for her, none of her protégées up to and including poor Sarah Hartley Lambert could ever be described as such. It was most reassuring for an older woman.

Tonight they had all been asked to the opening ball of the Season, and it was to be a tiara affair. There would be so many diamonds winking and blinking that by the time supper was served they would start to look quite common, and the sight of an unadorned head to appear quite enticing. Of course Daisy had seen it all before. The gentlemen, at first drawn only to the great glittering heads of the older women, would nevertheless be forced by etiquette to step onto the ballroom floor with younger heads, heads that were supported by youthful necks that had no need of pearl or diamond chokers to cover them, as did their mothers' or chaperones'.

And yet, despite having seen it all before, and so many, many times, Daisy knew that the game was already on, and she was already all too involved. She had to pair Sarah Hartley Lambert off with the best and the most suitable, or Mrs Hartley Lambert would not keep recommending Daisy to her friends in America.

Alas, so many American mothers had been put off titled Englishmen by the unhappiness of their offspring. So naive really, as if happiness in marriage was something that was to be expected out of life! Daisy sighed out loud and allowed her long, still elegant leg, now stockinged and fastened to a beautifully placed suspender to drop back onto the bed. She could honestly say that the thought of being happy *and* married had never, ever occurred to her; not once, not in her whole life. It simply had not arisen as a notion, not even when she was seventeen and terribly stupid. She had always far preferred her birds and her dogs to either of her two, now fortunately quite dead, husbands.

Husbands were so terribly, terribly – well, terrible, really. Nothing was ever enough for them. They must always have more of you than you wanted to give them. More love making, more attention to the menus, more listening, more flattering, and they never, ever thought how it was for *you*. They never thought about how tedious it was to be at their beck and call all the time, as if you were a servant and not a person. Always having to look beautiful for them, always having to look happy because you were married to *them*, always having to be thrilled that you were their wife, when really, particularly if they were married to someone like Daisy, they should be thrilled that they were your *husband*!

Feeling more than satisfied with the intelligence of her own thinking Daisy, now clad in her underpinnings, arose from her sumptuous bed with the great hand-sewn silk tapestry of her coat of arms behind it, and allowed Jenkins to finish dressing her. Tonight at the ball it would be Daisy's duty to make sure that Sarah Hartley Lambert danced every dance, that her card was full, that there would not be a moment when Daisy Lanford's protégée would be singled out as being without a partner. It did not matter whom Miss Hartley Lambert danced with at this her debut ball, but that she danced all night was imperative.

More than that, she must give the impression of looking more beautiful, more stunning, than any of the other debutantes. Daisy knew that Lady Medlar had Miss Edith O'Connor under her wing and that she would be this year's entry from Medlar House. Lady Medlar was always a formidable adversary, but, most satisfyingly, Daisy had heard that Miss O'Connor was less than beautiful and only interested in horses and hunting – in short, most completely and typically Irish.

And then again, at Lady Devenish's 'house of correction', as her Ascot house was jokingly referred to by fashionable wags, there had been staying, along with Edith O'Connor, a Miss Phyllis de Nugent. Now rumour had it that Miss de Nugent was a beauty, but that she had a character flaw and was wilful to the point of rudeness. It was such a satisfactory rumour that Daisy was inclined to believe it. And of course, if it was true, it would mean that Miss de Nugent might not be so much of a threat to Sarah Hartley Lambert's success as Daisy had first supposed.

The great thing about Sarah was that she was pliant in her attitudes, affectionate towards her mama, and reverential towards Daisy, all of which made Daisy feel oddly fond of her in a way that she would not normally feel towards a younger woman. And moreover, although she was too tall for the average Englishman's taste, there was no doubt that she did at least have charm, and that, coupled with a large fortune, in Daisy's experience very often took a girl a great deal further socially than beauty.

Whatever happened Daisy knew that tonight was all important and that Sarah must defeat all criticism from the moment she entered the ballroom, for it was not just the early bird that snatched the worm, in Daisy's experience it was, as it were, the early debutante too.

Not that the young men on offer this Season would be worms, not at all – they would all be aristocrats, officers on leave, heirs to great estates, with hardly grown moustaches and too young to have had much opportunity to meet the opposite sex, and they would definitely be scanning the ballroom for suitable mates. So much so that Daisy often thought, to herself only of course, that she would not be at all surprised one of these days to see the mashers entering ballrooms with binoculars around their necks, as they would at the racecourse, so openly did they quiz each new arrival at the ball.

'My lady is looking quite her old self.'

Now that she was finished with her labours Jenkins stood back and looked openly admiring of Daisy, which was really most unusual for her. This was the moment for Daisy to turn and stare at her best friend, and this time, dressed as she was for a private luncheon with an old flame, Daisy could only agree with both her dressing mirror and Jenkins. She did look quite herself. And although her former lover was old and overweight now, and although they had stayed friends (surely a miracle?), there was a real chance, provided he did not eat too much luncheon (not something on which Daisy would actually care to place a wager), that their charmed friendship might, considering how Daisy was looking that day, change back into a gentle afternoon *tendresse* – well, at any rate, it was certainly not out of the question. Not the way Daisy was looking.

The fashion that year was not particularly suited to the more mature woman, and yet, although Daisy's waist was no longer a charming eighteen inches, she nevertheless retained that peculiar aura that a beautiful woman will always emanate simply from having worn lovely things over a great period of time, as if the clothes themselves had somehow left some sort of permanent unseen imprint, as if they had somehow penetrated the pale skin of their wearer so that their elegance had seeped into her bones.

Today Daisy was wearing a straight walking coat in silk over a perfectly cut Regency style Empire gown, which gave a slimmer look to the hips. Her coat was cut three-quarter length, and the dress pleated to continue below it where the coat left off. Her hat was – well, it could only be described as enormous, as had been the fashion some years before. And of course quite heart stopping, once placed on Daisy's elegant head, its enormous ostrich plumes falling forward to within half an inch of its edge. The neck of the coat was filled with Daisy's famous pearls, row upon row of them, and of such a fine quality that they seemed somehow to shine upwards and give her pale skin an added lustre, as all good pearls must.

'My lady's gloves, my lady's umbrella, and there we are,' murmured Jenkins, as her mistress turned from the silver-backed mirror and made her way towards her bedroom door, ready at last for the world to see her as they both, maid and mistress, liked her to be seen – as perfectly turned out as any thoroughbred racehorse being walked round the paddocks at Ascot.

'Do you know, Jenkins, vis is what I particularly like. Ve start of ve Season. Everything so fresh, and even the trees in the Park seeming to make an extra effort to look better van ever. Vis is what I truly like.'

As well as the compliment of being asked to a particularly private luncheon with a particular old flame, Jenkins thought, and she made a note in her head to write up the observation in her secret diary, which she had managed to keep up despite all the exigencies of the Countess's demands and the travelling that their life involved.

Happily, not only Jenkins's diary, but also her thoughts, were hidden from her mistress, unlike the facts of her mistress's private life, to which Jenkins had always been and always would be privy. Daisy knew, as Jenkins knew, that her maid would never, ever, betray a confidence. There would be no scandalous detail artlessly disclosed after a house party, such as had been known to drop from the lips of other people's personal maids, or valets. Neither would Jenkins ever tell even the oldest of the servants where she had waited for her mistress, at whose houses, or with whom Daisy lunched or dined privately, for the simple reason that Jenkins was no fool. She trusted other servants as little as her mistress trusted men.

Daisy Lanford, Countess of Evesham, was Jenkins's work of art, as much as any painting that hung downstairs in the great saloon of the Eveshams' town address was part of some painter's oeuvre. It was Jenkins's pride to remain as she had always been – discreet. And in the end, she knew, it would be worth it, for Daisy would reward her, not just perhaps with a cottage on her estate, but with some of her beautiful things, and that would mean that Jenkins would know that she had done her duty, pleased her mistress, but, most of all, pleased herself. For Daisy as well as Jenkins knew that the maid was essential to her mistress. They were locked together in a relationship far more powerful than any she might have had with her husbands (least of all *them*) or her lovers, Royal or otherwise. If Daisy was a beautiful tree it was Jenkins who, like nature herself, placed the leaves upon her, and decreed not just when they should bloom, but when they should fall.

Jenkins followed her mistress down the grand staircase, five paces exactly behind, and watched with gimlet eyes as the menservants bowed to her, and the doors opened to her. Jenkins knew, as well as any, that those bows were shared by her, that those doors opened for her too, and that when the King's grey-blue eyes had, in years gone by, softened with appreciation at the sight of her mistress in the great plumed hat that she was still wearing, and when His Majesty had seen that her silhouette was as trim as any woman of her age, and his guttural voice had softened, it had been as much a compliment to Jenkins as it had been to Daisy. To say that to serve the old king in this way had been satisfying to a woman of her kind was to say the very least. Nothing could have given Jenkins greater satisfaction than to know that her mistress was also his. In France, as she well knew, when the old king had been alive, Daisy had been accorded the same status as his queen, so seriously did the French, quite rightly to her mind, take the status of king's mistress, or *maitresse en titre*, which was why Jenkins so often said 'we' in the servants' hall, and why it was accepted that she did so. Jenkins ruled the house as much as her mistress. Like Daisy's beauty, it was just an accepted fact.

Sarah, poor Sarah, Mrs Hartley Lambert sighed inwardly, what ever had the poor girl done to deserve to grow so tall? It was as if, Sarah being an only child, thanks to the unhappy early demise of her sainted father, it was as if nature had been determined to make up to Mrs Hartley Lambert, and so presented her with one big baby instead of several small ones.

Not that she did not at that moment look fine

and really rather handsome in her ball gown of white silk with its beaded hem and capped sleeves – very much à la mode and slightly Grecian in feel – because she did. Not that she did not have good thick dark hair, and a fine pair of blue eyes, but oh dear what a disadvantage when to see them even her mother had to step back and stare up at her until her neck nearly cricked. If only the Countess were proved to be wrong and there were some titled English gentlemen who did have a preference for statuesque girls, if only Sarah, at her first ball tonight, were danced with more times than her two English friends, then her mother's heart would be at ease for the rest of her days, of that Mrs Hartley Lambert was quite, quite sure.

'I so wish that you were coming with me, Mama dear.'

Sarah stared down at her mother, suddenly feeling bereft of confidence. Remembering the treatment she had been given at the hands of the Honourable Phyllis de Nugent and Miss Edith O'Connor did nothing to make her feel better.

'No, darling, I promised the Countess that I would leave all your chaperoning to her. It is part of our agreement. After all, I was by your side all during our stay in Paris, and that was quite sufficient. No, darling, it is altogether more fitting, here in London, if the Countess is your chaperon. She has the entrée to Court circles in London, which I have not. And really, you know, my rheumatism, since I came to London, has not been at all good. No, while you are out dining and dancing I shall have a nice rosewater and malmaison scented bath and a lie down, and that will keep me quite tranquil until you come back with all your news of the evening. When you return you will find me still awake with my light on. I shall be reading. You have only to scratch at my door, and I will call to you. Oh, darling, what excitement, your first ball. And with the Countess by your side, let alone Lady Devenish, you will not put a foot wrong. I dare say you will not be seated for so much as a second, your card full of names, all the – what does the Countess call the young men here? Oh yes, all the *mashers* ready to fight duels over you!'

Neither mother nor daughter was so stupid as not to know that this was all palpable nonsense, but it was well-intended nonsense, and so Sarah kissed her mother on the cheek, and straightening her back, and nodding to her maid to pick up her evening cloak and fan, she followed their hired steward down the grand staircase and so out into the street and to the waiting carriage that would take her round the corner to the Countess's town house. Following which they would go in stately fashion to dine with Lord and Lady Mount William and the rest of *le tout Londres*, as the fashionable and aristocratic were known, before going on to Lady Medlar's opening ball of the Season at Medlar House.

'God bless you, my poor child!'

From the first floor drawing room above, unbeknownst to her daughter, Mrs Hartley Lambert waved a little forlornly to Sarah's departing figure.

She could only thank God that she could pay the Countess to supervise Sarah's London Season, for assuredly she herself was simply not capable of such an undertaking. It had been quite faint-making enough to deal with the Countess over their financial negotiations, to pick up all her bills, to sign agreements for the expenditure needed to finance Sarah's coming-out ball, their innumerable outfits for Ascot (that was an event that not even Mrs Hartley Lambert would miss) and so on and so forth, but to have to bear the burden of the opening balls as well would have been simply too much. It was not just that she was herself a little shy of Society, and always had been, but also that she dreaded having to risk seeing her own daughter left languishing on a gilt chair behind the Countess, not a name scribbled in her card, while every other girl danced the night away. That she could not be asked to face.

Besides, she was shrewd enough to know that whatever money she dispensed, however much of her fortune she lavished on her daughter's London debut, if she herself appeared in the least bit gauche, or out of sorts socially at these opening events, it would be enough to enable the Countess to blame any failure of Sarah's to attract the right attentions on her mother's lack of social grace.

No, Mrs Hartley Lambert knew that she herself was best kept out of sight, best able to help her daughter by a judicious discretion as far as her own appearances at social events in and around town were concerned. Her time would come in June with Ascot and the great moment of Sarah's ball, when she would, she hoped, have the unquestionable delight of finding that her daughter's social success in England was by that time quite, quite assured. She sighed at the thought. It was most reassuring.

Sarah shivered. The intricacies of English dining had been brought home to her by Lady Devenish, and she thought she had not, as yet, made a *faux pas*, but there was still the ball ahead, still the truly dreadful notion, which would not be dispelled, that no-one would pencil his name in her card, no young officer come forward and ask for the next dance, no brilliant young man down from Oxford catch her eye and walking forward and bowing low over her hand (kissing was only for married women) write his name in the little tasselled dance card which hung from her white-gloved wrist beside her fan.

Despite Sarah's God's being very much an American one who she imagined might not like visiting England any more than she herself had really been able to up until now, she prayed to Him as she decorously and gracefully followed the Countess up the grand staircase of Medlar House and into the long gallery which led, eventually, to the ballroom. The opening ball of the Season had used to be the province of the Duchess of Salisbury, but since she had been gathered to her Maker the honours had passed to Lady Medlar, still, even at her age, one of the three great London hostesses who were, to everyone's minds, including the reigning political party, more than an influence on London, but in so many ways – London itself.

Nicknamed the 'Great Divider' since she had changed political sympathies and gone over to the Liberals, Lady Medlar was feared by duchess and debutante, social climber and politician alike. No believer in the softer, more compliant virtues usually associated with the fair sex, she was considered to be more overtly fearsome than any man would quite dare to be. A friend to none and a potential enemy to everyone, she had not spoken to her husband for more than twenty years, a situation which might have daunted a lesser character, but which seemed to add, in some strange way, a curious, almost satanic lustre to Augustine Medlar's reputation.

Aunt Tattie would often say, when Portia was enduring her own first London Season, 'If you had ever seen Augustine Medlar eating an ortolan, her great white teeth masticating the little bird's bones, Portia dearest, you would not, ever, wish to cross swords with her, believe me. Not ever.'

After which, to add drama to her statement, Aunt Tattie would shudder elaborately and drift off to work on a tapestry of medieval ladies awaiting their knights' return from the Crusades. A subject which to Portia, in some strange way, seemed to embody Aunt Tattie's life, whether at Bannerwick or at Tradescant House in London, for ever since the dark days of her crush on the tutor who had come to teach Portia at Bannerwick, Aunt Tattie's heart had remained firmly and obstinately unmoved by any other man.

In the intervening years, because she was not poor, Aunt Tattie had become quite famous for her inordinate sensitivity. It was generally thought that it was this characteristic which had kept her a maiden aunt and a spinster. Not that there had not been quite overt attentions paid to her by members of the opposite sex. At least one of the rectors of the local parishes had visited her for tea on a regular basis, not to mention a local magistrate who, although somewhat advanced in years, nevertheless managed to write to Aunt Tattie weekly, sometimes daily poems, most of which, it had seemed to Portia, had a tendency to begin with *Oh fairest one!*

If Mrs Hartley Lambert could not find it in herself to attend the Season's opening ball at Medlar House, such was not the case with the other mamas who had debutante daughters to present.

Naturally Portia was present at Medlar House that night, but despite the fact that Emily and Edith O'Connor were staying there for the Season Portia arrived with Phyllis in the anteroom to the ballroom several streams of people ahead of her old friend and her debutante daughter. The girls waved to each other, of course, Phyllis a little too vigorously, Portia thought, but then everything about Phyllis had always been a little too vigorous, so perhaps there was nothing to be done. Certainly

Lady Devenish had managed to work a few miracles, but not, alas, all.

Approaching the top of the staircase but not yet arrived on the landing leading to the ballroom, Daisy looked back down the great wide staircase with its ironwork and its marble steps now crowded with the occasionally great and the sometimes good. After all the trials and tribulations of the previous weeks it was most satisfactory to gaze proudly down at so very many tiaras, so very many jewels, so very many silk dresses, embroidered dresses, dresses of every kind and colour, but none at all that could ever be described as dull or inelegant. And the gentlemen too in their black waistcoats were more than elegant, they were superb. No doubt of it, it seemed to Daisy, it was as fine a sight as you could hope to find, and there was certainly no other nation that looked half so well in his evening clothes, do what they would, as an Englishman. Every other nation wore either too many medals or too vulgar a waistcoat, and of course, the English tailoring being what it was, there was nothing to beat it for making the dumpiest man look elegant.

Daisy touched Sarah Hartley Lambert on the arm. 'Everyone's here tonight, and everyone who is not here is certainly wishing they *were*, do you see, Miss Hartley Lambert? Vat is how privileged we are and we must always remember it.' She and her protégée resumed their slow progress up the staircase to the anteroom, which in turn led to the grand rooms that were decorated with the heavy blooms still favoured by Lady Medlar, despite the newer Japanese influence being felt in so many other fashionable houses.

Vast amounts of English lilac, pretty only for a very few hours when brought indoors, and therefore all the more treasured, spilled from the splendid vases in the anterooms and on the landings, and their subtle scent drifted down towards the waiting crowds of guests. To the gentlemen in their black waistcoats and immaculate tails, or their uniforms and decorations, to the older women in their tiaras set off by beaded and sculpted ball gowns, to the debutantes in their endless white, made up from fine muslin, or tulle, or sensuous silk, carrying their fans and their reticules, their dance cards looped over their gloved wrists, all of them doubtless suppressing an almost irresistible desire to yawn nervously, or tremble visibly, such was the importance of the occasion of their first Season's opening ball.

Pausing behind an elderly duchess and her party, Daisy again stared down the staircase to the newly arriving fashionable throng. Young debutantes at their first ball always rather reminded her of two-year-old fillies in the paddocks before the races. Groomed to within an inch, the shine and the glow of them making their eyes look larger, their hair more lustrous. Indeed their very grooming seemed to make them appear even younger and more vulnerable than they doubtless were, so that, what with the newly fashionable higher waistlines and narrower shapes, the dresses for the young had considerably less substance to them. And what with the newer, simplified vogue in hair, this year's crop of debutantes appealed more than ever to Daisy's experienced eyes as being just so many poor little lambs being led to the slaughter of marriage.

Marriage! Daisy sighed inwardly, remembering.

What a shock it was for all young, sensitive women of her day. At only seventeen or eighteen to be thrust up the aisle and down again by parents only too willing to find someone, anyone, suitable for their daughter. And then the ghastly fright of It all, followed by the dread of childbirth, itself followed by yet more childbirth, until such time as the *heir and the spare*, as the first two baby boys were now known in aristocratic circles, had been safely secured for the good of the title or the family line.

Of a sudden, despite looking at her most beautiful for some weeks, and feeling quite the same, as she gazed about her at the other women, both young and old, Daisy realised that she was only too glad to be through certain phases of her life. Even the loveliest of love affairs, affairs that could safely be undertaken once one's husband was satisfied that one had done one's duty to the family name by giving birth to the all-important sons, were hardly great compensation for the misery of what had gone before.

The unloveliness of married love was something from which few of her generation ever really recovered. Indeed, when the trials of childbirth were finally over, a great many women took to their beds, and feigned illness for the rest of their lives, very often for no better reason than to escape any further attentions from their husbands. Such poor sorts of creatures were utterly devoid of the kind of determined spirit possessed by Daisy herself, and yet in her heart of hearts Daisy, despite being so different, readily sympathised with them, knowing as she did that the men in their lives were probably incapable of anything but the heartiest selfishness, and that the marital side of their lives would have provided them with more fear and discomfort than they could have thought possible.

Despite all this, however, Daisy still had no hesitation in taking on this poor tall American gel and pushing her into the very situation that she, as a more than mature woman, knew very well would be at its best a matter of mere contentment, and at its worst would make a truly sensitive soul tremble. But really, there was nothing else to be done. And the reason there was nothing else to be done was that it was still as much a gel's fate to do as Society chose as it had ever been.

Miss Hartley Lambert would have to pretend, as her mother doubtless had, that, come what may, marriage had made her happy. She would have to have at least two boy babies for the sake of the family name, and she would have to smile and smile, and pretend and pretend in front of friends and family, Church and State, until such time as Society allowed her to have her fancy tickled by someone who was not her husband. Those were the rules, and, it seemed, always would be.

'My dear, just stay close to me, and I will see that you are looked after properly.'

Happily for Daisy, and indeed as it proved for Miss Hartley Lambert, the Countess had the command of certain more mature men, who, on seeing any of Daisy's protégées left on their gilt chair for far too long, would approach the wretched creature and scribble their names in her card – in return, of course, for a certain consideration, to be sent round to their clubs by the Countess at the end of the Season and then doubtless, and without hesitation, forwarded to the gentlemen's bookmakers, most particularly after Ascot.

'So, now we move forward.'

Sensing the young girl's nerves Daisy smiled at Sarah Hartley Lambert. Tall or not, the young American girl was so beautifully presented that even Mr Worth's old heart would have turned over with pleasure at the sight of her tricked out in the simplest gown that had surely ever come out of Paris?

The dress was of hand-made creamy white lace. It was almost, but not quite, a little reminiscent of the *merveilleuse* dresses that had burst upon the fashionable scene a few years before, but unlike the *merveilleuse* it had not the Grecian effect around the bust, nor the drapery held high underneath it, nor the full train. Rather it was short-trained, with a demure bodice set high, in thin lace, sleeves made of silk covered in the same lace in two columns either side, ending in a frill at the elbow, and then a neat wide belt of silk from which dropped a full skirt, lace-covered silk once more. The hair was looped up but set wider in the new way, and the shoes underneath the full skirt were hardly seen.

All in all, it was white, it was demure, but it nevertheless spoke of great wealth. Hardly any other girl of Daisy's acquaintance and of the same age as Miss Hartley Lambert could possibly afford a dress so richly made for the opening ball of the Season, however much she might yearn for one. Daisy knew, all too well, that all round the ballroom, seated on gilt chairs beside their chaperons for the evening, there would be handfuls of poor little shivering wretches who, unlike Miss Hartley Lambert, would be only too grateful to be tricked out in some old dress that had once belonged to their mother – or even their grandmother. Of course now that it was on its second or even third generation it would have been radically altered, usually completely re-tailored by some provincial dressmaker, the 'good' material used yet again for displaying the newest victim out on parade for the opening ball of the all-important Season, but that would not be making much difference to the wearer. She would have been told just how lucky she was to have a dress *at all*. Daisy had been a considerable heiress in her own right, with connections at Court and she knew not what, but that had not stopped her mother from presenting her at Court in a third-hand dress, admittedly newly embroidered, but nevertheless one which had seen other days, if not at Court, certainly in other ballrooms.

Indeed Daisy remembered how very grateful she had been for it, too, with its silken folds and its rare embroidery. But not nearly as grateful as she had been for the beauty she had inherited from that self-same grandmother, a beauty so young and so radiant that Daisy had become engaged to the catch of that particular year long before Ascot, which meant that her heavy diamond engagement ring had been on show for a satisfyingly long period of time, much to the envy of her rivals.

For the fact was that everyone, male and female alike, were rivals when it came to the Season. It was just how it was, and no-one of the same sex could trust another not to either cut in on them and sweep some little patrician beauty off to the shires or entrance some rich, titled gentleman into waltzing them into the conservatory, where, without hesitation, the debutante in question would accept an offer of marriage from a perfect stranger of whom her mama could only approve – just so long as he was not an Irish peer.

Hoary, hairy Irish peers with wild and worthless estates in remote parts of Ireland were *not* acceptable, unless of course the daughter was unearthly plain or had a reputation for bad temper, or worse. Not that Irish peers, however hirsute, would not be preferable to a foreigner. Inwardly Daisy sighed. A foreigner was not and would never seem a good idea to an English mama. To kiss your young daughter goodbye and watch her sail off to some foreign shore where heaven only knew what went on would never do if you had the slightest regard for your offspring. Everyone knew that foreigners had a way of locking girls up and making them have babies every year, and that they had little or no refinement when it came to marriage. No – by now, thank heavens, Daisy and Miss Hartley Lambert were nearing the top of the stairs and the receiving line – no, Ireland was really the very outer limit of what was acceptable in a husband, and even that was not uppermost in a mama's mind when presenting her daughter for the Season.

Not that everyone did not enjoy going to Ireland to let down their hair, because they did, but no concerned mother who loved her daughter in the proper way would want her to marry and settle there, or indeed in Scotland or Wales, or anywhere, when Daisy came to think of it, either remote or overseas. Although of course certain parts of the Empire, like India, had to be considered, always providing that the young couple would return laden with gold and jewels, not to mention valuable holdings that would keep them in luxury at their country estates for the next few generations.

So, when the dancing started tonight that was what was at stake. The young shivering innocents seated on their gilt chairs in their endless white dresses thought it was all about a gentleman dancing with you and falling in love, poor creatures. They thought the Season was all about beauty and love – they possessing the beauty, the gentlemen possessing the love – when in reality the older women in the room, the chaperons, the dowagers, knew that it was all about wealth, about titles, about acquiring the things of this world before your bloom wore off. Indeed some of the luckier young girls in the room, before many weeks had passed, would become wealthy to such a degree that there could never be a time when they would ever want again, for jewels, for land, for servants . . . Daisy paused in her thoughts, while nodding elegantly down the great staircase to someone in the crowd below. She had been *about* to add 'for happiness' – but really, happiness had nothing whatsoever to do with it, had it?

For instance, if someone had asked Daisy if she was 'happy' when she was Miss Hartley Lambert's age she would have answered that of *course* she was happy. Not to be happy if you were rich and titled would be ludicrous. Worse, it would be letting down the side. And far worse than that, it would be letting down one's *class*.

No, of course, if one had several houses and a stable full of hunters, if one had married a man with a title, if one had to change one's dress sometimes as much as four or five times a day, of course one was happy. One knew this because when one saw people in the streets, or in the countryside, who did not have such things, it was quite clear to one that they were *un*happy. They had to be. If they were not unhappy then there was something very wrong with them; they were lunatics, or simple at the very least.

Daisy had occasionally seen someone cheerful in the street outside, as her carriage passed them – or, nowadays, sometimes even her new shiny motor car – someone whose face had lit up while greeting a friend, or who was walking along arm in arm with her husband, or who was wheeling her perambulator off to some park with a beautiful bonny-looking baby seated in it, but really, they were not *normal*. They could not be. To be happy without possessing the kind of clothes and jewels, titles and estates, horses and carriages, motor cars and servants that Daisy had once possessed, before the awful decline of land values and other disasters, would be – well, it would be very real madness.

'Daisy, darling Daisy.'

It was the Duke of Connerton. Daisy smiled. It was always the Duke of Connerton. He had a crush on Daisy. He had always had a crush on Daisy. As a matter of fact he seemed to have had a crush on Daisy ever since she had met him out hunting when still a young gel. He was though, alas, very dull – more than that, he was stultifyingly dull. Still, he was at least a duke. Daisy eyed Miss Hartley Lambert, and at once, on cue, Sarah Hartley Lambert dropped into a really rather magnificent curtsy. (Congratulations, Lady Devenish!) In answer to Miss Hartley Lambert's curtsy the Duke inclined his head, his monocle keeping admirably steady as he looked poor nervous Miss Hartley Lambert up and down.

'Duke, may I introduce Miss Hartley Lambert? From New York.'

'Quite so.'

The two old hands exchanged looks, and at once Daisy could see the thought crossing the ducal mind. It was all too obvious to Daisy, who knew her Duke really rather well, that he was thinking, *The poor gel is really far too tall.*

Inwardly Daisy sighed. Thank heavens she had her 'paid retainers' as she called her retinue of men, some of whom, even now, she could see moving towards them, for without them Miss Hartley Lambert would be left seated on a gilt chair all evening. The fact that Miss Hartley Lambert was so tall, that no matter who was seated in front of her she would still have a good view of the dancing, would be small comfort indeed to her noble chaperon, or doubtless to her protégée. They both in their quite separate ways had a duty to perform.

As the opening ball of the Season progressed, Mrs Hartley Lambert had experienced no difficulty in keeping awake and waiting for the return of her daughter to their rented house in Mayfair.

She was quite naturally unable to sleep, being, as she was, full of that particular dread mixed with excitement that every mama must feel when her daughter is making her debut at a fashionable London ball.

Except, of course, it was worse for Mrs Hartley Lambert, for she had only one child, and that child a daughter, and, no matter how great their wealth, she knew as only mothers can that there was no way round it: Sarah had a grave and wonderful chance of making a great and brilliant match with a man born in the purple, a man of blue blood. Why was blood always 'blue' for English aristocrats, she wondered? At any rate, she knew that as the Countess of Evesham's protégée Sarah had a truly grand and brilliant chance of sweeping all before her. Tonight was the opening night of the battle, the campaign, the fight for the best for her beloved child.

So no wonder Mrs Hartley Lambert could not sleep for worrying. No wonder she could hardly read her Bible, *especially* her Bible, and having laid it carefully on her bedside table, for the benefit of the servants when they tidied in the morning, took something quite other out of the pile of books on the ivory-inlaid eighteenth-century *bonheur du jour* opposite her bed.

In place of the Bible Mrs Hartley Lambert had taken some really rather easier reading matter, namely *Chit Chat and Other Matters*, the reminiscences of Mrs Algernon Vere de Vere.

Mrs Vere de Vere had been at all the courts of all the crowned heads of Europe, observing and noting in her diary such riveting matters as the depth of the lace worn on the equerries' shirt cuffs and the number of horses that the Empress Eugénie had to draw her coach. While she was waiting for that all-important scratch at the door, for the delighted smile on the beloved offspring's face which would tell her that she had been a success, *Chit Chat and Other Matters* was considerably more interesting than the prognostications of persons by such names as Ezekiel on the matter of the world ending, or indeed the trials of Joseph when sold into Egypt. All in all, the only thing that could be said about them was that they were just – well, a trial, really.

Of a sudden, after what had seemed to be both a day and a night, there was that scratch at the door.

'Mama! Still awake! I thought you would be asleep long ago.'

'I hardly sleep, darling, you know that, especially in Europe. Europe induces in me a feeling of neurasthenia, of nervous exhaustion. There is not the same sense of elation as one can experience in one's own beloved New York, or indeed at Newport, where one can feel so very well, and somehow more cheerful. London is not cheerful, I find. It is sombre, it is grand, it is historic, but it is lacking in vim and vigour. One feels that the Tower of London, all its grim history, everything, is somehow still in the air, and this despite there being no fog to speak of at the moment.'

Mrs Hartley Lambert pushed nervously at her sleeping arrangements, and then patted her be-ribboned nightcap, thinking, of a sudden, that she could not tell from Sarah's face whether she had been a success or not. In fact, since she was still wearing her reading spectacles, she could tell nothing from Sarah's face at all.

She quickly took them off, and there, at last, was the beloved head, unadorned by anything but the smallest flower tucked into the chignon roll at the top. It was coming nearer and nearer to its doting mama, until there it was, as pretty as a picture, and glowing with that particular look which, Mrs Hartley Lambert immediately felt, could surely only come from some sort of success in a London ballroom? But, just to make sure, and having found her pinz nez comfortingly close to hand, she flicked her fingers quickly at her daughter, making an anxious little click, click, click with them, until Sarah drew quite close and, taking the dance card from her gloved wrist, placed it carefully in her mama's soft, round, plump hand.

Now the reading spectacles must be put on once more for inspection of the card.

'Darlingest, Lord Melbury! But surely he was a Prime Minister of England or some such, was he not?'

Sarah shook her head and smiled. 'No, Mama, his great-grandfather, I think you will find.'

'But darling, Sarah darling, here is Lord Velmont . . . and whose is this writing? Lord – who, darling?'

'Clanbridge. He is an Irish peer, the Countess said. Very hairy, very charming though. I liked him.'

'Yes, darling, but as I understand it from the

Countess, we do not go for an Irish peer unless quite desperate. Good hunting in Ireland, of course, but the rain! Endless, I believe. But. Sarah.' Her mother looked across at her daughter who was now standing at the window, the picture of grace in her white lace. 'My darlingest one, judging from this card it looks to me as if you have the whole of London at your feet already. My love, not one dance not taken. How proud I am of you. And you hardly in England more than a few weeks. What a feat for an American girl, and how proud I am of you,' she repeated happily. 'Not one single dance sat out, and every one of your partners a titled gentleman.'

Sarah turned from the window and smiled back at her mother. 'As long as it makes you happy, Mama, then I am happy.'

But her mother hardly heard her. She was too busy turning to the first dance on the card, once more starting to read through, and relish, the list of titled gentlemen who had danced with her beloved Sarah. It meant everything to Mrs Hartley Lambert, since her own reception by her husband's family twenty years before had not been unfriendly so much as hostile. It was the Hartley Lamberts' treatment of her, their despite of her, their going out of their way to treat their daughter-in-law in a way that they would not have dared to treat a maidservant, that, following the birth of her daughter, had determined her to reach for the heights when it came to Sarah's marriage. *No-one* was going to be able to look down on Sarah the way that the Hartley Lamberts had looked down on her mother. No-one was going to treat her like a maidservant. She would not be insulted daily, almost hourly, because of her poor origins.

From the first her mother was determined that Sarah was going to marry into an old family, one older than her in-laws' family, and not an old American family either, although that would not be unacceptable. She was going to marry into the British aristocracy and from that giddy height Mrs Hartley Lambert would at last be able to look down on the Hartley Lamberts of Newport, for ever and ever more.

Since she had come to Europe with Sarah, travelling in the grandest style, night after night Mrs Hartley Lambert would awake and put on her light and imagine herself able to call on all those Hartley Lambert cousins, all those Hartley Lambert aunts and uncles, flourishing, with the greatest enjoyment, her newly titled daughter under their noses. So much for looking down on *her*!

'Of course it makes me happy, darling.' Mrs Hartley Lambert put down the dance card very carefully on her bedside table and sighed. She felt as if she had just eaten one of her cook's hot pancakes just oozing maple syrup, and butter and cream.

'Good night, Mama.'

'Good night, darlingest. Be as good tomorrow as you were tonight and before long you will be married in Westminster Abbey with twenty-four attendants and the Archbishop of Canterbury to give the blessing.'

Sarah smiled, shut the door behind her, and then leant against it momentarily before giving out a tired and dreadfully unhappy little sigh. It was more than she could have done to have spoilt her mother's evening, perhaps her whole week, by telling her that every single one of those titled gentlemen who had scribbled their names in her dance card had been well over fifty, and in reality barely able to dance, let alone waltz, or even do the Bunny Hug let alone the tango. Indeed the notion of any of them even attempting a tango, or knowing what it was, brought a wry smile to Sarah's lips.

It was true that she had danced through the evening. It was true that, as the Countess smiled graciously, even proudly, to one and all from her chaperon's vantage point, her protégée had not had a moment to seat herself on her own gilt chair so thick and fast had come the stream of elderly men to scribble their names in Sarah's card. Meanwhile, her two former fellow pupils from Lady Devenish's tuition course had waltzed delightedly past Sarah, safely in the arms of much younger men.

Was it always to be like this? Was she only to attract the attentions of the elderly, via the Countess of Evesham?

Sarah picked up her skirt with one gloved hand and trailed almost aimlessly towards her own private suite with its large rooms filled with gilded furniture and vast portraits of someone else's ancestors, its patterned carpets, its chandeliers and its patiently waiting maid.

'Mrs Hartley Lambert must have been ever so pleased when she saw your dance card, miss,' ventured Corkie.

'Oh, yes, indeed she was.'

Sarah submitted gracefully to being undressed by the dutiful Corkie, until eventually she was able to seat herself in her satin robe and lawn nightgown in front of one of the many lively fires that were always kept burning in Sarah's rooms. For despite the fact that it was officially summer in London, the capital of England seemed a cold place to a former child of Newport, the buildings so grey in appearance, and so close to each other, each road so narrow, especially after the broad avenues and elegance of Paris.

'And the Countess of course, miss, she was ever so pleased, no doubt of it.'

Sarah's success at the ball, if it could be counted as such, was not just her own, she realised suddenly. It was her mama's, it was the Countess's, it was Lady Devenish's; it was the hairdresser's, the dressmaker's, the corsetiere's. It was everyone else's success, nothing to do with her. Her success had little to do with herself.

And yet as she lay in bed staring at the patterns that the dying embers of the fire were making on the ceiling miles above her head, Sarah could not help feeling grateful towards the Countess.

After all, given Sarah's height, which she understood was such a terrible handicap in British Society, she realised that she had, thanks to her patroness, actually escaped with her social life at the opening ball. She knew that, as she was an American girl – or, as the Countess referred to her, a *'Merican gel* – and had known no-one at all of her own generation in that ballroom, it would have been all too possible for her to have spent the whole evening seated behind the Countess a very lonely, stranded and isolated *'Merican gel*.

And a girl without a single partner, a girl with an empty dance card at the opening ball, would surely be shunned for the rest of the Season? At best it would be noticed and noted by all. Sarah was not so naive as not to sense, given the male herd complex, that all the younger men would shun her, doubtlessly assuming that she had, in the terms of the stable yard, a *known fault*. So all in all, she must feel only gratitude to the wise, and still beautiful, old Countess.

After all the Countess had made quite sure that Sarah Hartley Lambert had a full dance card, come what may, and would not be shunned by the pack. The pack would have noticed that Miss Hartley Lambert had not sat down for the whole of that opening ball. They would have noted that, despite her undoubted height, she had been danced with non-stop, her dance card filled from start to finish. Indeed by the end of the evening some of them were even to be seen queueing to scribble their names in her card, only to find it full. So, all in all, the clever Countess had, come what may, ensured her protégée some degree of continuing success, and Sarah knew it, and felt grateful.

She closed her eyes, shutting out the pretty patterns of the flickering flames on the ceiling far above her. Tomorrow morning she must be up betimes ready to ride out with the fashionable and the infamous up and down Rotten Row in Hyde Park, accompanied by not one groom, but two. Something which Sarah herself found embarrassingly ostentatious, but upon which her mother had insisted. She had also insisted, for this all-important show of wealth, on ordering for her daughter what Sarah thought must be the most expensive riding habit in the world. Not run up at Busvines, as so many others would have been, but made in Paris. It was dark green to set off Sarah's dark brown hair, and had the minutest silver threads running subtly through the stitching. The silver threads, thank heavens, could not be seen until the sunlight caught at them, at which point the idea was, apparently, that, without the onlooker's realising it, Sarah would catch the eye in a way that frost on a leaf in the early morning caught the eye, the French tailor had explained, with many a flourish of his arms as he elaborated on this scintillating fact.

Privately Sarah had found the riding habit what her Newport friends back home would call *shuddersome*. It was altogether too eye-catching to be quite nice, but her mama had fallen furiously in love with its Gallic subtleties, so that was what Sarah would be wearing in the morning, come what may, although she dearly hoped that she would not be wearing the plumed hat with the silvered band to go with it. There was another more discreet version without plumes or band, and she thought, beginning to fall asleep at last, that would surely be less eye-catching? Goodness only knew she was so tall on a horse, the very last thing she needed was to catch the eye with silver bands and heaven only knew what else.

'My dear.' The Countess was talking to Lady Medlar. 'Ve whole fing was a raging success. You are to be congratulated, Augustine, really you are. Those opening balls can be such a *disaster*. As we well remember, in the old days, the opening ball was so often so *rusty*. The orchestras had not been in the swing of fings for long enough, so ve music was dull and bad, and the caterers usually had not taken on enough servants, or the florists delivered enough blooms, and so on, ve whole fing, as I say, too *rusty* for words. And let us face it, Augustine, so important to remember things as they were, rather than as one would have liked it. The Duchess, if you remember, was always so *cross*-seeming at her opening ball! Whereas, nowadays, you, my dear, are by comparison ve epitome of grace and beauty. Really, you *are*.'

This speech was so unlike her old rival Daisy Lanford that Augustine Medlar found herself feeling completely wrong-footed, embarrassed, and indeed looking everywhere but at Daisy herself. She would, if she could, have liked to have asked, 'What on earth do you want, Daisy Lanford? What on earth do you want of me to come out with such *twaddle*?' But of course she could not. For, although Lady Medlar was the maker and breaker of reputations, although she sat, literally, beneath a gilded canopy to receive her guests at her afternoon At Homes during the whole livelong Season, even she would not have dared to be so impolite, or indeed so direct, to Daisy.

For, besides 'Little Mrs George' as Mrs Keppel had been known, no-one had been guaranteed to bring a smile to Edward VII's lips more quickly than Daisy. Whatever had been their affair of long ago, whatever had been their loving, their friendship had withstood the test of *love*, and that, as everyone knew, was the greatest test of all. It was well known among the middle-aged of their set that to love and to remain friends was even harder to achieve than that biblical ideal, the happy marriage.

No, despite everything, Daisy had been, and always would be in the world's eyes, the most adored of the old king's mistresses, and, no matter what happened, they had enjoyed too much happiness together for the rest of the world to forget.

Not that Daisy had not been a worry to all her devoted admirers. Indeed, throughout the previous decade she had fallen in and out of debt with such monotonous regularity that it had even come to

His Majesty's notice. More than once, knowing of her troubles, her former lover had brought in kind financial advisers to try to bring some sort of order to her chaotic life.

But no adviser could help Daisy, and while she remained, mercifully, above having to give 'tango teas' – the latest rage for the fast set – she had been forced to 'help' heiresses through the Season in return for having all her Ascot dresses paid for, and other remunerations. It was just a fact. Daisy, among many others of her kind, had suffered not just from the fall in land values, not just from the increase in taxes, but from her own inability to adjust to the fast-changing times. She had enjoyed too much for too long, and never counted the cost until a few years before when Messrs Coutts and Co. had finally brought home to her that she could no longer afford to go on as she had. Estates must be sold, albeit for yards below what should be their true value, old servants dismissed, and even horses put out to grass.

All this Augustine Medlar knew, and Daisy knew that she knew, but what Augustine still did *not* know was why Daisy was flattering her so uncharacteristically. Daisy never flattered *anyone*. What on earth could she possibly *want*?

Augustine leaned forward on her chair underneath its gilded canopy. Her curiosity was so intense that she really felt that should any more time elapse before she heard Daisy's intentions she thought she might have a fit of palpitations or burst her corsets. Of one thing both of them could be completely assured, and that was that Daisy was always up to *something*. And more than ever now that she had been forced to take foreign debutantes under her wing in order to pay for her own London Season. Everyone *knew* that nowadays Daisy could never afford to dress in new Worth gowns from Paris if they were not paid for by some *arriviste* mama from outside England.

'How may I help you, Daisy?' Augustine demanded, allowing her eyes to travel to the new arrivals at her afternoon At Home by way of pretending disinterest.

From the advantage of her raised dais she could see young men still placing their hats and canes in the corner of the room in the old way, the canes making a dull clatter, the hats too, as was the custom, being left at the side of the room, and never in the hall, unless it was one's own home.

Side by side with the young men came young ladies beautifully dressed in their walking clothes and escorted by their mamas similarly tricked out in the smaller, neater hats of the new era, the hobble skirts making it plain that they were dressed in the height of that year's fashion.

No so, however, the young officers in their strictly tailored uniforms, or the foreign diplomats in their strange, dark, always rather silken clothes. Nor indeed the members of parliament, looking rather too recently outfitted as Liberals always seemed to, still too new to power to have the easy air, the lived-in look of the older Tory men up from the Shires at the behest of their wives and daughters, their minds still at home on their estates, their worries over harvests and the falling price of land etching little lines under their eyes. And where once the *hauteur* of the newly arrived from the previous century would have marked their expressions, now there was only anxiety to be read.

Not that it mattered, to Augustine Medlar anyway. She cared only that they were all still there, everyone who was anyone, and as anxious as ever to be seen at her At Homes. All making their way, slowly or methodically, in whatever fashion they had elected, towards Lady Medlar's famous throne-like chair, with the dais giving it such an imperial air. She knew only too well that no-one in that room was able to put their hand on their heart and declare that they wanted nothing from Augustine Medlar. They were all there because they all, to a person, one way or another, wanted something from her; and that was what was so interesting to Augustine Medlar, to find out what it was precisely that they wanted, and then to deny or grant it to them, as the mood took her.

For that was what power was all about, the giving and the taking, according to one's whim, and never mind the consequences to the petitioners, never mind the hurt, never mind the gain. The power to raise or cut down was more sensual than love to Augustine Medlar, and more flattering to her ego than the heartiest compliment or the most ardent lover. Love she despised, and always had. Once suffered, love was thankfully to be set aside for the fascination only of the sentimental, or the foolish. Once one had one's babies, one simply ignored one's husband's mistresses, as one ignored one's husband's gambling debts; they were just a dull part of him, in which one took great care to take no interest whatsoever. It was common knowledge that England had enjoyed so little war for so long that the men were bored, and bored men went looking for mischief, which fortunately, since Society had at last organised itself properly over the last fifty years, they found in the arms of their mistresses in St John's Wood, or, if they were rather poorer, in the houses of somewhat cheaper women living at discreet addresses in Muswell or even Tulse Hill.

But – inwardly Augustine sighed – she must pay attention now for Daisy was answering Lady Medlar's question.

'You may not help *me,* Augustine, don't be silly!' Daisy gave her famously light musical laugh. 'You have never been able to help *me,* Augustine. Why, not even the King can help me, and you know that, of all people. *You* know that, or *should* do. No, of course you cannot help *me.*'

At this they both laughed, their eyes quite serious, because it was true. Daisy was beyond help. And anyway, they were both too honest not to admit to themselves that the very last person whom Augustine would want to help, even if she could, was Daisy. Looked at from a different vantage point, in some ways it was even possible that Daisy could help Augustine rather more effectively than Augustine could ever help Daisy.

The truth was that Daisy was vastly more popular in Court circles, and infinitely more admired. She had always had more allure, and of course was a beauty, which Augustine had never been. Augustine's face was too haughty, too cold, too altogether dominating, her lips suggesting not a pretty if pouting desire to be pleased by life, as Daisy's pretty mouth still did, but a sneering desire to put down the world, and naturally his wife, if she should so wish to do.

'The Duchess of Wokingham, Augustine. Is she to come to London for ve Season?' Daisy continued, after a small pause to allow for their mutual if somewhat humourless laughter.

Augustine's eyebrows, thin, still black, and very arched, did not now raise themselves gently, but shot up in surprise.

'I am really rather amazed that you of all people should enquire after the Duchess of Wokingham, my dear. You of all people asking after the Duchess! It is truly amazing.'

This time Augustine laughed on her own, her famously cold, dry laugh, a laugh that, it seemed of a sudden to her listener, was growing dangerously close to a witch's cackle, which, given that they were precisely the same age, was really rather worrying. For, despite the fact that Daisy did not like Augustine in the least, and probably never would, nevertheless they were of the same generation and Daisy did not enjoy seeing anyone of her own generation succumbing to age or infirmity, or even, by their behaviour, hinting at it.

'In vat case you amaze easily, Augustine, if I may say so,' Daisy retorted sharply. 'Ve Duchess has a son who is of a presentable age. She will be looking for a suitable gel for him, I imagine, although the Duchess's former life as a Gaiety Girl may of course mean vat she neglects her duties as a mother and stays, as she has so often been known to do in other years, on her country estates with the Duke and their six dogs. An occupation which, I may say, has never been known to bring about a good match for a boy, or a gel for vat matter. In our young day, Augustine, it would have been called neglecting our duty.'

At this Augustine Medlar smiled, if a slight baring of her teeth could be said to pass for a smile, Daisy thought petulantly. She hated to ask Augustine anything, even the time of day, let alone – least of all, dash it – a favour, but the fact of the matter was that there were very few ducal catches that Season, alas.

What there was, in grim reality, in the way of 'catches' was really very, very little. There were one or two hereditary knights, who were interesting, always providing of course that they had the money to keep up their estates, but not, alas, many marquesses or earls who could be said to be eligible or indeed remotely suitable. Some of the older boys had been killed in South Africa, and that too had had its effect on the depleted annual list. And others of course were known to have no interest in the opposite sex due, it was thought, to too much marrying of cousins in the first degree.

There *was* one elderly earl who always cropped up every year, and made Daisy sigh whenever some naive mama of some even more naive debutante mentioned him. He, it had to be said, did at least *turn up* for the Season, but since he had never been known to do more than dance with a girl, and since he was also known to have been a great favourite with a certain Royal personage, mamas everywhere had to be discreetly warned against him in the extraordinarily unlikely event of his having so far forgotten himself as to seek their daughter's hand in marriage.

The problem for the Countess was that in order to go forward at all, in order to send Mrs Hartley Lambert back to the United States with enthusiasm and, please the Lord, all-important recommendations to her fellow countrywomen to use Daisy's services, she had to find the most glittering match possible for the over-tall, although undoubtedly charming, young Sarah Hartley Lambert. And for once Daisy simply did not know where to begin. Which was why she was now standing like some common little petitioner at the foot of Augustine Medlar's wretched gilded and canopied throne asking for her help. A situation which that cold-hearted woman was quite evidently enjoying, but which Daisy was equally evidently loathing.

'So, my dear . . .'

Every time Augustine said 'my dear' to Daisy like that it seemed to her that it was like receiving a kick in her elegant ankle from one of Augustine's hand-made shoes.

'You have your eyes on George, the Wokinghams' eldest boy, the Marquis of Cordrey, for your 'Merican heiress, have you, Daisy? As well you might. Yet you did so well – was it two years ago? Yes. It must have been two years ago. You did so very well marrying off that plain little gel from Pittsburgh to the Earl of Rustington that I should have thought that would surely have been success enough for you? Your triumph in bringing off that match was the talk of London for some weeks, as I remember. I mean to say, the poor gel, she was so plain and so dull, but there. I understand that the union is a great success because they both enjoy sitting in swamps shooting duck in America.'

Daisy stared at Augustine as she rambled on with something close to hatred.

Oh the agony of it all! Having to bear Augustine's sadistic enjoyment, knowing that the catch of the Season, if he duly appeared that is, was some sort of cousin to Lady Medlar's husband, so that Augustine would doubtless be quite determined to have the *say so* over the Marquis of Cordrey, if she could.

Asking for Augustine's help, in however oblique a fashion, was such an agony that Daisy, in those few seconds that she stood before the Medlar throne, found herself feeling that she could have almost regretted that she had done as she had, and spent too much money too fast and too furiously throughout her giddy youth, and on into her middle years.

And yet not to continue in Society would mean that, now that she was more than middle-aged, no-one would even call on Daisy. She could see herself, and it was a hideous picture, *atrophying*.

Sitting perhaps by a window in some rented house in Mayfair – her own house having to be rented out to someone with more wealth. Watching helplessly as other, more fashionable personages walked past to At Homes which she herself could not afford to attend, on account of not having the clothes, the horses, or nowadays the motor cars, to trick out the once most celebrated beauty in London. It was an almost too bitter thought, even for Daisy, to remember how she had been, a famous beauty and the mistress and queen of the Prince of Wales's heart.

Almost, because to indulge in such thoughts could only end in that ghastliness of all ghastlinesses – lines down the side of the mouth. Deep etching down the side of the face such as she had noted in older women when she was young and giddy. For the moment Daisy was determined that 'lines' were something that your governess set you when you had been naughty and set fire to the footmen's coat tails on account of its having been a stormy day with nothing else much for a girl of any spirit to do.

No, Daisy knew, all too well, there was no alternative to the bitterness of having to place herself within Augustine's power, and although it was just a *little* like something in a nasty Greek fable, anything else was unthinkable. Daisy would rather die by her own hand than give up Society, of that she was quite, quite sure.

Unfortunately not only did Augustine know this fact, she also knew, and only too well, as all Society knew, that Daisy and the Duke and Duchess of Wokingham were, indeed *had* to be, implacable enemies. Although the Duchess was, it seemed, incapable of unkindness, nevertheless no-one could forget the history of the relationship between young May, before her marriage, and the Countess.

Of course Augustine would be the first to remember, as everyone would remember, the previous history of their relationship. How Herbert Forrester, a rich Yorkshireman with more money than most, had sponsored the future Duchess of Wokingham through the Season, for, it later transpired, the sole purpose of revenging themselves on Daisy who had quite purposefully failed to bring King Edward to their ball. As a consequence of this debacle the Forresters had lost any possible credibility in the eyes of London Society.

Daisy had humiliated Herbert and Jane Forrester, and Herbert Forrester in particular, being a Yorkshireman, had not forgiven her and in his turn had exacted a long-awaited revenge on the Countess.

Of course that was all years ago now, but the public scandal it had caused was still fresh in Society's all too long memory, that elephantine ability of the Court and other circles to remember and relish the thorough public trouncing that Daisy had eventually received at the hands of Herbert Forrester.

But with the tall, elegant although not particularly pretty Sarah Hartley Lambert under her wing, Daisy could see that she now had an opportunity to revenge herself in her turn on those self-same Forresters by smartly marrying off their protégée's ducal son to her protégée, the American heiress.

What a to-do that would be! How satisfactory if they could bring the Duke of Wokingham's son to the altar and marry him off to someone of *Daisy*'s choosing! In terms of Society, in terms of the ways of the world, it would be the human equivalent of winning the Ascot Gold Cup with a horse that you had bred yourself.

Few dukedoms could continue nowadays without the influx of American money. Everyone from the Marlboroughs to the – well – well – *everyone* who was anyone in the English aristocracy had gone after American money in the hope of gaining some kind of stay against the bailiffs battering down the doors of their ancestral homes. It was just a fact.

Happily, this was again something that both Augustine and Daisy well knew, the Wokinghams, although land rich, and still living in considerable style, had no holdings in American railways, or stocks and bonds. There had been no coal found underneath their land, no rich northern manufacturing empires backed their great houses and estates. Added to which, increasingly, was the concern that servants were no longer grateful to be in service to the nobility, as in former times. The rot had, everyone thought, started with such people as the Alderneys, who had begun a Society for the Rehabilitation of Old Retainers, which had shocked even the King. The very idea of helping old servants rather than old dogs was utterly alien to the English complex. And yet, shocking or not, the problem of a diminishing supply of servants would not go away.

And it was a vast problem for the aristocracy, for it meant that the ownership of houses as large as small townships had increasingly become a worry rather than a comfort. Kill as many cows, breed as many pigs, grow corn, and store hay, as they might on their estates, families like the Wokinghams were facing insuperable problems, *unless* – and given the propensity of the young to be so wilful and determined it was a big unless – they could marry off their sons to wealthy girls. It was the only thing that was left to them, and both Augustine and Daisy knew it. They also knew that Daisy's protégée was not the only heiress in town. There were others, and some of them were English, a fact which would endear them to someone such as the Duke of Wokingham more than a girl from Newport, however charming and well brought up.

'I will help you, Daisy, my dear.'

Again the 'my dear' from Augustine's thin lips

was like a kick in Daisy's elegant shins, and it was all she could do to refrain from wincing. Useless to remember what an appalling figure Augustine had cut on a horse, in contrast to Daisy's famous elegance. Pointless to reflect on how few names were scribbled in Augustine's dance cards when they were both young and in their salad days. Worthless too to think back to how desperate Augustine had been until she had duped Lord Medlar into marrying her. Such memories could not be relished when they both knew that Daisy had fallen into mountainous debt, and, if she was to carry on in the same vein as she had always carried on, must make a success of the Season and marry her American debutante to at the very least an Honourable.

'Now, my dear, my dear, dear Daisy . . .'

How many more 'my dears' would she get through before she came to the point? Daisy could feel the acid inside her burning and then rising to the point where she thought she might either scream or faint. It was too horrible to have to stand there with Augustine toying with her – yes, positively toying with her – in her sadistic and cruel way, but it had to be borne. Her problems with Messrs Coutts and Co. having once more arisen, and only too recently, it just had to be borne.

'Do you remember ve way you used to love to drown kittens when you came to stay wiv my parents at Wynyates, Augustine?' Daisy demanded suddenly, and with, for her, an almost unnatural ferocity.

This did, as least temporarily, put Augustine off her stroke.

'No – Daisy, did I? I can't believe that.'

Daisy smiled, kitten-like herself in her enjoyment. It was as if she had suddenly found a ball of wool to play with. Ha! She had succeeded in knocking the 'my dears' out of Augustine at last!

'Oh, yes, Augustine, my *dear*. Ve fact is that you so enjoyed drowning ve little day-old kittens vat the head gardener used to take pity on the cats and hide them from you. And what is more you were so famous for vis pastime that my father nicknamed you "Kitty Killer", which made darling Tum Tum, who was still Prince of Wales then, laugh a great deal, as I remember it. But of course we were all frightfully young then, were we not? Very young, and quite too, too tiresome, possibly, as well.'

This last reminder of how Augustine was remembered at Wynyates was the sound of Daisy's foot coming down good and hard. And it was a sharp reminder too that when all was said and done King Edward had been devoted to Daisy, and having had the King of England and Emperor of India on your side meant a great deal more than having the whole of the beastly Liberal Party together at the toe of your boot.

'What is it exactly that you want, Daisy?'

Daisy could see, and it was really very agreeable, that she had at last tired Augustine out. The great Lady Medlar was now ready to give in to whatever Daisy wanted in the way of a favour.

Still, not trusting anyone but themselves (and goodness knows if she did not know that they were both completely untrustworthy no-one did) Daisy leaned forward and whispered in Augustine's ear.

What she whispered was fascinating and enlightening to Lady Medlar, but whether she would remain on Daisy's side and do as she was being asked was quite another matter, and they both knew it.

Secrets

Phyllis lay in bed gazing up at her ceiling. It was early morning, too early even for the maid to come in and light her fire, too early too for the bath to be placed in front of the fire in the old-fashioned way, as it still was at Tradescant House. Too early indeed for her mother to come in and discuss with her the faults or virtues of the opening ball at Medlar House, but not too early for Phyllis to lie planning to go and visit *my secret Vice*, as she now called Richard Ward.

So far she had visited him upwards of half a dozen times, in complete secret. She would wait until her mother left the house on some social round, or to buy feathers or ribbons or some such, Evie following at a respectful distance, and then, on the pretext of fetching a book from the small library room which was situated on the same floor, she would skip upstairs, scratch at the door, unlock it in answer to his 'Come in' and go in to see him.

She had heard her mother saying, several times, that 'Richard', as she and Aunt Tattie called him, was 'improving'. Certainly he seemed to have gone from fury and fits of trembling to a quietened, almost over-subdued state, and this gentle-seeming passivity was what had drawn Phyllis to him. Also his eyes, which were sweet and kind but so bored that Phyllis could only feel sorry for him and want to help him pass the time, time which she knew all too well could creep by dreadfully slowly when no-one was around to keep you company. She herself had found time as slow as anything she could ever have imagined after her father had died. She had thought that she would literally die of boredom, what with the family away for months, sailing on the high seas, and only Evie and the dogs for company.

'You are my secret friend, are you not?' Richard Ward had asked, smiling at her sadly, the previous day. 'My secret friend, my little saviour, and you read to me so beautifully, it quite takes me back to the old days, do you know that?'

'The old days?'

'Yes, sailing together in your little boat, old whatshisname with us, and Henry your pug – remember how he took to sailing? That was a delight, that sailing, both of us together, such a delight. And you were always such a much better sport than my poor darling Elizabeth, who really did not care for sailing in the least, always fearing that her skirts would get damp. But not you, Portia, you were always springing to and from the boat to the bank, Henry at your heels. Dear Portia. What a fine time we had together.'

Phyllis had opened her mouth to say, 'Oh goodness, please, I am not Portia. I am *Phyllis*, her daughter,' but seeing the look of happy recollection on Richard Ward's face, and knowing that he had been suffering so terribly, in every way, she could not somehow bring herself to deny that she was Portia.

So, not wanting to disappoint him, she said nothing. Besides, she knew that she did look just like her mother, people had remarked on it many, many times. And, too, she was more than aware that, given the state of the family finances which always seemed to be spread precariously between house and stable, yacht and motor car, with very little left over for new clothing and what her mother called 'fripperies' – and the fact that many of the materials that made up Phyllis's remodelled clothes were taken from dresses found in the attics at Bannerwick – it was hardly surprising that Richard Ward had indeed mistaken her for his old childhood friend.

Even so, his calling her *Portia* was strangely thrilling. Phyllis had always envied her mother her ease of manner, her quiet determination, her way of handling everyone from the maids to the yachts with tact and discretion. So, what with one thing and another, she put off the moment of telling him that she was not her mother, reminding herself that since his mind had obviously been so dreadfully affected by the loss of his wife and daughter it was most likely that it had somehow returned to the past, and perhaps to that part of the past in particular where there would be no memory of his loss, but only the happy days of his youth with Portia.

Phyllis had chosen to read to him from a book that would amuse them both, and so had selected *The Pickwick Papers* from the tightly stocked room of books made available for guests at Tradescant House. She had already read it three or four times, and she was confident that she was quite able to read it well, simply because, as her father used to say, 'When you know a story the characters come towards you in all their colours, just like old friends.'

But alas, the *secret Vice*, being more used, perhaps, to sea shanties, or tales about ships and spice islands, or hostile natives, was not, Phyllis noticed, quite as fascinated by Mr Pickwick and his friends as she and her father had always been. Much as he complimented her on her style of reading at the start, it was not long before Richard Ward fell fast asleep.

Seeing this Phyllis left him, locking his door once more, and found herself dismally wandering the house for the rest of the morning, waiting for the moment when she would be changed by Evie into her riding habit and go to Hyde Park for her first public promenade on a beautiful chestnut hireling.

Fashionable promenades were still made in Hyde Park during the morning and afternoon. It was at this time that everyone, whatever their status, who prided themselves on being in the swim either rode or drove by, each leaning towards the others, each noting the other's turn-out, their horses, their carriages, their pairs, their fours, their riding habits, their companions, their hats, their plumes, their horses' bridles, their saddles, the paint on their coachwork. Despite the advent of the motor car, despite the King now going about in his fleet of motor cars, the fashionable still clung to the customof riding and driving carriages through and around Hyde Park of a morning and afternoon. It was too good a spectacle, too good a venue for showing off one's horses and clothes, one's mistresses and one's carriages, to abandon in favour of a motor car, however increasingly fashionable.

For the demi-monde of the day, the mistresses of the rich, it was especially important. The morning or afternoon ride was the moment when they could show off not just their horses and their riding, but their own silhouettes. It was a moment for searching out their rivals and noting them, each knowing that they were out to make an impression on the other's patron, no matter who. Most of all, everyone wanting to know *who* was *who*, especially if they were new to the fashionable cavalcade. Gentlemen could be seen greeting each other while staring from under their hats at approaching beauties, doubtless wondering if the time had come to swap their current *chère amie* for a more spectacular model.

Naturally enough, and even Phyllis knew this, no nice young woman would ever, *ever* notice a member of the demi-monde when out riding. It was not just that they were expected to ignore them, they were expected not to *see* them. As far as the unmarried young lady was concerned, the women from St John's Wood, or other similar environs, did not exist. Even if, like the famous 'Skittles', the former mistress of the Duke of Devonshire, they drove fast and furiously past in a gleaming phaeton with a pair of coal-black heifers following, Phyllis knew that she must not notice them. Least of all must she comment. The mistresses of the aristocracy might ride past without their clothes, or they might have flame-red hair and wear a riding habit with gold epaulettes, or ride a great black horse with a red bridle and saddle to match, but, as far as nice young ladies were concerned, they were not there. They did not exist.

Of course this did not stop those same innocent young ladies from seeing them from under their eyelashes. They might not turn their heads, or raise their eyebrows, but from under their eyelashes, as those other young women who had already chosen a rather different path in life rode past, whatever the embargoes laid down by their chaperons the young girls in question would make sure that they saw them. It was natural. Besides, some of them were too good to miss.

One in particular fascinated Phyllis. A tall blonde, as tall as a man, with wide shoulders, and invariably dressed in a replica of an officer's uniform. She was truly fascinating. More than that, it was rumoured that she was not exactly the same sex as Phyllis, although that was somewhat difficult to tell, since she wore gloves, covering that part of a person's anatomy impossible to disguise – the hands.

'She's called "the Colonel" because apparently she insists on wearing a uniform with the same pips as a colonel of a cavalry regiment,' Phyllis told Edith, as the blonde passed them that particular afternoon. 'My maid, Evie, told me that a few years ago the previous Prince of Wales noticed that whereas before when riding out in Rotten Row she always wore the uniform of a common soldier, which was permissible, she had changed her regular riding habit to that of a colonel. The Prince, being a stickler, felt that she had gone too far and the next time he caught sight of her he sent his equerry over to reprimand her. But apparently the equerry came back with the reply that His Royal Highness must not fret, because after all she was only a peacetime colonel, and would certainly resign her commission at the end of the Season if His Royal Highness so wished.

'What was the outcome of that, then?'

'Naturally enough, since she had provided him with an amusing moment, His Royal Highness did nothing about it, and so she carried on as she has to this day, an honorary colonel of a regiment of her own invention!'

'Oh my – Phyllis, no, please do look. Little Miss Hartley Lambert riding towards us and wearing a riding habit that would put even Skittles to shame!'

At that point, seeing a small party approaching, both girls reined in their horses, for in the party were two young officers accompanying the Duke of Connerton, and since all of them had met the night before at the opening ball at Medlar House, not to acknowledge them would have been discourteous in the extreme.

It seemed that they had also met Miss Hartley Lambert, because she too reined in her horse, and greeted them in her open way with 'Gentlemen! How good to meet you.'

This in itself was a breach of etiquette, for, as Phyllis and Edith knew only too well, it was not considered correct for young men to be addressed by a young lady first. The greeting was always meant to come from the men, who raised their hats courteously while the ladies merely nodded in return. It was also incorrect to say 'how good to meet you'. 'See you' was correct. No lady ever said 'meet'. A 'meet' was for hunting, not riding in Rotten Row. All this made it difficult for Phyllis not to titter, rather to the embarrassment of Edith, who could not help feeling a little sorry for Miss Hartley Lambert, even though she was not as proper as she should be – so tall and so gauche, and wearing such a terrible hat.

Sarah of course knew, as soon as she saw Phyllis tittering, that she had said something risible, although she had no idea what it could be.

It was not just that she could see her former fellow-pupil suppressing a smile; she could also feel the *just-wait-till-behind-your-back-we-tell-everyone-what-you-have-just-said* feeling. It was palpable. It was like a ripple in the water, it was like circles on a pond: she knew it would get wider and wider the moment she rode on. And, because she had lost the battle with her mother over a certain little matter, she could feel them carefully and wilfully *not* looking at – the *hat*.

'I don't think you know Miss Ha—' Phyllis began. 'I don't think you know Miss Ha—' She paused as everyone looked at her, waiting. 'Miss *Hatley* Lambert!' Phyllis finally finished, her face all innocence.

There was a great burst of laughter at this, the kind of laughter which the victim is forced to join in but, ultimately, is so wounding that they will probably, no matter where, no matter when, remember it for the rest of their lives.

'Hartley, actually, Hartley Lambert.' Sarah smiled, bravely, and went on smiling, bravely.

But it was too late, for thanks to Phyllis all their suppressed smiles had turned into unsuppressed laughter, and Phyllis, although she murmured an apology, was looking very pleased with herself.

'*Hartley* Lambert! Oh dear, of course, I am sorry! But you must admit, your hat does prompt such a mistake, Miss Hartley!'

That was not all that Sarah must admit. She must also admit openly that as of that moment her hat and Phyllis's joke were going to be laughed at in the mess, in the ballroom, in the clubs, everywhere.

She knew, only too well, that from now on she would be known as Sarah *Hatley* Lambert, and she knew they knew it, and it was all so shaming, and so embarrassing, that Sarah could have taken whatever armament was nearest to her and willingly killed herself at that moment.

But she did not. Instead she sat her horse, and she straightened herself to her full height, and she bowed her head to the young officers who were laughing so heartily and said, '*Touché*, sirs, ladies. It is, I know, a perfectly beastly hat, and you may be glad to know that I am about to return home and burn it. You have done well to make a joke of it, Miss de Nugent. For if this hat is not a bad joke, in line with your own, well, then the world is not round and the United States of America was not lost by a former King of England, and instead of being American, I would be rude and English, and mannerless, like yourselves.'

After which she wheeled her horse and headed back to the stables, her grooms, both of them, in hot pursuit, causing quite a flurry as they extended their trots to such a degree that they almost caused a party of newly arrived young ladies to take flight.

Sarah returned home immediately in the family carriage. And the hat itself was of course duly burned. But as she knew, and they knew – those others in the Park – she could not, alas, burn the joke too. The joke would stay around, possibly as long as she was in England.

She was, in some measure, she realised, as she watched the flames of the fire reaching up and slowly, far too slowly, nibbling and then eating at the wretched hat, in effect now ruined. Too late to curtsy beautifully at Court, to dance elegantly, or ride brilliantly. Too late for Worth gowns to detract from her height. Soon that greatest destroyer, that deflator of all that is possibly good, would be taking flight, setting alight everything that her mama and Lady Devenish had striven to create around her. Sarah was too intelligent not to know that no-one survived humour, ever. It had never been known.

'My darlingest one! Here you are! I have been looking for you all over the house. I do so hope that you had as wild a success as I wanted, and that you were as happy with your French riding habit as we all felt you looked going off?'

Sarah sprang up, half covering the fire with her outspread skirt, and doing a good imitation of chattering teeth, which must have looked really very strange since her mother kept their rented house at hothouse temperatures and her own rooms at only a few degrees under seventy-five, no matter what the weather outside, such was her horror of the cold, damp, English climate. A climate so inducive to melancholia, Sarah found, that had she not felt her recent humiliation at the hands of Phyllis de Nugent so keenly, she could almost have blamed the weather for her unendurable discomfiture and feelings of despair.

'Darlingest one!' her mama repeated, her arms wide open as if to embrace what she felt must have been a huge success for Sarah. 'The hat? Tell, oh do? The hat was a *succès fou, n'est-ce pas*?'

Sarah nodded silently, her skirt still spread out to cover the soft felt riding hat behind her now burning so merrily. The hat had indeed been a mad success, but not with her. It had been a mad success with her enemies, the Honourable Phyllis de Nugent and Miss Edith O'Connor, although to give her some kind of due Miss O'Connor had finally looked more than a little embarrassed at the behaviour of the others.

The hat had been considered so *madly* successful that it would doubtless continue to be a source of mirth for the rest of the Season.

'I knew it would be a success,' sighed Mrs Hartley Lambert. 'I knew it. I have always thought that there is nothing more eye-catching than silver reflecting the light, especially when the grooms have a touch of it too in their cockades, so that there is a winking and a blinking on either side of the equestrian.'

'Yes, Mama,' Sarah agreed, quietly, and found to her shame that she could wish, just for this one wretched moment in her life, although not for any other, that Lady Devenish had been her mother.

Lady Devenish had that quiet demeanour, that gentle humour, that understanding sort of way of going on with which Sarah found herself all too sympathetic.

Perhaps because she had grown so tall, which was considered such a handicap in a girl, even in America, Sarah had always wanted people not to notice her, had prayed *not* to be the centre of people's interest. It was just how she was. Her mother was quite different, perhaps because she herself had always been so pretty and so much the 'party piece'. Even when Sarah was young Mrs Hartley Lambert had been aware of her daughter's being so different from herself, always enthusiastically pushing her forward to excel at everything from skating to dancing. And to please her Sarah had applied herself to everything. In fact, looking back she could honestly say that she thought she had not altogether failed her mother, except in this one matter, this matter of people *noticing* her. But now, thanks to the hat, she had been noticed, and would be pointed out to everyone – 'Look, there goes Sarah *Hatley* Lambert!' Her chances of escaping from *that* joke were negligible, and she knew it.

Emily was experiencing that mild sense of dissatisfaction that all mothers of girls must feel from time to time. Now she came to think of it Edith was not, to her mother's mind anyway, quite graceful enough. Neither was she, in her mother's view, quite charming enough. Nor was she, as far as her mother's taste went, quite distinctive enough. She would not stand out in a crowd.

Indeed she had not, as far as Emily could ascertain, yet stood out in a drawing room, not to mention a ballroom. It was fair to say that up until now she had proved to be a disappointment to her mother.

Emily paused before considering her own looks in the mirror in front of her. It had to be said that she had always stood out in a crowd, principally of course because she had such a strong hair colour. Auburn was very noticeable, and when dressed in pink or red, very, very noticeable; indeed, outstandingly so. Lady Devenish had guided Emily's taste in that way, as later, did Daisy. Of course it was a long time ago, but they had undoubtedly guided Emily's taste most beautifully, not wishing her always to be seen in *green*, as Emily's mother would have wished. Much later her husband, Rory O'Connor, would always insist, one way or another, that she wore green.

'Is there not enough green in all Ireland that I have to wear it too?' Emily would groan whenever Rory returned from some expedition to Paris or London with green and more green materials for her delectation.

But there, now that Rory had elected to stay in Ireland with his country house politicking friends, his bad back and his habit of keeping company with poets, she could once more wear every sort of colour except green. Which was probably why she was looking so very fetching in a hat of palest pink which showed off her now quite snowy white hair with a fine dash.

White hair was so very flattering. Emily knew

this, of course. It made her skin look so fine and pink and perfect, and despite four children she still had a tall, graceful figure, the figure of a woman who had ridden hard all her life and never given best to any man. She might not be any Empress Elizabeth of Austria, but Emily was more than a match for anyone once mounted. And that was what she and Rory had had in common, their riding. And now they shared it no longer, since his disastrous fall out hunting. Indeed, it was a wonder to all and sundry that he could even walk again, and the fact that he did so was, she knew, despite the most terrible and constant pain.

Although, in common with the rest of the world, Emily could not like her hostess for the Season, she could not help liking Medlar House. It would be a strange sort of woman who could do anything but enjoy a household which employed, it was rumoured, anything up to sixty indoor servants. And an even stranger sort of woman who could not enjoy the luxury of being waited on hand and foot. Even her maid, Minnie, had her own servant, on call to help her whenever she wished. And although, admittedly, Polly was only a scrap of a thing, nevertheless her services, and the services of all the other servants, were something which Minnie, and Emily herself, were quite able to enjoy, feeling that they were in reality enjoying the hospitality of a minor monarch.

'Are you quite comfortable at Medlar House, Emily dearest?' asked Portia, and she leaned over the luncheon table towards her old friend.

'If by "comfortable" you mean am I enjoying feeling like the Vicereine of India every time I awake in the mornings, such is the luxury of our circumstances, then the answer is a decided yes, Portia, my dear. Yes, yes, and yes again.'

Portia smiled. Emily was looking magnificent that morning. As soon as she had entered Aunt Tattie's drawing room, Portia had known that she was in the presence of the old Emily. The old dashing sparkle had returned to her eyes, and she no longer had the slightly tired look that most mothers assume when around a daughter who is proving less than satisfactory.

'I have decided to enjoy myself in a most un-chaperon-like manner!' Emily's green eyes narrowed slightly as she followed Portia into the dining room. They were to lunch alone, which was most satisfactory, for it meant that they could catch up on all the latest news and at the same time form new plans, plans that would, they both hoped, push Edith and Phyllis more to the fore as the pace of the London Season increased and their hopes for their daughters, should they remain unengaged, decreased with equal speed.

'Pink is very becoming to you, Emily,' Portia murmured approvingly, while Emily's eyes rested on Portia's tasteful grey. She knew, as friends do, that nothing would induce Portia to leave off her demi-mourning for her darling Childhays. 'There will always be memories, will there not?' Portia continued. She smiled down the table at Emily, and as Emily smiled back, thinking that her old friend was referring to her widowed state, she added to Emily's surprise, 'I will always remember you in pink at Ascot, I think, with the most marvellous pink *cloques* on the heels of your shoes, and tiny pink rosebuds tucked in a fall down the front of your dress. What sighs of envy you provoked in all of us!'

'Not next to May, our present Duchess of Wokingham. Now there was a beauty if ever there was one. Is she come to London yet, by the by?'

'She is to arrive tomorrow, with her son. She has promised that they will be at their London address from noon, so we must both call, must we not, in the afternoon? The Duke joins them at the end of next week. London holds no interest for him nowadays, as it does not for men of country interests. He only really comes, she says in her last letter to me, to have himself fitted for new hunting boots, and such matters.'

The footman holding out the silver dish for Emily suddenly seemed unreasonably handsome, and the room in which they sat entirely heavenly. Emily very nearly leaped from her chair and started a bad imitation of a tango, such was her sudden feeling of joy in life, the sensation, which she had not experienced for years, of being yards younger than she knew herself to be, of being part of that hidden warmth which brought about spring.

'Yes, I will call with you. We can call together,' she agreed.

* * *

May was ready and waiting for them when they made their afternoon call the following day, and since she had arrived in London only a few hours before, and it seemed equally few others knew it, Portia and Emily were able to find their old friend, at first, quite alone, and this despite it being Thursday, which would normally be the Duchess of Wokingham's At Home day, when all the world, not to mention many of its wives, would be clambering past her steward and into her long narrow first floor drawing room overlooking Hyde Park.

'We are not in the least bit surprised to find you looking *younger* than ever, May, my dear!' Emily joked, kissing her old friend on both cheeks, and holding out her hands to show May off to Portia who was still standing behind her at the entrance to the drawing room. 'I mean, look, Portia! She is disgraceful, is she not? How can you manage to be married for so long and stay looking as though the bells are still pealing out their celebrations? And where is your beautiful son, of whom we have heard so much? Where are you hiding him?'

It was May's turn to blush. She had lost her battle to bring her son to town, and he would even now, she knew, be riding out in the company of his father the Duke, both of them doubtless congratulating each other on having escaped an extra week in London.

'George is coming to London next week, with his father. He stayed behind to help him on the estate.'

At this both Emily's and Portia's faces fell, as well they might, seeing that they were both the mothers of daughters, and May was the mother of a son of more or less the same age who must, as the whole world knew, since he was the heir to a dukedom, be both handsome and good company, not to mention elegant and charming.

'Boys, you know. They never want to come to London as much as daughters, I'm afraid.'

May shrugged her shoulders lightly, and tried not to look apologetic. After all she had not *promised* to bring George to town. She had said that she would, but she had not promised that he would be coming with her, although looking at her two old friends' faces she was sure that they must have counted on the young Marquis of Cordrey for an eligible addition to the ball that was to be given at Tradescant House in a fortnight's time.

'He is coming, of course. On Sunday night next.' May was busking it, as they would have called it backstage when she was a young actress. 'Yes, George is coming,' she added with more firmness than she felt, and at the same time she made a mental note to insist that her eldest son came to London on just that particular day, no matter what his father had to say on the matter. They must both come to London, and in good time to appear at the ball at Tradescant House. Not to do so would offend her dear friend Portia Childhays, a widow, a woman bringing out a daughter without a husband to support her, only an eccentric aunt to help her, which must be terrible. No, George must appear at the ball, no matter what.

There followed a slight pause in the proceedings, as must always follow a moment when no-one quite knows whether or not to believe in the preceding conversation.

'I was fitted in Paris, in February, for the Season, although the fashions are becoming a little too fantastical for my taste,' May murmured, as if to reassure her two friends that despite the rather old-fashioned attire she was at present sporting she was more prepared for the Season than they might have deduced from her afternoon dress – which, although a bit of an old favourite, nevertheless lacked immediacy.

After a short time during which they all sought to pick up the threads of their very different lives over the intervening years, footmen appeared with trays of silver upon which rested gold-rimmed teacups, and the vast London drawing room suddenly became a place of entertainment. Without much prompting, for it seemed as if from unseen sources they had been told that the Duchess was At Home, friends and relatives began to call. The clatter of hats and canes being placed in the corner of the room was followed by the murmur of greetings, and May moved backwards and forwards, lightly and gracefully, receiving, introducing, waving prettily.

And all the while Emily watched her with a slight degree of envy.

May had always been the most beautiful of the

three of them, and it had been no surprise to either Portia or herself that she had captured a future duke. And not just a future duke, but the whole of London Society, who it had to be faced dearly loved both beauty and charm. And since May had both, she now made a delightful duchess.

And, moreover, which was strange indeed considering the undoubted licence of the age, and the myriad follies and temptations of Society, if rumour were correct the Duke had remained faithful to his Duchess for all their married life, which, when all was said and done, expressed even more about the Duchess of Wokingham and her undoubted charms, both domestic and otherwise, than a thousand compliments to her beauty. To keep a duke tamed and happy was some feat, and everyone in London Society knew it, and, doubtless, envied it.

'Why do you sigh, Lady Emily O'Connor? Are you sad? You cannot be sad, not for a minute, I shall not allow it.'

'Who knows me? Do I know you, sir?'

The young man smiled as Emily turned. 'You would not know me, but I do know you. I have followed you on horseback over many a mile, Lady Emily. Captain Fortescue, Barrymore Fortescue – my friends call me Barry. I was named after my godfather, Lord Barrymore, a neighbour of your father's in Ireland, you will remember?'

As the dark head bent low over her gloved hand Emily felt a shiver of excitement zipping through her, but since she did not approve of such emotions in herself she said sternly, to the still bent head, 'I do not know you, young man. I know whom I know, believe me, and I do not know you.'

'No.' The young man straightened up, and his dark eyes gave every impression of glowing with admiration. 'As I said, you would not know me. I have only seen you out hunting, in Ireland. But to have seen you once is enough to make an everlasting impression, believe me, Lady Emily. Never since the Empress of Austria have I seen such a seat on a horse. You are not just elegance personified, Lady Emily, you are daring, you are Diana, you are a goddess on horseback.'

Happily for both of them, but most particularly for herself, Emily was well used to being praised for her seat on her horse. She knew herself to be a good horsewoman, although to be compared to the Empress of Austria was somewhat galling because, as she had gathered from her late father, the Empress, although dashing in the field, and gathering the admiration of everyone, was known to be daring to the point of foolhardiness, which Emily would never be.

Emily, being Irish, valued her horses far too much to ever risk them over some unsurmountable object, or to jump them blind, or any such nonsense. To Emily her horses were her friends, and she could not, would not, ever endanger them in order to hear the gasps of the throng behind, or be the toast of Leicestershire for *leppin' the unleppable*, as their old groom would have it.

'Captain Fortescue, may I deduce at least that

you have had a few days out with the Galway Blazers?'

'I certainly have, Lady Emily, and nearer to home I remember that you came over one year to Leicestershire, it must be four years ago? You were staying with the Ashley Montagues, as I remember it, for a fortnight's hunting. You rode an unrideable horse – a great iron grey it was. I remember that very well.'

'My, my, my, Captain Fortescue, you are not the only one to remember that horse, I remember him too, one *Jehu* by name, and that was what he thought himself at the time too, a god! Dear me, he thought he was the finest thing out, that horse. The conceit of him!'

The young captain's voice almost trembled with respect as he recalled, 'He was due to be shot as unrideable, and you arrived, and after only a day he was as tame as a canary in a cage. He was beautiful, and so were you, and what a sight you were together!'

Emily laughed suddenly at the memory. 'Ah, he was a gentle old thing, once you got to the heart of him. Just pretending what he did not feel, really, as so many big horses do, Captain Fortescue. Poor creature, it was just that he was frightened, had been frightened by some human being, somewhere, or at some time, and all he needed was someone to get up on him and tease him into remembering that he was a horse and not a god!' Emily laughed again. 'I had the measure of him only because I knew a horse just like him, many years before, when I was growing up at Glendarvan. Our groom, old Mikey, he brought him to my father's stable, and before long he was trotting about with all the young on his back for all the world as if he were a donkey on the beach at some Kerry resort. Ignorance, d'you see, Captain Fortescue, it is responsible for so much when it comes to horses. Most people, d'you see, are frightened of horses, and the bigger they are the more frightened, and you know how it is, they set about them, particularly your sex, and once you've set about a horse, well, there's little to be done, really, only everything to be *un*-done! All that I did was to make friends with old Jehu, and he went like a lamb for me. As a matter of fact they sent him after me, after I left Leicestershire, and he is even now alive and well and last seen taking my youngest daughter Valencia for many a mile at a fast clip, God bless him, for she is a sickly child at the best of times, and when she can't run about due to the wheezles and the sneezles, why Jehu can do it for her!'

'You sound so Irish when you talk of your horses.'

'I always say I was my father's second head groom, after Mikey. Brought up in the stables and learned stable ways.'

'And a seat on a horse such as I have never seen before, and doubtless will never see again.'

The look of extreme reverence on Captain Fortescue's face made Emily laugh a little too loudly.

'I am so sorry, Captain Fortescue.' She quickly took a handkerchief and waved it airily in front of her face. 'It was just that—'

He stared down at her, about to be offended.

'It is just that no-one has ever complimented me quite so extravagantly before. In fact my riding is – was – a source of ridicule in my family, really, when I look back. My mother you see was far more interested in the arts and so on, and my father was blind, so he never saw me ride. So really, your effusive compliments have come as rather a shock to me, Captain Fortescue.'

Captain Fortescue stared down solemnly into Emily's laughing green eyes. 'If only you would ride with me, it would make me the happiest man on earth, Lady Emily. I do assure you. Just once to ride beside you, anywhere, however tame, that would make my year, my life, as a matter of fact. I have carried the image of you in your green riding habit with your beautiful face, seated on your great hunters before me, always, ever and always, and I swear that I always will, I swear it.'

Emily dabbed lightly at her face and put her handkerchief away. Of a sudden the room seemed terribly hot, she did not know why.

'Oh, come come, Captain Fortescue. You go too far now, and besides, there are other young ladies in the room, nearer your age, if I may say so, who would be deeply complimented to ride out with you in Rotten Row of a morning. I am a mother, and a wife, after all—'

'No, no, you are nothing so mundane, and I

shall not let you be. You will never be anything ordinary, especially not on horseback. You are a *goddess*, Lady Emily. I promise you, I know. My mother was killed out hunting, and died happy, I am sure, such was her love for following hounds. But you – you far outstrip her prowess, I promise you. Your elegance, your way of moulding yourself to become part of the horse, is without parallel. Above all you are lightness and grace, your hands so delicate, your seat like a feather floating on the back of your steed. Has your husband had you painted on horseback, Lady Emily? I dearly hope so.'

'My husband – Mr O'Connor? No – no. He is quite a horseman himself, and besides, it would not occur to him. As a matter of fact he does not think particularly highly of my riding, at least I am not aware that he does. He has certainly never said so, not within my hearing, at any rate. He rather takes it for granted, as husbands must, I think. After all, they cannot be counted upon to be amazed every day of the year, can they?'

Barrymore Fortescue shook his head in open amazement his eyes widening in astonishment.

'If you were *my* wife, Lady Emily, I should have you and Jehu painted so high.' He nodded up towards the ceiling miles above them. 'And so wide.' Now he nodded to indicate the breadth of the room. 'And I should place flowers in front of my painting, and burn incense before it. If I were your husband, that is what I should do,' he ended, reverentially.

'Well, I dare say, Captain Fortescue, but since you are not we shall both just have to dream of such a painting. I assure you, it will never come to be!'

Emily had coloured at the passion with which the young army captain had spoken of the painting, and now she made to move away, but not before Captain Fortescue leaned forward and murmured, 'You will ride with me tomorrow, will you not? I beg of you. Just once, to ride beside you, would be more than I can tell you. It would be everything. Early in the morning? You know the place I keep my horses – two superb hacks – just near to the barracks. I expect you have hired from there when in London. Please come tomorrow. I will wait for you. I know you will love Brass Buttons especially. He is seventeen hands of chestnut muscle. I cannot wait to see you two together, and after that I shall commission a painting of you. Our secret, you know, Lady Emily, for if your husband cannot appreciate that you are a goddess on a horse, I, Barrymore Fortescue, can!'

After which he walked off to pick up his hat and cane from the corner of the room, leaving Emily murmuring to no-one in particular, 'But I am a married woman, I am only in London to present my daughter at Court, and so on and so forth.'

Presently Portia moved towards her, and together they left May's increasingly busy At Home, and returned in their smart carriages to their London addresses – Portia to Tradescant House, and Emily to Medlar House.

Here they were undressed by their maids, and subsequently, in quite elegant if not entirely new tea gowns, lay upon their beds while their maids moved around their rooms setting out their jewellery, their hair tongs, the underclothes, and all the other appropriate requisites for the evening, while their mistresses, unbeknownst to each other, both dreamed of other times, other years, when they were the same age as their daughters.

And both could not help realising that they were as yet not so old that love could not beckon at least one more time.

That Portia thought often of her reluctant house guest, Richard Ward, was not entirely surprising, for although she visited him every morning he was usually still hardly awake, staring ahead of him in such a bemused fashion while one of the valets set about shaving him as to give her to realise that his 'cure', if it was to be effective, was still far from being achieved. And yet she was not without hope, for the servants who waited on him during the day had told her that he became more and more 'himself' as the day drew on, and that by nighttime he was usually far less morose, and would ask for Portia, often.

'He usually asks for "Miss Tradescant", and in a most loquacious manner,' Evie had told Portia, proudly trying out yet another new word. 'I understand that is what is called a "time lapse", Lady Childhays. That's what that is, a "time lapse". He thinks you and him, that no time has passed and you are still the same young girl as what you once were. Which is sad, really, in'tit? I mean him thinking you are both still young, as when you both sailed together, that is sad, if not pathetic, I'd say, 'cos none of us is any younger, and some of us is a lot older than what we care to think of ourselves, although London can make some of us feel younger than we thought, I will say that. So perhaps the Vice Admiral is just feeling younger because he's here with you, in London? Could be, I will say. Anyfink is possible, in'tit?'

Evie's words, doomladen though they were intended to be, and which she often repeated, nevertheless gave Portia a glorious sort of feeling that she was indeed still the same age as she had been when she and Richard first sailed together at Bannerwick, Portia with her pug Henry at her feet, and Richard young and as handsome as no-one looking into his lined and red-veined face could possibly realise, alas, that he had once been.

They had enjoyed each other's company in those ways that are so particularly memorable, when each person has no great desire to break the splendid silence of the water and its ways with idle chatter, but will be happy only to listen to the sounds of the moorhens, or the curlews, or the kittiwakes, to the sounds of the sails creaking and moaning, as if the very effort of sailing were pulling on unseen muscles in their canvas, and they responding as people will who have not had any exercise at all of late.

Perhaps Richard could be better in time for our ball, here?

It was a silly thought, but such an exciting one that it made Portia pull her pillow up tighter under her chin and smile at the holland blinds some yards away that were flapping gently at the windows, while outside the house, London walked and trotted past the front door in all the glory of the summer weather and the heat and hustle of the new London Season. Portia started to dream of Richard Ward, quite recovered, perhaps even waltzing her round the ballroom below, once the rest of the guests had left.

Meanwhile further down Mayfair, closer to Piccadilly and the Ritz and Mr Selfridge's new emporium, Emily too lay staring at the holland blinds flapping gently against her bedroom windows. Next door, she thought, lay Edith, doubtless hoping against hope that she would have enough partners at the ball that night, whereas her mother was lying wondering whether or not to meet Captain Barrymore Fortescue, a young man at least ten years younger than herself, out riding in the early morning in Rotten Row.

It was unthinkable of course. She was a married woman, and her husband an invalid back in Ireland. No lady would contemplate riding out with a younger man in such circumstances, would they? Most especially not Emily who, while she had always been more than dashing on a horse, had also been more than proper when off one. It was all fine and fair to receive fulsome compliments from foolish young men, and, it had to be faced, to be quite pleased by them, but to take them seriously would be foolishness indeed, and to activate the wishes of foolish young men, madness.

No, there was no point in beating about the bush. There was no going back to the girlish days of riding out on over-groomed hacks hoping to meet up with passionate young men, because of course one never did, not even in the dim days of one's youth, and so there would be even less chance of such a romantic occurrence now. Indeed, there was no supposing that life would be any different now from the way it had been then, however much couples might these days be shocking the world with the tango and the Bunny Hug. No, she would be sensible, she would not meet Captain Barrymore Fortescue, not at any time, not at any livery stables near to the barracks. The very idea was preposterous.

For a start they would have to meet so early that no-one at Medlar House, least of all Minnie or young Edith, would know of Emily's leaving the house and making good her escape, possibly by hackney, to the Park. And then there would be the problem of returning unseen, perhaps when the women were breakfasting in their rooms and all the men downstairs enjoying a leisurely four-course breakfast over newspapers and coffee. It would indeed be more than a little difficult to arrive back in one's room in one's riding habit, unbeknownst to anyone.

On the other hand, of course, if one *were* going to do it one would merely leave Minnie a note that one was not to be disturbed and then return before the appointed hour when one had said one *was* to be disturbed. And of course if one locked one's bedroom door no-one would know, if one took the key, *which* side the door had been locked from, which meant that one really might remain undisturbed.

Even so, if it was out of the question, then it was out of the question, and no more to be said or thought on the matter. And if there was no more to be said or thought on the matter, then one simply must not speak or think, even to oneself, about it. It would have to be a forbidden subject.

Like Portia, although she did not know it, Emily now hugged her pillow tighter as she thought of Captain Barrymore Fortescue's darkly glowing eyes, and of his passionate adoration of her seat on a horse. It had been flattering. That was all, she told herself, her pillow now doubled and held even tighter to her face. It had been flattering, and very kind in its way, of course. To compliment an older woman in such an extravagant manner was kind and flattering, but it was also rather endearing.

Yes, that was the word, 'endearing'. The way he had recalled her seat's being as light as a feather, the glowing reference to her hands, had been very flattering, but now she must forget about it, or else she would be in danger of having her head turned, and that, after all, for a mother and a wife such as herself would be quite, quite absurd.

But even as she shut her eyes and allowed

herself to drift off into one of the loveliest sleeps that she had enjoyed in a long while Emily could hear Captain Barrymore Fortescue's rich rounded tones saying, and so persuasively too, *You will ride with me tomorrow, will you not? You will love Brass Buttons—*

She always did have a weakness for a horse called Buttons. She remembered her first pony, Bright Button, and then there was that lovely Buttons at home, a strapping bay gelding – he had been such a ride. Remembering him was a joy.

Seconds later Emily was fast asleep and when Minnie came to wake her preparatory to dressing her for dinner and later a ball, she thought that she had never seen Lady Emily look lovelier. Her long white hair, once such a deep auburn, streaming down her back, seemed suddenly to be more blonde than white, and her skin as young as that of any girl enjoying her first London Season.

'You could pass as a debutante yourself, Lady Emily,' Minnie said as she raised her curling tongs to feel the heat, and Emily tied her tea gown around her once more. 'Sure you're as beautiful as any of 'em, and I dare say always will be more beautiful than they will be at your age. No-one would take you for being more than eighteen, I'd say, that's how beautiful you're looking since you came to London and left all your cares behind you, in Ireland, where let's face it cares seem to have come thick and fast of late, what with the politics, and the people determined to be rid of the likes of us, and houses set on fire, and horses stolen, not to mention Mr O'Connor's being so poorly with his bad back, and I know not what.'

Of a sudden the 'Mr O'Connor' to whom Minnie was referring seemed as remote from Emily as he must do from her maid. Emily loved Rory, of course she did, but she could not remember him as she should. She could remember that she was married to him, and that they had children, but she could not remember him as he was, or had been. Emily closed her eyes. She must bring Rory to her, she must remember how delightful he was, bring him back, before it was too late, and she did something foolish.

The Tradescant family doctor was about to begin examining Richard Ward with his usual *I'll-be-the-best-judge-of-this* doctorly expression.

Unable to bear his company for longer than was strictly necessary, Portia left him to it, closing the bedroom door behind him and traversing the sitting room next to it. As she did so she noticed a copy of *The Pickwick Papers* left to one side of Richard's chair. She picked it up and opened it at the bookmark. When they were young she had always teased Richard that he did not read, but such, obviously, was the tedium of staying upstairs locked in his room, day after day, slowly recovering his senses, that he had obviously taken to reading out of both boredom and perhaps desperation.

'Did you bring this book in to the Vice Admiral, Evie?'

Evie, who was busy polishing the pictures around the room, shook her head, uninterested.

'Oh no, Lady Childhays. I haven't got on to proper long books yet, you knows that better than anyone. No books yet, I haven't. I'm still just learning *words*.' She turned back to her dusting with a pitying expression.

Portia replaced the book, at the same time making a mental note to ask Richard if he was enjoying reading at long, long last. Whether he was or not, there was no doubt at all that the fact that he was reading meant that he must be getting better, more alert, more aware of his surroundings, and that was good.

'Lady Childhays.' Dr Bentley cleared his throat. 'The Vice Admiral is a great deal better. He has passed a point that I had hoped to see him pass in, say, another month's time, a point where the body has ceased to call on certain elements to provide its energies and now started to build up its own reserves—'

'You mean,' said Portia calmly, 'that the alcohol has passed out of his system?'

'Not necessarily . . .'

'That the energy created by the alcohol has passed out of his system and he has now begun to make his own energies?'

'Not necessarily . . .'

'What do you mean then, might I ask, Dr Bentley?'

'I mean that the Vice Admiral is beginning to respond to the process of isolation and a good diet, and that he is going to be able to live a normal life quite soon, just as long as he never touches, er, ahem.'

'Alcohol?'

'Not necessarily just alcohol, anything at all with any kind of stimulus in its contents. Even, say, Christmas pudding, or a brandy snap, or certain cough mixtures. They will all cause the craving to return, and once he is drunk I am afraid that we would once more be facing this more extreme treatment, the isolation, and the strict diet of meat and vegetables, fruit and custards.'

'I see.' Mentally Portia found that she had now changed Dr Bentley's name to *Dr Not Necessarily*. His obvious loathing of any suggestion or addition to his monologue made her wonder, as she allowed him to continue with his generalisations uninterrupted, what sort of life, if any, his wife might enjoy. She imagined their day-to-day dialogue.

His wife might say, *Breakfast is a good meal to start off the day, my dear.*

'Not necessarily,' would come her husband's reply.

Are we not lucky to have two healthy children?

'Not necessarily, my dear.'

Fresh air is good for us, would you not agree?

'Not necessarily.'

What on earth could a poor Mrs Not Necessarily make of such a man?

Since he was finishing his lecture now, and had presumably every intention of leaving, Portia hoped, she only half heard his recommendation that Richard be allowed downstairs in another week, providing that he maintained his good progress.

Even so, Portia, with an unquestionable feeling of relief, followed him, until at long last they were both in the corridor outside and could lock the door behind them, leaving the key, as usual, in the lock for the convenience of the servants arriving with meals and newspapers and other items.

It was as they made their way downstairs again that Portia turned and looked back up at Dr Bentley, unable to contain a mischievous curiosity.

'Are you married, by the way, Dr Bentley?'

'No, Lady Childhays, I am not.'

There was a small silence as they continued on their way, and then Portia, unable to resist further temptation, turned once again. 'Probably just as well, considering how busy you are, what with one thing and another. I suppose you have a very busy practice?'

Dr Bentley paused. Portia waited until, the pause having grown to a positive hiatus, she thought she must resign herself to final disappointment.

'Not necessarily,' the doctor pronounced at last, bringing on, without his knowing it, an uncontrollable fit of the giggles from Lady Childhays.

To cover the moment, she hastened away with a strangled excuse, leaving Aunt Tattie to settle his account, and make the usual observances that people find it so necessary to make to doctors –

endless thanks, and appreciations, just as if they were not paying for the services of the wretched man, just as if he was not doing his job, executing his professional occupation in precisely the same way that everyone else executed theirs. Except, with regard to the other professions, no-one seemed to bother to be so fulsome in their thanks or so craven in their attitude. Why, sometimes, the way people treated them, it was as if doctors were gods, and not just professional men.

Still, as Portia hurried off to find the steward and talk over his instructions for the ball, not to mention suggesting to him the idea of taking Richard to be fitted with some evening clothes, she could not help feeling elated.

Richard was going to get better! They might even dance together at the ball in a fortnight's time. It did not seem possible, but even as she sang a little ditty that they had used to sing together as the boat sailed safely home towards Bannerwick in the dear old days, Portia knew that she was not pinning false hopes on the future.

After all, Evie had said, and many times, that the Vice Admiral did nothing but talk about 'Miss Tradescant'. It seemed that just as Portia had not forgotten Richard Ward, he too had not forgotten her.

That night, at the ball which followed the inevitable dinner, Emily sat among the usual set of dowagers and chaperons knowing that she looked as she felt, positively radiant.

Edith too was looking really rather splendid, and was, Emily was glad to see, much sought after by all the young men, and this despite the fact that she was no beauty, in her mother's opinion, although there was no doubt that she had an attractive air about her, and looked sparkling and vivacious when spoken to. However, although all the young men sashayed over to her and insisted on writing their names in her card, their enthusiasm only seemed to last for one dance. Not that anyone was permitted more than two dances anyway, but even so, no young man seemed over-enthusiastic when it came to putting his name down for the second. What was worse, no-one ever, ever returned to place his name in her card on another evening. It was too galling for words.

Tonight this was particularly noticeable, so on their way home Emily decided to tackle her daughter.

'What kind of questions do you allow the young men you dance with to ask, Edith, dear?

'Oh, just the usual you know, the usual things that young men always talk about.'

'You will oblige me by giving me an example,' Emily insisted, despite the fact that Minnie was present and pretending to stare out of the window.

'They always ask me where I live and I always say "Ireland", and when they say *How too too* or some other silly reply, I say, "Yes and I wish I was back there rather than dancing here with such a dull Englishman as you!"'

Emily half closed her eyes, and then opened them again.

'I think, my dear, we had better have a talk with each other, and soon, really I do. Obviously Lady Devenish's tuition and attentions extended to everything except the proper kinds of conversations for a young woman to be having while dancing. You must flatter young men, Edith, really you must. You must learn to flatter young men, especially English men.'

'Oh, I don't care, Mama, really I do not. I don't like England. I wish only to be back in Ireland with Valencia and you and Papa, dancing in the hall with all the servants.'

'Ah yes, we all remember that day, do we not? That was a grand sort of day, the day of the storm, and the ceilidh in the hall at Glendarvan.'

This, accompanied by a sigh of pleasure, came from Minnie in the corner of the coach, which made Emily immediately want to rap her maid over the wrists with her fan.

'It may be what you feel about England and dancing, but conversations, socially, should never reflect one's feelings. Never, ever, do you hear, my dear Edith? Why, if all conversation did reflect people's feelings, people everywhere would be coming up to people everywhere else and saying such things as "My, you look mighty ugly today". Or "Whatever made you buy that hideous little hat?" Or "What a stupid face you have!" No, no, no. Tomorrow we must practise together making proper conversations, and you will please pay attention, and thereby I trust gain the devotion of some poor young man, somewhere. Or at least encourage one of them to dance with you *twice*! Great heavens, Edith, it is becoming quite noticeable that you only ever enjoy a dance once with one young man. It will be the talk of the town soon, really it will be, if you do not learn to flatter in your remarks, and soon.'

Edith said nothing in reply, but turned her uneven profile towards the window. Her lower lip protruded, an ominous sign, Emily knew.

Staring at her briefly, and feeling as she did her usual frustration as far as Edith was concerned, Emily suddenly did not care. She suddenly did not care one single little sigh if anyone danced with Edith once, twice or even a dozen times, no, she was quite, quite sure she did not even so much as half a sigh. Tomorrow she would go riding with the Captain Barrymore Fortescue, in her very best and most beautifully cut Busvines riding habit, and she would not care a hoot, let alone a rap, or a perch.

Captain Barrymore Fortescue was going to be allowed to admire her equestrianism, and she was going to enjoy showing it off to him too. She had not enjoyed any of her time in London with Edith, and her daughter's reluctance to behave as a nice girl should or could was enough to make her mother feel that she could not and would not tolerate any more. Instead Emily would ride out on Brass Buttons, and let the world think what it would. She would, for once, do as she wanted, just as Edith was always intent on doing whatever came into *her* head. Two could play at that game, and as far as Emily was concerned two were going to play at that game too.

'What was that you said, Mama?' Edith turned her cool, almost arrogant gaze on her mother.

'I said nothing.'

'Oh, really? I thought you said "humph".'

'Why on earth should I say such a thing, Edith? I have better manners than you, my dear, I do assure you. Only a hoyden and a frump would make such a sound, believe me.'

Edith dropped her eyes. They both knew that Emily had indeed said 'humph' and quite loudly too. But why she had said it, like so much in their lives, in everyone's lives, was a secret.

Intrigues

Things were not going well for Daisy. She was the first to admit this to the most important person in her life, namely herself. For a start Mrs Hartley Lambert would not be held back any more, and this was proving a disaster for poor Sarah.

Mrs Hartley Lambert would not be held back for the simple reason that she wanted to witness her daughter's great success for herself. She had become perfectly tired of being kept, as it were, behind drapes, and really, considering how much she was laying out in monetary terms for her daughter to do the London Season, no-one, least of all Daisy, could blame her.

'I cannot bring myself to blame her, *really* I cannot,' Daisy told Jenkins's back as the maid poured water into the brass bath in front of the inevitable fire, always lit in Daisy's bedroom wherever she was, at whatever time of year. 'After all, the poor woman is laying out *thousands* and *thousands* of pounds – or is it dollars? – on the Season. Anyway, whether it is dollars or pounds, the fact is vat she is, and let us face it, Jenkins, and it does have to be faced, vat is not nothing, even in this age of endless extravagance.'

'No, my lady,' Jenkins agreed, turning towards the great bed on which Daisy was still lying, and clearing her throat pointedly. 'My lady's bath is now ready for her, if my lady will walk towards it.'

'And, Jenkins, that is *another* thing to which I should draw both our attentions,' Daisy continued, still gazing past her maid and the waiting bath, and frowning. '*Why* is she putting out *thousands* and *thousands* for poor Miss Hartley Lambert? Because, Jenkins, because she has a positive bee in her bonnet vat the poor girl must marry better than her Hartley Lambert cousins in 'Merica. And what is more she is positively determined that she must return with her to the United States and parade her under their noses as the wife of some pasha-type from England, don'tcher know!'

'Yes, my lady, so you have said, my lady.'

Daisy determinedly ignored Jenkins's hearty sigh, as she always did when she was using her maid as a butt for her thoughts.

'But I mean to say, Jenkins! One cannot *guarantee* such fings, however much money is laid out, one cannot guarantee it, can one? One can only do one's very best, and hope for the same, Jenkins, for uvver people to do ver best, and so on and so forth, ad infinitum, Jenkins.'

Jenkins nodded sagely. She knew only too well what was at the centre of this heart-rending speech of her ladyship's and that was the fact that only yesterday Mrs Hartley Lambert had called on them, in full fig, on a dozy, sunny afternoon when my lady was just about to change into her tea gown and take a nap.

It had not been a good time for anyone, let alone Daisy, who, at that particular hour, was used to looking forward to a glass of madeira and a piece of fortifying fruit cake rather than an indignant American mama who complained loudly and vociferously that her Sarah, to her certain knowledge, had not yet been danced with by any man under the age of fifty-five.

'Titled they may be, my lady, but young and suitable they are *not*!' Mrs Hartley Lambert had thundered at Daisy.

It had all been most unseemly, if not indecorous, besides being not at all the sort of thing to which the Countess of Evesham was used.

'Last year's gel, Miss Springfield Digby, and Mrs Springfield Digby had no complaints, Mrs Hartley Lambert. And they, if you remember, recommended me to you, for my fine services and my connections at Court. Indeed as I remember it Miss Springfield Digby finally managed a very nice little marquis, and is now a very sweet little marchioness herself, and they fish together quite happily. As I recall, she did not complain at all, but then she was not as—'

'As what, Countess? She was not as – *what*?'

Daisy had dabbed at her forehead with a small, lace-edged lawn handkerchief, from behind which she then allowed one terrible, tired word to escape. '*Tall!*'

There had been a short pause after that.

They both knew that Sarah was disastrously handicapped in this way. That her prospects were not to be judged alongside those of the former Miss Springfield Digby, who had been, if anything, petite in the extreme, and therefore plucked off the bough of that year's debutantes as soon as she was able to be fitted with a diamond engagement ring.

Mrs Hartley Lambert had paled, but had recovered herself. She had continued, a little more calmly, 'I am not interested in any girl except my own. My Sarah is being made to look unwanted by the young gentlemen of this town, and I will not have that. See to it, Countess, or I shall personally want to know the reason why. I do not want to see her circling the ballrooms of any more London houses in the arms of some white-whiskered old gentleman, not now, not tonight, not at any time. It is starting to make her look ridiculous in the extreme, and I will not have that. Why even in Paris she managed to dance with two or three younger gentlemen, and since their revolution French men have become really quite *small*. If smaller French people could dance with my Sarah, so can smaller English people, Countess. See to it. I have paid you enough to line your pockets for at least another dozen London Seasons.'

After she had left, still in a great huff, Jenkins, who had been listening at a side door as was her wont, had let herself back into the drawing room just in time to see her mistress pulling the drawing room bell so hard and long that the embroidered piece attached to it had come off in her hand. After which she had thrown it at Jenkins, and herself upon a nearby sofa.

Being Daisy, of course, and, as Jenkins knew only too well, redoubtable in the extreme, she did not moan unnecessarily, or feel sorry for herself. She did not complain that she had never been so insulted in all her life, because, apart from anything else, both she and Jenkins knew that she had often been just as insulted, by bankers, by husbands, even by her son. Instead she went straight to the heart of the matter.

'She is so tall,' she had cried to the steadily burning log fire, to Jenkins, to the portrait of an ancestor placed over the chimneypiece. 'She is as tall as ve lamp post outside vat window! I cannot cut off her legs, now can I? Besides. Most of this year's young men are not tall, in fact a great many are really rather small, albeit not French, and what is worse they are quite likely to remain as small at the end of the Season as they were when they started out. And it has to be faced, Jenkins, when all is said and done, if I cannot cut off Miss Hartley Lambert's legs, I cannot either stretch the eligible young men so vat they at least reach up to her chin.'

There had been a short pause, during which Daisy tapped her foot upon the polished wooden floor as regularly as any young drummer in the band of the Household Cavalry.

'The young men know that they look ridiculous alongside Miss Hartley Lambert. They know they look just like Shetland ponies beside a carthorse. Not vat Miss Hartley Lambert is a carthorse, but she is so *tall*! She is as tall as a carthorse might be, as I say, if put beside a Shetland pony.'

Now, with the same problem besetting her, indeed making her mind crease with the burden of it, Daisy wandered almost aimlessly towards her bath. She stepped into it and sat down, allowing Jenkins to soap one of her feet while she lay back in the water and counted off on the fingers of one hand how many of the *taller*, younger men she could lure into dancing at least once with the luckless, hapless, Sarah Hartley Lambert.

'Lord Severington's son, John. Lord Morpeth's son, John. The Marquis of Heveningham's son, John – is there any member of our aristocracy, by the way, Jenkins, who is *not* called John?'

'No, my lady,' replied Jenkins mechanically, picking up Daisy's other foot and soaping it almost too liberally with the great sponge from the South Seas that had been brought back for her ladyship many years before by someone very special, so special that Jenkins knew my lady would have long ago forgotten his name, as she had forgotten the names of so many of her admirers. However, she still appreciated the sponge.

'I dare say I must not give up hope, Jenkins. I daresay I really must not, really I must not. I must put my best foot forward.' As Jenkins replaced the second of these in the bath water and began to soap one of Daisy's arms, she went on, almost desperately, 'I must just think of something, Jenkins, or some*one* who could help me get the thing going for Miss Hartley Lambert before the Season is closed and everyone fled back to the country, and the whole thing is a complete and utter failure.'

'The trouble is, my lady, Miss Hartley Lambert has a joke out against her,' Jenkins remarked, replacing the first of her ladyship's thoroughly washed arms back in the water, and going round to the other side of the bath to soap the second long, elegant, white arm.

'I beg your pardon, Jenkins? What is vat you just said?'

'I said, my lady, the trouble is not that Miss Hartley Lambert is so tall, begging your pardon, my lady, but that she has a joke out against her. It is going the rounds, as they say, and even the servants here, even they make the joke now. And you know how it is, my lady. Once there is a joke out against you during the Season, there is little to be done. It is not the kind of thing a person can see coming on, a joke, but there it is, once it is there, there is nothing to be done, my lady.'

Daisy sat up abruptly in the water, splashing it on the carpet around the bath, and smacked the surface with her hand.

'What joke, Jenkins? What have you heard? And where did you hear it?'

'I heard it first when my lady was at luncheon.

I believe, now I recall it, it was from the Marchioness of Ovington's maid who had it from a relative of mine who shall remain unnamed, for obvious reasons, but who is not given to telling pork pies – that is, lies, my lady. Really they are not.'

Jenkins fell silent, too busy mopping up the spilt water to carry on, and too obstinate too, Daisy knew, to carry on unless Daisy begged her so to do.

'Carry on, Jenkins, please.'

Daisy arose from her bath and summoned her towel by waving both her arms towards her body, which she always did and no doubt, Jenkins thought, possibly always would.

'Carry on, Jenkins, tell me at once. What is it vat you are on about? What is this joke, please? About Miss Hartley Lambert? Tell me, at once.'

She stepped out onto the white fluffy bath mat that Jenkins now laid before her and allowed Jenkins, as always, to wrap her in a large, monogrammed bath towel.

'Tell me the joke, Jenkins, at *once,*' Daisy repeated.

'Well, my lady,' Jenkins said, pursing her lips, knowing that she had all Daisy's attention for the first time for many a long day. 'It seems that Miss Hartley Lambert went riding in a very – dare I say it – *common* . . . well, no, in a very *unsuitable* hat.'

'Yes? Well, vat is not so unusual. We all have had hats that have made us look ridiculous at some time or another, have we not, Jenkins? I well remember a plum-coloured beauty vat my late husband threw on the fire of a street vendor some Seasons ago, and there was vat ghastly monstrosity he brought me back from Paris when we were first married, all tulle bows and butterflies. Oh, no, Jenkins, we have all had nasty hats. Vat is not so very unusual I should have said, not at all.'

'Yes, my lady, but this hat was particularly vulgar, my lady. It had silver in it, and her riding habit too. Apparently it is – at least so it was rumoured – apparently it was *français*!'

She should have told me! I would have warned her, the French cannot make riding habits. Everything else, but not riding habits! They go too far. They are too romantic for the strict tailoring necessary for a riding habit. It is just a fact. Oh, my heavens, what a disaster. Disaster of all disasters. If only I had known. I had not stopped to think that she would be even tempted by such a habit!

Daisy started to walk up and down, swathed in her bath towel, as she accused herself in her thoughts and suppressed a desire to swear out loud in a most unladylike way.

Jenkins watched her ladyship carefully before continuing. It was always best to watch my lady until she calmed down a little, because, apart from anything else, she seldom heard even Jenkins when she was in one of her pets.

'Apparently the hat was all too like that worn by a certain kind of lady to attract the attention of a certain kind of gentleman,' Jenkins finally continued, just a little relentlessly, because part of her was rather enjoying, as it always did, this particular little piece of mild gossip. 'And too, it seems, my lady, that the grooms wore silver cockades in their hats to match her riding habit, all chosen by Mrs Hartley Lambert in a fit of excitement in Paris, they tell me. At any rate, it seems that it was difficult for anyone to miss seeing all this silver everywhere, what with Miss Hartley Lambert being so tall, and her grooms too, apparently.'

'Worse and worse!'

'Oh yes, and it seems, my lady, that not only did no-one miss seeing poor Miss Hartley Lambert tricked out as if she was only newly housed in St John's Wood, if not Tulse Hill, by some obliging gentleman – in other words not looking as a young innocent girl should look, my lady – but she bumped into a party of friends coming from the other direction. It was that Miss Phyllis de Nugent, Lady Childhays' daughter, and that other young lady. Anyway, it seems that as soon as she saw the monstrosity on her head, Miss Phyllis introduced the young men with them to Miss Hartley Lambert not as Miss Hartley but as Miss *Hat*ley Lambert.'

Daisy sat down on the edge of her bed.

'No, oh no, don't tell me this,' she groaned, wringing her hands at the thought of how much that was done could not now be undone.

But her maid was still enjoying herself too much to stop.

'So naturally, the hat being so very prominent

on this very tall person, now known as Miss *Hat*ley Lambert, they all burst into unkind laughter, my lady.' Jenkins paused, and something close to a smile, or that could possibly pass as a smile, appeared, briefly, on her thin lips. 'And as you know there is none so unkind as the fashionable, my lady. We know that, you and I, with our experience from the past. There is none so ready to laugh at others like what the fashionable will do, none at all, even though I say it who is only a maid. We know, my lady, do we not, just how the modish can laugh at one's expense, and how one can only hope that their memories will pass, and with them the memory of one's past.'

Jenkins sniffed, but she also smiled again, remembering the moment of horrible disgrace years ago when a certain Mr Herbert Forrester had brought about the disgrace of that celebrated beauty, Daisy, Countess of Evesham. And how everyone had laughed, for several Seasons, and not just behind her back, in front of her face too, and in front of Jenkins – for servants suffered alongside their mistresses in these matters – although no-one seemed to realise it.

There was a long silence, a long and terrible silence, and then, frowning and furious at the same time, not a pretty sight despite her undoubted elegance and still evident beauty, even to her devoted Jenkins, Daisy let out a screech of anger.

'Vat is so terrible! Oh, poor Miss Hartley Lambert. What a terrible joke to be going the rounds at her expense. To be called *Hat*ley. Oh, poor, poor Miss Hartley Lambert.' There was another long and terrible silence, and then, 'But it won't go away now, will it, Jenkins? Not for a single tiny little minute, because jokes like vat do not go away, do they? They stay around for years and years and years, and no-one ever forgets them, sometimes for several generations. Sometimes they even get written up in books and newspapers. Oh, poor Miss Hartley Lambert. But nothing to be done now, Jenkins. We might as well call on Mrs Hartley Lambert and hand in the towel. I have never understood which towel, but hand it in I fear we must.'

At this she handed Jenkins back her own towel and gratefully accepted a gown in its place. 'I shall have to be honest with the poor woman. I shall have to tell all, Jenkins, really I will.'

Jenkins allowed this remark to go unanswered for a good minute, and then again what passed for a smile for Jenkins played about her thin lips.

'I was thinking, my lady, that there must be something that we could do in return to Miss Phyllis de Nugent, to pay her out. It should not be difficult, given that she has the reputation, even with her own maid, for running about wherever and whenever she should not, and spending time with persons what she should not, and so on, and so on. It should not be that difficult to pay this Miss de Nugent out, no, I should not think it should be at all difficult to land her in some warm, if not hot water.'

'I hardly think so, Jenkins. Miss de Nugent is a clever little thing, if not very pleasant, as I understand it from Lady Devenish. She was most unkind to Miss Hartley Lambert when they were being taught their "say sos and say nots", or so Lady Devenish hinted. It seems that the poor girl was so spoilt by her father, when he was alive that is, that now they can do nothing with her.'

Daisy sat down at her dressing table but avoided her reflection in the glass, because without any powder or paint and in one of her pets she knew that she would be looking like something the cat might bring in, and perhaps not even the cat. Possibly a decent sort of cat might avoid bringing in something that looked as raggedy as Daisy felt she must be looking.

'No, I am very much afraid, Jenkins, vat we shall have to make our way to the Hartley Lamberts and give back the undoubtedly large amounts she has generously donated to me in the hope, the very forlorn hope, Jenkins, vat I should be able to snap up a titled gentleman for poor Miss Sarah.'

'I am, myself, against handing in the towel,' Jenkins announced, at the same time folding yet another of Daisy's large, monogrammed items even as she pronounced her point of view. 'We have never yet handed in the towel, no matter what the circumstances. No, I think we should gird up our loins,' she held up one of Daisy's silk stockings to the light to examine it for flaws, 'and buckle on our swords—'

'Vat is quite enough, Jenkins. Quite enough analogies or whatever ve wretched things are called for one unholy morning, *thank* you!'

'Snap on our armour, get back on our steeds,' Jenkins continued, ruthlessly ignoring her mistress while holding up another silk item to the light. 'And we shall take fire to fight fire. Before it is too late, we shall have to think of something like a joke at Miss de Nugent's expense, and that way we would perhaps save the situation for Miss Hartley Lambert. Either that or we shall plant something in her house to disgrace her. We shall not rest until we have revenged ourselves, my lady. After all, we are old hands, are we not? And Miss de Nugent, she is only young and stupid.'

Daisy turned from studiously avoiding the sight of herself in the mirror.

'Jenkins, you are a genius. Of course! Fight fire with fire! She has burned us, we shall scald her back. Of course! We shall do exactly vat and we shall do it at *once*. Except, Jenkins, I am not very good at jokes. As a matter of fact jokes have never been my forte, as you might have noticed, Jenkins. Could we not – perhaps we could find someone who was good at jokes?'

'Never you mind that, my lady, just put it all out of your mind. I know just who to ask, and I will do so – on your behalf.'

'Could you, Jenkins?'

'Yes, my lady. I knows someone, someone in the household of Lady Childhays, someone who will put me in the picture, and then we can get back at her, as we shall, my lady. Just leave it to Jenkins. Jenkins knows what to do, and Jenkins always will.'

'Oh, Jenkins, you are a wonder.'

'Yes, my lady.'

There was a long silence following this outburst of flattery, and then, unprompted, as Jenkins slowly drew on Daisy's silk stockings, and clipped them to their suspenders, Daisy remembered that it would probably be just as well to show herself to be more heartily grateful than ever to her maid.

'Oh, and Jenkins, you know that silver cream jug you so admired the other day? How about if I put that together with the samovar – in my will, I mean? For you, to be left to you?'

'Thank you, my lady.'

Jenkins turned back to my lady's wardrobe. Any more London Seasons like this one and she might well end up being the grateful recipient of half the Evesham silver. It was not entirely impossible, she thought, feeling suddenly, for Jenkins, really quite smug.

Phyllis of course had grown careless about her visits to her *secret Vice*, but it was not her mother who had noticed, it was her maid. Evie, who had known Phyllis since she was a child, but not particularly liked her for the past couple of years, had also noted the presence of *The Pickwick Papers* in the Vice Admiral's room.

She had noticed it, but unlike Lady Childhays she had also noticed that the bookmark, a silk one made by Portia herself, one of many sewn during a particularly snowy winter in the country, was moving slowly forward, page by page into the centre of the book. Someone, for it was certainly not the Vice Admiral, who took little interest even in the newspapers, was reading to him.

It was an irresistible temptation to follow her charge. But Miss de Nugent, Evie often thought, had eyes in the back of her head, and no sooner had Evie decided to tail her of a morning when there were no other servants about, and Lady Childhays was out having a fitting for her ball gown, or paying morning calls, than, the maid noted, the visits or the readings seemed to suddenly stop, and the bookmark in *The Pickwick Papers* remained firmly at the same page as the day before.

So Evie knew that Miss Phyllis must be paying secret visits to the Vice Admiral, but she simply could not catch her at it.

'She is elusive, that one!' Evie informed her dictionary every night, while trying to look up yet another word to learn. 'She is *elusive*. She is cunning as a vixen. She is . . .' She paused, leaning over her beloved book. 'She is – precocious too, that's what she is!' She thumbed through the book once more, attempting to look up the word despite being unsure of its spelling. 'No, that's wrong. No, she is – she is just elusive, that will have to do for the moment. Elusive, and cunning too.'

She lay back against her one pillow. She knew that the wretched girl was paying visits to the upstairs room. She knew that she was spending time alone with the Vice Admiral. It was just a question of catching her at it. Sometimes she thought she could scent a whiff of her perfume on the air, or see a thread from her dress. But of course now that the Vice Admiral was allowed out of his room to take turns around the gardens, or if it was raining around the ballroom, it had become more difficult to know, for, while these bouts of exercise were always taken at a time when no-one was about, nevertheless the more sane and less incomprehensible Vice Admiral Ward became, the less certain Evie was that her suspicions were well founded.

More than anything it was the look in Miss Phyllis's eyes, the spring to her step that betrayed her to her now less than devoted maid.

But this was all before Evie had been, of a sudden, and from the shadows of the lower end of the overcrowded servants' room, approached by one of the valets after supper the previous evening.

He was a cunning kind of rascal was Evans. He had what Evie could only call a 'lurgy look to him'. Much more the kind of man to be found working in a London house. Not at all the type to take himself off to the country. He was for hire all right was Evans. And not only that, but he had a hard look to him, and none of the maids trusted him, or liked him, with good reason, Evie had heard.

So Evie was less than happy when the man approached her, but something in his manner, the hardness of his eyes, the cunning of him, had made her stop and listen to what he had to say none the less.

'A certain personage, Miss Evie, has approached me wanting my help. An old acquaintance like from Wales, a long time ago. A Biblical amount of time, I should say. But here's how it was, it seems. Our mothers' brothers were cousins, or some such. Anyway, once upon a time our grandfathers were both Valley, and that is enough, wouldn't you say, Miss Evie? It is enough for us Taffies to have relatives in the Valley in common, I would say, myself, I would.'

For herself Evie had not wanted to say, nor cared to do so. She had not been in service all her life, or more to the point *lasted* in service all her life – without a breath of scandal, what was more – without developing a sixth sense of danger, of what should or should not be avoided. This sixth sense was essential for servants. They had to be aware of what might be about to happen, before it happened, if they were to survive. Without it, Evie was all too aware, she herself could not have avoided accusations of theft, or breakages. She could not have avoided wandering hands – butler's hands, steward's hands, footmen's hands, sometimes even, alas, guests' hands – without that beloved sixth sense of something that was about to happen that would not be to her credit.

Being a servant meant that you were never so poor that you did not eat, but it also meant that you never slept quite easy in your bed either.

There was always, in a big, rich house especially, someone new arriving, someone who could be out for you, or out for your job, or simply an evil mischief-maker who just liked to make life uncomfortable for other people.

No, 'Miss Evie' had not survived all those years with Lady Childhays by being an innocent idiot.

So, now, staring into what seemed to her to be Evans's cunning eyes, made worse by drinking too much porter, Evie stood quite still, her expression one of cold reserve, her dislike for the man quite evident. But she nevertheless did not move away, for she knew that he had something to tell her – that beloved sixth sense again – and for some reason that she could not name she knew that what Evans had to say might involve either Lady Childhays, or Miss Phyllis, or possibly both. After all, there was more to the London Season, and all the servants knew it, than just the frills and the folderols. There was politicking everywhere, downstairs as well as up.

There had been, in past Seasons, as Evie well knew, enough excitements to make the Gunpowder Plot pale into relative insignificance. There had been the planting of stolen jewellery on several famous occasions. Also the planting or sending of letters – letters filled with ridicule for husbands who were ineffectual in the bedroom or, worse, husbands who were known to like their own sex. There had been gambling debts unpaid, and notes redeemed behind backs; there had been mistresses unceremoniously dumped, only, to the fury of their former lovers, to end up in more select, and sometimes even royal, beds.

And all this, all the essentials, as always, accomplished not by the protagonists of the dramas themselves, but by their servants. After all who else but the servants could run to and fro between the houses with messages for assignations, or warnings of dangers to come?

In one case it was rumoured there had even been a specially made underground passage involved, and servants running to and fro underneath the road between the houses connected by it. Running possibly with amorous notes, or blackmail letters, or just with flowers and love tokens. It was the servants more than anyone who were privy to the sighs and the groans of the lovelorn, or the recently forsaken. It was the valet who held the sore head of the cuckolded husband, and the maid who put burnt feathers under the nose of her mistress when it was discovered that she had committed the only sin for which Society would never forgive her – namely to be *found out*.

Sometimes Evie thought that the intrigues of the older generation were one of the main ingredients of the Season, that it was the love affairs of the older women, more even than the marrying of their wretched daughters, that brought the wives and mistresses so eagerly to town every Season with such monotonous regularity. After all, a love affair in the country was an impossibility, given that even the early denuding of a gardenia flower was commented on, by everyone, all the time.

No, by and large, everyone knew that love affairs were for busy London. For cities where the population wrestled and jostled past the people involved, and they were able to escape unnoticed by any but themselves, at least for a little while.

And of course the love affairs were always conducted by the most respectable in front of, sometimes, the most cunning and eager for gain – namely their servants. For some reason many Society people thought that their servants were either deaf or blind, and not as self-serving as themselves, and so were quite happy to conduct their love affairs in front of those same all-seeing, all-hearing witnesses, to the delight of their employees who could not, quite understandably given their low pay, but seek to find some profit for themselves in their new-found knowledge.

The look in Evans's eyes was therefore not unfamiliar to Evie. It told of some sort of gain for himself, some monetary accruement with which, judging from his breath, he would be subscribing to a further pint or two of porter rather than to a new edition of the Holy Bible.

Any minute now, Evie realised, she too would be expected to display that same gleam of *avarice* – another new word – yes, avarice and greed that was positively glowing in Evans's porter-ridden eyes.

'So this same relative, as you might call them, wants my help. And they are quite prepared to pay for it too, and doubtless yours as well Miss Evie. I have not any doubt on that score. She has taken the situation that badly, has this personage in question, that she is quite prepared to pay for just and honest retribution, and most handsomely, I am sure, Miss Evie.'

'And from what source is this wealth to come? Not criminal, I would hope?'

'No, indeed, Miss Evie, not criminal, nothing like that, God bless you. No, you need have no fear on that score, and what's more, God bless her, she does not mind to what lengths we go to obtain this quite just retribution. No, God bless you, you need not worry on that account.'

'I have no idea why God should come into this conversation at such regular intervals, really I have not. If I were you, Evans, I should leave Him well out of it. He might impinge on your conscience during the conversation and stop the very words in your mouth. Or He might overhear you, and strike you down for thinking or planning something that might not be to the whole advantage of this household. That's what God might do, Evans, so I should leave Him out of it, really I would.'

'You're a very good woman, Miss Evie. The best, I would say. And loyal, I knows that. To Lady Childhays, that is, but not I think to Miss Phyllis, who if I may say so is not at all the thing, and quite likely, to my way of thinking, to bring disgrace on the family, if what I have heard of her has anything to do with it.'

Evie's attitude to Evans changed in an instant. Evans was obviously a great deal shrewder than she had at first realised, and while he might have an understandable weakness for porter, on the other hand it was obviously not so great that he had not spotted the black sheep at Tradescant House.

Evans now leaned towards Evie, who braved the smell of the porter the better to hear the rest of his speech.

'I have seen potential disgrace in a certain party's behaviour.' He looked behind them, and then went on, his voice even lower, 'I have seen, for myself, mind, behaviour such as is reprehensible in a young lady well brought up. What with her visiting, on her own too, the Vice Admiral, morning after morning after morning, if what I have heard and seen on occasion is the truth. And that is not all, I believe. For before this, as I understand it, the young lady set about disgracing a certain other person's protég— pro— protég—'

'Protégée. It's a French word, Evans. It means someone what is being protected by you, or being looked after in some way.'

'I never was one for foreign languages. For a Welshman, mind, learning English was bad enough, I tell you.' He smiled briefly. 'Anyway, this friend of mine, her mistress has not taken kindly to what has happened to her – you know, protégée – and that, and she wants you to do something about it. She wants you to retaliate on their behalf, on behalf of her mistress and herself. She wants you to punish Miss Phyllis for them. And, Miss Evie, knowing how much she gets under all our fingernails, perhaps for us too, do you not think? For she has not left us entirely unmarked, has she, Miss Phyllis? And let us face it, there are some who might blame you for her behaviour, which is too terrible to think of, but as I understand it it is not unusual for the maid to be blamed for the young mistress's carryings-on. Not keeping a proper eye, and so on, and so forth.'

Evie prided herself on her good nature, on her ability to forgive and forget. At least, until that moment she always had, but now, faced with the reality of Miss Phyllis's deception, of knowing that she had not been mistaken in her charge, that she *had* been visiting the Admiral, and *alone*, she felt a well of indignation, a positive ball of fire, of fury, that she had seldom felt before.

She had always suspected Miss Phyllis, too much the favourite of her father in Evie's opinion, of being a spoilt hussy, a madam, a hoity-toity deceiving little number not worthy of her mother's love and devotion, and now here was the positive proof.

'In what way did she disgrace your friend's protégée, Evans?' Evie asked, her eyes narrow and hard, and her heart still beating with fury.

Evans looked grave now, so grave that Evie could not even guess at what he was about to say.

'She made a joke at her expense, would you know, Miss Evie? A cruel joke about her hat, when they were out riding, and as a consequence the poor young lady has only to enter a ballroom, or go riding in Rotten Row – even without the hat –

to meet with laughter, and conniving surreptitious laughter at that.'

'A joke?'

There was a small silence, and then Evie's eyes, already narrowed, became, it seemed to Evans of a sudden, like slits in the medieval castle that was her face. The nose the tower, the mouth the moat, and the eyes now slits in the walls of the building, ready to rain down arrows on Miss Phyllis, the viper in her poor mother's, as well as her poor devoted maid's, bosom.

'That would be Miss Phyllis all over, do you know that, Mr Evans?'

Evie sighed heavily, and so did Evans, she with fury at her charge, and he with satisfaction that she had for the first time elevated him to 'Mr'.

'Yes,' Evie continued, 'that would be Miss Phyllis all over. Always knows best, and always has done. Always ready to put a spoke in someone else's wheels, and never at her own expense. Well, well, well, so now, on behalf of your friend and her mistress, we had better put a spoke in *her* wheels, Mr Evans, had we not?'

Evans smiled and held out a large, lined fist. 'Shake my hand on it, Miss Evie. You feel the same as I do, mind. What we might call *a positive surge of honest indignation*. After all, why should this poor protégée, this luckless young girl, see, the innocent young lady, be the butt of a joke and have her chances ruined by Miss Phyllis? I ask you, why should she?'

'Indeed, Mr Evans, precisely my own feelings

on the subject, and always will be, I promise you. Miss Phyllis is a wanton and a deceiver, and as such we must act in our own best lights, and I for one cannot wait. She has been a thorn in my side all her life, and now I shall be quite happy to ram a spoke in any or all of her wheels, that I can assure you.'

'We are as one, Miss Evie, as one.'

Honesty of intent, belief in the goodness of their intention, and unity of purpose shone out of both their eyes as they pumped each other's hands up and down, so much so that Evie quite forgot in the excitement of the moment to ask just what her cut of the prize might be, but only agreed to meet with a plan in mind the following day.

Aunt Tattie was feeling vaguely excited. It was not just that she had been included in all the plans for the forthcoming ball for darling little Phyllis, but she had become more and more the confidante of her house guest, Richard Ward.

It had come about in a most gentle way, which was just as well, since Tattie always did have a marked preference for gentle ways in everything.

She had been seated, as she was daily, with her new prayer book – *Thoughts On Piety by A Monsignor* – when the Vice Admiral had been brought into the newly sunny garden by Evans, who was acting as his valet.

They had not spoken at first. He had taken turn and turn about, and Aunt Tattie had noted, from beneath her still quite long eyelashes, that he was walking perfectly steadily, and that he had a less flushed look to his face, and that all in all he was looking a great deal less like her brother Lampard, and a great deal more like a normal English gentleman.

The next day, at the usual quiet hour, they had repeated the same routine. Aunt Tattie seated in the same place, and still on the same (rather laboured) thought of the undoubtedly inestimable Monsignor, and the Vice Admiral toddling past at really quite a good clip, when she raised her eyes, and this time allowed herself to speak. She thought, since it was her garden in which he was exercising, that it was perfectly permissible to engage him in conversation of some sort or another, for when all was said and done they could not very well continue to ignore each other without both seeming rude.

He must have thought the same, for he stopped and turned round and came to rest in front of her Arts and Crafts bench.

'Miss Tatiana, how very kind of you to hail me in this manner. I have not stopped to talk when I saw you here reading, for I know from dear little Portia, my daily visitor, that you are only newly converted to a High Faith, and therefore have to do much studying.'

'That is all too true, Portia is quite right,' Aunt Tattie replied, her face still grave from the struggle with the worthy but unnamed Monsignor's cumbersome thoughts. 'All too true. But to be honest with you, Mr Ward, I am finding these thoughts, although very, very worthy, very, very tiresome too. For, you see, they are the kinds of thoughts that might occur to the clergy, but certainly do not occur to the normal human being going about their appointed tasks, if you see what I mean? They are, even to a person of my known sensitivity, just a little too high flown. I am, when all is said and done, only a human being, and too much of this world, I fear, whereas the Monsignor seems to be of quite another.'

Richard Ward smiled, and as his hostess patted the wooden Arts and Crafts and, to him, really rather strangely shaped chair placed carefully in front of her own bench, he nodded dismissal to his valet and sat down upon it, gratefully. For much as he had enjoyed, in the previous weeks, young Portia's flying visits in the mornings, much as he had even quite enjoyed her reading to him from some book or another, as the mists of alcoholism had gradually cleared from his mind he could not wait to sit and talk to this dear personage from the dim and distant past. He remembered Aunt Tattie and her brother Uncle Lampard so well, from the dear days of Bannerwick, and it seemed to him, as he seated himself beside her, that the dear lady had, like Portia, not changed at all, that she was still as she had been exactly, and at that moment he too felt the same.

And it was such a healing thought. It was as if the past had never been and he was young and vibrant, and his parents were still alive and he in love with life. And yet the mere mention of religion, alas, brought back more sombre thoughts too, which could not be avoided.

'I have not much respect for religion myself, Aunt Tattie, at least in recent times. Not since the loss of my beloved wife and daughter. For if God chose to take persons so dear and so good from this world – from me – then I have no time for God, I am afraid.'

Aunt Tattie nodded. 'That is quite understandable, young Richard Ward. If I were you I should feel precisely the same, but when the healing time has come and gone, as it surely will come and go, and there is hardly a trace of even a scar, then I would say that you will come to terms with the fact that God has to let even the sea, even the tides and the storms, have their way. All He can do is offer you the healing. Otherwise we should all become like sleepwalkers, should we not? Just sleepwalking our way through life to the tune of His playing, and because He loves us He would not want that.'

'It seems to me that I have been asleep this past year, so little of it can I remember,' Richard told her, with a sudden piercingly sober look. 'That at least is true. And you are right, perhaps the sinking of that ship, that terrible loss of life, had nothing to do with the Almighty and everything to do with man. And it was my fault that my beloved little family were on that same so-called unsinkable ship, my idea to send them to America – my treat. My conceit, if you like.'

Aunt Tattie put out her hand suddenly and patted Richard's still bronzed hand.

'My dear Richard Ward, it is not given to us to mete out our own punishments. You must now learn to forgive yourself. Every day, if you will, for my sake and your own, you must try repeating the words *I forgive myself* three times when you rise, three times when you take turns around my garden after we have had our conversation, which I hope we will continue to do, and then three times at the end of the day. And, if you will, you must start now. It is never too early to start a good habit, you know.'

Richard paled slightly and then reddened. 'Come, come, Aunt Tattie. Not out loud, surely?'

'Out loud,' said Aunt Tattie firmly.

'I forgive – myself. Hmm. I, er, forgive myself. And. I forgive myself!'

'Well, now, there you are. You feel stupid now, but later you will feel better. And believe you me, that is no more than I feel after trying to follow this essay of the good Monsignor's "On Awaking". Why, Richard, if we did as the Monsignor here advises,' Aunt Tattie started to knot the wooden beads about her waist around her hand, 'we would still be going through the act of getting up as the sun was setting. There would be no time to live, no time to eat, no time for anything, except rising! I am not an insensitive person, but really, the Monsignor goes too far, even for me. Now, don't forget your little repetition, and I will see you here tomorrow, same time, same place, and we will talk some more.'

After their conversation Richard Ward returned to his room, and although the valet still locked the door he felt strangely at peace. Knowing that he still had a friend in Portia's aunt meant so very much to him. He knew that Portia was doing all she could for him, but somehow the presence of her aunt in the house, and her insistence on his repeating the words *I forgive myself,* seemed to him to bode well, and for the first time he found himself staring out of the window of his rooms on to the busy London street below, not thinking of the dark past, but of Aunt Tattie in her strange medieval clothes staring into his eyes, but with such a kind expression in her own that for the first time since he waved goodbye to his beloved wife and daughter, saw their figures growing smaller and smaller as the great ship sailed off to meet with catastrophe, a small voice inside his head whispered that there might at last be a little hope come into his life, and that although it might only be the size of a pinprick it was, nevertheless, that most glorious of feelings without which there is only darkness.

Of a sudden it was almost as if the past had started to forgive him.

Feeling much better than he had for what now seemed years, he started to walk about his rooms, touching pictures and straightening them, humming a little, thinking over the past weeks. Idly he passed the table where he kept his various mementoes, his cigars and matches, his snuffbox, a pocket knife, some money, his card case and other small items, and glancing down he saw that there was a letter partially hidden by his card case and snuffbox.

It had been left poking out a little behind the two different shaped silver boxes, just enough for him to see, but certainly no-one else.

I must see you, soon. I will unlock the door tonight. Meet me in the ballroom. P.

It had not taken Evie long to work out, with the help of the less than estimable Evans, that the Vice Admiral must have a crush on Miss Phyllis. That being so, it would be something indeed if they could fake a note to him, and signing it 'P' set up a meeting between himself and Miss Phyllis, and then, having sent the same request to Lady Childhays, *Meet me in the ballroom tonight*, signed it with the initial 'R', make sure that Miss Phyllis's mother would come upon the old man and the young girl. Miss Phyllis would be thoroughly disgraced and doubtless banished to Bannerwick and left to the patronage of her elderly relatives for the rest of her natural.

'It will do him for Lady Childhays, of course,' said Evie, sagely, to Mr Evans, 'but that can't be helped, considering. No, it can't be helped at all. But what it will do, for good and all, is Miss Phyllis. That will be as right a spoke in her wheels as anyone could wish, the deceiving hussy.'

The truth was that Evie had never really forgiven Miss Phyllis for not going on the sailing trip with the rest of her family, a trip which should have left the maid free to study her books and improve herself, time which she had mentally set aside for herself alone.

'I don't suppose he will know her handwriting, will he, now?'

'Not from Adam – or rather, in this case, *Evie*'s own!'

They had a short laugh about that.

'Besides, I can fake Miss Phyllis's hand soon as look at her; her handwriting's just like one of us servants', not all like what a gentlewoman's should be. She never had any interest at all in her books and lessons, always out riding or sailing with her father, was Miss Phyllis. And of course Lord Childhays indulged her in everything, seeing that she was the first born and he had wanted a son. Until her brother came along, he treated her more as a boy than a girl, I always think. But of course when they wanted her to go round the world with them, on a true adventure, she had to be different, didn't she? She had to stay at home and make herself the bane of my life instead! The one time I could have looked forward to being on my own, to study my books and that, she had to land herself on me. But then that is Miss Phyllis all over.'

Now Richard stared at the handwritten note. It was scrawled in blue ink across one of Portia's cards – *Lady Childhays, London.*

Why should anyone wish to meet him alone, and why in the ballroom? It was not conventional.

More than that, it would not be kind to his hosts, to Aunt Tattie and that nice friend of hers, the other woman, whoever she was, who occasionally popped her head round the door in the company of the doctor.

Not that he did not find Portia as attractive as he had always done, spirited and fine, but Richard was too much of a gentleman, too sober now, and the road back to sanity he had traversed over the past weeks had been too hard by far, for his ever to wish to return to any kind of hysterical state.

So, no, he could not respond to such an invitation. Perhaps the very act of sobering up had been just about as much as his poor old mind and body could take, for he had no wish to be alone with a young girl.

With the feeling that his intelligence was slowly awakening, and the past slipping into a less confused state, as soon as Evans, the valet, came back into his rooms with a good, hearty supper laid out for him, Richard handed him a note in a plain envelope.

'Please give this to Lady Childhays on my behalf, would you?'

Evans was momentarily confused. Miss Phyllis, surely? But then he remembered the card Evie had taken from Lady Childhays' writing case, and so, with a strange little smile he took the note from the Vice Admiral, and having laid out his dinner for him in the proper manner let himself out of the room. He locked the door and quickly undid the envelope, the flap of which, in the correct way, remained slipped into place, rather than gummed – a polite custom with well brought up people, giving as it did the responsibility of trust to the bearer of the letter.

But Evans was not trustworthy, and would never attempt to be so. It was not his way, and so he held the card from within the envelope between his fingers only seconds after he had taken the note from the Vice Admiral.

He read Richard Ward's carefully penned words with a sinking heart.

No, my dear. I could not possibly meet anyone in the ballroom, let alone a young person such as yourself. R.

Evans started not to run, but to hurtle down the stairs towards the servants' quarters in the basement. The one thing that he and Evie had not reckoned on was that Richard Ward would prove to be not just a Vice Admiral, but a gentleman too! How inconvenient! How unlikely! He almost fell into the servants' dining room, and beckoned Evie as unostentatiously as he could.

'Things, Miss Evie,' he said, speaking out of the corner of his mouth, to the relief of Evie, for it seemed to her that the smell of cheap porter was permanent around Mr Evans. 'Things have gone sadly awry. The gentleman in question has read the note and is refusing to act upon it, with the result that the wretched man is all set to leave Miss Phyllis standing around on her own, alas, uncompromised! Her reputation thoroughly intact, which is not at all what we wanted for the little jumped-up hussy, is it, Miss Evie?'

Evie thought quickly. Mr Evans was right. Miss Phyllis, to whom they had naturally written a note on behalf of Richard Ward, was indeed going to be left thoroughly uncompromised, and now it was too late to stop certain events from hurtling forward to who knew what end.

'Nothing to be done, Mr Evans, except wait and see and hope for the best, as always, in the best of all possible worlds.'

'Yes, Miss Evie, but not quite what we were hoping for, when all is said and done, would you say?'

'Not quite,' Evie agreed. 'But then what is?'

'It might all end in disaster.'

'Doubtless, it might. Or it might not.'

'I rather fancy that if I had a wager on the outcome, my money would be going on the first option rather than the second, Miss Evie.'

Evie turned away from him, walking back to the bench where she normally sat when off duty, to her knitting and her thoughts.

'I am afraid I rather agree with you, Mr Evans.'

Evans frowned to himself as he watched Miss Evie hurrying away. He turned to go back to the men's quarters feeling really rather wretched.

Captain Barrymore Fortescue could hardly believe his eyes. Of course he had hoped, but only in a very faint way, when all was said and done, that Lady Emily would turn up to ride with him in the early morning, in Rotten Row, but he had not really believed that she would.

'Lady Emily!'

He sprang forward from the shelter of the stable on seeing her, so tall, so slender, so much the horsewoman standing in front of him in the summer sunshine of an early London morning. And as his eyes grew wide with appreciation he knew that particular excitement of the young lover-to-be. He could hardly believe his luck, but now that he had his goddess firmly within his sights he knew at once that he would not let her go again, not for all the gold of the Indies, not for all the silk in China, not for all the other married women who had previously passed through his bed.

'Lady Emily, I say, this is too, too of you, really it is!'

Emily looked up into Captain Fortescue's passionate young dark eyes. He would not know it, but she could hardly bring herself to believe that she was there either.

'Yes, I know, Captain Fortescue, I agree with you. It is really too, too of me, but too, too what of me? I dare say neither of us can bring ourselves to find the right word, but there it is. I am here, and so are you. Now where is Bright Buttons, or whatever he is called, and where your mount?'

Barrymore Fortescue snapped his fingers and his groom came running.

'Bring out Bright Buttons for her ladyship, Buckston, and take her to the mounting block.'

'You will do no such thing, Buckston,' Emily put in. 'You will bring out Bright Buttons and lead him up to me, please.' After which she turned and eyed Captain Fortescue with a bright, hard look. 'No equestrian I know uses a mounting block, Captain Fortescue, unless they are *injured* in some way, or excessively old.'

Captain Fortescue reddened, knowing at once from the look in Lady Emily's brilliant green eyes that he had made a cracking ass of himself. Of course! A horsewoman such as Lady Emily would naturally despise a mounting block. She would spurn such an aid. It would be for 'coffee housers', as the ladies who trailed along at the back of a hunt were known. It would be for 'lilting Lydias', women who hacked gently and slowly around the Park, not for the Dianas of the chase, for the goddesses of equestrianism, to have their horses brought to a block to allow them to scramble aboard as if their mounts were so many omnibuses or tram cars. No, just a hand such as Buckston was holding out to her now, and the placing of the noble, slender foot in that hand, an *allez oop*, and an equestrian such as Lady Emily would be seated aboard Bright Buttons as lightly as any feather now floating from the Serpentine towards the barracks.

And so their ride began, with Lady Emily a little ahead, stern and silent, her green riding habit showing off her tall, slender figure, her silken white hair startling beneath her elegant hat, and the expression on her face one of cold disapproval, as if she could not, after such a *faux pas*, believe that she was out hacking of a summer morning with someone so positively idiotic as Captain Fortescue.

Barrymore knew himself to be handsome, and a well-known seducer of beautiful married women, and until that moment he had never found himself at a loss for words. How could he recover his footing with this goddess of the chase whose seat he had so admired in Ireland, those few seasons ago? How could he impress on her that he wished he had had his tongue cut out rather than have so offended her by suggesting that she would be the kind of woman to need a mounting block?

'Come on, Captain Fortescue. The Park is empty of anyone but a few cavalry types. I'll race you to that bench over there, and if you get caught you can pay the fine, and if I get caught I shall plead a bolting horse!'

She kicked Bright Buttons lightly and at the same time her hands, as light as her seat was balanced, tightened a little, and the horse flew from under her, and even as he flew Emily gave a shout of laughter, as Barrymore, too late, attempted to follow on his slower mount. Carrying more weight he knew that he had not a hope, for she had gone from a walk to a fast canter in a matter of seconds.

Watching her from behind, too far behind, Barrymore knew that Lady Emily had stolen a march on him and it would be difficult, most likely impossible, to recover any ground. Weaving between the Park trees, pretending, as he was well positioned to observe from behind, to be a helpless woman quite out of control, Lady Emily cantered faster and faster. In and out of the trees she bent her willing young horse as supple as a sapling, herself gurgling with laughter, until finally her mount took off towards the Serpentine, towards the wild fowl, towards no-one and nothing, Barrymore following at an admiring distance.

Finally, of course, as is always the way with pranks on horseback, she went too far. It was inevitable, really, and what was more he had a feeling that it was what she, at least, wanted. He closed his eyes and sat back, waiting for disaster, as with a gay laugh she took off in front of a Park bench, jumping it with miles to spare between Bright Buttons's hooves and what looked like an old man still seated upon it.

But Captain Fortescue need not have worried. His goddess of the dawn, his equestrian heroine, seemed to know both her steed and the poor creature on the bench, for she safely landed on the other side, and seemingly satisfied at last that she had finally had some sport drew Bright Buttons to a perfect, cavalry halt, turned him on a sixpence, and walked him decorously back to the captain.

'I – er – I am quite stuck for words, Lady Emily. Is that personage on that bench – well, I imagine that he too is somewhat – er – somewhat stuck for words too, Lady Emily!'

'Not at all, Captain Fortescue. That personage, as you describe him, is fast asleep, in a drunken stupor as a matter of fact. I thought Bright Buttons might wake him up, or that he might hear us sailing over the top of him, but he did not. He is still, if you observe, seated in precisely the same position, having I would think enjoyed far too much alcohol for far too long.'

She turned her horse towards home, laughing appreciatively at her own escapade.

'I am, you see, having been brought up in the west of Ireland, quite an expert when it comes to the *slump* of a man with too much drink taken. A genius, in fact. Otherwise, sure, I would never have lepped the bench the way I did. But I speak too soon. Oh, dear, here comes the law!'

The policeman, Barrymore thought, ruefully, afterwards, had not a hope, for the moment he approached her Lady Emily let out a huge and hearty sigh of relief and began a speech which she had obviously made on some other occasion, such was the fine and steady stream of words she addressed half to himself and half to the hapless officer of the law.

'Oh, but, Captain Fortescue, you were so brave. And I was so frightened! I have never known Bright Buttons to behave so badly before! He must have been stung by a young bee. I always think that in May or early June the sting of *young* bees is so much worse. Yes, I do declare. Look, officer, would you not say that would be the mark of a bee, just there – on his hind quarters? Yes, there it is! Oh, poor, poor little horse, what a dreadful thing to happen to him, of all people. Of all horses, you know, officer, this darling one is the best behaved. And yet, see, one sting of a bee and he is off like a bolt from a gun! And jumping a bench too! I mean the nerve of him! The very nerve of him! I would not know what to do with myself if I did not know that this horse is normally an angel. More than an angel, an archangel. And the captain here, so brave in galloping after me, coming to my rescue. I do not know what I should have done had I not heard that rattle of his horse's hooves behind me. Would I have been able to stop myself? I think not. Why, I might have ended up, just think, officer, in the Serpentine there! Swimming around, perhaps even *drowned*! Indeed, I might have drowned if it had not been for the two of you, so brave and so kind, coming to my rescue, *willing* to come to my rescue. Dear, oh my! Really, I think I might faint at the very thought of the might-have-been. Worse, the probably-would-have-been!'

The officer of the law who had witnessed the jumping of the bench now, and, Barrymore thought, really rather understandably, of a sudden appeared to have entirely forgotten why he had approached the two equestrians whom he had found so far out of their ground in a place where only pedestrians were normally meant to be discovered. This was quite obvious from the way he was frowning, and then frowning some more, and then patting Lady Emily's horse, and frowning yet again. For if Lady Emily had not herself drowned, it was all too obvious to Barrymore that the poor officer had been thoroughly submerged, not by water, but by words.

So many words, such a torrent of words, that, as happens when people are found wandering after an accident, it could be that after witnessing such an escapade and being exposed to such an avalanche of verbiage the poor man had lost his memory altogether.

Lady Emily now leaned down from her horse, and before the poor officer could say more than 'Er um' she kissed her gloved hand to him.

'Officer, I shall always remember your kindness in coming after me, in worrying over the danger I was in. And you, I know, will always remember the terrible harm that can be caused by such a little thing as a young bee's sting on a sunny summer morning, will you not?'

Staring up into those great green eyes the officer stood back, nodding slowly and happily.

'Why, ma'am, of course. Always. A terrible thing a bee sting, particularly a young bee, as you so wisely said, ma'am. God bless you and keep you safe.'

'And you too! I am sure that we can all rest easy in our beds as long as we have policemen like you ready and eager to be of assistance to helpless women such as myself.'

After which pious thought Lady Emily pressed her riding boot to the side of Bright Buttons, and with one more kiss of her gloved hand over her shoulder to the admiring and now utterly devoted officer, she walked off to the safer sand of Rotten

Row, and so on towards the barracks and the livery stables.

'Such a nice man,' she remarked, her eyes widening and more innocent by the minute as Barrymore caught up with her. 'So understanding. And terrible about the bee, didn't you think? So sudden, such a thing.'

Barrymore went to open his mouth, and then closed it again. A few minutes later he remarked in a tone that he had never known himself use before, 'You are quite, quite wonderful. You are quite the most wonderful creature I have ever known, and I am, and shall always remain, and never will not be in love with you.'

At this Lady Emily merely laughed, but the look in her green eyes registered that she had heard him, and – who knew – even appreciated his sincerity.

The light from the now quite old-fashioned gas lamps that were flickering into life in the old blue and gold painted ballrooms was necessarily eerie, and Phyllis could not help shivering as she made her way down the stone and iron staircase to the lower floor. Ballrooms, like swimming pools, like boathouses, like all places built for certain kinds of enjoyments at certain times of day or night, when empty, had an echoing feeling. As if once left on their own they enjoyed some secret life, as if unseen and perhaps ghostly figures might suddenly appear to enjoy themselves, use the pool or the ballroom, or take out a boat, when the normal world had quite gone away.

Phyllis had received a note from Richard, written on one of her mother's cards: *Meet me in the ballroom at eleven tonight. R.*

She had not expected such a note, and having not seen him for some few days, due to the exigencies of the Season, too many engagements, too many fittings for Ascot and so on, she had been more than surprised.

And then, too, following the shock of finding the card under her favourite lawn pillow, she had felt guilty, for she knew that he had no idea who she really was, since she had never disabused him of the notion that she was not Portia, her mother, but Phyllis the daughter.

It had been fun visiting the old tar to start with, because she was bored, and doing something wicked, like slipping in and out of the Vice Admiral's room unbeknownst to anyone, and reading to the poor old thing while he sprawled about gradually and painfully recovering his senses, had been an adventure. Just as going to sit with her father's mastiff, a wholly forbidden exercise, when all the servants were out, had been an adventure, but an adventure which, when you discovered that the dog would not harm a fly, rapidly became dull and eventually just silly.

And that was the worst thing about this note: it made her feel silly. She did not want to continue reading to the old boy any more, or even to see him much again, and for a very good reason. The previous evening she had danced not once but twice with a certain young man, who had utterly and completely taken her fancy. Better than everything, he made her laugh, and she made him laugh. He was the second son of a second son, and he had a passion for sailing, and one more ball, one more dance, and, Phyllis was quite sure, he would waltz her into the conservatory and ask her to become Mrs Edwin Vessey.

But, despite this extraordinary and desperately exciting occurrence, an occurrence that had driven everything except Edwin and his beautiful blond looks from Phyllis's mind, she could not say no to meeting her boring beastly *secret Vice*, because she was afraid he might tell her mother, or Evie, or that horrid valet Evans, of her solo visits to him, when she had read to him, and let him think she was her mother.

So here she was, standing shivering and alone and clinging to her silk shawl, his note in her pocket, and the memory of how stupid she had been all too clear in her mind.

Of a sudden there was a sound from above.

It was the unmistakable sound of a door opening and a pair of shoes, not heavy-soled men's shoes or boots either, coming downstairs. The footsteps were light, indeed so light that they could only belong to someone feminine. The gas lamps were still flickering into life and so it was easy for Phyllis to shrink back behind one of the large pillars and wait to see which female it might be who was coming down to the ballroom at precisely the same time as herself.

The figure came slowly and carefully down the stairs, as if it was afraid of whom it might be about to meet.

'Richard Ward? Young Richard Ward?' a voice called out, and echoed, dully, around the old ballroom.

Phyllis knew just who it was to whom that voice belonged, but how that person came to be there, calling for the Vice Admiral she could not imagine.

She shrank back behind the pillar, hoping against hope that the female person in question would not come in search of Richard Ward and find her instead, which would mean that she would be forced to tell her why she, Phyllis, was also there, waiting for the same person.

Eventually, having called a few more times, looking every now and then at her fob watch, the person in question sighed. Turning out the gas lights, one by agonising one, she left the old, blue ballroom, closed the double doors at the top of the stairs quietly, and left Phyllis below in utter and complete darkness.

Feeling her way across the well-polished ballroom floor, bit by little bit, and then equally bit by little bit, quite agonisingly, up the staircase to those same double doors, Phyllis found herself promising God that she would rather die by her own hand than deceive anyone ever again.

Somehow, she hardly knew how, she eventually reached her room, but only by little dashes from one doorway to another, as figures that she never realised flitted about the house at such a late hour seemed to cross and recross halls, corridors and landings. Maids, valets, someone she had not even realised was staying in the house creeping downstairs and letting himself into the dining room, obviously to help himself to the port. She saw them all. Someone else – Evie she thought – she heard scratching on her mother's door, and she even saw that awful Evans creeping down the back stairs, obviously on his way back to the servants' quarters, which, cramped though they were, nevertheless housed half a dozen or more men during the height of the Season.

At last Phyllis, after what seemed to her to be a lifetime of adventures, reached her own bedroom and sitting room. Flinging herself through the doors and onto her bed, she found herself almost crying with the relief of being back where she belonged. She had no idea why that wretched Vice Admiral Ward had sent her a note, and as she lit a spill from the spill vase and set it to his horrid card, she promised herself that she would never break Society's laws again. She had learned her lesson, and very nearly the hard way, for she knew that if he had arrived down in that ballroom, and if that female person had seen them together and alone, she, Phyllis de Nugent, would have been utterly ruined, her reputation lost for ever.

If to be ten minutes without your maid meant that you faced ruin, what would have happened if she had been found with a single, middle-aged man? There would not have been a hope in a million of someone like Edwin's taking her into a conservatory, any conservatory, and asking for her hand.

Worse than that, she would have been known throughout Society as *damaged goods*, and sent home, not even home to her father's house but possibly to live with Aunt Tattie at Bannerwick, to a lifetime of sewing samplers and suchlike activities, which was to say to a life of doom and wasted hopes.

As the smoke arose from that wretched card and it fell into satisfying little black shreds, and eventually totally disintegrated in the hearth, Phyllis decided, for the first time since her father died, that she would try to be as good as she could – as good as she thought her mother to be – for she knew now that just for derring-do, and from boredom, she had very nearly ruined her whole life.

She undressed herself, laying out her clothes on the chair in a modest sequence, ready for the morning, and even remembering to kneel and say her prayers.

The last of which, whispered, and necessarily very personal, ran, *And thank you, God, for not letting Aunt Tattie see me! Thank you a million, million times, and I will always be good from now on, for ever and ever. Amen.*

After which she hopped into bed and, pulling the covers up to her chin, fell asleep remembering Edwin and how they had danced and laughed together, and how she had confided to him how much she hated the Season and wished only to be back in the countryside, and how he had felt exactly the same. And how their eyes had met, knowing, at once, that they were that strange thing, twin souls, and that very soon they would not have to even bother to voice their thoughts, they were so alike.

PART TWO

Giving Back

Herbert Forrester sighed and looked out of the window, away from the invitation that was resting in his hand. His darling May, now Duchess of Wokingham, had never forgotten them, and nor would she, he dared say.

In his hand, and the reason for his reverie, was an invitation to Mr and Mrs Herbert Forrester from 'The Duke and Duchess of Wokingham', in other words May and her dear husband, to a great, grand ball in their London house.

Of course Herbert would not be going, and nor would his beloved Jane, not just because of the latter's determination to avoid seeing or hearing from May and 'her set', as dear Jane would sometimes refer to them, but for other reasons, reasons that Herbert could not reveal to anyone.

As a matter of fact he was only too thankful that his Jane had such a bee in her bonnet about the Wokinghams. For, and here again Herbert sighed, it made it so much easier to give a reasonable excuse to his beloved for not going to London. If he pandered, happily, to Jane's aversion to fashionable London folk, she would never suspect the real reason why Herbert would not be making the long journey to enjoy the Wokinghams' ball, which he knew would be attended by everyone who was anyone, including King George and Queen Mary, and members of the aristocracy and the government; and doubtless enjoyed by them too.

No, Jane was never to know why they were not going down to London, why they would not be hiring a town house for the week, why he would not be taking her to buy her the most beautiful gown she could ever wish for, why he would not be hiring the best and most expensive jewellery from some ageing aristocrat for her to wear. No, he would rather take his own life than ever let his Jane know that she was not long for this world.

'My dear.' Jane bustled into the first floor drawing room. Mid-morning she was always bustling, it seemed to Herbert. Seeing the invitation in her husband's hand, she put her head on one side, and looked questioningly at him. 'My dear, anything of particular interest?'

'No, my love. Nothing to concern ourselves with, you will be very well glad to hear. No, just our May feeling kindly towards us, as always, and sending us an invitation to the ball they are giving in London next month. But—'

'We shan't be going, shall we, Herbert?'

A gleam of something close to terror appeared in his wife's honest brown eyes as Herbert turned from the window to look at her.

'Good Lord, no, my love. Why, I know, better

than you even, that a visit to London is as agreeable to you as having a tooth pulled!'

They both laughed, and as Jane did so she gave a little light cough, and waved a fan, one of the many she had collected, to be found on all the small tables crowding the room.

'Oh, you are so right, Herbert. That is exactly how it is for me. Going to London is tantamount to having a tooth pulled!'

She gave another little wave of the fan, and another little cough, and then, putting her head on one side, she said, 'It's nice we are so alike in our tastes, isn't it, Herbert? I can't imagine you being married to a woman who liked gadding about and going to London all the time.'

Herbert hesitated. He hated to tell Jane any kind of untruth, but the fact was that it was she, and not he, who had such a particular taste for the quiet life, and did not like London. To humour her, however, he always played along with the myth, amounting now almost to legend, that he did not enjoy parties or dressing up and going out to socialise.

Mind you, it was true that York more than satisfied his needs. They went on visits to friends who lived some way outside the city, particularly during the short and blessed break known as the Yorkshire Summer. And then in the winter they visited each other for games of cards and suchlike activities, and dinners – there were good dinners cooked in friends' houses, no denying that, no denying it at all.

'No, you're right, love,' Herbert replied at last. 'I enjoy our life here, and our friends, more than I can say. And I have no real desire to be anywhere except in your company.'

This last was certainly true. He had no desire to be with anyone but his Jane, particularly since the doctor had told him of her incipient illness, knowledge which, their doctor had stressed, must be kept from her if she was to survive as long as they hoped. If she was to survive the coming summer, she must never even suspect that she had more than a little infection which 'brought her down' some days, or that the pills she took were more than just 'strengthening' pills made from various livers and so on.

'I doubt that she will last another winter, Mr Forrester, but let us take one day at a time, and no more and no less, eh?' At which his old friend had squeezed Herbert's arm. 'I know what it is like to lose one's wife, and believe me, I had rather it had been me than her, in my own case. A man alone is rather a pathetic creature, I always think. We don't do well on our own, we men. But there, I am lucky, as you are. I have a daughter.'

'What shall I tell Jane, though? What should I tell her?' Herbert's eyes had filled with tears. 'I don't want her frightened. I won't have her frightened.'

'And no reason she should be. No, far better to keep one's loved one in ignorance. Woe to the man or woman who takes it upon themselves to act like God and pronounce on someone else's life span.

These modern doctors who turn round with "You've got a week", what do they know? Why not ten days, rather than a week? Why not a fortnight? They should keep their mouths shut, not pronounce on us all as if they were the Almighty.'

Herbert had agreed with his doctor wholeheartedly and then, having shaken each other's hands, and avoided the sadness in each other's eyes, he had turned on his heel and instead of returning to his office he had made straight for his club in the centre of the city, and sent a note to Jane telling her he was called away for a couple of days on business to Bradford, after which he had taken a train to that same city, booked into an hotel near the station and started to drink.

He had never, to his certain memory, been so drunk since May's mother Ruby had died. He had been drunk then, but not as drunk as he had become after seeing his doctor and hearing about his Jane.

But then he had taken the train back to York once more, and put up at his club, where he sobered up, and down, and pulled himself together in such a way that he swore, from that day onwards, he would never allow himself more than a glass of whisky after dinner. Never would he let Jane see the panic, the fear, that her imminent demise had brought about within him. With this resolution had to come, as he well knew, an unshakable decision not to allow himself more than a nightcap of whisky 'before retiring'.

Too much wine, one glass of porter too much, it

did not matter, truly, what it was, but he was certain that if he became in any way intoxicated he would risk lowering his guard, and might, inadvertently, allow Jane to see what she must not know. Or, if he became morose from drink, she might just *sense* that he knew something that she did not. The problem was that they were so close that sometimes it seemed to him that she was able to read his thoughts, almost before he had thought them.

'So, dinner as usual tonight? I mean at the usual hour, Herbert, my love?'

'Why, yes, love, that would be everything I could wish, a quiet dinner for two, just you and I. I could not want for more.'

But the truth was that he *could* want for more, and did. He wanted more and more, and never-ending, dinners and luncheons with his beloved, his darling Jane, opposite him.

After all, it was for Jane that he had turned down the attentions of Daisy, the beautiful Countess of Evesham. That was something for which he had not been forgiven, quite naturally, by the Countess. And after all, no real man could have said, all that time ago, that the stunning Daisy clad only in a tea gown and silk stockings was not a temptation, and to say any different was so much hogie pogie.

Herbert had not been tempted, not because he *could* not have been tempted, but solely and simply because he *would* not be tempted. Nothing would induce him to be unfaithful to his beloved

Jane. She was the light of his life, and though he had loved his first love, Ruby, with all his heart, he could never have been tempted to marry her. Ruby and he had youth and adventure in common, they had a poor background in common, they had a wish to succeed in common, but they did not and never would have had marriage in mind, even though he had saved young Ruby from drowning when, as a young child, she fell into the river.

I must just take each dinner and each luncheon, as they come. I must pretend to myself that there will be another million dinners and luncheons to come. Just as if my life with Jane was beginning and not, which is the truth, ending. That is what I must do.

Jane stared across the table at Herbert. 'What, still not fancying wine with your meal, our Herbert?' she asked, her head once more on one side as he covered his wine glass with his hand.

'No. It is since the influenza in the winter, I think. It right put me off my wines, and I want nothing more than my whisky before I retire, love.'

Jane straightened up and laughed. 'I don't believe you, Herbert Forrester!'

Herbert remembered to keep his eyes calm as he stared across the heavily embroidered luncheon cloth at his still pretty wife.

'And why is that?'

'Because, quite simply, you did not have the influenza in the winter, Herbert. *I* did!'

Herbert smiled. 'I know you did, love, and ever

since then you have suffered from your little cough and your breathlessness, but you see I had it too, when I had to go to Bradford that time, remember? It come on quite suddenly, and I was right poorly, I tell you. I did not want to worry you, since you yourself were below par, but I had two or three days of feeling quite unlike myself in Bradford, and when I came back somehow my taste buds could no longer support the idea of wine. That is what I think happened. I think the bout of influenza took away my liking for wine.'

'Oh well, Herbert, never mind, eh? What is not missed is of no matter. I, on the other hand, have decided that I might feel better for a glass of red wine once or twice a day.' She nodded towards her wine glass, but seeing Herbert's anxiety as the maid filled up her wine glass she went on, 'It's all right. I checked with Dr Leonard, and he said there is nothing at all amiss with my taking a little fortifying red wine twice a day. In fact, he thinks it positively beneficial.'

'In that case, I will be tempted to join you in a glass, and that way we can drink to each other twice a day, my own love!'

Jane smiled delightedly. For when all was said and done there was no real pleasure in enjoying wine on one's own. She nodded to one of the maids, who quickly took the wine round to Herbert's side of the table.

'Herbert.' Jane raised her glass. 'Let's drink to each other, love. And to our future together, don't you think, dearest?'

Two raised glasses, two smiles, and one heart at least feeling as if it were sinking like a stone.

As he raised his glass to drink her poor health, everything to do with Jane that he so loved seemed of a sudden to be a burden to poor Herbert. Her pretty ways, a burden. Her smile, her sweet smile, that too a sorrowful burden, at the thought of how few days there were to come during which he might enjoy it. Her clothes, always so bright and so crisp, seemed to mock the sad thoughts that would not go away. And then there was her unselfishness. This business of her taking up wine again was most probably because she thought *he* had given it up for *her* sake. It was all so beautiful, and so sad.

'You never liked wine before, did you, Jane?'

'No,' she admitted, and then she frowned. 'No, I never did, but I don't know why, I do now. It makes me feel better, stronger even.'

'That's good, then.'

'Yes. Something else we can share. Herbert. Not that we don't share so much already.'

'We've been lucky, haven't we, Jane? We've hardly been apart, all our lives. What a thing that has been, our lives spent always so much together!'

'And still so much more to which we can look forward, Herbert. So much more.'

'That's right, love. So much.'

'And summer is here.'

'Yes, love. Summer is here.'

'And the birds are singing.'

'Yes, love, the birds are singing.'

'And I have a new dress from London, just arrived.'

'Have you, love? I can't wait to see it.'

They smiled at each other, but just for a brief second, he could not have said why, Herbert had the idea that he glimpsed tears in Jane's eyes.

Aunt Tattie was waiting, quite eagerly, for Richard Ward to arrive in the garden. She did not know what to say to him. It was all so strange. A young man his age . . . well, he was forty, she supposed. Anyway, he was much younger than herself, and sending her a note on Portia's London card with an invitation to meet her in the ballroom!

Why should he wish to do such a thing? She thought he might have some burden, perhaps some new sorrow that he wished to tell her about when no-one else was about; or he might have something that he wished to give her quite privately, without Evans or someone seeing, some treasure that he wanted her to safeguard. Men did trust her, she had noticed that over the years. Even Lampard had trusted her, with so many secrets, far too many, that she had really rather he had not. But there, he was her brother, and when all was said and done a brother was a brother.

She had found the note on her bedroom table, just after she and Portia had decided to swap rooms, because she found it so very difficult to sleep in London, and her room overlooked the main street outside, and what with the windows open on a hot summer night and the sound of the carriages arriving and departing, and the street cries in the morning, there was always something to disturb her.

Well, to cut a long story short, at all events she had truly had enough of not sleeping, London or no London. So Portia, such was her sweet nature, had suggested swapping rooms, and after they had duly rehung all their clothes in fresh wardrobes and the maids had damp-dusted and swept and all that, Aunt Tattie had found this card from Richard Ward hidden under her pillow.

Of course she had not wanted to go to meet him, but she had thought it must be her duty to do so, and so she had taken herself off to the ballroom and then, the silly man, he had not turned up!

Why, she had wondered, go to all the trouble of writing her a hastily scrawled note only to fail to materialise? She thought it must be all part of his poor condition. Her brother Lampard, suffering from the same condition, had been terribly hither and thither, and still was. He hardly knew the time of day, or the year or the month, he had grown so bad of late. Happily he had some devoted servants who took care of him night and day now, and so he was what her mother's cook would call *out of your hair, Miss Tradescant, thank goodness*. And it was true that he was out of her hair now, but such could not be said for Richard Ward.

As Aunt Tattie went over and over, again and again, the strange behaviour of her reluctant house guest, downstairs in the servants' dining room

Evie and Evans were looking at each other sombrely, in the true knowledge that they had both, as Evans put it succinctly, 'made a hell of a hash of it, Miss Evie. But then we was not to know that the Vice Admiral would be such a gentleman, was we?'

'No, that is true.'

'And you was not to know that Miss Tradescant and Lady Childhays would, of a sudden, decide to swap their rooms, was you? We was not to know that you placed the note just where the wrong woman could take it up. And now here we are, back at the start of it all, and no better off if you ask me. What am I to tell my relative, that is what I would like to know? She is wanting to hear something she is, and she can't be blamed, can she now? Not for wanting some news of retribution for the destruction of the social ease of this – er – protégée.'

'Quite right, Mr Evans,' Evie agreed. 'I would feel the same in her position, wanting to know that something was going to happen by way of revenge, I would and all. It is only natural.'

'That is what it is, Miss Evie, natural. Revenge is natural. You are kicked in the shins by someone, it's only natural that you want to kick that person's shins back. I know it's not Biblical, that I will agree, but it is natural, really it is.'

Slowly, oh so slowly, after this heartfelt statement from Mr Evans, a plan came into Evie's mind, and it was a good one, of that she was suddenly quite sure. She turned to the valet.

'There is one thing that has happened, Mr Evans, which we did not think of. I don't exactly know why it has happened, but something has changed our Miss Phyllis, beyond anyone's dreams. She is a different girl today than what she was a few days ago. Which leads me to think that we may well be still able to do something to retrieve this situation. If Miss Phyllis has turned over some sort of a leaf, we might induce her, of her own free will, to make amends to this poor young lady.'

'Meanwhile,' said Evans, going to the window and looking upwards and out towards the garden, 'look at the Admiral seated beside Miss Tradescant. That was not exactly what we intended, was it? Those two becoming intimate!'

They both started to laugh, because really, when all was said and done, it was funny. Just one of the many small, amusing, or sometimes tragic dramas that played themselves out during the Season.

'Do sit,' Aunt Tattie commanded. As obedient as a spaniel or a lap dog the Vice Admiral sat down on the strangely shaped Arts and Crafts chair opposite her own strangely shaped bench. 'Good. Now we can begin to talk. I can never talk when a man is towering above me. Tell me,' went on Aunt Tattie, 'do you think you might have something on your mind that you wish to tell me, young Richard Ward?'

Richard shook his head. He had nothing on his

mind except the idea, and it was an exciting one, that Portia had been eager and willing to meet him quite alone in the ballroom downstairs. It had never occurred to him, wreck of a man that he was, that Portia could still, after all this time, find him exciting, that she would want to meet him alone. He had thought of her so often when he was at sea, and after he was married – when he probably should not have thought of her at all – and now here they were in London, and Portia had sent him a little note urging him to meet her for some reason that he could only surmise.

'I wish to tell you that coming here and being with you, in your house, with everyone that I once knew in my youth, has turned me round. Such kindness, such unheard-of kindness – I cannot tell you what it has meant to me.'

Aunt Tattie's grasp on the beads around her waist tightened, and tightened once more again, until she was almost cutting herself in two. She did not wish to boast, but she knew that what Richard Ward was saying was only the truth. She knew that she and Portia had been the instruments of his salvation in a perfectly practical manner, in a way that was not elucidated by the wretched Monsignor in his essays, in his roundabout, *seventeen times around the bushes and cannot understand a word of it* way.

'So, that is why you wanted to meet me?' Aunt Tattie's eyes filled with tears.

'That is why I wanted to meet you,' Richard agreed innocently. 'To tell you that you, and

Portia, have literally saved my life. That you have taken a drunken old tar and turned him round. And every day I have said those words you taught me, and every day, few of them though there have been, I have become better and better. You are kindness, you are thoughtfulness itself, and that is why I wanted so much to meet you again, to tell you that.'

Aunt Tattie patted his hand. 'Dear young Richard Ward. What a fine fellow you are once more!' She stared into the handsome face, now substantially less florid, the eyes clear once more, the speech utterly coherent.

Richard laughed. 'Now you go too far, Aunt Tattie!'

'Not that you were not always a fine fellow, but now, here, I see you as you were in the dear old days at Bannerwick, a fine, upstanding, honest fellow with such a passion for sailing and for boats, as to put everything else out of your mind. And Portia too, of course, *she* has never lost her passion for boats. Sailing halfway round the world with just the crew and her children for company. She did that, you know, after – after her poor husband was gathered.'

'Poor man. To close his eyes for ever on Portia's beautiful face, how terrible for him.'

Richard said the words sincerely and without embarrassment, and for a while they were both silent, as people of different ages can be silent together, knowing that they understand each other across the generations, appreciating each other as other souls nearer in age sometimes cannot find the time or the will to do.

'Of course. But to return to the present. You are better, that is all that matters. You are whole again, and likely to remain so. And, you know, Portia will be down in a minute, and we can take luncheon out here, in the garden. That will be amusing, I think. Always, indoors in London, halfway through the Season I begin to feel . . . shut in. Hemmed in, quite tired of the indoor life, don't you agree?'

At the mention of Portia's name Aunt Tattie sensed Richard Ward growing worried and restless. He was certainly becoming tense, if the movement of his feet, the crossing and recrossing of his legs, was anything to go by.

'Yes,' she said again, 'Portia will be down to join us any minute and we will be able to take luncheon outside. I have instructed the servants. And do not fret, there will be nothing in the food to bring on your former indisposition. Meanwhile, let us have some lemonade, ice cold and freshly made.' She rang the small, silver, finely wrought eighteenth-century bell in front of her and smiled encouragingly at Richard Ward.

I will be here to see you through the next phase of your life, whatever it is, her smile told him, while at the same time her thoughts ran ahead to the idea that she would never bother to read essays on being good again. They made you feel too *wicked.* No, in future she would confine her ideas to doing. To do good was to follow your heart sincerely, and really, reading about how to go on was about as much good as reading a receipt in a cookery book, appreciating it to the full, and then failing to make the blessed dish.

Upstairs Evie was facing her mistress, and, for her sins, telling an enormous lie. And what was worse Miss Phyllis was witnessing her doing it, and they were both wriggling and squirming in front of Lady Childhays' honest gaze, while at the same time not looking to each other for help.

'I was readin' *The Pickwick Papers* to the Vice Admiral, my lady. It was nothing to do with Miss Phyllis here, bless her, not at all. It was me that was sneaking in and out and reading to him for all I was worth.'

'*You*, Evie?'

Portia did not believe a word of it. She knew, and all too well, that Phyllis had been up to something of late. She had been so good, so docile, so willing to do or say anything Portia had asked of her, that her mother had become convinced that she was 'up to something'.

For that reason her suspicions had alighted on the book. Supposing that Phyllis had been going in to see Richard Ward all alone? Supposing she had been reading to an unmarried man, a widower, herself unmarried? It would mean that her reputation was lost. It would mean that she was ruined. The bookmark told all. That and the fact that young Phyllis was now being such an angel.

'Yes, my lady, it was me. I thought, and I am

sorry if it was wrong, but I thought, and Mr Evans too, that it would do him good to listen to someone readin' to him, and all that sort of thing. And seeing that it is such a very amusing book it seemed to me that it might buck him up, begging your pardon, my lady.'

Portia's eyes, large, grey and discerning, moved from the maid's face to her daughter's. She knew that they were both lying, and she was determined to prove it. She had to get to the bottom of the whole matter. More than that, she had to find out if Phyllis's reputation was quite ruined, which she well suspected it might be. Besides, Evie had told her, some weeks ago, that she was not 'on' reading books yet, only learning new words. However, fearing some hysterical outburst if she reminded the maid of this, Portia took another tack.

'Very well, Evie, let us call up Mr Evans, and let him substantiate your story, shall we? If, as you say, he witnessed your reading to the Vice Admiral, if it was indeed you.'

She rang the bell to the side of the door, and after what seemed to everyone to be hours, not minutes, the valet appeared at the door of the suite of rooms, panting and breathless, and fully expecting to see the Vice Admiral rather than her ladyship as the summoner on the bell.

'Oh, my lady, Miss Phyllis, Miss Evie, I thought it was sir that had summoned me. I never realised it was you ladies, begging your pardon, my lady.'

'No need, Evans. I just wanted you to confirm what Evie and Miss Phyllis here have just told me.'

'Which is?'

'Which is that Evie has been reading *The Pickwick Papers* to the Vice Admiral?'

Without a flicker, for he was such an accomplished liar, and would always remain so, Evans thought proudly, he immediately answered Lady Childhays. 'Why, of course. But I was always in and round the place, my lady. There was no harm to it. These days the man is quite back to himself, but in previous days it was very soothing to him, I do assure you, my lady. Really, like a little child is soothed by reading to it at night, my lady. And, too, when his mind was liable to wander and he would sometimes imagine he was on the bridge of his ship, and suchlike nonsense, some of those early days in particular, he was held to his chair by the story, I always thought. So, all in all, I was very grateful to Miss Evie here, my lady. As you may well imagine, my lady.'

Portia knew that Evans too was lying, but that there was little she could do about it. More than that, she did not care to pursue the matter any further, for the truth of it was that since the servants were able, and for some reason only too willing, to back up Phyllis, her reputation to all intents and purposes was now quite safe. Had they not been willing and able to do so an ugly rumour about Lady Childhays' daughter's being damaged goods would have been set in train, and within a few days, as had happened before in previous Seasons, she would have had to send Phyllis packing, all her chances of making not just a good match, but any match, quite ruined. It was a very frail thing, a reputation, so frail as to be like gossamer, although of course, once safely married, a young woman was able to enjoy a liberty not known to many single people of any age.

'Good. Well, then, it is all settled, once and for all. And I can only thank you for taking such trouble with our house guest, who is now, as you may all have seen, quite cured of his ailment, and likely to remain so for the foreseeable future. Indeed, on that subject, I must thank you both, Evie and Evans, for all that you have so patiently done for him. I hope his cure is reward enough, but I intend that it will not be. I shall make sure of that, at the end of the month, I promise you.'

'Thank you, my lady.'

Answering in chorus though they might, and smile innocently and sweetly though Phyllis might, Portia did not believe a word from any of them. She knew that they were all up to something, or had been up to something. But it was all over now, and nothing to be done, and what was better, nothing to be proved.

She turned to Phyllis after the servants had left them, and in a very different and somewhat puzzled tone said, 'Now, my dear, I have received a note from Mrs Edward *Vessey*. It seems that her son, Edwin, has requested an interview with your papa, which, alas, is of course not possible. She wishes, therefore, to know to whom her son might apply for his interview. Which guardian must he speak to? I mean to say. Do you know anything of this? Has he made his feelings clear in any way? I saw nothing of note at last night's ball, only that he has now danced *twice* with you at three consecutive balls, which must mean something, I suppose?'

Phyllis blushed to the roots of her hair. She and Edwin had decided to evade the interest of the crowded ballrooms and what Edwin called 'the awful dash to the dread conservatory!' and between them had agreed to his going straight for the all too terrifying interview with Phyllis's guardian.

A visible look of relief came into Portia's eyes as she realised, of a sudden, that her only daughter had at long last, it seemed like weeks and weeks to her mother, succumbed to the honourable intentions of a well brought up young man who, if not titled, was at least from a good family. Edwin Vessey was tall, blond, and utterly charming and if she had heard the truth about him, his only vice was the writing of poetry in his spare time. He was not a gambler or a womaniser, he was young and kind, and he would be, Portia suddenly thought, quite perfect for Phyllis.

'Oh, my dear. Phyllis, my dear.' Tears came into Portia's eyes quite involuntarily. 'Has it as last *happened*? A nice young man taking a positive interest? Never mind that he is only a second son of a second son, he is a nice young man, and you both looked so charming, such a couple, when you were waltzing the other evening, that I must say I did find myself hoping. Besides which, Aunt Tattie has known of his family for ever and more, I know. For centuries probably, knowing Aunt Tattie!'

'Yes, Mama, but Edwin and I did not know whom he should request an interview of, so – so his mama volunteered to write to you on his behalf. For as you know, his father too is no longer with us.'

'Very proper of him,' Portia replied briskly, her thoughts galloping ahead to a London wedding, ten attendants, and a honeymoon on her beloved yacht, which she would of course lend. 'I am very much afraid, though, dear, that your guardian is Uncle Lampard. It is to him that your Edwin must apply for his interview.'

They both looked at each other, suddenly comrades in arms in the often embarrassing battle of life, for if Phyllis's Great-uncle Lampard was not a sore embarrassment then King Edward VII had been a completely faithful husband and Portia's maiden name had not been Tradescant.

'I shall have to write back to Mrs Vessey and inform her, but – my dearest, do warn your suitor, will you? I mean we both know Uncle Lampard. Well, we know what we know, at the very least, and unlike the Vice Admiral's, his habits are quite unchanged.'

Portia nodded, brisk and to the point once more, and yet her heart was as light as it had not been since Childie had been taken from her. Phyllis with a proper suitor, it was too marvellous.

Phyllis in love, it was almost unbelievable. More than that, a beautiful young man in love with Phyllis. She turned by the stairs.

'We are taking luncheon in the garden, Aunt Tattie and the Vice Admiral and myself, but it will be rather dull for you, my dear. Why not ask Evie to bring yours up on a nice tray to your sitting room? It would be better for you, to avoid too much excitement, and also you must rest before tonight's entertainments. Oh, and one more thing, Phyllis. I am so happy for you, really I am.'

Phyllis smiled, her heart suddenly seeming to take off, not unfortunately for Portia because of some dutiful feeling towards her mother, nor from pride that she had at last compensated her beloved parent for all the love she had shown her daughter while she was growing up, but because in her mind's eye she suddenly saw Edwin. It was as if he was standing between her mother and herself, and his bonny looks and merry eyes, and his *goodness,* seemed to fill the room. He was just such an absolute sweetheart! He was so much nicer than herself that Phyllis knew without any doubt that he would make her nicer too, and that would be quite something, surely?

Portia too smiled at her daughter, but no more than Phyllis did she smile from pride that Phyllis was at last the kind of daughter for which all mothers must long – good, kind and honourable. Rather she smiled because she too thought of Edwin, and it seemed to her suddenly that with the new generation England would, despite the

Bunny Hop, the tango and who knew what else, somehow or another carry on as it was meant to do, with handsome young men marrying spirited young girls, and all would not be lost.

'Edwin is in the army, Mama, as you know, but I dare say he will come out soon and we can settle down in the country and have masses of dogs and horses, and never mind the rest of the world.'

'I dare say you will, darling. No-one wants war.'

'No. Besides, Edwin says he is not the stuff of heroes! Although I can't quite believe that. But still, I must go and tell him that he has to see Uncle Lampard. Oh, I say, poor Edwin!'

'Yes, poor Edwin!'

They both laughed, and Phyllis kissed her hand to her departing mother, and then heaving a great sigh of relief turned towards her room, and Evie. She knew just how much of her happiness she in fact owed her maid, and Evans too, now, and knowing servants she knew that she would, all too soon, have to pay for it. But with what, and how, she did not yet know.

'Ah, Evie.'

Evie's sharp-nosed face appeared round Phyllis's sitting room door, but she did not smile, only went to the table that Phyllis had pulled out and planted the great mahogany tray bearing Phyllis's luncheon upon it before turning with a sigh of relief back to the door, which she now closed.

'There's some nice fish under that cover, Miss Phyllis, boiled fish with parsley sauce, and some nice creamed potato *à la française*, and also some consommé and some Melba toast, and a cream vanilla junket freshly made by Cook. So tuck in and no more of your nonsense.'

'Yes, Evie, of course.'

Phyllis sat down to the gate-legged table, all docility, and at once took her white linen napkin upon her knee and started to sip, delicately, at her consommé, stopping every now and then to butter her Melba toast.

'Now then, Miss Phyllis, we all know what we have all been up to, do we not?'

Phyllis nodded.

'And we all know that we owe Mr Evans a great deal – more than a great deal. We most likely owe him our lives and our hopes for the future too, I would say, would you not, Miss Phyllis?'

Again Phyllis nodded, but kept her gaze on her soup. She had no wish to stare into Evie's eyes, any more than she thought Evie would wish to stare into hers. They had both told lies, and they both knew at least a little of why those lies had come about. It was all to do with Phyllis's love of daring and her wish to flout Society's laws.

'I have been a disgrace, I know it, Evie,' Phyllis said simply, 'but I am a changed person now. I have met someone for whom I would do anything, so I have every reason to become a nicer, better person. Love makes you very humble, Evie, really it does.'

'Not the Admiral, surely? You cannot love the Vice Admiral, Miss Phyllis. He is much too old for you!'

Phyllis started to laugh. 'Oh no, bless you, not the Vice Admiral. Good heavens, Evie, I only went to his – I only did what I did, you know, read to him and all that, because – because – because I was so *bored*, and you know how it is – if you are bored and cross you do naughty things.'

'It might have cost you your reputation, ruined your life, Miss Phyllis, you know that?'

'Yes,' Phyllis agreed, quietly. 'But thanks to you and Evans it has not. Now,' she turned from the table, 'what can I do for you, and Evans, Evie? To pay you back for your loyalty?'

'You *can* do something . . .'

Phyllis waited, and thinking of how much of her pin money it would take to satisfy Evans and Evie her heart sank a little. It would be goodbye to new hats and gloves for quite a while, even hat pins, she imagined.

'You can undo the harm you did when you made that joke against poor Miss Hartley Lambert when you were all out riding that time.'

Phyllis reddened. 'Was it that bad?'

'You know it was, Miss Phyllis. Why, everyone calls her "Miss *Hatley* Lambert" behind her back now, you know they do.'

'To be honest, I had not realised, really I had not.'

'No, well, seeing how you are – or were – I am not surprised at all,' Evie stated, determined to be ruthless and tactless while she could.

'It was the hat – it was terrible. But it was only meant as a joke, Evie, really. It was not meant to be particularly cruel. It was just such a terrible hat.'

'Everyone has terrible hats some time, Miss Phyllis. You wait, I dare say you will have a hat or two that would make a sailor blush once you're married and your husband insists on choosing them for you in Paris or somewhere. Just you wait.'

'I dare say you are right, Evie. And you have given me an idea as to how I may make amends to Miss Hartley Lambert and resurrect the joke – but this time against Miss O'Connor and myself.'

Portia had been in such a flurry because of Phyllis and – in her mother's mind at any rate – her imminent engagement, that she fairly flung herself down the stairs towards the garden without a thought to her appearance, with the result that she appeared, dishevelled and not at all the thing, and already late, at Aunt Tattie's luncheon table.

She did not know it, but the fact that she did not have time to make herself appear as groomed and matronly as she should succeeded only in making her look younger and more attractive than she had looked for many a long month – in fact, her aunt thought, since poor Childie had been gathered.

Cheeks a little too pink and shiny, hair straying from its normally soigné and well-arranged chignon, she burst into the garden without hesitation, thinking only of how rude she must appear to Aunt Tattie and the servants, if not to poor Richard. And so she burst upon the quiet, pretty luncheon scene so nicely arranged in the garden as a child might burst through a wicket gate.

Richard Ward, whose true vision of the world had only just been restored, stared at her for a few seconds. He could not remember who she was for a moment, and then he realised – the woman in front of him was Portia. His Portia, returned to him after all these years! Grown just a little older, of course – a trick of the light upstairs had suggested to him that she had no grey hairs when of course, like himself, she had more than a few – but this did not matter. Now he came to look up at her, his heart beating at a very irregular pace (as indeed any gentleman's will who has received a note from a lady asking him to meet her at a late hour in a deserted ballroom), he realised that she was, to all intents and purposes, still his dear old Portia. Still impulsive, still with the same pair of clear grey eyes, still firm of purpose (he could tell that from the set of her mouth, which had always been most attractive to him), and yet ready to laugh at herself, as she was now as she quickly tried to brush dog hair from her skirt and apologise to Aunt Tattie at one and the same time.

'Aunt Tattie, you will not send to the Pope in Rome I hope, that I am once again late for luncheon?'

Aunt Tattie, who had so far recovered from her Italian conversion as to be able to find humour in life once more, smiled, if a little demurely. 'Oh, I dare say even His Holiness has been late for luncheon or dinner at some time or another,' she murmured, at once putting her guests at their ease, for if there was one thing that scared an Englishman more than the mention of a Frenchman, it was the mention of the papacy.

'Very good, Aunt Tattie, very good,' Richard murmured, but, to the old lady's all too evident satisfaction, he had eyes only for Portia.

In York Herbert Forrester was saying, 'My dear love, I thought we should go for a drive in my new motor car today. Would not that be a bit of gaiety for two old folk? Bit of a spin, a bit of a drive, seeing all the world at up to – who knows – twenty miles an hour or whatever?'

Jane looked up from her sewing, and smiled. 'Why, Herbert, that would be the greatest fun. Do let us.'

'You will have to wrap up nice and warm, love. Get Hoskins to put out your warmest coat, and a nice motoring hat and veil, because although it is hot now, given a speed of ten or fifteen miles an hour the pace hots up and the air cools down, believe me.'

Herbert stood up, relieved to be doing something, and at the same time anxious that Jane should not suffer from his desire to do anything rather than watch her.

It seemed to him that he had been watching her, hour by hour, minute by minute, almost for the past two months, and every hour and every minute she had looked more and more frail. The shadows under her eyes had grown deeper and her small, irritating cough more frequent, until he had found himself praying, day after day, that God would take him before his poor Jane.

'I will have them bring the motor cars round to the front, and you meet me on the front steps. No need to bring Hoskins. We can do without her if we have the chauffeurs with us, and two cars in case of breakdown. No need to take more than that, I shouldn't have thought.'

'It seems ever so funny, Herbert, to always have to take out two motor cars instead of one, when only two people wish to travel!'

Jane started to laugh, and at the same time, as always, the short, dry cough started up again, and she had recourse to yet more of her poor little lace-edged handkerchiefs.

It was keeping the anxiety out of his eyes that was such a terrible trial for Herbert. It was keeping that look of *you are normal and fine and everyone else feels like you do* look in his eyes that made him, sometimes, just go right down the garden, where there was no fear of anyone's hearing him, and burst into unmanly tears, howling the ruddy place down until he could howl no more, before returning to the house, his cheeks mopped, the look of calm in his eyes once more in place.

'I will meet you at the front, then, dearest, in as much time as it takes you to put on your motoring clothes and those chauffeurs of mine to bring themselves and their motors round to the front steps.'

Herbert kissed Jane's all too cold forehead, and fairly fell out of their drawing room, stumbling over his own feet in his hurry to get out of the house and into the air outside. Somehow, when they were outside and active, he could pretend that Jane was really healthy, that she was going to live as long as anyone else, that she was going to make her three score years and ten, with him, and they were going to be Darby and Joan, and all that kind of thing. He could make himself believe it when he was back in the good old outside, facing the horizon and enjoying fresh air. Inside, well, inside was different. Inside meant that he just looked at Jane, his beloved, and saw the wretched disease making her ever frailer, ever more vulnerable, taking her nearer and nearer to that point where he would no longer hear the beloved voice, see the sweet smile, or enjoy the quiet calm of her company.

'Here we go!' The chauffeur started up their motor and, with a wave to the motor car behind, they set off at a splendid speed.

Jane shut her eyes, despite the protection of her motoring veil. They must be going at ten or twelve miles an hour already! It did not seem possible! She laughed out loud at the speed, and staring into Herbert's eyes as he sat beside her she imagined they were eighteen or twenty again, he taking her on one of the 'turns' at the local fun fair, and both of them laughing, for no good reason, and for every reason too: for the joy of living, for the happiness of the moment, in the knowledge that they were still in love and as much twin souls as ever.

'Faster, faster,' Herbert urged their chauffeur, all the while glancing behind at the other car following and waving to the driver in a commanding way to imitate their speed. 'We could reach twenty miles an hour without blowing anything, couldn't we?' he shouted over the sound of the summer breeze which now seemed, to Jane anyway, to be as loud as a gale. 'Come on, man, faster than the wind. We could make a record here, if we but tried!'

So enthusiastic was he, so immersed in the marvel of the moment, the open road, the motor cars both increasing their speed, the chauffeurs doing as he bid, that Herbert took his eyes off Jane. It was only natural, after all. Seconds before she had been holding on to her hat and laughing, better than he had seen her look for weeks, what with the excitement of the day, and the joy of being outside. But then, as the needle of the speedometer climbed steadily higher, passing fifteen, edging up and up, and the motor car lurched forward with the effort of attaining the speed being asked of it, changing gear and pulling up the hill in front, Jane's head fell back. Still smiling, what with the joy of motoring and of being beside Herbert, she felt a sudden crushing pain. As she did so she put a gloved hand up to her breast, her eyes suddenly seeing the countryside fading, lurching, tilting, until at last it fragmented into tiny pieces and was gone from her vision, and there was only darkness before a wonderful light came towards her, slowly at first, but at last enveloping her for ever.

Aunt Tattie had pretended that she had to go inside to fetch a shawl which everyone realised she had no need of considering the temperature in London that early afternoon must have been at least in the upper seventies. But nevertheless she went inside, and did not come back for many minutes, pretending to call for her *griffon bruxelloise* – her funny little dog, by name of Pecksniff, a quite new arrival at the London house, and already a great favourite with both the servants and herself.

'Portia, I am so sorry that I have been such an inconvenience to yourself and Aunt Tattie,' Richard blurted out, suddenly breaking the silence of the London afternoon that had followed the old lady's disappearance inside. 'I cannot thank you both enough for what you have done for me, and why you have done it I cannot think. But done it you have, between the two of you. In your gentle but firm hands I have become whole again.'

'We did it because we have always had a great affection for you, Richard, you know that.' Portia smiled, and tried to pin yet another straying piece of hair back into place, while at the same time wishing that Richard did not appear now to be as youthful and as handsome to her as he had ever done when they were young.

'Affection! That is a strong word coming from you, Portia!'

He was teasing her of course, because they both knew that Portia was, for her sex, in fact extraordinarily reticent, at least as far as her emotions were concerned.

'Do you miss Lord Childhays? You must miss him so much.'

'Oh, I do,' Portia agreed, feeling guilty because, if the truth were known, it had been a week or so now since she had got up and spent the day thinking of him, wondering what he would have done in this circumstance or that. 'I do. But you know how it is, Richard. We have to live, and while I have often wanted not to live, since he was taken, I am still here, and that has to be faced. I am still here.'

Richard put out his hand suddenly and placed it over Portia's. Bespectacled and watching keenly from a first floor window inside the house, Aunt Tattie, Pecksniff in her arms, noted this and decided not to return to the garden for at least another ten minutes.

'I for one am very glad that you are still here, Portia, and I am only sorry that I did not meet you when . . .'

Portia was thinking back to when they were young. 'Oh, don't worry. I didn't mind, really. In fact I quite understood.'

'I knew you would. You have always been my soulmate. I knew that when we were sailing. I knew that I would never have to explain anything to you.'

'People come into one's life . . . and there is not a good moment, sometimes.'

'Exactly so – and besides, I would not have wished anyone to know that is – you know.'

This was vague enough, and masculine enough, to make Portia quite content to think that he also was referring back to when they were young. She remembered that day so well, and how stupid she had felt clambering all over the Wards' garden, going to meet Richard, only to find, or rather to see, him with Miss Cecil.

'Aunt Tattie has been understanding itself, really she has. She seems to know how one feels without one's saying anything and almost before one has finished thinking something. And she is so practical.'

'We all love Aunt Tattie – Phyllis is devoted to her, despite her conversion to Rome!' Portia smiled.

'Phyllis?'

'Yes – my daughter, Phyllis.'

'Oh, of course. I haven't met her yet, have I?'

'No. Not yet. She is a good girl, now, and about to become engaged, I am happy to say. But she has been quite a handful, I am *un*happy to tell you. Very much her father's daughter. But now – well, now, at last, she has fallen in love and we have high hopes something will come of it, so all's well that ends well.'

'I shall look forward to meeting her.'

'Oh, and by the way, Richard – I know all about

Evie coming to read to you, and I do not mind, really. It was quite understandable.'

'Evie?' Richard frowned. He vaguely remembered someone coming in and reading to him in the past weeks, but he had felt terrible, crucified by an appalling thirst, and plagued with nightmares of a kind that even now were dreadful to remember. So bad had that time been that he would not have known, frankly, if it was the devil come to read to him. He only remembered that being read to always had the same effect on him, it made him fall asleep.

'I thought of you often, during these last terrible weeks. And do you know something, Portia?'

Portia turned to look at him.

'Sometimes I even thought it was *you* reading to me. So much were you in my mind, so clearly did I see you in my mind's eye, that I really thought you were in the room with me.'

Portia paused. A thought occurred to her, and a memory of Evie and Evans, and Phyllis, their limbs twitching with guilt. Of a sudden the picture of them all came swimming towards her, but then, being a kind-hearted and above all a practical woman, she turned away from both the thought and the memory, and after a short pause she said, quietly, 'And I have thought of you too, Richard, of how much you must have been suffering. But I also thought that you were best left in charge of your own ship. You know how it is, just like at sea, one man only at the helm.'

'And you were right, Portia. I was best left. I

had to fight the demons on my own. I had to see them down, and finally, I hope, put them to flight for ever.'

At that moment Aunt Tattie, judging that she had left the two childhood friends together long enough, now re-appeared bringing with her Pecksniff, who proved, as do all small puppies, to be a welcome diversion, running about the garden and disappearing under bushes, finding himself suddenly, to his surprise, only to disappear again, before discovering something even more alarming attached to his body, something which had to be pounced upon, told off and barked at – namely, his tail.

'I do so love a new puppy,' Aunt Tattie murmured, trying not to notice that, in fact, she was the only person watching Pecksniff, and that the two other persons present in the sunlit garden had eyes only for each other. She knew this because, as people do who want only to stare into each other's souls, they were both staring at her in a superhuman effort not to give themselves away. 'Yes,' Aunt Tattie continued, her eyes still on Pecksniff, 'a new puppy is just so riveting, I always think. Have you noticed, they always seem so dreadfully surprised to find that they have tails!'

But no-one replied, as she knew they would not, for they were being what Aunt Tattie sometimes called *noisily silent*.

Of course Herbert knew, as soon as she slumped forward clutching at the front of her dress, that his

Jane had been taken from him. And in a way he was glad that he had taken her out, even if he should be blamed for so doing, later, by others, because the last memory he had of Jane was of her laughing, and enjoying herself, and in truth he had known, day by wretched day, how frail she had become, and that in fact she had no real hope of enjoying the rest of the summer.

And so he had helped to lay her out. Nothing but the best would do for his darling, her favourite blue silk, her pearls around her neck and in her ears. He would have everything as he knew she had wanted it.

She had also, it transpired, written a last letter to him, to be found once she had been gathered to the next world.

My dearest of dears, my dearest of all loves, my Herbert,

I know, and have known for some time now, that I am not long for this world, and in knowing this, and that you have been at such pains to keep it from me, my love for you has if anything grown not to the size of this world, but in truth to the size of the next.

How you have borne your sorrow around me so bravely, my dearest love, I shall never know, but bear it you have, and with so much kindness, with such unselfishness, even down to your giving up wine for my sake!

I never thought I could love you more, my darling Herbert, than I did on my wedding day, or when our little daughter was born, or on any of those happy, happy days that we have enjoyed together, but now in my unhappiness at leaving you I have found that I have loved you more than I could have thought possible.

We will meet again soon, my dearest of loves, in at least as happy a place as we have enjoyed in this world, and when you close your beloved eyes for the last time in this world may my spirit be the first to welcome you in the next.

Your Jane.

And now Herbert was left within his own world once more, but without his Jane. He had money, he had property, he had a daughter, he had friends and a small circle of business acquaintances, but he had no Jane, so, as he realised in the weeks following her funeral, in reality, he had nothing.

It was as if the whole world was just a vast empty space. It was as if he had been left in the icy wastes, or on the savannah, or the tundra, or the prairie, with nothing but a feeling of endless uninhabited space. Walk and walk as he might, in whichever direction, there was just more of the same.

And walk he did, every afternoon, unable to bear looking at the motor cars he had once been so proud to drive. He set off towards the countryside outside the old city of York, towards the moors to which he and Jane had gone so often to picnic and enjoy themselves. Once reached, and no matter what the weather, he would walk on determinedly, not returning to the house until only the hall boy was left up to greet him, and a lonely supper on a tray awaiting him before the unlit library fire. It was hopeless to think that the loneliness would ever go away, so hopeless that not even the birth of a grandchild did anything to lift his spirits more than temporarily.

The truth was that he had no interest in life now that Jane was gone, and before many weeks were out, as happens with loneliness, he started to look as he felt, haggard and uninterested. His eyes, once large and life-loving, seemed to have sunk into his head, his hair thinned, and his clothes hung off him as his appetite for food disappeared as quickly as his appetite for life.

For some hearts one touch alone can awaken and not break their thrilling strings.

He had no idea where he had found that quotation from many years before, but he saw to it now that it was put on what was to be his and Jane's shared grave.

As is natural for they who mourn, on Sundays he would not leave the graveside of his beloved Jane but sat beside its freshly dug earth and talked to the one he could no longer see, reminding her of all the happy times, all their shared memories, shaking his head in amazement sometimes, frequently laughing, and occasionally allowing the tears to roll down his now sunken cheeks as he pitied himself for the loss of his so-great love.

* * *

'It cannot go on, sir, really it cannot. You will do yourself an injury, really you will.'

It seemed to Herbert at that moment, although he was standing in his own library, in his own house in York, that he was awaking to a voice still nagging him as if he had awoken from some dream of loneliness to a reality of irritation.

To his disappointment, as was always true of his state nowadays, he found that he was still on this earth. Worse, he was being lectured by his son-in-law, a worthy enough and kind young man, and one who worked diligently enough for his father-in-law, but not someone who could understand the old and their problems, not a person who could appreciate how, with death, the life can go out of the bereaved, taking with it all that ever mattered, that made life worth living. That was not something which his worthy son-in-law could appreciate, however upright and honest he was, however well intentioned and sincere.

'I beg your pardon. I am sorry, I was miles away.'

Herbert's son-in-law returned to the subject. After all, it was his duty. He had promised Louisa to do all that he could to persuade her father to start looking after himself. And, indeed, he could quite see why Louisa was so upset about her father now that he stood in the same room with him, only a few feet away from what now seemed to him to be a crumbling rock.

His father-in-law, in just a few weeks, had started to look dreadful. Even his clothes, once so proudly kept and worn with flair and dash, would now be considered a disgrace to a much less prosperous man than Herbert Forrester, Esquire, the owner of not just one prosperous mill, but several, not to mention property in York and London, and shares in railways, and who knew what.

'You are suffering something terrible, Mr Forrester,' stated Herbert's reverential son-in-law, 'and we thought, leastways our Louisa did, that a good big change, a complete change of scene like, might do you more good than you think. You know travel is meant to be so beneficial at these times? It is thought to be a good cure for sorrow, or so Louisa said, and goodness she has suffered in the past, has our Louisa, she has known suffering all right.'

Herbert looked dully at this young man who had married his daughter, and thought to himself, *What the hell does he know about suffering, or pain? He married the boss's daughter and now he's feathered his own nest all right, has our Louisa's young man. No, he'll never starve, he won't, thanks to the sweat of his father-in-law.*

But then, after the poor young man had gone, a mite crestfallen as he always seemed to be after being in his father-in-law's company, Herbert began to think about what Louisa had sent her husband to tell him, her counsel by proxy, as it were.

Maybe our Louisa *was* right to remind him that travel was the traditional cure for a broken heart. Certainly it might be a good idea to leave *York.*

Certainly that might be a good idea. He could shut up the house, and leave it, and go on to London, where he could think again as to just how or where he should travel. He did not want to return to fashionable London, that had too many bad memories for him, but as an investment, some time ago, he had bought several town houses in more remote spots, far from Mayfair and Piccadilly, and well away from the stamping grounds of the rich and grand. Two were in an elegant terrace of houses in Kensington, which was still some way away from the fashionable world. Kensington, formerly a village, was now reaching out towards London proper and providing discreet and genteel housing for literary folk and artistic types, as well as, at the less prosperous end, for retired governesses and suchlike.

The two houses Herbert had bought were in a state of some disrepair, needing modernising in a way that was now quite acceptable even for less fashionable folk. He could put in electricity and the telephone, and he could put in proper bathrooms – he had seen quite a few of the newer type of bathroom when staying with a business acquaintance the previous year – all marble, and made in splendid modern shapes. One of the bathrooms actually had its bath sunk into the floor, and another faced out towards the view so that the owner could see across his land to his horses and sheep at grass. Well, whatever he would decide on in the way of taste, there was no doubt that Herbert could do the two houses up. That would take up a bit of his time, and then he could sell one and keep the other to await his return from his travels.

Anyway, it would take him away from York, and that after all was the first consideration. And then bullying and chivvying the builders, arguing the toss with some jumped-up young architect, that too would take his mind off his sorrow. And perhaps too, in genteel Kensington, so very different from York, he would start to see the world less as an eternal loneliness, start to be able to consider to where he should take himself off – perhaps the South Sea islands, or America, the Wild West, that sort of thing. What with the journeying and the sailing, it would do for a few months, that kind of scheme. Something would happen, he felt, if he could only get himself going. All in all, and it was a sobering, even an ageing, thought, Louisa had been right, he *must* start himself moving again, and soon.

Then, of course, another thought occurred as he lit his first cigar for many weeks. It was no good living in the past, because the past did not, and could not, give back. But, what was much worse, you could not give back to the past. By moving on, somehow, some way, he could and would keep his Jane for ever locked into his heart; by trying to keep going he would be giving back to her memory.

After all, when all was said and done, his darling Jane would not want to look down at her Herbert from the next world and see him in the state into which he had allowed himself to slip.

He stood in front of the hall mirror and stared at himself. The truth was that if Jane were here she would give a little cry of horror at the sight of him. Her hand would fly up to her mouth at the sight of his sunken eyes, his pale skin, his unkempt clothes, and then she would give a little scream. He could just see her doing it. After which she would start running about, and amid a torrent of words she would ring the bell to the side of the hall fireplace and shout for the maids, and tell someone to take Mr Forrester's bath and put it in his room at once. She would call for hot broth, and a nice glass of red wine. She would do all those things, and more. Now, if he were to keep her memory alive, and be as she would have him be, he must act as he would if she were here.

In other words he must restore himself, and then he must move on. It was the only way. To do anything else would be to desecrate her memory, and their shared memories. To behave otherwise would be to let their happiness together slide off as if it had never been, and that would never do. Not in a million years would that ever, ever do.

Within the week, Herbert promised himself, now quite determined, he would make sure to have shut up the house, left instructions for flowers to be placed weekly upon Jane's beloved grave, and himself made his way to London. But first he would have some hot broth sent to the library, and then some red wine. And then he would take a bath, and have himself shaved, and his hair cut, and a new shirt put out, and a clean set of clothes, not this black suit and black tie, which, he realised in a second of horror, despite the pleadings of his manservant he just might not have changed out of since the funeral, or only shortly after. It certainly looked like it.

Hours later he regarded himself, fairly transformed from the wreck he had been when his son-in-law called, and he could hear Jane's voice saying *Oh, Herbert, that white shirt with that stiff collar – I do so love to see that cut of collar on you, really I do.*

As he raised his eyes to heaven before falling asleep late that night Herbert knew that it had not been Louisa who had sent his son-in-law round to him, but Jane. He blew her a kiss high above the clouds and fell asleep with her name on his lips, but this time, instead of crying himself to sleep, he found he was smiling, for he knew that his wife, as always, was looking after him, making sure that he was going to make a good fist of it.

That was what she always used to say when they were young. *Don't matter, our Herbert, if you don't make a success of something, just so long as you've made a good fist of it.*

Comings and Goings

How she came by the clothes that she wore that afternoon Emily would never remember, but come by them she did. And of course, as always happens, whether one is dressing in costume for a play or a ball, being transformed into a different woman, a woman who, when she turned towards the cheval mirror in her hotel room, looked like no-one she had ever seen or met, increased Emily's excitement a hundredfold.

She had chosen black, and to offset the black silk of the high-necked jacket and belted skirt, itself discreetly swathed in such an old-fashioned way towards a cage at the back, she wore a large hat with a white veil, and white lace gloves. Half mourning, whole mourning – but the real morning outside her hotel room was bright with sunshine, and as she stepped out into it, leaning lightly on her white-laced black silk parasol, Emily's green eyes were bright with the excitement of the moment.

It was heaven to walk along, slowly, staring into unknown shop windows, the displays within shielded from the sun by blinds outside and inside by lace curtains looped and swathed, which gave the interiors a weird dark look that made the stuffs for sale seem eminently undesirable, whereas those same goods in other hands, displayed perhaps in some shop near Piccadilly, would have looked infinitely alluring.

And yet as she walked, in her disguise, Emily found that the years had fled and she was now more than ever the outrageous Lady Emily. She half wished that Portia was with her and that she too was disguised, and both of them laughing. This thought, though, led to another more salutary and at the same time more day-to-day one – namely that Portia was a widow, and she would never want now to climb back into black clothes. She would not find it amusing in the least. Emily sighed. Conscience did indeed make cowards of them all, and really, now she came to think of it, she should turn back, and hurry off in another direction rather than meet Barrymore here, he too disguised, he had promised her – both of them laughing – in clothes that would not be the dress of a gentleman.

Seconds after becoming quite sure that she would indeed now hurry back to the hotel, change, and go home, Emily caught sight of what could only be a bookmaker – or a person selling comestibles from door to door, something of that nature – and he was coming straight up to her, undeceived by her heavy disguise, and kissing her hand.

And of course as soon as she saw the dark sparkling eyes, Emily knew straight away that it was Barrymore and that she could no more go back to the hotel and home to Medlar House than she could give up riding fast to hounds.

'Madam, may I make myself known to you? I am your husband, Mr Smith Barrymore!'

It would be out of character to start to laugh straight away at the handsome rogue standing in front of her, and so Emily knew that she had to resist, and that despite the white veiling, and the black clothes, to even smile would be to somehow give the game away, for both of them.

'Good morning, husband dear! I am surprised you knew me, since I am dressed in clothes that you have not, to my certain knowledge, ever seen before.'

'I know, dear,' Barrymore agreed, his face quite straight. 'But see here, I have sold at least six of those new typewriting machines to a number of luckless personages in remote and run-down businesses around these parts, and now I feel that it is high time to take my beloved little wife—'

'Now, dear, here I must stop you, for little I ain't, Mr Smith Barrymore – which is evidently why you spotted me, despite my discreet clothes.'

Barrymore's eyes glittered as he looked down at Emily, holding her white-gloved hand tightly in his crooked arm.

'No, naturally. You are quite right, dear, you are not little. You are tall and slender and I would know your divine figure wherever I saw you.

Whoever you were with, and whatever you were wearing, I would always know you.'

His tone was one of light banter, but his eyes although they pretended to mock and tease her also said *no clothes can disguise your body from me*, which made Emily feel as if she was walking along beside him clad only in her underpinnings, her silk stockings and her suspenders, her elegant little tight laced button boots, and nothing else at all.

It was her moment of surrender. Long before they reached the restaurant where they were to have luncheon together, long before she lifted the white veil of her secondhand hat, confident that no-one they knew would recognise them in this remote area of Chelsea, long before they started to eat their food, slowly and appreciatively, talking of everything but love, and drink their wine, slowly and sensuously, thinking only of it, Emily had made love with Barrymore.

In her mind's eye she saw herself walking back to that little hotel where she had booked and paid for their bedroom and sitting room, her veil dropped, her eyes looking only ahead. She saw herself nodding briefly to the hotel clerk, walking slowly up the stairs in front of Barrymore, inserting the key in the lock, and walking ahead of him into the sitting room, where, one by one, she drew first the blinds and then the curtains, and then, turning, stood quite still.

She would allow him to lift her veil and look at her, and then he would remove her hat, and next unbutton her tight little black silk top, and put his hands to her corseted breasts which would make her sigh just a little. Next would fall her long white hair, silken pale strands to her waist, and then she would put up her hands to his face and pull him to her.

Now, still in heaven but looking at him dreamily over lunch, she could see how young and healthy his skin was, how dark his hair, and how brilliant, as always, his eyes. She could appreciate his mouth, lips that curved upwards always ready to smile or to laugh, white teeth, slim waist, long legs. He was a bouquet of a young man, and the look in his eyes told her that she was, as yet, not old.

'Come, dear.' He turned when they eventually left the restaurant, and held out his arm, and Emily slipped her white-gloved hand into it, now feeling as if they were really married, just a nice middle-class couple come to London for their wedding anniversary, celebrating in style, enjoying a lobster luncheon together and then sauntering back to their hotel to make love. That was how easy it had all become, and soon she would discover that because of that very easiness, that closeness in temperament, each revelling in the same sense of humour, each loving to ride hard and make love hard too, Emily was soon – too soon – to discover that giving up Barrymore was impossible. That making love with him was not just out of this world, it was shocking in its intensity. She was not seduced by him, or he by her, they were, in reality, drugged by each other.

And as day after day passed, and she found herself making any excuse to meet him, somewhere, anywhere, as she slipped off early from some soirée, or left Edith in Portia's charge, or May's, or anyone's – as Edith's mother took hansom cabs, or rode out at ridiculous times to meet Barrymore in Rotten Row, little knowing that what seemed so private to her was in fact all too public to everyone else, her daughter was making plans to run back to Ireland.

For May coming to London for the Season was always both a delight and a duty. The delight was in seeing pretty clothes, and beautiful people wearing them, for there was no doubt about it, London at the height of the Season was filled to the brim with more beautiful people than the vast arrangements of flowers at her London home could hold arum lilies or malmaisons.

This particular morning May was looking at her best, and feeling at her worst. She could not get her son to join her in London – not even it would seem for their own ball. Well, yes, he would come up in the company of his equally leaden-footed father for the Wokingham ball, but only for their ball. He would not come for anything else, such was his loathing for London, and he would not stay more than a handful of nights before he must fly back to their estates with his father, on the pretext that what with the fall in land prices and heaven only knew what else, he must be seen to work the land alongside the men on the estate, or they would all, according to the naughty wretch, give up their tied cottages and flee to the city where work was far more plentiful, and better paid.

The problem, of course – and the reason why not even May's new primrose lace-trimmed morning dress with its splendidly cut skirt of *peau de soie* and its stiff tight belt of the same could stop her feeling out of sorts – was that May knew that her son was *utterly* right, which in itself was infuriating.

The fact was that unless people did take up more what May would call Artsy Craftsy attitudes to their land, and while not exactly sitting down to get drunk with their labourers – or insisting on their eating with you in the dining room and other nonsenses that some over-liberal souls had already gone in for – unless they were seen to be getting their hands dirty, the families on the estates *would* up sticks and flee to the cities. After all, even a hansom cab driver was better paid than a farm hand.

May had enjoyed too much of a hard life when she was growing up – always at the beck and call of stern nuns, and not really knowing why she had been left to be brought up in a convent until her mysterious patron, Herbert Forrester, suddenly turned up and took over her life – not to sympathise with the predicament of the poorly paid estate workers. But Herbert Forrester had transformed her life, turning it into something of a fairy tale, a romance which had its ending, in essence, when she became Duchess of Wokingham. And although she did not go around in a glass coach, she did now own a golden one (only used by the family for coronations) and she did have footmen, quite a number, although none of them had enjoyed a former life, she imagined, as a rat.

All this was occupying her mind in one way or another as she sat, her personal maid by her side, in the smaller of the two large drawing rooms which the family enjoyed at their London house.

'My, my, my, but Miss O'Connor is about to be late, is she not?'

Her maid looked up from her stitching and nodded slightly, as was her wont. 'Yes, Your Grace.'

At that moment, a footman came in, bowed, and announced 'Miss O'Connor'.

May, still seated, turned to her maid. 'You may go now, Cropper, and leave us alone. Tell the footman not to bother with the fire while I am with Miss O'Connor, but to bring us some lemonade, and some sort of sweet biscuit – almond, I think. Tell them to bring us some of Mrs Aylmer's sweet almond biscuits.'

Of course May knew all about Emily's daughter Edith O'Connor, but nevertheless she could not but be disappointed when she saw her. She was not at all the beauty, as her mother had always been, and indeed still was. Far from it, in fact. Miss O'Connor was small, and dark, like her father May supposed, and with none of her mother's splendid colouring. Rather pale, in fact, and the profile, far from being classical, was most uneven. Only her eyes were magnificent, a pair of almost startling hazel eyes that, May supposed because she was wearing blue, looked almost violet at one minute and strangely mosaic and alluring and hazel at another. Surrounded by thick black lashes, which were so long and thick that they seemed to cast a shadow when she looked down, the eyes were jewel-like, and more than made up for the rest of her face, as did her hair, which was thick and dark, and worn in a splendid chignon, a little old-fashioned, but noticeably styled under her fashionable forward-tilted hat.

'My dear Miss O'Connor, how delightful to see you.'

Edith curtsied deeply to the still young Duchess of Wokingham, at the same time thinking for perhaps the hundredth time that she would always be grateful, in the end, to Lady Devenish for dinning into her the importance of grace and deportment. Without dear Lady Devenish, Edith thought, she might have sunk without trace in London Society, whereas she had finally, in the last week, even managed to bob about a bit, and was heard to be mentioned by the Duke of Connerton as having a 'very pretty way with her', which certainly would not have been possible before her 'say so and say not' weeks with Lady Devenish.

May rearranged her own skirts in a more satisfactory way, her small white elegant hands hardly able to bend themselves to the task, such were the size of the Wokingham rings – or *rocks* as she and John always jokingly called them.

'How is your dear mama? I saw her briefly at the Albany ball last night, but we hardly had a second, I am afraid. She is looking magnificent, of course, but then she always has looked magnificent.'

May stopped suddenly. She had not been an actress, for however short a time, for nothing. Indeed she had had to continue practising that same art as a duchess. The result was that she knew immediately, without being able to say why, that she was now walking, if not jumping, conversationally speaking, on eggshells, for as soon as she had mentioned Emily her daughter had looked as if May had taken up a gun from under the silk cushions beside her and pointed it at her.

'My dear,' May dropped her voice immediately, 'first let us have some lemonade and almond biscuits and then you must tell me everything.'

The thick black lashes now lowered themselves over the magnificent eyes and a sigh escaped the slender blue figure seated on the Knole sofa opposite her.

May knew at once that she was right, and quickly going to the bell she pulled it to hasten the footman. She had little enough time this morning as it was, but if she was going to hear a confidence, or help this delightful young gel in some way, then the lemonade must arrive *tout de suite*!

'Very well, now, lemonade.'

The footman poured it, and while he was

normally too quick and tripped over his large feet, now, May noticed, he seemed to take for ever, as if he sensed that by lingering he might gain some little piece of knowledge. First one glass, drip by little drip, and then the next. May found her foot tapping with impatience on the old wooden floor, but then her eyes suddenly met Miss O'Connor's, and for no reason other than to cheer her May promptly crossed hers behind the footman's back, which, she was glad to see, made Miss O'Connor bite her lip hard in her effort not to laugh. When the door had shut behind the footman at last, the girl could not but help explode with laughter.

'Oh, but isn't that servants all over, I find, do you not?' May too was laughing, but at the same time she took care not to raise her voice above a whisper. Silently, she stood up, and on tiptoe, her small, perfectly clad feet making tiny, graceful steps, she went to the door, and wrenched it quickly open. Then she shut it again, walked back to her sofa and re-seated herself. 'I always do that,' she said, quite matter of factly, before giving a little sigh of satisfaction and starting to nibble an almond biscuit. 'The servants always listen at doors. Our conversations are music to their ears, poor dears. I know that, but I like *them* to know that *I* know that they do it, d'you see?' She smiled, and then putting her head on one side she said, 'So? Shall we now continue? More soberly, more seriously, having gained a short moment of privacy, which is hard enough in these sorts of households, goodness knows!'

Edith too smiled, quite spontaneously and possibly for the first time in the last twenty-four hours. The whole world seemed to have put its weight on her back these last days, but of a sudden, seated alone with this delightful little woman with her beautiful blond china doll looks, and her mischievous ways, Edith felt that now only half the weight of the world was on her shoulders.

'You are so kind to see me. You must have so much else to occupy you. But, you see, in all honesty I did not know whom to talk to about – about – my *mama*. And then I suddenly thought of you. I have been used, you see, in Ireland, to having my papa, but he is not here, and there was no-one else to whom I could think of turning.'

May found her heart sinking. She had known as soon as she saw this dear young thing that something terrible was bothering her, and then she had sensed that just the mere mention of Emily was too much. Now, here she was, saying exactly what May had most feared, that there *was* something wrong with Emily.

'Of course, of course, you do quite right to come to me. Most especially if your mama is – not at all the thing?'

'No, Duchess, she is not at all the thing. She is not herself. Not at all herself. And I am too young, and altogether too much of a disappointment to her, too like my papa in fact, to ever be likely to have any influence with her. I had thought to approach my friend's mother, Lady Childhays, but I understand from Phyllis, from Miss de

Nugent, that *her* mama is – not exactly herself nowadays either.'

May had straightened herself and the expression in her eyes had gone from one of settled seriousness to one of deep gravity. Everyone who loved May, and there were a great many of them, knew that except at funerals May's eyes rarely looked grave, but they did now, for if there was anything sadder than the sight of the young with the burden of their parents upon their shoulders, she did not know of it.

'Tell me, my dear. You can trust me, I promise you. Your mama and I have known each other for *so long*. Is she ill? And Portia – Lady Childhays – is she, too? We are none of us getting any younger, it has to be said, although of course we all still think of ourselves, as the middle-aged are apt to do, as little spring lambs.'

'They are both suffering, Lady Childhays and Lady Emily, from the same malady,' said Edith, and even to her own ears she sounded just like her father. She could hear him saying just such a thing, describing the state of the two mothers in just such a way, only his voice would have the lilt of the Irish, and his eyes would be serious but not desperate as Edith knew the expression in her own must surely be.

May's hand crept up to the lace at her throat, but it was the only outward sign of her anxiety. 'Namely, my dear?'

'They are both suffering' – Edith dropped her voice – 'from – love!'

'Never say so!'

'Lady Childhays it seems has fallen in love with an old friend – Vice Admiral Ward, whom she rescued from a terrible situation, and they now have an understanding, as I believe it is called, but this is not be talked about, except by Phyllis – Miss de Nugent. She knows, and their maid, Evie, and now of course I know, but no-one else but us, and you now, of course, Duchess. That is all.'

'Well, quite.' May could not help seeing the fun of the situation, for all that the poor gel seated opposite her was sporting an expression that would do service for an undertaker. 'So, let us see – the *maid* knows, and *yourself*, and *myself*, and Lady Childhays' *daughter*, and obviously her *aunt*, and all their servants, for once the *maid* knows everyone below stairs knows – so, really, that means the news is quite out, and all London knows! No need to post it in any of the "future intended" columns!'

They both laughed.

'Well, I do see.' Edith nodded, still smiling. 'To continue, however. It is really very understandable, and not at all out of the way, that they should have feelings for each other, two old friends, et cetera, et cetera. And, since Lady Childhays is a widow, that is perfectly proper too, I would assume. After all, one cannot mourn one's husband for ever, can one, Duchess?'

'I do not suppose you can.' May waved her handkerchief in front of her face for a second, thinking quickly. This was not after all quite as terrible as she had dreaded to hear, surely?

'Well.' Edith paused, frowning, considering this. 'Well, I think one could mourn someone for ever, but I am not sure that it would be quite right, not finally, although completely understandable. For some people there is only one person, would you not say?'

'I would indeed,' May agreed warmly. 'And so this is the situation of Lady Childhays, and you say that your mama is also suffering from the same condition—' She stopped suddenly, realising, but not adding, *but she is married still, and your papa alive.* Instead her gaze flew to the large eyes opposite hers, and she shifted her position. 'My dear, but how terrible for you. I mean to say, you know this for a fact, obviously, or you would not have come to me in this way?'

'It seems that the whole of London knows it for a fact, Duchess, and that is precisely why I have come to you. Lady Childhays, you see, what with the engagement of Phyllis, of Miss de Nugent, and herself so delightfully placed, is feeling happier than she has done for years. I could not go to *her*. It would not seem quite right, do you see? Despite her being my mama's friend. Besides, I do not think *I* have the best reputation with Lady Childhays, having larked about so dreadfully when staying with Lady Devenish.'

'I dare say everyone larks about when staying with Lady Devenish. I dare say there is not a debutante of any spirit who does not lark about when being made to laugh to the sound of a piano and I know not what. But to return to this other matter. How do you know that the whole of London is privy to this matter, my dear?'

'My maid.' Edith knew that she need say little more. They both knew that those two words said everything. Minnie had come to Edith with the news, which she herself, it seemed, had garnered from the servants' hall of all places. That alone had been a searing pain, the knowledge that her mother was the object of common gossip and ridicule below stairs.

'Your maid.' May's voice dropped once again, and she half turned as if suspecting that other ears would now be pressed to the keyhole of the door.

'Not the dear old lady who is outside in the hall, but Minnie – our old faithful from Ireland. She was told on the best authority, it seems.'

'Well, there indeed is the worst of it, is it not? For once one's maid is coming to one with news then one is only too amazed not to read it next in the Personal Column of *The Times*.' May laughed shortly, but this time without humour. 'Who is the other person involved? A married person, I trust?'

'No, alas, Duchess, not a married person, that is the worst of it. It is a very handsome young officer, a Captain Barrymore Fortescue.'

'But this is madness!' May's voice now was hardly above a whisper. After all, it was at her own At Home that the couple had met. 'One simply cannot risk one's reputation in this way, and one certainly should not – not with an unmarried daughter.' May made a small sound between a sigh and a gasp, and then she went on just a little more hurriedly, 'Not that you will remain un-engaged for long, my dear. You are not the sort to remain on any shelf for very long, I do assure you.'

Edith looked at the Duchess with her candid gaze, but evidently she was undeceived by the older woman's optimism for she said in an even tone, 'You are very kind, Duchess, but you and I both know that having a mother with, let us say, a certain reputation, making something of a scandal, will not be exactly enticing to any young man. Add to that the uncertain future of Ireland, and I *am* Irish, and my undoubtedly plain looks, and I will certainly not represent a bargain to any nice young man.' She smiled before continuing. 'Not that I am asking for sympathy for myself, for I am not. I know that I have done nothing at all to help myself. Although I will say I had no wish to do the London Season, and I begged Mama not to indulge in it for my sake. Dublin would have been quite enough – I am afraid the London Season is of no interest to me. I am far too like my father. I came here practically dragged by my hair, and now here I am, halfway through the wretched caper and having made a bad-tempered display at practically every ball only the victim of my own folly, for whatever happens now I have no hope at all of making a match, least of all with my mama seeming to have lost her head over a younger man, and an unmarried one at that.'

'It is not your fault that you have not enjoyed the Season, my dear. I dare say many a gel of spirit has not enjoyed her first London Season. But, and this is always to be remembered, very often a second Season, or even a third, does the trick, and she can then become quite comfortably engaged. I know it happened to Lady Curzon – her success was not until later, as I remember it, while I myself – why, I was on the London stage! And the Duke the other side of the footlights. Always in the same seat! Can you imagine any less likely way to become a duchess? But there, it is all a long time ago, and we older ladies can become dull company by always looking back instead of forward.'

May had rattled on a bit, going by the conversational highways and byways as she had, for a good reason, because it gave her time to think, and to think as she could while she talked. This again was a habit of the stage where the acting or dancing went on inexorably, and it had to be faced very often quite mechanically, while one's eyes took in such matters as the number of persons in the audience that night, or the fashionable crowd in the boxes, or one's fellow members of the cast, in case they should be in a mind to trip one up or make one laugh just as one was meant to be beginning one's number.

'This has the makings of a disaster, but it has to be a disaster that can be averted, my dear. I saw your mama fleetingly last night, as a matter of fact, and she did seem in perfect high spirits.'

Edith looked so sombre at this that May stood up and went to sit beside her.

'I have a plan, my dear. I shall ask your mama for permission for you to come and stay here, with me, tomorrow night, for the ball. We will have dinner and then go down to the ballroom. At dinner I will make sure to place Captain Barrymore Fortescue next to a certain lady who, I am sure, will prove to be most attractive to him. I have often found that men, when thinking they are furiously in love with one person, turn out to be just as furiously in love with another the very next minute. This lady is older, as is your mama, but she can break a young man's heart as soon as look at him, as they say.'

'But what of Mama?'

'I think you will find that your mama will have returned to Ireland, that she will discover, of a sudden, on the receipt of a telegram, that she is badly needed. That is why I will gain her permission for you to stay here, for the rest of the Season if need be. It will be a whole lot jollier for you, and since my son and husband will have turned tail and left again for the country the night after our ball, a whole lot jollier for me too. Bless you, I only wish I had a daughter as lovely as you, really I do. Now you must leave me, but rest assured that this whole matter will be at an end within a very few days. Older women often feel neglected, and sometimes they have been. It is all very understandable, and love is a great seducer!'

They both laughed, almost too heartily, with relief at this lighthearted remark.

'But also a deceiver.' May's head was once more

on one side. 'Sometimes it is not only difficult for a woman not to be flattered, it is impossible. But the moment passes, and life resumes its usual rhythms. One gets up, one goes to bed, one worries about one's son, or one's horses, or the harvest, and the moment passes.'

'Have – have you . . .' Edith stopped. For a minute she had thought she was back in the library at Glendarvan with her father and they were having the kind of conversation that fathers did not normally have with their daughters, but he was always happy, for some reason, to have with Edith.

'No, my dear, never! I know myself to be far too fortunate in every way to ever look to either side of my marriage. My upbringing was loveless, and so when the Duke came to me and asked me to marry him I knew that not only was I the happiest girl in the world, I was also the luckiest. And having been, for a short time, on the stage, I knew that *luck* is to be treasured, and one should take nothing for granted, not a happy day, not a morning of sunshine, least of all a good audience! So will you come to stay with us, here? Or would it be too dull for you?'

'I should love to, but will you really ask Mama for me?'

'At once.'

May gave Edith a quick, bright smile, and as they walked to the door she found herself saying, 'My dear, if you will, take your maid and go to luncheon somewhere out, and do a little shopping.

I have accounts at all the pretty places, and you may charge all manner of things to me. Buy yourself a new parasol, or a fetching hat, anything you care to, and forget about going back to Medlar House until four o'clock, by which time I think you will find that your mama will have left for Ireland.'

It was not that May felt indignant, or indeed morally outraged, she had seen too much of life to entertain those feelings, but as she called for Harper to follow her, and for the Duchess's London carriage to be brought round to the front steps, and arranged all the other little details that leaving one's London house incurred, she certainly felt – well, *flustered*.

Emily and she had always been close, and she simply could not understand, after all the innocence of her friend's behaviour in their youth, the dreadful come-uppance she had suffered at the hands of Daisy, Countess of Evesham, and her banishment back to Ireland under a quite false cloud, how Emily, of all people, could behave in this way, and her poor daughter be made to suffer for it! All in all, it was *flustering*, there was no other word for it.

May could have jumped from the top step outside the double front doors into the carriage when it eventually drew up, so great was her sense of fluster and urgency, and once the carriage drew away from the house it was quite claustrophobic inside the blue satin-lined coach, for she had no-one to whom she could talk about this horrid state of affairs.

Even had she wanted to talk to her travelling maid about Lady Emily – which she certainly did not – Harper being Harper would not have shown the slightest interest. Harper took no interest in anyone's affairs except her own. May had long ago resigned herself to only talking either *at* Harper – giving her instructions and so forth – or *to* Harper, which meant that they had ten minutes on Harper's favourite subject, namely Harper.

What made matters worse, of course, was the fact that Emily was staying at Medlar House. It would be very difficult for May to brush past Augustine Medlar without being required to say three bags full nine times over, and May did so hate that, no matter what. She had never felt able to be at all close to the ladies who ran political salons, any more than she thought she could feel close to people who were able to break their poor children's hearts by bringing disgrace to their family names.

Once arrived at Medlar House, all these emotions brought May up to Emily's suite of rooms on the second floor at something close to a gallop. Somehow she had avoided Augustine Medlar, but now she realised that she was about to become lost in the corridor of guests' rooms. She turned to Harper, and Harper, with her maid's sixth sense of the where and how of the layout of houses, which came, May supposed, from having to accompany her mistress to strange houses all over Europe, wheeled round at once and, fairly charging off, somehow found Minnie.

Looking into the Duchess of Wokingham's eyes Minnie found that it was no good pretending, any more than it was any good the Duchess pretending to Minnie. May's upbringing and stage experience was far too deeply rooted in reality for her not to know when someone else was on to a scandal, and Minnie did not have the guile to even want to pretend anything more than she felt – namely undisguised panic at the disintegration of her mistress's reputation.

Reputations were *everything*, and everyone knew it.

'Your young mistress, Miss Edith O'Connor, is coming to stay with the Duke and myself at Wokingham House. As to Lady Emily, I think you will find she is going to go back to Ireland.'

Minnie swallowed hard, and then slowly bowed her greying head of thick curly hair with the starched hat set upon its top, once, twice, three times, as if she was praying at Mass.

'I knows that, Your Grace. I am very well aware of that, and myself too. Why, did Lady Emily not receive the communication only this morning, and terrible news it is too. I have only just finished her packing.'

May stared at the small Irish maid with her freckled face and honest, tear-filled eyes. It was simply not possible. May had wanted to send a telegram to Emily, she had planned to send a telegram to Emily, but she had not yet sent the telegram saying COME BACK TO IRELAND AT ONCE STOP O'CONNOR.

So how had it happened that Emily had received news and was now packed up and ready?

She took several steps back from the small Irishwoman, and then said, thinking quickly, 'Oh, I am confused, to say the least. Well. Then it is fortunate that Harper is here to take Miss Edith's portmanteaux back to Wokingham House, would you not say, Minnie?'

'Oh, I would, ma'am, for it would be a terrible thing, in my opinion, for Miss Edith to have to drop the curtains on her dancin' for the sakes of the terrible news from home. It is not as if there is not another way, for of course there is, and Miss Edith has had enough in her youth, what with the nursing of Miss Valencia, and the good and the bad that comes from that. Always worrying about her little sister so much that she never wanted even to go hunting in case she should come back and find her taken. And then not wanting to come to England for fear of the same, and always misbehaving in the hope that she could go back to Miss Valencia. Well, is not that enough? I would say, begging your pardon, Your Grace, that is quite enough to be going along with, and there are many others that would agree with me.'

'I am sure, Minnie. And now, please, lead me to Lady Emily, for we have much to discuss.'

May made a small gesture as if to indicate that her old friend's rooms lay ahead of her down the corridor, but as it turned out they were behind her.

They both turned, and leaving Harper to wait to be shown to Miss Edith's rooms May walked quickly after the little Irishwoman, her own sixth sense at its most alert. For why and how Emily could have received any sort of telegraphic communication before May had sent it, not even her stage training could tell the flustered Duchess of Wokingham.

'The Duchess of Wokingham, my lady!'

May swept in to Emily's rooms determinedly. Emily had always been a great deal taller than May but May, she always felt, was just as determined. While she might not fancy galloping across country at every minute of the day, she knew that rules were rules, and that Lady Emily was in the process of flouting them, which, in the little Duchess's less than humble opinion, would not do.

'So you have heard.'

Emily turned, and May saw at once that she was in her travelling clothes, and paler than pale, as if she had been terribly ill, and she could not help feeling heartsick. Her old friend was as much changed from the bubbling happy individual of the previous night as could possibly be imagined.

Why was love so awfully, awfully painful, she wondered, of a sudden. She herself had never known the pain of it, only the happiness. She and John had been chalk and cheese, oil and water, to look at and certainly to listen to, but he had been impassioned by her, first on the theatrical stage, and then on the stage of life, and, it had to be faced, that was more than satisfactory for May. She had done very little to encourage him, in fact just carried on doing what she had wanted to do, namely acting, and he had found her somehow, married her, and taken her back to his family home where they had truly as nearly as is possible with human beings, lived happily ever after.

'I never believe anything until I hear it from the personalities involved,' May replied evenly, after a few seconds, and very much on her guard, not knowing into what deep waters she was dipping her small foot. 'To do so would be wrong – the theatre teaches you that, if nothing else.'

'Well, it is after all unbelievable, but only to be expected.' Emily started to wring her already gloved hands. 'I warned Rory. Time and time again, I warned him that getting mixed up with country house politicking would be either dull, or dangerous, and now – she went to the window, looking out onto the tranquil scene below – 'now it has turned out to be both dull and finally, fatally, dangerous.'

'Dull? In what way?'

'You do not know, why should you, what I had to put up with before I came here from Ireland. Nothing but caterwauling and lecturing and people conspiring and planning, and then re-conspiring and changing all the previous plans, and all of it muddled and muddleheaded, and a great deal of it dangerous talk that can only lead to sorrow. Nothing to which you can honestly put your hand on heart and say, "Well now, that does sound a good idea." Oh no, just talk, talk, talk. And about what? Dear heavens, they could have all turned a hundred acres of bog turf to sweet loam in the time they used up in talking, and to much better effect, I would say, and most sane people would agree with me.'

'So it is politicking that causes you to return to Ireland of a sudden? Are you needed by your husband?'

May felt it safe to venture in this direction, although she knew that the ground beneath her words was liable to suddenly give way and Emily to explode, such was the look of mingled sorrow and fury in her old friend's eyes.

'Politicking sooner or later turns to deeds, but deeds of any worth are seldom attached to high-flown notions and no practicalities.' Emily snapped the lock on her father's old worn Gladstone bag with its small gold coronet and initial P, and turned sad eyes on May. 'What Ireland needs is prosperity, not politics. It needs a collective policy, it needs investments, but it is neglected, neglected, and neglected still more. We will be driven from it now, and our kind not likely to come back, yet at Glendarvan we have done nothing but try to improve and give employment, and Rory, whatever his present stupidities, knew the land better than any. All gone to ashes, but thank God at least the children and Rory and the servants, and the horses of course, have been spared. And – would you believe it? – the children's toys.'

Now May was truly lost. She had arrived at Medlar House all prepared to read the riot act to her old friend, in whatever diplomatic but firm way she possibly could, and instead she had found that this same friend was already preparing to leave the capital and head back to the west of Ireland.

'My family have been in Ireland for four hundred years. Does not that give us as much right to live there as anyone? Besides, who is to say who can live in whose country after so much time? And do we not say we are Irish? Have we not been christened and raised there? And I married to a man with the name of O'Connor and still they came and razed Glendarvan to the ground in the name of some so-called cause. Not a brick of it left, not a painting, not a piece of china, nothing. Just the stables and the horses – which does at least mean we can get out and go north, which we shall now do.'

May stared at Emily. So this was the subject of the communication of which Minnie had spoken? This was why Emily was leaving so suddenly, nothing to do with Captain Barrymore Fortescue and everything to do with Ireland and its political unrest.

'Oh, Emily, my dear, I am so very sorry. How too terrible for you. Has this been known for many days?'

'It happened two or more days ago, but I have only just heard of it. And I am to leave at once, for as you can imagine there is so much to be done.

Happily our house at Bangor, by the seaside in the north, is ready and waiting and we shall go there at once. As I say, at least we have the horses and the carriages to take us there, and the children and the servants are safe.'

'I was come here – I *came* here – as a matter of fact to ask your permission for Edith to stay in London with me, with us. We have so much to which to commit ourselves in the way of social engagements, and it seems a pity, given that this is her first London Season, that she should not be presented. Our son as you know is to make his first Court appearance with the Duke, and then we have our ball tomorrow night, which should be an exciting event. Costume, you know – such a rage at the moment – everyone is to be in fantastic costume! It should be very glamorous. And if it is not, well then I shall want to know why! All in all, what with Ascot and other events, it would be such a joy to chaperon Edith, whom I understand to be a girl of great charm.'

'You understand? But I thought Minnie said Edith was coming to see you this morning?'

'Oh, she did, but only for a minute or so, and then she went off shopping with her maid. We exchanged a few pleasantries and sipped lemonade and then I promised to run around here and ask you the favour of leaving her with us, for the duration of the Season, as 'twere.'

May's head was on one side, and her voice was at its most charming, but Emily did not seem to notice. Seizing her Gladstone bag she walked up to her old friend and caught May's slender arm in her own gloved hand.

'Oh, May, I do feel that God is punishing me, that Glendarvan has been razed to the ground by these rogues simply and solely to punish me for my sins. I have sinned so dreadfully, and as if it were not enough that poor Rory has so much in the way of pain, now he has no house.'

Emily was too stern a character to cry or feel sorry for herself, but looking at her now May knew that she was suffering the most dreadful remorse, and she sympathised with her.

Who had not, perhaps on the death of a friend, or even a pet dog, wrung their hands as she was doing and asked themselves whether they could not have done more? May had felt such emotions too often not to put out her own hand, and placing it over Emily's gloved one she looked up into her friend's beautiful great green eyes, and said, 'Hush, now. No use in continuing with this talk, believe me, no use at all.'

'No use at all,' Emily repeated dully, nodding her head. 'No, of course, there *is* no use, but still I am unable to stop thinking in this way. I am being punished for my sins. I should have returned to Glendarvan long ago. I lingered too long in London—'

'Remember you had to chaperon Edith through her first London Season. You could not have gone home.'

'Edith!' The name seemed to be wrenched from Emily. 'My poor darling Edith *hates* London. *She* never wanted to come. She never wanted to leave little Valencia, who is now it seems quite ill from the smoke affecting her chest, and what with her weak heart . . .' She stopped. 'No, it is no use. I am leaping my fences before I reach them. I am seeing a ditch before I come to it, miles before. If I think like this before I have even set foot back in Ireland I will have gone mad by the time I reach the ruins of my poor family home. Oh, but, May, just think – the paintings alone! Would it not have been better if they had *taken* everything? The paintings, the statues, they could at least have given someone *else* pleasure, but to set fire to it all? And for what reason? Hatred, alone, an uncontrollable hatred. God forbid that Rory seeks vengeance. I do not think that he will, not given his temperament, not given his history. No, we will go north, to Bangor, and we will be happy again. People matter, not things.'

Her speech over, Emily seemed to have calmed herself, and seeing this May leaned forward and kissed her gently on the cheek.

'You are right. It is people who matter, not things. And may I take it, since you are leaving so precipitately, that you are quite happy for Edith to stay on with us at Wokingham House?'

'Of course! If she wishes! Anything you like! But I must go now.' Emily, once more in a tearing hurry, leaned forward in her turn and kissed May briefly before remembering one more item. 'Oh, and May – I have a letter. I wonder if you could see to it yourself, if you could place it in the appropriate hands without its going through a third party?'

May nodded, and took the letter without even glancing down at the name written in Emily's bold writing across the envelope.

As it turned out it was the only mistake she made during the whole interview. Knowing each other as they had when they were young, which is to say when they were at their most vulnerable and innocent, as soon as Emily saw that May had simply taken the envelope and slipped it into her small reticule she realised that May knew everything. Her old friend had been too unsurprised by the request to deliver what must be a private letter to be in ignorance of her affair.

'You know?' Again the green eyes stared into May's brilliant blue orbs.

May could not lie. 'Yes.'

'Who?' The word burst from Emily, and she reddened. 'Everyone? The whole of London? Who?'

'No, no.' May put out a reassuring hand. 'No. The servants. No-one else. Not yet. And now – not ever. No-one else shall know, I shall see to it. I will buy more silence than you can imagine. Please, rely on me for this. I am your friend. It will not go further than tittle-tattle and servants' gossip below stairs and so on, truly. Put it from your mind.'

Emily sighed. For all that she wished that she had not sinned, for all that she knew that God had punished her, and she had now lost Glendarvan and possibly every family treasure that she had ever loved, just seeing Barrymore's name in her own writing across the envelope as she passed it to May had made her heart contract.

The truth was that she had loved that passionate young man, and for a few hot afternoons she had been young again, and carefree. Even now, knowing how splendid that had been, how it had made her feet float and not touch the ground, how he had adored and loved her, how he had admired and worshipped her – even with Glendarvan gone she could not regret having loved him. She should, but she could not. She must, and yet again she did not. She would not be being honest if she did not admit at least to herself that she would never look back on that brief time without thrilling to it, knowing that it would never come again, that she would never feel so young again, be so much in possession of all her senses.

'Do not groan so, Emily dearest, you will make another home.' May was patting her back now, and Emily had not even been aware that she had made any sound.

'Yes, I will. You are right.'

Emily turned and walked to the door without looking back, wishing that she was as innocent and kind as May. Every step she took was as if her shoes were filled with lead, and every part of her body longed to be that letter which those hands would hold, that envelope which those fingers would unseal. She longed to be the very words that she had written to him just so that she could enjoy the passionate look in those brown eyes as he read, and thinking that he would hold the letter to his dear face to smell her scent and kiss her words she longed to be the paper too.

She turned towards May at the door. 'Goodbye. Take care of Edith, she's a good girl at heart, you know. You will find that out.'

May nodded, realising just a little of what Emily must be feeling but happy too that she could not feel it more exactly. Unmarried love was so painful, while married love brought so much happiness, such contentment, such security.

There and then she resolved that she must find her son the same happiness as she and John had enjoyed. If she was right in her summary of Miss Edith O'Connor's character, George might indeed find it with her.

First of all firsts, she thought, already feeling a little less fraught on the carriage ride home, she must not at any turn praise Edith to George. There was nothing worse than the feeling that someone was being pushed towards you. That was the first of all firsts.

And then again, she must be casual, she must not say 'I cannot wait for you to meet the delightful Miss O'Connor', rather the reverse. She would say something faintly damning, like 'Poor little Miss O'Connor, such a tragedy. First she has no success so far in the Season, not being a beauty, and second she now has no home in Ireland because rogues have razed it to the ground.'

That was how she would approach the whole matter of George and Edith O'Connor. Although, and here she had second thoughts, it would probably be far better if no-one apprised Edith O'Connor of the demise of the family home until after the Wokingham Costume Ball. Really, bad news could always wait, and it would only spoil the ball. Or, worse, Edith might return to Ireland before George's mother had been able to introduce her to George.

Daisy was still of a mind to throw in the towel, or whatever the horrid expression was, as far as Sarah Hartley Lambert, and indeed Mrs Hartley Lambert, was concerned. Not content with being the butt of this really silly remark – it could hardly be called an amusing joke – Sarah Hartley Lambert must now add fuel to the laughter it seemed, by riding out with Miss de Nugent and Miss O'Connor, all of them now tricked out in hats more suitable to the demi-monde than to nice young ladies.

'What do vey think vey were *doing*, Jenkins?' Daisy demanded. 'Why, I hear vat even the King and Queen have heard about it, although vat I cannot believe, for surely even kings and queens have better things to do than listen to idle gossip about debutantes giggling in Rotten Row, do you not think?'

'Yes, my lady.'

'And you are quite right, Jenkins, as always. Kings and queens do have better things to do, so vat I cannot believe.'

'No, my lady.'

Daisy raised her chin in order to allow Jenkins to lower the great diamond necklace, once the property of her mother-in-law, and place it reverentially against Daisy's skin. Then, slowly, oh so slowly, because old jewellery could be dreadfully chilly, she did up the clasp.

Now they both stared with some satsifaction at the dull glow of those perfect old diamonds so beautifully placed around Daisy's still elegant neck.

'They are dear, are they not, Jenkins? These old diamonds are very dear. Dear old friends. And they do glow so, do they not? They are so old they are like old silver, which has a perfect dullness. Like perfect conversations which must always be a little on ve dull side in order to show up ve wit to come, these diamonds are just a little on ve dull side until they catch the light, and then they really burst into life.'

'They are perfect, my lady. Quite perfect. Especially around my lady's neck.'

'Well, who else's neck would they go round, Jenkins, may I ask? Who else's, please?'

Jenkins looked sideways at Daisy in the looking glass. She knew just how jumpy her mistress was, and why. They had enjoyed little or no success with this latest American heiress, Sarah Hartley Lambert, and now, by all accounts, at least by Evans's account, all three young ladies had made a dreadful stir. It seemed it was meant to be a prank to redeem Miss Sarah and squash the silly joke about her, but it had sadly backfired and now fashionable people everywhere had gone from mocking Miss Sarah to being outright shocked by her and her antics.

Everyone knew that it really did not do to make exhibitions of themselves in purple and orange hats (everyone knew what kind of women wore either purple or orange), and as for trotting demurely down Rotten Row at the height of the fashionable hour wearing them, well, it was the kind of thing that, in her ladyship's day at any rate, would have been enough to send the three of them packing.

Happily one of them was rumoured to be engaged already, and the other had been taken under the wing of the Duchess of Wokingham, which was itself a social panacea – once under the protection of a duchess few debutantes had much to worry about.

This left only Miss Sarah, Daisy's protégée, in the centre once more of the very worst kind of attention.

It was a headache and they both knew it, and now, tonight, it was the Duchess of Wokingham's ball, and Daisy had to find dancing partners of a suitable nature for the young American girl whose mother was now threatening to return to Newport and close not only her doors but the doors of all her friends to Daisy. And that, Jenkins knew, they could frankly not afford. For a handful of London Seasons now her mistress had only just kept going, only just kept her beautiful head above water, with the help of the American heiresses and their mothers, and now it seemed only too likely that it was about to be all over.

'I have collared two or three young men, but really, Jenkins, they are all about as suitable as a footman. All of them younger sons, and some of them younger sons of younger sons, and you know what that means – tea thrice brewed and no title, my old nanny used to say!'

Jenkins smiled, coldly, all the while concentrating on the next and most elaborate of her tasks, taking what the Countess called the Family Fender from its great coroneted leather box, and lowering it onto her ladyship's head. It had to be placed just so, with a cushion of hair to prevent it from hurting my lady's head.

As it was she never returned from a ball, or an opening of Parliament, without moaning that it was too heavy and really she had no idea why people so coveted them. At the Coronation, my lady, as was her right, had worn not only her usual regalia, along with all the other peeresses, but also her tiara, which Jenkins had thought excessive, but then hers was not to reason why.

If all the ladies of consequence wanted to look as mad as hatters, that was their business. It was certainly not for their maids to comment, although that did not stop them thinking their thoughts, some of them less than reverent, Jenkins was glad to say.

'You see, Jenkins,' Daisy continued, watching eagle-eyed through the looking glass as the tiara was fixed in place by the maid's still nimble fingers, 'I have to find someone suitable for Miss Sarah, or this will be our last Season, and neither of us would want that, would we?'

'No, my lady,' Jenkins agreed, although even as she said the words it seemed to her that, in her mind's eye, she could see her sister's cottage nestling in the little Devon village.

She could see the brass kettle on the hob, and the fire in the chintz-covered sitting room. She could see the horse brasses around that same fire, some of which Jenkins had bought as presents for her sister in return for being looked after on her week off once a year. She could see the walk down to the beach which would be so nice before tea, she could feel the rumble of her stomach as she turned from the beach with her sister and they went back to home-cooked stew and dumplings in the alcove of the cottage kitchen.

Her sister had written of all these things, as well as her desire to see her sister retired with her.

We will be known as 'the two Misses Jenkins' in the village, I dare say, but you will not mind that.

Of a sudden, to be known as anything at all in a village seemed to Jenkins only too appealing. She would no longer be a maid, but a person. Perhaps the vicar on Sundays would know her name? Perhaps she would walk through the village and people would nod and wave to her? It was almost unimaginable to Jenkins, so long had she been in service, it was almost, but not quite, unimaginable.

'Ow! Jenkins! Ow! Really! You are losing your

touch, really you are! Be careful. I shall be going to ve Wokingham Ball without a head if vis goes on for very much longer!'

'Most appropriate since you are dressed as Marie Antoinette, my lady.'

Daisy's expression in the looking glass turned momentarily sour and Jenkins turned away, wishing for the first time in her life that her sister had not written to her of all the jollities that retirement could offer, and all the benefits too.

Their father had left them both enough to buy that cottage together, and really she should do as her sister was asking her, before she grew too old to be able to enjoy her freedom, before she forgot that once upon a time she had actually answered to her given name, not just her surname. She had actually answered to Betsy. People had called *Betsy!* and she had come running.

Daisy must have sensed something of her maid's thoughts, they were after all an old partnership, for she turned to Jenkins a moment or two later and said, 'I am sorry, Jenkins, really I am. I should not take it out on you because I have lost my touch. But the truth is, Jenkins, I have, and I have been thinking I should retire from Society now, you know, before people start to notice. I do not want to be one of those old countesses who are the laughing stock of Society, Jenkins. You remember ve Countess of Bradstock when we were both young? Oh dear me, Jenkins, if her tiara fell off once it must have fallen off her poor old head fifty times, and at ve most embarrassing moments. And then she would fall fast asleep during the entrée, or start to get up to go during the hors d'oeuvres. I really do not want vat to happen to me, Jenkins. It would let us both down, would it not? It would make us both appear ridiculous to be trying to carry on in ve face of – well, we know what!'

They both froze suddenly, Jenkins in the middle of warming the curling tongs and Daisy in the act of holding up one of her rings to make sure it had no fluff at the back.

It was as they both hesitated that a small truth started to appear, at first quite a long way away on the far horizon of time, but then it came nearer and nearer until both mistress and maid found themselves staring at it, unable to avoid its startlingly bright presence. They had grown older, and suddenly they both knew it.

'Shall vis be our last Season together, Jenkins, do you think?'

'Never say never, my lady, and never say die, but it could or could not be. We shall see what we shall see, my lady.'

There was a small pause as they both now stared at Daisy's reflection. She looked impossibly beautiful. Older of course, but still very elegant and quite, quite lovely, the features still even, the figure more rounded but still heartbreakingly fragile somehow. And of course the blue and silver eighteenth-century costume, the powdering of her hair that Jenkins was about to effect, it was all so unspeakably glamorous.

'I heard that one of the Howards has spent literally thousands of pounds on his costume for this evening, Jenkins. It is covered in amethysts and pearls, in the Elizabethan manner. And at least three of the ladies we know are coming as Madame de Pompadour. So awfully strange, do you not think, vat we are all so fascinated by costume balls these last years? As if we are not content to be ourselves any more, as if we have to dress up as someone else to make ourselves more interesting. Ever since King Edward died, I fink, do you not, Jenkins?'

'Yes, my lady.'

'And did you hear that the Duke of Balniel has insisted on tiny diamonds sewn all over his jacket of beaten gold? And there are tiny sapphires on his sleeves. But he has not the legs for hosiery, did you know that, Jenkins?'

'Yes, my lady.'

Jenkins had started powdering Daisy's hair, carefully and beautifully with small dabs of a small but effective powder puff. Now swathed in protective capes, Daisy watched her a little mistily in the mirror, for however careful Jenkins was the powder still escaped into the air, giving the whole scene a feel of yesterday. This was the first time for an age that Daisy had seen herself white-haired, and she realised that the whole effect could be really rather flattering.

'No tiara, Jenkins. I have decided I shall not wear the Family Fender.' Daisy started to remove it from her head. 'It looks old-fashioned. Instead

I will wear the sapphire piece from India. Why not?'

'Yes, my lady. The Fender might be a little too modern for Marie Antoinette, I do agree. If it is the old-fashioned effect that my lady is going for, we will have to put aside the Family Fender.'

Having coiffed my lady to suit the Fender, Jenkins sighed inwardly and once more applied herself to combing and fitting the sapphire piece.

Really, that cottage, its fire, the kettle on the hob, all the sounds of the sea outside, was beckoning to her in such a fashion that of a sudden she knew she had grown too old to dance attendance on the Countess any more.

'Mmm.' Daisy turned at last from her reflection. 'Vat is what I have always loved about you, Jenkins, do you know? Your ability to sum up in a few words what we are both thinking and leave us both none ve wiser!'

Daisy laughed suddenly, but Jenkins, having effected a complete change of hairstyle in under twenty minutes, feigned deafness, too busy trying to find her mistress's jewel-encrusted evening reticule to really care to add anything. Even if she had, Daisy thought, staring at her own still elegant arms in their evening gloves with their row upon row of diamond bracelets, it would be about as reasonable as the Evesham family motto: *What Has Been Has Often Been Before*.

Trust the Eveshams to come up with a tangle of words that had nothing to do with anything that Daisy could see. Such nonsense, like so many family mottos, when you really thought about them. And, like so much, it only really looked good in Latin.

'By the way, my lady, the letter that came from the Duchess of Wokingham, I believe it was. Came round by hand a short while ago. Shall I put it in the safe with your tiara?'

'Yes, thank you, Jenkins.'

They both knew that it had not been a letter from the Duchess but a small parcel of large, unused, quite new, five-pound notes. The letter was Jenkins's polite way of putting things.

Now mistress and maid prepared to descend to the hall where the other servants would be waiting to applaud the Countess when she appeared, never more so than tonight when she was intent on appearing so regal. It was always such a lovely moment, this business of descending the staircase and hearing the maids in particular making the old house ring out with the sound of their enthusiastic clapping. Tonight, however, both mistress and maid were aware that such moments might be going to become rarer and rarer for them, until eventually they were gone for ever, the two of them leaving the Season without a trace. For who would remember Jenkins, or perhaps even the Countess, in years to come? Who would remember the way my lady wore her clothes, her elegance, her way of walking? The turn of her head, her sparkling eyes, her delightful laugh?

To Daisy the sudden sound of the servants'

applause was deliciously soothing, and it lifted her like the sound of the sea outside one's bedroom at Broadstairs. As she started to descend the stairs, head erect, her eyes never looking down, not once – the true test of the Great Beauty – Daisy allowed herself to enjoy this lovely moment with a new intensity, in the knowledge that it might indeed, after all, be her last. As a great actress should, Daisy realised, as the applause grew in volume (mostly nowadays directed towards her jewellery rather than her beauty, she always thought) she must at last contemplate leaving the stage before her meteor dropped to earth.

From now on, it had to be faced, old age beckoned. She was no fool; she knew, all too well, how cruelly old women could be treated by the fashionable and the clever. Not for her the snide remarks, the whispers behind the fans, the *ah but you should have seen her when she was young*. She was not yet old, but she was not young either. She must leave with grace, with dignity, above all at a moment when she would be missed. She owed that to herself. She owed it to her two deceased husbands, to her son whom she hardly ever saw, to her servants, but above all to Jenkins whose work of art she had been for so long.

Terrible for Jenkins to be pinning on her tiara when perhaps she would be in need not just of the fashionable 'mouse' but of a wig too! Dreadful for Jenkins if she had to go on pretending that my lady was still young. Such a strain. As she stepped past her loyal servants, Daisy determined not to take her thoughts any further. The point was that after so many years in loyal service, she must not ask too much more of the redoubtable Jenkins.

They did not like each other at all, they never had, but they relied upon each other. Above all, Daisy knew she must free herself, before it was too late. She must learn to be not Daisy, the Countess, but someone gentler, quieter, without a 'name'.

She stepped into her carriage. Very well, it was an old-fashioned carriage, and her coachman's legs were really rather bent, but goodness it was splendid, and she still had it drawn by four horses, despising anything less. And not for her the tawdriness of a motorised vehicle and all those silly veils. She was Daisy, she was famous for going about in her own splendid carriage drawn by a team of matching grey horses. That at least she would see to it would remain unchanged.

She sat back against the plush interior, and in the growing light of the street lamps, only recently abandoned by the lamp-lighters, she looked with love on her London, and the London which had always loved her. Perhaps she had not been as popular with the people as Nell Gwynn, say, but goodness she had been, and was still, loved! Even now people cheered and waved when they saw her arriving.

Hansom cab drivers still tipped their hats and whips at her carriage. They knew style when they saw it, and they knew that the Countess was not just the epitome of the old style, she was that best of all possible bests, the famous great beauty.

Ahead of her lay the Wokingham Ball.

She would arrive decorously, towards the last, doubtless placed beside that dratted old bore the Duke of Connerton, or some such, but, her reputation still intact, she would naturally command as much attention as any royal. And why should she not? She had been loved by Royalty, she had made Royalty laugh, she had cheered Royalty through many a dull hour. She deserved to be thought of as royal, because, when all was said and done, she had been.

But now as the horses dropped their pace to a walk and the lights and flares around Wokingham House lit the now darkening evening, and flunkies ran to open carriage doors, their white stockings somehow staying as bright as the lights, Daisy sighed with contentment. It was all still there. Style, grandeur, aplomb, a sense of how to be, a sense of reaching out to something better – it was all still there, waiting for her.

Something else was waiting for her too, and it was not until she took her place at dinner that Daisy saw what it was.

Of a sudden, as a pair of brilliant brown eyes smiled into hers, Daisy was not quite so sure that she was ready for retirement, at least not until the end of the Season, but quite, quite sure that one way or another she could help out her hostess, the Duchess, who had so obligingly sent her round a 'little gift' earlier in the day.

As soon as she saw those brilliant brown eyes Daisy was quite determined to help out the Duchess in any way she could. For the wretched Augustine Medlar, despite all her smiles and promises, had been about as much help to Daisy as salmon in the wrong month.

The Ball

There were many other guests to account for, all making their way, by one means or another, to the Duchess of Wokingham's Costume Ball. So many coming up from the country, or recently arrived, that the livery stables were filled to overcrowding with horses being washed down, or brushed off, or teams being changed. It was a busy, busy day for everyone in every trade, from jewels to dresses, from flowers to wine, with everyone happy that the weather was continuing fine, and all knowing that the Wokingham Ball was always one of the centrepieces of the Season, and nothing that happened there ever went unnoticed.

George, Marquis of Cordrey, in common with most sons was the least enthusiastic participant in his mother's ball. The fact was that he had not wanted to come up to London at all, even for a few days, and everyone who knew George knew it. His father knew it, his mother knew it, his valet knew it. He actually thought his dogs knew it. Of course, saying goodbye to them was the very worst of going to London. Long before he patted their heads and gave instructions to the grooms as to what they liked and when they liked it, and asked his valet to make sure that one of the hall boys kept an eye on them too, his dogs knew that George was leaving for London.

Of course, he had his 'sleeve dog', as all good huntsmen must. A sleeve dog was a small dog, in his case a Japanese butterfly dog, that could, when necessary, be tucked into one's coat when out riding, just its little head left sticking out while one cantered along the walls of the estate enjoying the early morning stretch, feeling oneself to be the luckiest devil alive, and knowing it too. One's sleeve dog was the only one of one's dogs allowed upstairs; that was why it was so necessary to one. And, more than that, without it one would have to face the unimaginable, hours inside a house (which was bad enough) *without a dog*.

At least he could take Misty to London with him. That was his one and only consolation. She tucked nicely into his coat on the journey down, and once at Wokingham House he was able to jump up the steps with her and into his rooms without his mother seeing, and then run her round the place to take the edge off his misery at being in London.

He knew that he was not in his mother's good books, so in order to be diplomatic he left little Misty shut in his bedroom and went straight down to the drawing room to see her.

'Ah, George.'

George loved his mother because she was

beautiful and she was kind, and he knew that she would guess he would have brought Misty to London, that even now Misty was probably chewing a perfectly priceless leg of a perfectly priceless piece of furniture, but that neither of them really cared.

However, despite loving his mother, George always wished that she would not sound quite so surprised when she saw him. It was as if she still could not get over the fact of him. As if she had suddenly come across him, like Moses, mewling among the reeds.

He kissed her hand, and she smiled at him. George knew that smile. It made him wary.

'How's Misty?' she asked, all innocence.

'She's very well, Mama, thank you.'

'Oh, well, that is good. As long as you have not brought her up here – she does chew everything so, George, you know that. The gilt of one whole Louise Quinze chair, Cropper told me, last Season.' May managed to make her eyes large and keep her face straight. 'Dreading our ball again, are you, George? It is at least costume this year!'

May's head was cocked to one side, which her son knew was a further sign of mischief afoot. His mother only put her head on one side when she was planning something.

'Of course not, Mama. You know how much I look forward to the ball.'

George walked to the window. He knew that he should feel grateful for the view of London from Wokingham House, but the truth of it was that it always made him think, not of the loveliness of the architecture opposite, but of the greyness of it all compared to the green fields and blossoming trees in the country.

'We have a house guest, George. I know you will be kind to her. She does not know it yet, and you must not mention it – I am to break the news tomorrow morning – but her family home in Ireland has been razed to the ground. Too terrible for them, but we wish her to enjoy the ball tonight without that sorrow on her.'

'How frightful.'

'Yes, it is horrid. And George, there is another thing. She does need someone to be nice to her. She is a very, very plain gel, and no-one, so far, has really paid her much attention. It is only a little thing, but after the King has led off the ball with me, and Papa followed with the Queen, will you be kind enough to follow with her? She is after all our house guest for the rest of the Season, if she will stay, which is very doubtful, although I hope she will. Will you lead her out? It would be such a compliment to her. Please do this for me, despite her being so very, very plain.'

Inside George groaned. Up to London, which was bad enough, a night spent dancing instead of seated in the library at home enjoying a book and a glass of wine, and now dancing with an ugly girl!

'Of course, Mama. I will do whatever you want, providing you will not mind my returning to the country tomorrow.'

'You can't go tomorrow George, that is far too

soon. You have to come to Court. You must stay at least a week, you know you must.'

It was their way of bargaining, and they both knew it.

'Not a week, Mama, please. How will I go on? There is nothing to do in London during the day except dance attendance on dowagers at soirées, and the last time I did so one of them passed out on me and I nearly suffocated.'

'George, dearest boy, that was a small incident, and if you are man enough to fall off your horses out hunting then you are perfectly man enough to have dowagers fall on you while you take tea. Do not tell me you lack social courage, or I will think you as much a coward as a man who shirks fighting for his country. People need all forms of courage, you know, not just courage in battle.'

May had scored, and they both knew it. George coloured. It was true. He did lack social courage, but, and this was a big 'but' as far as he was concerned, he was damned if he would let his mother see that he did. Not now that she had pointed it up, he would not. He turned away, his face setting. Damn it, women like his mother always seemed to get their way. Which was right, he supposed, since they ran the servants and set the tone of everything, but even so – a whole week in London!

'We will meet here in the drawing room before dinner. We dine in the Long Room, and then we go down for the ball. So, I expect you will want to go and stretch your legs before all this. Why not go out in the Park on a hireling and ogle a few of the prettier equestrians?'

'I was thinking I might go to Burlington Arcade. There must be a cravat or two there that I could fancy, I shouldn't wonder.'

May's head was on one side once again, and she smiled, always a danger sign, as George well knew.

'Oh, but I told the old chap up at the livery stables that you would take out one of his hirelings. I rather fancy he is to have it ready for you at half past two.'

Again George groaned inwardly. His mother was always ahead of the game. She seemed to know young men too well.

'But riding in the Park is such tame stuff, Mama.'

'Oh, I agree, George. It is, of course, but an awful lot of what you will pass on horseback in the Park is far from tame, I do assure you. Luncheon is in the small dining room at one, by the way.'

With which May left George to chew the cud and eventually, in high dudgeon, dash back upstairs to give Misty a hearty dish of chicken.

After leaving her son May sped away, well satisfied with the ground that she had prepared for George's meeting with Edith. She fairly flew up the stairs to her rooms, first of all to make sure that Edith had settled in all right, and secondly to make sure that the costume she had ordered for her had arrived, that her new house guest liked it, and what was more that it fitted.

The short answer was that the costume had arrived, but as soon as she burst in on Edith, May sensed at once that there was something wrong. What could the matter be? The box lay unopened on the bed and Cropper, the Duchess's much treasured, highly trained personal maid, was looking as if she had just been told off.

'Ah, so the costume has arrived. But there has been no time to open the box yet?' May looked at the two people in the room with her innocent questioning gaze. 'So. Obviously it has *only* just arrived, and so we need to unwrap it. Scissors please, Cropper.'

Cropper, a small, stout northern woman with friendly brown eyes and a figure like a toby jug, went thankfully to the dressing table and after a few seconds duly produced a pair of scissors to cut the ribbons on the box.

Edith stared at the gown when the Duchess took it out of its box as if she had never thought to own a dress like it, which indeed she had not. Up until now her dresses had been made up of old white dresses and more old white dresses, very suitable for a debutante, her mother had kept telling her, and indeed, as the run of things went, Edith had found that most young girls up from the Shires were dressed just as simply as herself. With the occasional exception of mothers like Mrs Hartley Lambert, and a few others, most parents did not think it worth tricking out their daughters in expensive dresses for ball after ball. Once they were married it was quite different; then their husbands were supposed to supply them with a large dress allowance and they were meant to vie with other people's wives to be the best dressed. That was how it was. No father would give a vast sum for a single dress, until perhaps her wedding day, and even then they were usually heard to heave a large and hearty sigh of relief when the girl in question declared that she would far rather wear her mother's wedding dress.

'*Et violà!*' With Cropper's expert help May laid out the costume. It could not have been more suitable if it tried. 'It is a copy of the Winterhalter dress worn by the Empress Eugénie, and I really think it could not be more beautiful,' May said, as she and Cropper spread out the hoops and the immense petticoats, and then, at last, the dress. 'It is quite, quite lovely, I think, and it was to be worn by Miss Prudence Mahon, but she had to be whisked back to America, for all sorts of reasons. I suddenly remembered her mother pleading with me to find someone to wear it, and then herself taking off for the United States and leaving it behind in the charge of Mrs Binty in Dover Street. So here it is. For one night, Edith dearest, you are going to be not a duchess, not a queen, but an empress!'

Cropper looked to Edith, and then at the dress, and then back to Edith again.

'I wonder if it isn't gonna need a touch of altering along the bust line, Your Grace, so I best get it on her, and then run it into the sewing room.'

'Come, Edith,' said May, suddenly suspecting

that the young girl was feeling just like George downstairs, fearful of stepping into the limelight. 'I am one of your godmothers, as you probably know, so this is your coming out present from myself and the Duke. And I am only sorry we were not in London sooner, so that we could have been of *use* sooner.'

Pale-faced and unable to believe that she was really going to wear such a dress, Edith stepped towards the two women.

'Hold out your arms.'

Edith held out her arms and May and Cropper held the dress against her.

'Perfect,' May said, smiling happily. 'Quite perfect. I always say, from having been on the stage – no, I am afraid I always *boast* that I can judge a girl's measurements from fifty yards. It becomes rather a habit, do you see, from being backstage and so on. Costumes go missing, other people take what is yours and try to wear it, and then you have to take other people's because they are wearing yours – oh, you know how it is. It goes on and on, backstage I mean. So that you end up being able to spot a costume's size at twenty paces!'

The dress was of a tasteful pale blue, Pompadour blue, and cut across the front into a sculpted and rounded vee, the wide sleeves caught up with pale pink silk roses, the same outlining the front of the dress. The waist was small and tight, and set off the enormous skirt which lay above not just the hoop but also a mountain of petticoats.

May said to Cropper, 'How beautiful it all is, and how beautiful Miss O'Connor is going to look in it. Come, let us dress her in the hoop and petticoats and then throw the dress over the top, in the accepted manner.'

She walked Edith firmly to the looking glass, and Edith could hardly believe her eyes. She would never have thought that a dress, any dress, could so change a person. What was more, the dress was so beautiful that she felt she would have to live up to it, unlike the dresses her mama had put her in, which had made her feel mousy and ill at ease, if not grousy and out of sorts.

'I shall leave you now, my dear, to have a rest. Cropper will look after the dress alteration, it is only tiny. And everything will be just so, you wait and see. And Edith, you must understand, this is a gift, you know, from the Duke and me. No, we do not want to be thanked, we just want you to feel happy in it. And if you do not, why, you can choose something else. Possibly one of your own dresses, something familiar, if you do not wish to be in costume. It is just more lively if you are.'

'I love the dress, more than I can tell you.' Edith loved it so much that she did not want to get out of it.

'Cropper will dress your hair in the larger way that was so fashionable then. It will look very fine, you can be sure of that.'

Cropper was more than a help to Edith, she was a friend, or at least she became a friend in a very few minutes.

'Tell you what, Miss O'Connor, why not let me undress you here and now and lie down on the bed in your tea gown?'

'I have no tea gown, I am afraid. I have only a wrap.'

'Well, never mind, eh? I will hurry along and borrow one from the Duchess. She has a wardrobe full that she keeps not just for herself but for anyone staying, too. She is that generous, you know, Her Grace. It comes from having been an actress, I always think, used to bunking up and sharing when she was younger. She never has forgotten her days behind the footlights neither, bless her.'

Cropper hurried off and was astonished, if not shocked, to find when she came back that Edith had undressed herself without her help.

'Well, well, miss, that was very good of you, really it was, to help me out in this way,' she said, covering her embarrassment at seeing a young woman of Edith's background fending for herself. 'Still. There was no need, I do assure you. We are more than happy to dress and undress guests, as you may imagine. Used to all sorts here, too.'

She held out a tea gown, Japanese in style, and as soon as Edith put it on she felt exotic, which was hardly surprising given that it had much gold and black embroidery on it, not to mention butterflies on the sleeves and collar. She laughed suddenly, looking at herself in the looking glass, Cropper standing behind her.

'I feel as though I ought to have a knitting needle through my hair.'

'And so you shall if you should want it, although judging from this picture the Duchess has just given me it will not be quite in keeping, I shouldn't have thought, not with the Empress,' Cropper said, and she stared for a second at Edith's face reflected in the mirror.

Edith turned away, thinking that the maid must be staring at her uneven profile or her less than classical features, but Cropper, very gently, turned her back.

'No, no, Miss O'Connor, if you don't mind. I must study your face in order to arrange your hair for you tonight. Would you mind if I washed it for you in an hour or so, and dressed it myself?'

'No, of course not. I am afraid that between us Minnie and I – that is my maid – usually make a bit of a bird's nest of it, you know. It does seem to frizz so, but in the wrong places, I find. Never where I would like, at the front, but always wispy bits escaping at the side.'

Cropper smiled, patting the young girl lightly on her back, realising of a sudden how much she needed mothering, poor soul. She had been neglected in all the refined areas where a young girl should never be neglected.

'I have all sorts of potions and lotions that I use to take out frizz where it is not wanted, and I am a dab hand with the curling tongs, I think you will find, even if it is myself that says so. I have never had no complaints as yet when I dressed a lady's hair, I will say. Probably spoken too soon, but I have not – yet. See, you have a heart-shaped face, and that is very becoming to a certain style. And your hair is beautiful, really quite lovely. You don't mind my saying that, do you?'

'My hair?' Edith looked astonished. 'But my mama has always said that my hair is too fine, and the colour not very interesting. Hers, you see, was auburn, and now is a wonderful white. Very flattering, as you may imagine.'

'Yes,' Cropper agreed, obediently, but not really listening because in her experience very few mothers knew how to turn out their daughters in any kind of style that suited them, starting as they did usually with their own looks and their own style which was usually two generations out of date. The corsets that she had been obliged to throw out that some poor young girls were expected to sport under their clothes! They were hardly worth thinking about, except to remember that some of them once they reached the kitchen dustbins were discovered to be so ancient and so antiquated that they had even made Cook split her sides with laughter at their antiquity.

Such poor creatures, some of these girls were who were sent up to London to do their social stint! Some of them did not seem to know what time of day it was. Very often their mothers had died and they had only grandmothers to bring them up. Fathers were never interested, of course. It was a wonder that they were ever married off to anyone.

Many had been the time when Cropper, seeing the contents of some debutante's portmanteaux, had found herself thinking that she would not have been surprised if the girl had been sent up from the country tricked out in a white wig and a silk dress with panniers, and a box of black patches to stick on their faces. Really! What some country families thought would pass as clothes for their daughters for the London Season did not bear thinking about.

'Now then, miss, lie you down on that bed and leave all the rest to Cropper. That's right, shut your eyes and feel quite free to think and breathe yourself into a little bit of sleep. Like when you was little, miss, you know? And your gran came and read to you in the afternoons. One of the best times of day, I always think. Nothing to touch it, except late at night, that's another lovely time for all of us, what with hot milk and biscuits and a warm bed, don't you think?'

But Cropper was speaking to herself, for when she looked over towards the bed the poor young girl was fast asleep under the cover and looking, with her hair down, more like ten years of age than the seventeen or so that she was meant to be, her long dark hair falling free, and, if Cropper was not mistaken, a contented smile on her sweet little face.

'Poor thing,' the maid thought to herself as she tiptoed about the room setting up all her lotions and potions preparatory to beginning what promised to be a lengthy transformation. 'As I understand it, her mother's had a tragedy and had to return home and the Duchess has taken her under her wing. Could not be worse really. But then that is the Duchess all over, always taking on some cause or another, or some lost sheep, or some ageing person. Dear me, all these years! When I think back, the house was always full of them back in the country. Luckily the Duke was more realistic and very often, realising that the Duchess was being taken for a sop, would gently send them on their way.'

She stared again over to the bed. Different here, though. This Miss O'Connor, she was a nice young girl, and by the time Cropper had finished with her she was going to be a beauty, or Cropper would want to know the reason why.

What seemed like hours later but was in fact only a little more than an hour, Edith woke up to see Cropper seated and sewing, and said, 'Oh dear, I had such a bad dream. I thought I smelled burning! Goodness, how nice to be awake.'

Cropper stared at her, momentarily startled, and then she said, 'Well now, Miss Edith – you don't mind me calling you that? No? Well, now that you are awake, we may begin.'

She set aside her sewing, which Edith could see was something with ribbons and a piece of lace, a little like the dress that had arrived in that huge box. Cropper held out her hand to Edith, who took it, half marvelling as she always did at the roughness of maids' hands, at the feeling that those hands had seldom been out of water or free from soap of one kind or another at any time of their life.

'Do you like being a maid, Cropper?' Edith turned her beautiful eyes on the older woman.

'I beg your pardon, miss? Do I like being a maid? Why, Miss O'Connor, you're not one of those Liberals, are you? Begging your pardon, miss, but really! What a question! Of course I likes being a maid. I get more happiness out of what I do than the Duchess gets out of what she does, I sometimes thinks. More variety, you see. Her Grace, as I see it, often has to do many tedious things that she had rather not, but she must, and without complaining, because that is what duchesses do.'

She paused, nodding, obviously agreeing with herself most heartily.

'But me, I only do what I like doing. Dressing hair, handling fine clothes, sewing confections of one kind or another, using my imagination for my coiffures. There's nothing that I am not asked to do, and nothing I do that I do not enjoy, or would be without. Long may our lives here last, miss, really. Long may these years continue, for without this house and these families people like me would not have the fun that we have. We are never lonely – bend your head over the basin, Miss Edith – we are never without friends, or a roof over our heads, or fine food to eat. We are cared for until we die. Do I enjoy being a maid, miss?' Cropper started to feel the water in one of the copper jugs. 'I like it better than anything I care to think of. Why, last Season Her Grace gave us all a week off at the end. Caused a scandal among her friends, I can tell you, but she did. And' – Cropper leaned forward – 'she only gave me a fur hat and tippet, can you imagine? Oh, she's terrible she is. Liable to give away the clothes she stands up in if you're not careful. I have to keep a hold on her, a tight rein sometimes, but she just laughs. *I know, Cropper, I know!* That's all she says – well, that's all she *has* to say, because she knows that I am the one with the common sense, and she is the one what gets run off with by her feelings.'

Cropper gave a great amused laugh as Edith felt the warm water from one of several metal jugs tipping over her head, followed by a cold lotion that Cropper told her was her special mix, and then a rinse of camomile tea, another rinse of a flower water, and finally boiled rain water, which Cropper said was perfect for fine hair.

'I do so like your hair, Miss Edith. Now bend down in front of that fire while I comb it through and dry it for you. My goodness, but it is good and thick, and squeaky – can you hear it squeak.'

Minnie was no trained maid like Cropper, and now, as Edith submitted to the professional maid's attentions, she started to appreciate the difference between being looked after by a proper lady's maid and a maid who could iron and wash and lay out clothes, but do little else of any consequence. Cropper dried Edith's hair and brushed it, strand by little strand so that it turned from being vaguely frizzy to a shining mass of dark, catching the light and showing off its suddenly apparent auburn tints.

Then came the dressing and the undressing.

First Cropper must dress her in new underwear,

bundling up Edith's old corset in some newspaper and throwing it into the wastebin, which made them both laugh, Edith almost shocked, Cropper highly satisfied. Then Edith lay down on the bed and Cropper dressed her in the new underclothes, lacing her into a new corset before slipping the hoop, the petticoats and finally the fabulous dress over her head. Next she promptly and properly threw a protective cape over her charge.

'Have to try dressing your hair for a few minutes to suit the style of dress.'

She murmured and muttered and pulled Edith's hair up, pinning a 'mouse' as she called it under the back to make the whole effect grander, then combing the hair over it and trying various ornaments.

'The Duchess sent up some diamond stars for you, but I don't know so much, they might – no. Maybe if we position two just here at the back it will complement your short train. Mmm, and this little nonsense I have made could be quite effective at the front. Mmm, maybe not. Just the stars, but not at the back, to the side. No, to the front.'

During all this Edith stood quite, quite still and her face was a study in docility. She had never had anyone make such a fuss over her before, and she found it perfectly delicious.

'Cropper, you are too kind, really you are.'

Cropper was not listening.

'Now, what I am going to do now must not make you cross. It's one of those things that I find always bring luck. I am going to ask you to face outward, away from the mirror, and not look at yourself at all until I have finished. When I have finished I shall put on your shoes, and you shut your eyes and I walk you to that cheval mirror over there, see? But first we are going to take everything off and you are going to lie down on that bed again and compose yourself once more, for if you don't I think you will find that you might become too flushed, and I don't want that, and nor do you. Makes a young lady look as if she has been at the sherry wine! It's only natural to feel nervous before the Duchess's ball. After all, it is one of the great events of the Season.'

Wonderingly Edith sank back once more onto the vast bed and stared up at the ceiling, her feelings a mixture of awe at Cropper's professionalism and fascination at how persons such as the Duchess were looked after. Was this what happened every evening when the Duchess was prepared for a ball, or even a dinner? She supposed it must be.

No wonder therefore that the Duchess looked so composed always, so on top of things, with such a spring in her step, for to be looked after and treasured in this way must be to become the person that you were meant to be, to become the person Society meant you to be. Long before you left your apartment, or put a foot on the top step of the stairs leading down to the public rooms, you had already been transformed.

How important it must be to be groomed in this

way if you were from a great family, or held in esteem. It meant that you were like a horse, all shiny and tricked out in your best before you were pulled out of the stable. No matter if you finally reached home mud bespattered, you started out spring-heeled with life and exuberance.

And that was just how Edith felt at that moment, and she was not even dressed yet. She felt exuberant, ready to tackle any situation, just because Cropper had given her confidence in herself. No wonder Cropper loved her work. She must see the change she could make, not just in people's clothes, but in their personalities. Edith could feel that she herself had changed already. She felt more rounded, unlike anything she had yet felt, nearer to heaven; and she was still not fully dressed.

Downstairs George was tickling Misty's tum, and groaning inwardly to himself. He had gone, on his mother's directions, to the livery stable, and he had dutifully ridden out in Rotten Row, and dull to the point of extinction it had been. How flat Hyde Park was after riding round the estate, and how over-dressed the girls and women. He had not wanted to look at any of them. They were all exotic birds of paradise, he was sure, but not to his taste. All waiting to be seen by someone and as a consequence, to his eyes, tawdry. Not that he did not have all the normal red-blooded reactions, but when he was in London he longed to find someone who would just be normal towards him.

As soon as he was introduced as 'the Marquis of Cordrey' all the debutantes simpered and the demi-monde glittered. *Future duke, future duke.* It was almost like a drum roll so loud were their thoughts.

Like most little boys George had dreams while he was growing up. His dream had been to be a knight in shining armour, and unknown to anyone, disguised as a tramp or some such, do great deeds. In this way he would meet a beautiful young girl who would not know who he was and would marry him just for himself. No more bowing and scraping, just two people at ease in a world which would be like a great park, full of birds and wild things.

'But instead,' he now told Misty, picking up the little Japanese dog and popping her into his silk dressing gown, 'instead I have to lead out some plain Jane from Ireland who is going to wink and blink at me like candles on a Christmas tree, and I shall have to pretend that she is my fairy princess. Oh, what a dreadfully dull thing it is to be in London, and in the summer! It is about as much fun as waiting to be shaved, which I am.'

His valet came into the room, bowl, hot water, brush and razor at the ready. He looked at George and knew at once that 'we', as he always referred to George, was 'having a fit of the piques'.

'Oh dear, my lord. Staring at your feet and talking to yourself. In a fret, I see.'

'How very perceptive of you, Frear.' George looked up and smiled, freeing Misty from the comforting warmth of his silk dressing gown.

'Mind your lordship's dog, this water isn't half hot.'

'Misty! Basket!'

The little dog jumped into her basket on command as George stared at his valet in the looking glass before which they were both now positioned, one seated, one standing.

'Is it too much to wish that one might enjoy one's week in London, my lord?'

'In short, Frear, much too much! Far too much! So much too much that I think you may well find my lordship standing outside in the courtyard waiting for a livery coach to take me back to the country.'

Frear started to lather his young master's face vigorously.

'The trouble with you, if I may say so, my lord . . .'

'You may.' George swallowed some of the foaming shaving soap and quickly shut his mouth against the bitter taste.

'. . . is that you never give town a chance. Country, country is all you allow for, and really, a week a year, just the ball and Ascot, is not much for Her Grace to ask of you, my lord, really it isn't.'

George was about to open his mouth to protest when he remembered the awfulness of the soapy taste in his mouth, and his lips remained firmly pressed together.

'You see, my lord, London is just like everything. You have to give it a chance. And you, if I may say so, my lord, never give it a chance, and that will not make things any easier for you. You will never find a bride in the country, my lord. It has never been known. What girl of spirit would want to languish in the country when she can come to London for the Season? There is no such person. Keep still, my lord. I have no wish to cut short your time in London by violent means.'

'I suspect you of talking to my mother, Frear,' George protested, when Frear had finally finished shaving him. 'This is propaganda. Next thing we know you will be singing the praises of ugly girls from Ireland and so on and so forth. I shall never fall for a girl who is not a country lover. She must be much happier in the country than in town, as I am.'

'But even this Diana of the chase will want to come to town sometimes.'

'Why, Frear, why?'

Frear looked up in the middle of putting away his shaving materials, each tool carefully cleaned and dried, and neatly replaced in its appropriate leather casing. 'Your lordship was saying?'

'I asked you,' said George, standing up, 'why on earth a country-loving woman would want to come to town.'

There was a short pause, and then Frear, at last satisfied that his shaving paraphernalia was as beautiful as the day it was born, turned to the Marquis and with a small theatrical gesture, for which he was famed below stairs, said in a reverential tone, 'Hats!'

'I beg your pardon, Frear.'

'Hats, my lord. A woman must always come to London for her hats. If she does not come to London for her hats she will fade away. A woman in the provinces can never look beautiful if she is not wearing that season's hats.'

George frowned, suddenly impressed. The first thing his mother did when she came to London was to invite the milliners round. And good God, they certainly did come round, in their droves, in their dozens. And the hours spent trying on the hats, Cropper fussing around her as if both their lives depended on it.

'Do you know, Frear, I think you might have something there. And it is certainly true, when one goes to the races in the south the first thing one notices is the stylish set of the ladies' hats, and quite the reverse in the provinces . . .'

'Where they are always half a season, if not a whole season, behind the times, my lord.'

George sat down in one of the armchairs scattered around his rooms as Frear started to lay out his evening clothes. 'So that is why my mother is always so insistent on coming to town in the early summer. Not just the ball, and Ascot, but the hats. And the hats are not just for Ascot, but for all the year round, until the next Season.'

'A woman,' stated Frear, knowing that he was winning on all fronts, but all the same laying out his lordship's silver costume with proper reverence, 'can be out of fashion with her clothes, even two seasons behind, but not with her hats. Hats change quicker than any other item of clothing. Gentlemen's hats too, if you notice. I have had to order you a whole new set, from the usual source. I mean, my lord, imagine if you, or your father, had not changed a few years back to the tighter, more curly brim? How would you have looked? Imagine if you had not changed from the curly brim to your present—'

'I see what you mean, Frear,' George interrupted staring ahead of him. 'We would look cracking asses, as usual. I mean, really. It would be the talk of the clubs, would it not, to be going around in some fusty Chesterfield sort of outfit.'

George found himself imagining the scene, his father and himself checking into their clubs wearing ghastly checked trousers with one of those straight coats and a topper. They would both look like his grandfather, or something. 'Do you know,' he went on, after a few minutes, 'I am very grateful to you, Frear. You really have put me straight about a great deal.' Frear made a deprecating sort of sound and breathed on the old-fashioned silvered evening pumps. 'No, really, Frear. You have been most generous in your counsel, I see that. I understand London in quite a different way now. It keeps one up to the mark, stops one atrophying, and so on.'

'No need to start indulging in any of the smart talk, though, my lord.'

'You mean saying "too, too" every five seconds, Frear?'

'Precisely, my lord. Smart talk, like hats, always

dates one dreadfully. It is best avoided, really it is. From what I have seen, in the early days, looking after His Grace, clothes must be kept up to muster, but not language. Language must be a guiding rule, and it cannot be modish. It sticks, my lord. Smart talk sticks, and then it dates one. So. Now, are we ready for our bath?'

George, who had taken Misty on his knee, a habit of his when he was much struck by a new and startling thought, put her down again and back in her basket.

'Yes, Frear. Quite ready.'

Somehow not even the thought of dancing with his mother's lame duck, whatever her name was, the ugly little thing from Ireland, could now put him off London. In fact, by the time he climbed into his marble bath and lay back in the steam allowing Frear to wash his hair for him, George had quite made up his mind to stay in London after Ascot. That was how much Frear had impressed him with his little talk.

'You are one in a million, Frear, really you are. One in a million.'

'Yes, my lord, I know. Now is my lord aware that the Duchess wishes him to go to the ball dressed as Oberon, King of the Fairies?'

George closed his eyes. Just when everything had seemed to be righting itself, too.

'So that is what that silver stuff on the bed is meant to be?'

'Happily my lord has the figure for it!'

'But not the taste for it, Frear.'

And George sighed as more soap, this time from his hair, found its way into his mouth.

While George was enjoying his talk with the best valet in London, and his father, due to May's insistence that he 'send Frear to the boy', was having to make do with an underling who only just managed to shave His Grace without cutting him, May herself was struggling to bath and change with only the help of a tweeny.

'Do not fret yourself, Perkins, I am perfectly able to dress myself, and coif myself too. Just try to handle the button hook without skinning me, and if you have difficulty with the corseting, a boot in the back, as my old dresser used to say, is as good as a kipper for breakfast on tour!'

'Yes, my lady.' Perkins smiled, weakly.

Perkins, thought May, sighing inwardly, had a very weak smile as well as a fear of doing anything well. Happily, having loaned the estimable, irreplaceable Cropper to Miss Edith, May knew, from her acting and dancing and singing days, how to costume herself.

Of course she would not look as good at Perkins's hands as she would when Cropper was in attendance, and certainly not as relaxed, for five minutes of Perkins was enough to bring on a fit of the laudanums. And she could handle herself, but not her hair. Her hair would have to be finally finished by Cropper, and only Cropper. Cropper would have to fix her headdress into place, and Cropper would have to brush the final strands covering over the 'mouse' and pin, and pin the fine blond hair again. That May could not, and moreover would not, attempt to do.

Normally the whole procedure of getting bathed and dressed seemed to take only minutes, or at any rate not more than an hour or so, but this evening, with Perkins wibbling about, dropping the button hook, breaking one of the laces on May's brand new health corset, holding up her silk stockings to the light for such an age that it seemed to May at any rate that they might well have faded by the time she laid them out on the ottoman, it seemed to take for ever.

'Perkins.' May stared hard at her hands in a very pointed way, so as not to take in the broken string on the brand new health corset, and instead moved one of her large diamond rings so that it caught the light, first this way and then that. You will find another health corset just where you found the first one, and no need to fret yourself, we still have plenty of time to spare.'

Of course they had nothing of the sort, but it would not help the situation if May pointed this out. It would only make Perkins panic, and the idea of Perkins panicking was even worse than the reality of Perkins thinking she was maintaining her standards as well as Cropper.

Once more May sighed inwardly, a heartfelt sigh that was even heavier than the first. She felt really very virtuous, if not saintly, for to lend one's maid on the night of one's ball to a poor Irish girl who tomorrow would have to be told the most dreadful news was, when all was said and done, quite a bit of a sacrifice, even if May did know how to dress herself, which, it had to be faced, not many duchesses did. She only hoped that when she saw Miss Edith, fresh from Cropper's expert hands, they would all consider her little act of unselfishness entirely worthwhile.

'No, Perkins, I said the health corset. That is not a health corset, in fact it is not even a corset, it is a – it is one of my oldest – no, do not fuss yourself. Possibly better if I lay everything out for myself, and you just stand behind me when I dress and try hard not to break the strings on this new health corset this time. No. The button hook, it turns this way, do you see? If you turn it that way you will wrench off the button.' As Perkins did so, May half closed her eyes.

'Oh dear, Your Grace, I really am ever so sorry.'

'Yes, well, never mind. No, never mind, no really, please. It does not matter, please do not cry, Perkins, really. It is only a button on a boot. I am not wearing boots under my ball gown, I do assure you.' May held up her evening shoes. 'See? And there is no need to button them. The hook was for— I tell you what, once I am in my underpinnings why do we not wait for Cropper, and she can finish me off? No, please, do not fret yourself. You have poured the water in the bath really very nicely, no really. No, the temperature is perfectly fine, really. I like it on the cold side before a ball. One does not want to open a ball flush-faced, does one? Gives one quite the wrong air, I always think.'

May scrubbed herself vigorously, watched by the far from estimable Perkins who now stood right down the other end of the room holding out a towel, as if she expected Her Grace to leap out of the bath like a gazelle and run down the room to snatch it from her trembling hands.

Having rinsed herself, May stood up, climbed out of the bath, and held out her arms, her lips now chattering from the cold.

'It is quite safe to bring the towel now, Perkins, if you would.' Perkins hesitated. Finally, closing her eyes and giving vent to her frustration May barked, 'Now!'

Perkins ran to her, towel at the ready.

'Good. Now, Perkins, run to the curling tongs and start to heat them. Cropper will be here any minute and she will be wondering what on earth I am doing still in my birthday suit.'

As soon as Cropper arrived and saw Her Grace still in her underpinnings, Perkins behind her lacing her so slowly that Cropper could tell at once from Her Grace's face that she was about to explode, she said, 'Very well, Perkins, thank you, you may go.'

Perkins went to the door, her feet trailing. Cropper gave the tweeny's back the briefest of looks, and then she too barked, 'Now!'

Cropper looked at Her Grace. Cropper's nimble fingers had Her Grace tightly laced by the time the door was shut, and they both started to laugh.

'I had to pretend to be you, Cropper,' May confided. 'It was the only way. I had to fairly bark at Perkins finally, and then she did manage to hurry up, just a little.'

'Lordy, Your Grace, Perkins is about as much use to herself, or anyone else for that matter, as a piece of burned suet. Dear oh dear. I only took her on here for the sake of her poor mother who was near to killing her with a carving knife, and that is the truth.'

'Perhaps we should take her back to the country with us?'

'Yes, Your Grace, and perhaps not. Perkins is the sort that would faint at the sight of a cow.'

'Oh, well. Now tell me – how is Miss Edith?'

There was a pause as Cropper held the curling tongs up to her face to feel the temperature, and then put them away from her, and then took them up again, and then away again, until finally her upper lip told her what she wanted to know, that they were quite ready for her ladyship's hair.

'I think Your Grace will be satisfied. I have sat her on a travelling rug in the middle of her room and told her not to move until I come back. She is to stay as still as a dead leaf until you have seen her.'

'Of course, in that gown, it is truly difficult to sit, isn't it?'

'Oh, don't worry, Your Grace, I arranged her dress all around her. It is magnificent. What a bit of luck, Your Grace, to find that, just when you wanted something so quick. That is luck when you need it, it truly is.'

Finally, in half the time that it had taken Perkins to break the strings on the health corset and fill the bath with tepid water, not to mention rip a button off one of May's kid walking boots, Cropper had the Duchess ready for her ball.

The dress was heavily draped at the top, swathed with lace, the sleeves covering the upper arms draped and caught at intervals so that they looked like part of the top. Caught up under the bust and falling from it was a long silken cord ending with a tassel, and under the high bust the dress was very fitted, in contrast to the sleeves and top. From there it fell in silken folds over the hips, becoming elaborate – a swirling skirt which when the wearer was walking could also be seen to have a train at the back.

All in all, and in pale yellow, it was both feminine and dramatic.

'The tiara is so heavy, I always forget,' May murmured, 'just how heavy diamonds can be.'

'Your Grace has never looked lovelier.'

Cropper always said that. It was part of a ritual, and it was most kind, but it was a little like *madame est servi!* coming from a French housekeeper; it was customary, and had nothing to do with how May was actually looking. Even so, it was nice.

'Lead the way to the debutante, Cropper,' May commanded, very much the duchess. 'She is meant to be the Empress Eugénie, and I am meant to be the Empress Josephine, so we shall surely be quite a powerful duo!'

'Yes, Your Grace. I will walk ahead of you, i

you don't mind. Make sure she's not been up to mischief in my absence.'

Cropper hurried on ahead to Edith's suite, so that by the time May arrived she had her charge standing up beautifully straight, the diamond stars in her hair showing up the auburn lights, and her dress spread out behind her. Her gloved hands held a fan, naturally, and Cropper had tied her dance card to her wrist, ready for the ball.

May, having been all too flustered by her own preparations, was half dreading what she should see. After all, it was quite possible that the dress she had found for Edith to wear was unsuitable, or unflattering, so she was far from expecting what she was presented with when she rounded the corner of the double doors leading into her house guest's rooms.

It would have been difficult for a more phlegmatic character than May not to have smiled with delight when she saw Miss Edith O'Connor that night. Possibly Mr Sargent's skill with brushes and paint on canvas could do justice to the glow of her dark hair, to the creamy skin set off by the beautiful materials. The diamonds in her hair looked so thoroughly at home that had she not possessed such fine eyes the onlooker might have gazed at the stars in her hair rather than those in her eyes. She looked beautiful, and she knew it.

'Come, my dear,' May told her. 'Follow me down to the drawing room where the gentlemen are waiting for us.'

Edith, although well schooled by now in the art

of entering a drawing room in evening dress, found her heart beating excitedly. She had never felt so pretty, or so warmed. She had never received such attentions, such generosity. Her mama was kind enough, and Minnie the same, but they had never taken such trouble over her, or encouraged her to think of herself as in any way a beauty, in fact far from it. Her mama had encouraged her to make the best of herself, but the underlying message was always that she would never be the beauty her mother was and so making the best of herself was all she could do.

And yet here she was now, following the Duchess of Wokingham down the grand marble staircase of Wokingham House and through the series of great double doors to be greeted by the Duke and his son.

In the drawing room, George was feeling more relaxed than he had ever done in London. Frear had made him understand, once and for all, just how important London and the Season really were; how one could make a cracking ass of oneself if one did not listen to one's mother. One did not have to go round saying "too, too" or anything of that nature, but one did have to come up for the Season. It was just one of those things. Never mind the Park was dull and full of the kinds of girls that either bored him or frightened him to death, it had to be done. Never mind that he was going to have to lead out this ugly duckling from Ireland, he would do it. From now on, thanks to Frear, he would do it, and do his best to do it properly.

'Ah, George. John, dearest. I do not think either of you have met Miss Edith O'Connor, have you?'

The Duke and his son turned polite eyes towards the Duchess and her young house guest. George's jaw dropped when he saw the ugly duckling from Ireland. In fact, May was only too happy to see, not only did his jaw drop at the sight of Miss Edith O'Connor in her sumptuous dress with diamond stars in her hair, but his eyes took on the stare of someone who has just been struck by lightning.

With proper humour May introduced them.

'Oberon, King of the Fairies, meet the Empress Eugénie.'

Edith dropped into a full and beautiful curtsy, a curtsy of which poor Lady Devenish would have been immensely proud and approving. The two men bowed. They all stared for a second or two, not Edith of course, but May at the men and the men at Edith.

'I say, George, you had better put your name in Miss O'Connor's card while you can. There will not be a space anywhere as soon as the other guests arrive,' his father murmured, smiling approvingly. He did not like coming to London either, but when he saw his wife in her tiara and young gels like Miss Edith looking as fresh and beautiful as a bunch of flowers, well, there was no doubt about it, the journey did seem worthwhile.

'Miss O'Connor – or rather I should say Empress – would you mind leading off the dance with me, after the King and Queen and the parents, that is? Would you mind awfully?'

Edith smiled and George saw with gratitude that she had really pretty small white teeth.

'Would you like to write your name, Your Majesty?'

George bent his dark head. She had such a pretty voice! Just a little Irish lilt to it, and nothing wrong with that. He wrote CORDREY and then in brackets Oberon beside the first dance, and then quickly, a few numbers later, he wrote CORDREY again. Only two dances allowed, and to ask for that was, they both knew, just a little shocking!

If anyone had told George this morning, when he was down in the dumps and thinking that only Misty was going to give him any pleasure while in wretched London, that he would have been walking on air by dinner time, he would not have believed them.

'May I take you in to dinner, too, Miss O'Connor? Please say I may?'

'No, George, you may not,' his mother instructed him, overhearing. 'I am sorry to tell you but you are to take the Countess of Evesham in to dinner.'

George groaned under his breath, and Edith smiled at him.

She was saying nothing more. She did not have to. For the first time in her life she knew that she was looking beautiful. She did not have to glance in the old silver-backed mirrors that were placed around the damask-walled room for confirmation, she had only to look into the Marquis of Cordrey's blue eyes.

May smiled at John and he smiled back at his wife, for they had both noticed the moment.

'Well, well,' said her husband. 'You certainly have transformed your ugly duckling, my dearest heart.'

'Had I told George that she was a beauty he would have gone quite the other way,' May said, laughing and fanning herself as they went to the top of the room to prepare to greet their guests, whose carriages they could hear even now arriving as the flunkeys in the great hall below flung open the doors. 'But telling him she was plain and unfortunate and making sure she was far from it when I brought her up to you, well, was it not better, after all?'

'You are perfect,' sighed John. 'But then I always knew that. The first time I saw you, I said you were perfect, and that was from the other side of the footlights too. Good eye for a horse, good eye for a girl, it runs in the family, I always think.'

May forbore to say that something must have gone sadly wrong with his father, in the light of the old duchess, but instead said, 'I think that Stilley Street will be beckoning very soon, do you not, John? I have that feeling. And if it does, will they have your approval?'

'If she is as good as she is beautiful, which I am sure, knowing you, that she is, why not? There is good blood there, on her mother's side, and a bit of Celtic never did anyone any harm.'

'Precisely my feelings, John . . . Good evening, good evening.'

They began to greet each of their dinner guests, who were now queueing up the stairs, being announced, moving forward slowly and properly.

'Ah, Stilley Street, our bridal suite . . .'

For a second they glanced at each other, between greetings, and then they smiled. Just the sound of that address took them back to those wonderful afternoons of making love, and burning crumpets, and doing all those silly things that lovers rejoice to do, which stay in the mind for ever.

'It's all ahead of them . . .'

The Duke was dressed as one of his ancestors, very handsome in a white wig and white stockings, and an old velvet gold-embroidered jacket with frothing lace under his chin and at his wrists. He felt very attractive until he sat down and his lace kept getting into the way of his eating.

'Glad fashion has changed,' he told the lady on his right, who happened to be the Queen. 'Can't keep the lace out of me hors d'oeuvres.'

Lower down the table Daisy was having a fine time seated between George and young Captain Barrymore. She knew, regretfully, that it was her duty to charm Captain Barrymore, but no more, and that being so she charmed him most effectively, right through dinner, and into the ballroom. In fact Daisy charmed both young men until, despite her being of an age to have given birth to both of them, they finally parted from her in the ballroom with vague feelings of regret. When an older woman sets out to charm a younger man, he tends to stay charmed, but when Daisy set out to charm a younger man he tended to stay mesmerised.

'I only wish that I could open the ball with you,' George told her, not meaning it, since he was well aware that he was promised to Miss O'Connor, and yet meaning it too, because being with Daisy made him feel a hundred times more confident than being with someone his own age.

'You do not at all,' Daisy told him. 'Besides, I am, as always, promised to the Duke of Connerton.' The expression in her eyes was so grave and at the same time so falsely innocent that George began to laugh. 'I know,' Daisy agreed, and she fanned herself, smiling. 'But there, someone has to take him on!'

To Captain Barrymore Fortescue, whom she hardly knew of course, she said, 'I know just the person who will not be embarrassed by your height, Captain Fortescue.'

This was just a little squashing, but since the young man was so handsome as to be almost incredible, and she knew he was all too full of his own charms, and had a reputation with the ladies, Daisy felt quite safe.

'I had no idea that my height was embarrassing,' the young captain protested.

'But of course you have. Most gels will get a crick in their necks just looking at you, or trying to look at you. You are far too tall, and that being so

I will have to find you a gel who will not mind your being such a beanpole. Really, Captain, you are not so much a dancing partner as a liability, particularly now that you are dressed as the Prince Regent. In those tall heels I want to become a woodsman and cut you down.' Daisy saw with satisfaction that, of a sudden, the young captain looked just that, very much a young captain, so she turned, and catching sight of her soon to be former protégée, Miss Sarah Hartley Lambert, she beckoned her over.

'Miss Hartley Lambert, allow me to introduce Captain Barrymore Fortescue to you. Thanks to his costume and his high-heeled shoes the poor fellow, as you can see, Miss Hartley Lambert, has quite outgrown himself, but I know you will allow him to put his name in your card for the first waltz.'

Daisy gazed from one to the other of these two impossibly tall people with such a sense of relief that she felt quite faint, and she was suddenly glad that she was not to chaperon anyone ever again. It was really too much, and not worth the candle – worth nothing at all, finally, because even when you brought about a successful match, just as in Shakespeare, everyone thought it was really of their own volition, and no-one was grateful, and if you failed, well, everyone was set against you for the rest of their lives. So, no, she was all too thankful to be stopping.

And when, a few minutes later, she was led on to the floor by the Duke of Connerton, she could not wait for her dancing days to be over too. But, and here was the joy, with her last Season in sight, with the door closing on her reign as a great personality of her day, with retirement from all giddy nonsense hovering on the horizon, she had at last, with one last and final flourish, found Miss Hartley Lambert someone who did not make her feel as if she were a lamp post.

The King was leading the Duchess onto the floor, the Duke was leading out the Queen, and the orchestra was beginning a stately and beautiful waltz. Soon it would all be over for her, but not, she hoped, for all these beautiful young people. Not for George, now dancing with Edith O'Connor, not for Phyllis dancing with Edwin Vessey, not for any of these golden couples circling to what seemed to Daisy to be a heart-breakingly slow waltz, as if – well, as if it were not just her last waltz, but theirs too.

Daisy turned away from the thought. She would have none of that, and besides, the Duke of Connerton was treading on her foot, and it was difficult to be sad when someone had just landed right in the middle of one of one's best silver-embroidered shoes.

She looked down at her foot as they both paused. She had last worn these slippers for just such a ball, and someone had done exactly the same thing, trodden right in the middle of one of them. She started to waltz again, and then she started to laugh.

'My dear, I am so sorry.'

'I know, Dukey, I know, but you need not be, I assure you.' She continued to laugh. 'You know how it is! I suddenly remembered that the last person who trod on one of these shoes was you – at a costume ball in 1899!'

The Duke smiled. He never laughed, but he did love Daisy, always had.

Meanwhile Sarah was saying to Captain Barrymore Fortescue, tongue in cheek, 'I am so glad to only have one dance with you, Captain Fortescue.'

He was shocked, she could see that, and stared down at her with mixed feelings while she laughed and waved her fan about her face, mocking his embarrassment, knowing him for what he was, a ladies' man and a rogue.

'Why would you be so glad, Miss Hartley Lambert? I must confess to being hurt at the very idea.'

'I am glad because you have such a very bad reputation, Captain. Being American, I only like tall, upstanding young men, preferably with Puritan ancestors who sailed to the New World on the *Mayflower*.'

Sarah was being partly ironical, and partly truthful. She had heard all about Captain Barrymore Fortescue from Corkie, her maid. She knew, as most people did apparently, all about his affair with Edith's mother, and she wanted none of him, as a consequence of which, she could appreciate at once, he was instantaneously interested in her, as was always the way with a ladies' man.

'Miss Hartley Lambert, I know I am not what I should be, that I have not been as I should have been, but I do assure you that the events of the past weeks have brought me to my knees, as it were. I have been badly burned. My feelings for another, whom I imagined I loved, have been quite overturned, and I realise now what a cracking ass I made of myself, and how conceited and foolish I was to think that I could – well, suffice it to say that I have vowed to turn over a new leaf, and try to become the kind of person who, if not exactly the kind of Puritan to which you refer will be as near as dammit – sorry, as near as possible – a better person. I want to be good now, I know. For the first time I have had my heart broken, and I would hate that to ever happen again. I have come very near to causing terrible hurt. Too near.'

Sarah nodded, not believing him but enjoying the pain in his eyes. He had behaved disgracefully, and the whole of London knew it.

'You are a good dancer,' she conceded. 'That at least is something.'

'When I am with someone with such kind eyes as yours I want to be good at everything, not just dancing. Why have I not met you before?'

Sarah laughed. 'I dare say if you had met me before your fascination with a certain person has been such that you would not have noticed me anyway, Captain Fortescue, and you are holding me too tight. It is not correct.'

'I am sorry. I did not mean to.' He released his

grip a little, but his eyes remained on Sarah's face, and then he said, looking suddenly less contrite and a good deal more himself, 'I say, Miss Hartley Lambert, you dance like a dream. Will you let me teach you the tango?'

Sarah stared up at him. The tango? This was fast talk indeed.

'I very much doubt it.'

'Very well, marry me then, and I will teach you the tango and no-one could stop us, just imagine! You are perfect for modern dancing.'

'From what I have heard you do need to be married to do the tango,' Sarah admitted ruefully.

They both laughed, and for a second their eyes met in an unspoken conspiracy. A whole vista had suddenly opened up to them both, a married world where they could both tango, or Bunny Hug, or – well, anything, and no-one could stop them.

'If we were married,' Barrymore went on, dreamily, 'we could have our own private tango club, and telephones in every room, and fast cars outside the front door, imagine?'

'Is that how you see marriage, Captain?'

'Don't you, Miss Hartley Lambert?'

Sarah stared up at him. It was suddenly mesmerising, the thought of marriage being fun. It had never occurred to her that marriage could be fun, or that people who were married did have fun. She had thought of marriage as dull and confusing, and having to put up with much that you would not tolerate in any other state, but she had never before thought that it might be amusing.

'If you married me we would have a house filled with laughter, and life would be one long tango, I promise you that, Miss Hartley Lambert.'

'Our children would be too tall,' Sarah told him, impulsively, and then, realising that she had said too much, she looked away, colouring. It was her turn to be embarrassed. 'Although I believe the Countess told my mother that in England the nurses give the babies gin to keep them small, so that would take care of that problem,' she went on gamely.

The waltz came to an end, but it was difficult for either of them to bow or curtsy, they were laughing so much. As far as ballroom conventions were concerned they had both gone too far and they knew it, but they had also become united in humour, conspirators, a little naughty, set against the rest of the world. He leaned forward and scribbled his name once more in her card, and underneath in tiny letters he wrote *Tango, tango, tango with me!*

Sarah turned away from him. Neither her mother, nor the Countess, nor the all-important Corkie would approve of him as a choice, surely? Sarah started to dance once more, this time with the poor old Duke of Connerton, and she glanced sideways to her former partner who was waltzing past her with Miss O'Connor. Seeing him with another girl in his arms Sarah felt a stab of jealousy, which vanished quickly as he passed her murmuring, 'Takes two to tango, particularly if the orchestra is playing a waltz.'

Sarah pretended not to hear, but because he was so much taller than Edith O'Connor and she was so much taller than the Duke, she was quite able to see his mischievous expression, and that was what stayed in her mind long after the ball was over and she went home. It was his droll expression and the memory of their laughter that kept her awake half the night, so that when Corkie woke her as usual with her cup of hot chocolate she said to her young mistress, 'My, you look as if you have been awake all night, Miss Sarah. I'll have to put tea leaves under your eyes.'

Of a sudden Sarah realised that tea leaves were not going to be a cure for the particular ailment from which she now knew herself to be suffering.

Old Friends

Herbert had come to London, or at least to Kensington, for no other reason than to escape the loneliness of York. The more people stopped him to commiserate, the more people avoided his eyes when he alighted from his motor car, or a hansom cab, the more his loneliness seen through their eyes became etched in black for the sufferer.

His echoing footsteps around his house seemed to say, 'You are alone, you are alone.' The servants looked at him, particularly the female servants, as if they expected him to grow horns and a tail. Being a man, their eyes said, he would not know how they felt; being a man, their eyes went on, he would not know how to put menus together, or talk to Cook, or cast an eye around a room and know immediately what was needed, dusting or sweeping, tidying or flowers. And it was true, being a man, he now felt as helpless as a baby. For thirty-five years he and Jane had gone their separate ways, knowing that each bore the other's burden in a very different manner. His was business and the making of their fortunes, hers the care of their daughter and their home. It had been satisfactory all round, and both, in their very different ways, had appreciated each other, had known, without any doubt at all, they could be *counted on*.

That was what he now missed, someone whom he could count on, someone whom he could turn to knowing that she would be only a step or two behind him, knowing that she would listen, that she would care how he felt, above all that she would tolerate his moods. For to feel grumpy on your own, to feel sad on your own, to think about the problems of the world on your own, was about as interesting or amusing as eating and drinking on your own.

'That is good!'

He found himself turning every now and then to try to catch one of the servants' eyes when he took his luncheon or his dinner. Or, alone in his club, he found himself looking around at the other tables, lamely trying to catch the eye of another luncher or diner, failing, more often than not, and in failure being left to feel a fool. So all in all, Herbert alighted outside the two houses he had bought but as yet not seen with as light a heart as was possible in the circumstances. Here at least there was no possible chance of anyone's either looking away or crossing the street when they saw him, or stepping back, which was often worse, to commiserate with him. Here he was just another sombrely dressed businessman with a black band on his arm, just another north countryman who had bought two houses, one of which he proposed to live in.

'Mr Forrester?'

A sprucely dressed gentleman was waiting for him on the top step of the large house. Looking up at him, and at the two houses, Herbert was glad to see that the agent for the family who had sold him the property did at least look respectable, which was not always the case with the agents of these old families. He was relieved to see, too, that the façade of both houses was broad, and not just substantial; they were, to all intents and purposes, imposing. And there was only a spread of about six or eight of them in the whole road, which meant that when he stepped inside the hall of the first the general air was one of importance and comfort. Of course they were not grand, like Medlar House, and they were not two spits from Piccadilly either. They were not in Mayfair at all, but they were well built, with porticoes and suchlike, probably only fifty years old, but good and solid for all that, and although there was no fancy plasterwork there were good mouldings and high ceilings, and when he followed the agent upstairs he was pleased to note that the stairs were shallow and the staircase broad, as were the landings. Nice broad landings with good deep architraves to the doors, and the first floor drawing rooms, while not embellished with gold and panelling, were gracious rooms with good big fireplaces, and they ran from back to front of the house and had sets of four windows which looked out towards Kensington Gardens.

'I like these houses. No need to show me the one next door, I gather it is just the same as this, is it not?'

Herbert lit a cigar, such was the relief he was feeling at discovering that, despite buying from a distance, he had bought some good, even quite respectable property.

'Are we quite sure that we do not want to see next door as well?'

'Well, we are rather,' said Herbert, smiling suddenly at the dapper little man standing to the side of him. He was smiling for the first time for weeks, and he went on smiling thinking of how Jane, were she with him, would laugh with him afterwards and possibly mimic the man: *Are we sure that we do not want to see next door?* He could hear her laughing and doing a bad imitation of a southern accent. 'There is no point, you see. I will see the builders in the morning and let them work out what is to be done. Meanwhile I am off to my hotel, and you back to your office, no doubt?'

'We do not have an office. We have chambers. We are acting as agents, but we are in fact lawyers. I am a junior partner.'

'Well,' said Herbert dryly, 'please do not let us stop us returning to our chambers, shall we?' He waited, fingering the innumerable sets of keys that he had just been handed, until the man reached the door, and then he said, pulling on his cigar, 'Just as well I liked them, the houses, that is, would you not say? Just as well I liked them, eh?'

The man nodded briefly, and with a last disapproving look at Herbert's cigar, which was meant to give Herbert to understand that he was of the old school and did not approve of cigars outside the smoking room, he was gone, leaving Herbert to wander freely around the house. His house.

It was a queer feeling, and despite his undoubted state of grief, an exciting one. To be all alone in an unfamiliar house was always odd, and left you with a feeling of trespass, even when you knew that the house in which you were tiptoeing was in fact your own.

Walking slowly, his echoing footsteps giving him a feeling of excitement, Herbert started to explore the house, marking out in his mind, and making notes, at last, on his second tour, as to which rooms he would use for what.

Obviously the first floor would be the drawing room, and there would have to be a small dining area, and a butler's pantry for when he dined alone, for he wanted no more of sitting at the head of a large piece of mahogany and staring down at an empty place. And then above would be his bedroom and bathroom and dressing room. He could take out some walls to make the whole of that floor his own, make it spacious and masculine. He would buy large mahogany furniture, wardrobes and chests of drawers. He had seen all manner of pieces in various catalogues, some of them really quite innovative. Pieces that Jane would have looked at and then firmly shaken her head.

'Too Artsy and Craftsy for me, our Herbert, too much silver inlay. And those large corner decorations, vulgar, I call those, and expensive too.'

Now, all alone, Herbert thought, looking around as if someone could hear his ruminations, he would experiment with his own taste for the first time in his life. He would probably end up with a nightmare interior, but, at all events, he would at least have had some fun.

And suddenly it came to him that despite everything he had done in his life, he had never had the opportunity to become *mad*, as in mad as May butter, or mad as a hatter, or just lunatic. No, he had always been sensible and reliable. He had never changed his style of dress, never worn something like a straw hat with jodhpurs. As a matter of fact he had never worn jodhpurs. He could not ride. He might ride. He might ride every day in Rotten Row, or he might learn to drive a team of horses, too fast, from London to Newmarket, or from Newmarket to London.

Having reached the top of the house he sat down suddenly on one of the broad window sills. The room in which he sat had obviously been, and would be again, a maid's room. Except – he pulled on his cigar once more – except he did not think he wanted to employ maids any more.

No, he suddenly realised, he did not really like employing maids. He would employ only *male* servants. They were easier to deal with, less likely to carry criticism in their eyes, or give you back chat, silently, as maids seemed so adept at doing.

And there would be no nonsense either with male guests, which, he had understood from Jane, could be such a nuisance to deal with, always having to send in the old and the ugly, in case there was hanky panky on offer.

All these thoughts, some of which he would act upon, and others which he quite obviously would not, brightened Herbert, as new thoughts do, bringing with them a feeling that his future had been repainted in stronger colours. He descended to the hall once more, resolved to keep looking ahead, just kicking on, not looking to either side, and above all not looking back.

The builders he called upon the next morning were a well-established firm, owned by an old friend, and so Mr Forrester was greeted with some warmth. Herbert knew very well that his friend would have been sure to tell the builder that Herbert Forrester was a rich man, and that if he called the builder must pay attention to him, make a fuss of him, allow him his head.

Once inside the man's office Herbert lit his first cigar of the morning, knowing that he would not be asked to go outside; he was the customer, after all. But Mr Blundell did not turn a hair, but looked appreciatively on as if he *expected* persons like Herbert Forrester to light cigars and smoke them whenever they wished, which gave Herbert the feeling that he was really going to like this fellow, that he was what Herbert called a *goodly* fellow.

'To begin with, Mr Blundell, and I hope this will

not upset you, I must tell you I am a man of no taste.' As Blundell smiled and looked disbelieving, he continued, 'No, really, I have no taste at all. That is the bad thing. The good thing is I do at least know it, and let us face it, Mr Blundell, that *is* a good thing, is it not? For I bet you a dime to a dollar, as the Americans say, that most of your clients think that they have taste at least as good as Mr Lutyens's, and will not take advice on any point.'

At this Mr Blundell did not smile, so Herbert knew at once that he had hit the nail on the head.

'I used to know persons of fashion, at a certain point of my life, but quite briefly, as you may imagine,' Herbert continued. 'After all, I am not really the type to be taken up, except for a few seconds, by respectable and fashionable people.' Blundell attempted to look disbelieving again, but Herbert went on, 'But there was one thing I really admired about them. Most of them were like me, they knew that they had no taste. They knew that if they wanted their houses to look like anything better than bedlam they should invite someone of taste to help them. Last night, when I walked round the property I have just bought in Kensington, I had a mind to do it all myself. I could see it all as I thought it ought to be. And then, as I say, I thought back to the days when I mixed, albeit briefly, with persons of fashion, and I realised I could make a blunder. Worse, I could throw good money after bad and the whole thing would still be a disaster. So, reluctantly, I realised that I needed someone to help me with my decorations, widower that I am now, Mr Blundell. Are you that person, do you think?'

Mr Blundell shook his head. 'Oh, no, Mr Forrester. I would never see fit to advise others on their choices of interiors. I am a builder. I will help you make your house warm and comfortable and take orders for whatever you wish, but I would never help another choose. It would be presumptuous.'

Herbert pulled on his cigar. 'This is very good news, Mr Blundell. In fact this is the best news I have heard in a long time. You see, my question, as you doubtless realised, or maybe you did not, was a trap. Should you have said yes I would have known you for a greedy wretch who would stop at nothing to make a shilling, but by saying no you have shown yourself to be an honest fellow who, like me, knows his limitations. Now, I must hurry, because I have an appointment back at my house, with just such a person as I need. A person of taste, Mr Blundell. An old friend, as a matter of fact, the Duchess of Wokingham. I gather from the Society columns that it was her ball last night in London. A great grand affair, a costume ball – so much the rage now, as I understand it – but not for the likes of me or you, I am afraid, Mr Blundell.'

It was only as Herbert turned at the door, as Blundell was opening it for him, and shook the man's hand that he realised that he had thrown the poor fellow into a dreadful muddle, first declaring himself to be ignorant and unfashionable, and seconds later hurrying off to meet a duchess.

'Oh well,' Herbert thought to himself as he stepped quickly into a hansom cab, and the horse in his turn stepped on it, 'there is nothing to be done about anything, really, and if we are all understandable, and everyone knows what we are, then there is no excitement to life.'

Excitement that was what he wanted, what he needed, to take the edge off his sorrow, excitement and change of circumstances. And perhaps he would not have to go to the South Sea islands to find it after all.

The ball had been such a success that May could hardly believe the flowers that were arriving in the hall below. There had been something special about it this year, some feeling that they must all enjoy these dear days of summer, now, before it was too late. She had felt it, and in some strange way she could sense that everyone else had felt it too. There were nightingales singing in the trees as the guests arrived, there were candles glowing and flunkeys running, the gold on their uniforms catching the light of the flares in the courtyard and the sound of the murmur of the guests as they had waited to go up the stairs, but it had all been somehow different, this year, with less of a sense of a ritual, more of a sense of clinging on to the present before the future arrived.

Royalty had been present and led off the ball which had been a triumph of jewels and costumes. The papers had written of the thousands spent on jewelled designs from the past, but most important of all, more important than anything else in the whole world, George had fallen in love. And Edith had fallen in love, and their second dance together might have been an assignation in the conservatory so apparent had been their attraction.

Cropper had done really very well by the young gel. Not even May, who was used to Cropper's genius at transformation, would have recognised in Edith, with her shining hair, her tiny waist, above all her glowing look, the really rather sad creature that had first come to see May to talk about her mother. Gone was the awkwardness that so often characterised those that had been told they were not beautiful, gone the feeling that she was an 'also ran', a 'no hoper' someone who was just marking time until she could return to Ireland and her horses and dogs, and in their place had arrived an undoubted beauty. Very well, her profile would never be classical, but frankly May thought a tip-tilted nose was really very appealing, and of course her eyes were quite magnificent, and they, more than the nose, would always be a woman's centrepiece.

Thinking on all this May made a note to make sure some of the flowers that were arriving found their way not to hospitals but to Cropper's room. Not that she would appreciate them, Cropper did not appreciate flowers in bedrooms, but she would enjoy the compliment.

'Harper!' May called for her travelling maid.

'Harper! Lay out my new blue coat and skirt with the matching hat and ostrich plumes, would you, please?'

'Yes, Your Grace.'

'We are going to Kensington this morning, Harper. That will be an adventure for you, will it not?'

'Kensington?' Harper's jaw dropped down to her lace-up black shoes. 'Whatever for? Why should we be going to Kensington, Your Grace?'

'I have to see an old friend, Harper. He is alas now a widower, and it is very sad indeed, so I have to go and see him. He is my godfather, of sorts.'

'But Kensington, Your Grace! I mean to say, I have a cousin who lives in Kensington!'

'I dare say, Harper. That does not mean that persons such as myself cannot visit, does it?'

'Well, no, Your Grace, of course not. She is a very nice lady, now you ask, which you did not, but – does Cropper know of this?'

'Cropper? No, Harper, Cropper does not know of this, and nor should she. It would not do to shock Cropper too much, after the success of the ball. And she will no doubt be having her hands full, very soon.'

May smiled to herself as she waited for Harper to lay out her clothes. Very soon, she imagined, Cropper would be dancing attendance on young Edith, dressing her hair for a Westminster wedding.

'I should imagine that Your Grace will not be

wanting to take the carriage to Kensington? Make too much display, would it not, Your Grace?'

May thought for a second. 'No, we will take a hansom cab. I say, Harps, what an adventure!' May gave a girlish laugh. 'I have not taken a hansom cab for such a while.'

'And no more have I,' said Harper, with some feeling. 'I hope I like it.'

May sighed. There was Harper, at it again, me, me, me, and nothing else but me.

'I was sick once in a hansom, Your Grace.'

Quite honestly, May thought to herself, if Harper had not been a dresser in the theatre, if she had not been her personal maid at the Gaiety and all that, she could never have tolerated her. As it was she had to, and as it was, Harper would have to tolerate May, hansom and all.

'You dare be sick in the hansom, Harper, and I will drop the curtain on you for ever.'

'Yes, Your Grace.'

Looking down from his sparsely furnished first floor drawing room Herbert was delighted to spot a hansom cab drawing up. This would be his May all over, no clattering out to Kensington in a blooming great family coach with four horses drawing it, but a discreet hansom drawing up outside his house. She would have known, May would, that it would draw too much attention to Herbert's new house if a great coach with the family coat of arms drew up outside, and he hardly moved in except for a few sticks of furniture that had been in store on the other side of the river, and a bed of course.

'Jepson!' Herbert called down to his manservant, also newly arrived from York. 'Jepson, to the front door, please. The Duchess is here.'

The door opened before she could ring the bell. May smiled. 'Good morning, Jepson. Good to see you in London, I am sure. Stay here, Harper.' May nodded at a small hall chair. 'Stay here and keep an eye on' – with a look around the bare hall and a laugh – 'on nothing at all!'

They all laughed at this.

Jepson, who had been Herbert's manservant since he was knee high to a grasshopper, had known May since she was far from being a duchess. Now they looked at each other afresh, taking in the changes in hair and faces since last seen.

'Lead the way, Jepson,' the Duchess told him. 'Lead the way to dear Mr Forrester.'

Up the stairs she fairly sprang after Jepson, in as good and happy a mood as she had ever been, and only just remembering in time, as she reached the turn of the stairs, that poor Herbert Forrester was in mourning, and any unseemly display of joy and merriment would be quite out of place.

'May.' Herbert bent over her hand. 'Thank you for your condolence letter. Brief and to the point, and not bringing in your own losses, whatever they may have been, which so many condolence letters see fit to do. *I well remember the day my poor mother was taken from us* . . . Oh, dear, as if a person in mourning wants to hear about someone else's loss! Why, to look at a pile of condolence letters you would honestly think that the whole world was dead.'

They both laughed, and May was relieved that Herbert could be so very honest, for she could not help also feeling inwardly shocked at the sad and much aged appearance of her dear old friend.

Not wanting to dwell on the changes in him, May turned quickly on her heel and walked off down the room, exclaiming at the pretty proportions and wondering what Herbert might make of it, for, as she well knew from Jane, Herbert had always left 'that sort of thing' to his much loved wife.

'My, but what a pretty room this is.'

'I know, May. As a matter of fact, as I expect you appreciate, this is a very pretty house. They are both pretty houses, but, May, what am I, a poor widower, with only money and no taste, to do with them? If I call in someone to help me whom I do not know, it will be murder. And after I thought about it last night I realised I will be sure to choose the wrong person, someone with no taste, who will want to put Japanese prints and peacock feathers everywhere. Which is why I called you in, young May. To help out your poor old Herbert Forrester . . .'

May smiled at that. Herbert was a wise old thing; he knew that duchess though she was May still loved being called 'young May'. It took them both back to that wonderful day when Mr Herbert

Forrester arrived up in the convent and May was brought into the nuns' parlour and everyone could see that this young and beautiful girl – thank heavens that she had been beautiful – was going to be rescued by the rich and affable Mr Forrester.

'I thought you wrote to me because you wanted to see your old friend.'

'I wanted you to *help* your old friend. I have the cheque book and you have the taste, I should have thought. Oh, May, I have gone too far, haven't I? Why did I buy two houses?'

'For a very good reason.' May put her head to one side.

'Which is?'

'Something that will make itself known to us in due course, I dare say. So, one is to sell, and one is to keep. Needs must make them very different then, dear old friend.'

'Oh, yes. I should like to sell the one next door, as you may imagine, to someone convivial, someone who will enjoy proximity, but not prove to be inquisitive and a nuisance. And while I am on this subject, May, now I am a widower I find I am fed to the teeth, if you will forgive the expression, with nosey young maids staring at my plate to see if I have "finished up", or creeping down the corridors in front of me waving feather dusters the moment I appear, or frowning at the smell of my cigars. So, I have been thinking I will only have male servants.'

'Very sensible. They will not have ambitions

which is always good. And you, what are you going to do?'

May turned and faced Herbert, sensing immediately that he had the look of a traveller in his eye.

'I am going to go abroad, to that German spa that is so fashionable, and then on to the South of France, and then back here. I shall be gone only a short time.'

'That is a perfectly splendid idea,' May told him, nodding, although in reality her mind was already far away, as women's minds are liable to be, trotting off towards damasks and cool linens, beautiful mahogany furniture and fine ornaments; everything, in fact, that had to do with the house.

'You are as good as you are beautiful, May love, and I have always said so.'

'Now you go too far,' May murmured. And then, leaning forward, she said, 'Now – I have such exciting news! I do believe that George has fallen in love with my dear friend Emily O'Connor's daughter.'

'Fancy!' Herbert's heart contracted a little. Everyone was in love. The whole world was in love, and he was still in love, but *his* love was not here, or there, but somewhere above him, looking down. Oh, Jane! How much he missed her.

'It is good news, is it not, Mr Forrester?'

'It is perfectly splendid news, perfectly splendid, and we shall all be very happy to dance at their wedding, I am sure. I only wish . . .' He stopped, and looked away.

'The start of the Little Season,' May continued, pretending not to notice the tears in his eyes. 'Yes, I think the Little Season, as some now call it, will be a good time for them to marry. George has not proposed yet, but from the look in his eye it will not be long before he does.'

'Wait until I return from my travels, will you?'

'Why, it would be impossible not to do so!'

Herbert kissed May's gloved hand once more, or at least he bent low over it. 'Very well, Duchess love, so for Herbert it will be the spa and then France, and then back here for an autumn wedding.'

'Exactly so.' This time it was May who leaned forward and kissed her old guardian on the cheek. 'Go tomorrow, but come back as soon as you wish. And do not forget that if you are not happy with my choices, well, we can change it all again.'

Herbert paused. 'I will tell you something, our May, something for which I have a hankering, in which my Jane would never indulge me. I do have a hankering for one of those cupboards from Liberty with the silver adornments, you know? Big square silver decorations on them, they have. I quite fancy one of those.'

May hesitated. She knew precisely the sort of cupboard Herbert was describing; a writer friend of the Wokinghams had just such a one. She would not have chosen it for herself, not in a million years, but when all was said and done it was not her house, and seeing the look of longing in Herbert's eyes, the pressed-against-the-window look of a small boy who is watching a train set in the display but knows that he will never be allowed the toy, she smiled.

'I know just the one! We shall start with that, dear old friend. We shall start with your cupboard and work round it, shall we?'

'Do you think, our May?'

'Oh, I do. We will make a feature of your cupboard.' She turned and looked round the room. 'Here, perhaps?'

'Yes, that would be nice.'

May turned back to her dear Herbert Forrester and for a few satisfying seconds she was quite sure that he had colour in his cheeks, that he looked fuller, and taller, and that at the idea of the cupboard with the great silver squares on it, and the great silver buckles at its centre, his newly stooped shoulders had straightened a little again.

Daisy had enjoyed the Wokingham ball perhaps more than she had enjoyed any ball for many a long Season. There was no doubt but that the Duchess had been very clever to seat her next to Captain Barrymore Fortescue. It was to make clear the fact, obviously, that he was now a reformed character. Indeed, he could talk of nothing but how wretched Lady Emily had made him feel. The fact that he felt safe to do so was, she supposed, really rather flattering, and yet it was annoying too, because really Daisy was never interested in other women, let alone another woman who had charmed this handsome young man.

'Yes, but now you must stop feeling this pain, and open the doors of your heart to someone else,' Daisy ordered him within a very few minutes.

It was absurd, of course. All love affairs now, to Daisy, seemed just a little absurd, all involvements of the heart the same. Yet, staring into the deep, dark brown eyes of the incredibly handsome Captain Barrymore Fortescue, Daisy had started to feel just a trifle sympathetic towards Lady Emily, for all that she had never liked her, even when she was young.

It would have been too easy to entrap him, Daisy realised, staring at the ceiling as Jenkins fussed around her with her hot chocolate – ever a favourite for the Countess in the morning – and murmured some nonsense about a disaster in Ireland, and Lady Emily's house razed to the ground, and so on. (Nothing was truly so surprising when it came to Ireland, really.) Quickly dismissing any idea of pretending shock at the news, Daisy continued to stare up at the ceiling high above.

She was aware of the change that had taken place in her, Daisy, the great beauty, the person for whom people stood on chairs just to catch a glimpse of her beautiful face. The change that had come about in her had everything to do with a kind of growing fatigue, but also a strange contentment, as if, socially, she had fought the good fight, and had now finished her course.

In the old days of course she would have given Captain Barrymore Fortescue to understand that it was perfectly in order for him to call on her for 'tea in the library'. That was how it had always been termed. 'Tea in the library.' And then of course when the ardent young men did call, the servants would all be out, *tout d'un coup*. There would, of a sudden, be only a sleepy afternoon hall boy to let in one of these same ardent young men, and 'tea' would indeed be in the library, and my lady in her tea gown, draping herself, gracefully and discreetly, across a chaise-longue. After some very pleasant diversions between caller and hostess there would indeed be 'tea', but only after an interlude of passionate love-making.

Young male visitors who called at teatime had to earn their eclairs, Daisy was glad to remember.

It had been a perfectly beautiful way of going on, but it was only a way of going on, it was not a way of *life*, as Daisy would always have been the first to admit. Her generation had always understood that 'love' was a diversion, not a marital requirement. Once married a woman could choose her own way of going on, her own pleasures, and her husband, as discreet as herself if he were sensible, would do as she did, and never dream of being around their London house at teatime. It had not been known. Husbands went elsewhere during the Season, to St John's Wood perhaps, or to another address, similar to his own, to have 'tea' with another married woman who needed to be diverted, just like his wife.

In this way the status quo was observed and the

boat never rocked. It was best; and of course it meant that the name continued, because the children were conceived with proper blood lines, and had parents who did not have silly ideas about 'love' but recognised that first they had to do their duty and have children, and only after that could they pleasure themselves, as much or as often as they wished, always providing they did not make a scandal.

Oh, no, it was the best way, by far the best way. Daisy sighed, quite loudly, so that Jenkins looked round suddenly, obviously forgetting that she was meant to be too busy to listen to Daisy.

Now, however, Daisy sensed that there was trouble afoot among the young. It was not just the tango clubs and the skating rinks and all those other shocking elements that had come into play, but that the young nowadays seemed more ardent, much more sincere, less aware of the rules of how to go on, even to think that love and marriage went together, which, it had to be faced, it had never, ever done, at least not for long.

'Jenkins?'

'Yes, my lady?'

'I think I have found the answer to our problem with Miss Hartley Lambert.'

'Yes, my lady. Well, there is often a way out of the knottiest maze if we think of it, my lady. A thin thread that will lead us to a new dawn, a guide from above—'

'Yes, Jenkins,' Daisy snapped, interrupting, for really she had been too late to bed to take too many more of Jenkins's wretched bromides, or old saws, or whatever they were that she was forever spouting. 'The thing is, Jenkins, Captain Barrymore Fortescue, a very handsome younger son of an earl, is going loose, as they say, and I really think he would be just ve thing for Miss Sarah.'

'But Miss Hartley Lambert is about to return to the United States of America, I understand from the grapevine, my lady.'

They both knew what the 'grapevine' was, and also that Jenkins was always the first to hear anything on it, for the simple reason that she had been around long enough to be known as both a source for the usual river of gossip that the Season generated, its sometime tributary and, on a bad day, the mouth that disgorges itself finally into the sea.

'What!'

Daisy sprang out of bed, throwing aside the monogrammed linen sheets with a force that threw up a strange powdery dust into the summer sunshine that was beaming in from under the raised holland blinds.

'Yes, my lady.'

Daisy could swear that Jenkins was almost smiling. As a matter of fact, on their bad days Daisy could *always* imagine Jenkins almost smiling, particularly when Daisy had her head chopped off and held up to the delighted crowd, Jenkins, in Daisy's imagination, would be in the centre of it all, smiling delightedly.

'How do you *know* vis, Jenkins?'

Of a sudden Daisy's huge sacrifice of the previous night, guiding the wretched tall Sarah towards the even taller Captain Barrymore Fortescue, whom she herself could easily have enjoyed before tea in the library any day of the week, was threatening to be of little or no consequence at all. If the wretched Miss Hartley Lambert left for America her sacrifice would all have been for nothing.

'Mrs Hartley Lambert's maid had it from Miss Hartley Lambert's maid. Oh, yes, my lady.' Again the smile threatened as Daisy's face became like thunder. 'Miss Hartley Lambert has told her mother that she has had enough of London and dancing endless waltzes with old men, and yesterday afternoon they ordered their tickets for the return journey. The best suites, of course, on the best liner, and sixteen trunks to be brought down from the attics at once, not to mention fifteen hat boxes, and other portmanteaux—'

'Oh, *fing!*'

Daisy stamped her foot at Jenkins, and they stared at each other. This was bad news indeed, and they both knew it. When Daisy stamped her foot and shouted *fing!* it was bad news to beat the band, almost as bad as when the old king's beringed fingers used to start to tap the table in front of him and he cleared his throat, which meant that he was bored enough to order a lobster tea.

'Very well, Jenkins.' Daisy was pacing. 'Forget the bath, forget everything except some clothes and all the usual.'

All the usual meant curling tongs, corsets, stockings, suspenders, button hooks for boots and gloves, hat – very, very large – a longer jacket, three-quarter, and a skirt with tiny pleats falling just below that same straighter jacket. All a few years older than they should be, but still much more suited to Daisy than any new-fangled hobble skirts or some such, which would make her look just like mutton dressed as poor little lambkins.

'Very well, my lady.'

'And Jenkins, forget the carriage. I will take a hansom. It will be quicker. Oh, and Jenkins. You, of course, will come too.'

'Would not my lady prefer to take Laker?'

'No,' said Daisy, lying down on the bed to be dressed. 'My lady would not prefer to take Laker, absolutely not. My lady is going to take Jenkins.' This time it was Daisy's turn to smile grimly. 'Because Jenkins heard it on the grapevine, did she not, so Jenkins is going to hear some more, but this time from the horse's mouth.'

'Yes, my lady.'

Jenkins started to heat up the curling tongs, and if she had employed a cross word such as *fing!* she would definitely at that moment have expressed it quite loudly.

Fing, fing, fing! Morning was her time of luxury. When my lady was out on her calls, that was time set aside by Jenkins for doing what Jenkins liked, and they both knew it. It was her time for reading my lady's newspaper, and for going to the servants' hall and listening to the newest, or latest, on the grapevine.

It had been May's idea that George should tell poor Edith the news about Glendarvan. Of course Edith had known, from May, of Emily's sudden departure for Ireland, but since she thought that this was to prevent a scandal she had not missed her mother at all. In fact, Emily being such a very strong character, Edith had, and she was too honest not to acknowledge this, been only too relieved that her mother had returned to Ireland without her. Away from her mother, Edith had been able to deceive herself into thinking that she herself was quite changed, and just got on with the business of the ball by pretending that she was a new and altogether different person. It was as if the Wokingham ball was her very first, and, it had to be faced, she had been a success, no-one knowing, as she was led onto the ball-room floor, or at least only slowly realising, that she was in fact the very same Miss Edith O'Connor who had been around since the beginning of the Season.

Now, as Edith went to meet the Duke and his son in the library, she had no idea of the true reason behind the invitation to join them. She knew of course that she was in love, and that she was in all likelihood loved back, unimaginable as it seemed, by someone who was so kind and so shy that Edith could only feel protective towards him.

As she made her way downstairs Edith was not to know that May had thought it best that the bad news from home should be broken to her by someone of her own age. Seeing how very taken George had been with young Edith O'Connor, May had thought too, that such a test for George, with all his shy attitudes, and for Edith who was so unsure of herself, would prove to be a bond between them. After all, if George was to take Edith into his life for ever, if Edith was to surrender herself to George for eternity, there would be no greater proof of George's sensitivity than his breaking the news of the destruction of her beloved family home.

The Duke, while approving of the scheme, had however insisted on being with his son, for father and son were close, and the Duke had sensed that the presence of an older man in the room might also steady Miss O'Connor. He imagined that Edith would not give way while there was another man present, so that the impact of the bad news would be somehow lessened. After all, it was often true that the very fact of having to control oneself, in front of children, or in front of adults, could bring with it a new energy, at the very least a diversion, like exercise on a cold day.

And so that was how Edith heard that Glendarvan, her beloved home, and all her possessions there, had been destroyed, and for no better reason than, as the Duke said gently, 'an act of hatred, no more, my dear. Just an act of senseless hatred by ignorant lunatics, for your father and your family are much loved in that part of the country and we are all well aware of that.'

Edith stared across the room at the two tall, kind Englishmen, not quite able to take in the whole dreadful nature of the news.

'Should I return to Ireland at once?' she asked, her heart sinking at the idea that she might have to leave Wokingham House, where, it suddenly seemed to her, she had started, perhaps for the first time in her life, to find real happiness. 'Will my papa and mama not want me to be with them at this moment?'

Father and son looked at each other, and then at her, and finally the Duke said in his slow, deliberate, shy fashion. 'My dear, you must do as you think fit, of course. But I think your mama expressed the wish that you would stay with us, here at Wokingham House, until such time as she sent for you. They are all to go north at once, to their house at Bangor, and there she will make for you all a new home.'

Edith looked at George. How awkward! She could not but be honest. The feeling of relief at what the Duke had said was immense. She did not want to leave George, or Wokingham House, or the dear Duchess, or even the Duke, one bit. And although she loved Bangor, she could not wish herself at that moment away from George.

The Duke cleared his throat and walked over to the window. He did not want to make things awkward between George and this lovely girl, but really, it had been worth a little distortion of the truth when he saw the look in George's eyes when young Miss Edith O'Connor had come into the room.

He had felt the same, of course, exactly the same as George was feeling at this moment when he first saw his darling May tripping onto the stage singing some silly little number. That had been it for him. He had been destroyed for ever as far as the opposite sex was concerned. Never looked at another woman.

It was obviously a family weakness, falling in love and knowing what you wanted straight away, knowing that the girl in front of you was all you would ever want.

'I feel it might be my duty to go to Mama and help her. On the other hand,' Edith looked across at George, 'if, as the Duke says, Mama expressed a wish that I should stay on in London, and finish the Season, then perhaps that is what I should do?'

'It is as Papa said,' George reiterated, knowing that his father had been over-generous with the truth, for George's sake. 'Lady Emily wanted you to stay on with us and finish your Season, going to Court and all that. And I have to say, you must know, that I wish it too.'

The Duke was still staring, diplomatically, out of the window. Edith would be blushing now, he knew. All young girls blushed when they heard that particular tone in a young man's voice. All passion and commitment, and the voice alone quite obviously infused with love.

'Well, if you think that is what Mama wanted . . .'

'Of course it is. She wanted you to stay here and she wanted my mother to present you at Court.'

The Duke turned at the window and walked back to Edith. He knew from his wife that, thank God, a scandal had only just been prevented, that May's old friend Lady Emily had made a cracking ass of herself over some young captain, unmarried, indiscreet, and totally unsuitable. But now the whole affair was over, thank heavens, the past the past, and no more to be said on the matter.

'Well, if you really think . . .' Edith's voice tailed off. Glendarvan quite gone. Never to see it again The thought was impossible. 'My sister, Valencia?' she added, suddenly.

'Quite well,' the Duke said, almost too quickly 'We heard last night. They are all perfectly fine and moving north.'

They had heard nothing of the sort, and George knew it and his father knew that he knew it because he threw him a quick look.

'Was that wise, Papa?' George asked later, after Edith had gone to her room.

'No, but I think it must be true. After all,' the Duke said drily, 'if it were not true we should surely have heard to the contrary, and at once your mother and Lady Emily being so very intimate.'

George nodded, still staring at the door through which his goddess had just passed. He turned to his father. 'You know, of course, how I feel about that enchanting creature who has just left us, Papa?'

'Yes, dear boy.' The Duke's hand came to rest on his shoulder. 'Of course I do.' They looked at each other shyly. 'Good luck, my boy. I hope she will consent. I think you could make each other very happy, and so does your mama. And make yourself happy too, by the way!' They shook hands.

'I thought I would dance with her at the ball tonight, and take her straight to the conservatory after a turn around the floor.'

'Splendid. Quite splendid. And then, when all this ghastliness over Glendarvan is finished, you can take her north and ask permission of her father. I believe he is a nice enough fellow – some funny ideas, though, I hear. You know, a bit on the poetic side since his hunting accident, but there. Edith will be too busy here in England to trouble herself with such matters, thank God. And you too, doubtless. You will still I am afraid have the estate to run with me, but of course you must have your own house. That is *de rigueur*. Cannot have you both living with us. That would never do.'

George looked at his father. He was the best of fellows. Seemed to understand everything before one had to say too much.

'Oh, and by the way, George, your grandmother's ring. I think you will find it is in the safe in your mother's dressing room. Very nice sapphire of the first water. She left it to you for just such an occasion.'

The Duke turned back to the window, thinking ahead as even fathers do when a wedding is in the air. He must start to plan the fireworks on the estate. All the workers and their families must come to a big party with fireworks.

And then he would make sure that the Dower House was made ready for them when they came back from their honeymoon, and Stilley Street of course. The Duchess still kept that just as it was when *they* first went there. Her little doll's house he always thought of it. His Duchess's doll's house, all bright colours and pantries with brass kettles and a sitting room with a brown leather chair, a bit worn now, and a patterned carpet, and velvet moleskin-coloured curtains at the windows as well as clean white nets. Ah me. He sighed, and turned, but George had gone. Impatient, no doubt to find that ring of his grandmother's! Oh yes, he would be impatient all right, and then of course he would be restless until tonight came. How happy they would make each other was up to them, but today at least was one of the good days and to be remembered as such.

A thought struck the Duke as the footmen flun open the library doors for him.

He had not told Frear. He must go at once an tell Frear. It would never do not to tell Frear. Afte all, Frear, well, he always did put George straight, whenever the Duke wanted him to. Had not he put George straight this time? Good heavens, without Frear, the boy might not even be engaged!

No, he must tell Frear. Or there would be all hell to pay!

New Beginnings

The feeling that she was being punished for he sins had never left Emily until she saw the gat lodges of their seaside house at Bangor. Of sudden it seemed to her that God might hav forgiven her so-great passion for Captai Barrymore Fortescue. She turned to Valencia an sought her hand underneath the travelling rug.

'Oh, look, Valencia, the sea. We shall get yo quite well again, here, darlin' dote, I know. Pink cheeked and rounded of eye. You will become a fit as a hunter.'

Valencia clutched her little terrier to her an smiled. It had been terrible for them all, the hous and everything gone, but there had been goo things too, no toys burned, and no animals hur and while they would all miss the paintings an books, she supposed, the animals were mo important.

'Look!' As the servants fell ahead of them in the Victorian house, thankful to have arrived last, her mother turned to Valencia. 'A parc already!' They both stared at it. Somehow the fa that there was a parcel waiting, and that it had her name on it, *Miss Valencia O'Connor*, made Bangor seem as if it was home already.

'Open it, dearest, quick. It might be something nice.'

Emily turned to find a pair of scissors, a knife – anything sharp. She knew from the writing on the brown paper that the parcel must be from Edith in London, and that a surprise was just what Valencia needed. She had feared so much for the child's already frail health that she had fully expected her to be at death's door when she arrived back from England. But children were as unpredictable, it seemed, as their parents, and whereas such a strange and horrible twist of fate might have been expected to make Valencia more of an invalid, in fact the danger, and the excitement too, it had to be faced, had seemed to trigger in her a resilience that no-one had ever suspected was there.

And, too, perhaps the fact that attention had been taken from her, that everyone's eyes had turned away from 'poor little sick Valencia', had also been of some benefit to the youngest of the O'Connor children.

'Why can one never find a knife or scissors when there is a parcel to be opened? Oh, look, dearest, let's try spearing the string with this paper knife.'

They wiggled the paper knife hard and in the end the string, weakened by their enthusiasm, gave way at last, and Valencia was able to scrape off the sealing wax, and tug off the brown paper, and the box presented itself.

Valencia looked up into Emily's face and her voice was barely above a whisper.

'I think it might be a London hat.' She had lost what little colour she had, just staring at the box, her heart beating faster than ever. She pushed her hair up a little from her forehead. 'Supposing,' she asked her silent mother, 'supposing it is a hat from London?'

'Well,' said Emily, quietly. 'Well, and if it is?'

Valencia's great green eyes, so like Emily's own, stared back up at her mother.

'It might not fit.'

'Nor it might,' Emily agreed, after a moment.

Neither of them moved.

'Shall I open the box? Even if it does not fit, you could wear it, could you not, Mama? It need not be wasted, after all, need it?'

'No, of course it need not.' Emily's face was as serious as that of her daughter.

'We can look at it together if we are quite sure that it would not be wasted?'

'Yes, we can.'

The childish hands, smooth and white, stretched out to the box and she pulled at the lid.

A cloud of tissue paper seemed to envelop the room in which they stood, and the young girl pulled excitedly at the contents of the cloud, pulling out a hat, a gorgeous green velvet hat with great green ostrich plumes.

'Shall I put it on?' Her face was as grave as a bishop as she held it.

'Well you might try it on, if you had a mind to do so.' Emily did not move. Not for her to spoil the moment, but to stand still and pray silently, *Please help the hat to fit!*

Valencia reached up and put the hat on, and then, since it did not seem to want to fall to her nose and leave her blinded, she walked in stately, disbelieving fashion to the old silver-backed looking glass on the opposite wall, and climbed onto a small stool to stare at herself.

She had not grown very tall, despite her twelve years. It was as if nature had singled her out to give her the permanent look of a youngest child. But now, with the hat, with the great green plumes of ostrich feather floating above her, she had height, she had grandeur. She was suddenly older.

She climbed back down off the stool and walked straight up to her mother to kiss her. 'I can't kiss Edith, so I'll kiss you!'

They both laughed, and then Emily swung her round a little, making the feathers move this way and that.

'I think we will be happy here, Mama, really I do. And look . . .' Valencia pointed to the window. 'There's the sea. It will make my chest better, and we will be a family gain.'

'Have we not been a family?' Emily stared across at her youngest, startled.

Valencia shook her head. 'No, Mama, we have

not. Not since papa hurt himself and you and he could not agree about – well, you could not agree about anything. Here, by the sea, we can go bathing, and we can play croquet out there on the lawn, and Papa will not miss his hunting because there is none to miss, and Edith will come back from London, and we can put on plays in the great hall out there. And Papa can buy himself an organ, because he is always saying he will and now he can. We can be a family again!'

Emily smiled, her heart contracting. Children noticed everything. Well, not everything, she hoped. Her mind ran to Edith. Please God she had never noticed her mother's lapse. If she had, whatever would she think? Emily turned away from the thought, only to return to it. If Edith knew of the affair, really there was nothing to think, except that her mother was a human being, and weak, and that after all had been all too evident of late.

Daisy fairly swept into Mrs Hartley Lambert's drawing room, leaving the panting Jenkins, who was looking no less cross than when they had left the house, in the hall.

'Countess!'

Daisy had no idea why Mrs Hartley Lambert always addressed her as if they were both in a Russian novel, but there, she did, and nothing to be done about it at this late stage.

'I had to see you, Mrs Hartley Lambert.'

The American woman turned away. 'I have no

idea why, Countess. After all, the whole Season, as far as Sarah is concerned, is a complete failure. Sarah has not found one convivial dancing partner. She is, apparently, feeling more wretched than she has ever done—'

'Until last night.'

'I beg your pardon?'

'Last night, Mrs Hartley Lambert, your daughter at last found someone—' It was on the tip of Daisy's tongue to say, mischievously, *taller*, but she resisted the temptation. Mrs Hartley Lambert was really not humorous enough to understand a light remark made in passing. She would think Daisy was being sarcastic. It would not be seemly. 'Last night, I saw Miss Hartley Lambert falling in love, and what is better, I saw her being fallen in love with! No, really, I did. I saw two young people . . .' Daisy closed her eyes melodramatically. 'I saw two young people waltzing around a ballroom with eyes only for each other. A tall young man with a beautiful Merican gel in his arms for whom he had eyes only – for her.'

Daisy paused, knowing that she had somehow run into a grammatical cul-de-sac, but not really caring, as Mrs Hartley Lambert's lace-edged handkerchief dabbed at her lips.

'Are you sure of this, Countess?'

'As sure as I am vat . . .' Daisy hesitated again, about to say *vat I was the late King Edward's mistress*, but she resisted that temptation too. Again, Mrs Hartley Lambert would not understand. Indeed, she would find it shocking. She would not comprehend the status of being a king's mistress, or, in Daisy's case, more precisely the mistress of the Prince of Wales. 'As sure as I am vat we have a king upon the throne and that this ring of mine is an emerald.' Daisy pulled off her glove dramatically, exposing a large emerald surrounded by diamonds. 'Vat is how sure I am. Now, where is Miss Hartley Lambert?'

'Sarah is not yet down.' Her mother glanced at the clock. 'As a matter of fact she is usually down by now. Although she breakfasts in her room, we like to be here together by ten o'clock. But of course the ball last night made her late, and, too, I have given orders for everyone to pack up the house, as we are to return to America. She may well be packing.'

'Or she may be lying in bed dreaming of Captain Barrymore Fortescue!'

'I beg your pardon? Captain Barrymore . . .'

'Tall, stunningly handsome, an army officer and ve second son of an earl.'

'Tall, you say? And an earl!'

'No, he is not an earl. His father is.'

'Even so.' Mrs Hartley Lambert's handkerchie returned to dab her lips. 'Sarah has said nothing o this to me. But of course I have not seen her! My my, my! Tall and an earl in the family, you say Where is Sarah?'

She went quickly to the bell and pulled it s many times that Daisy thought for a second that sh must have had practice as a bell ringer in a church

Outside in the hall Jenkins was sitting staring at the wall. It was usually very dull to be left in the hall while her ladyship went in for one of her little dramas during the Season, and normally she would have put her ear to the door, despite the presence of the hall boy. But today she could not be bothered. She was not even interested, a fact that was as surprising to her as it would have been to my lady. Jenkins was making up her mind, and when a person is busy making up their mind, it is after all perfectly understandable that they should be interested only in themselves.

'Lah-di-dah, lah-di-dah,' Jenkins said out loud suddenly.

The hall boy stared at her. 'I beg your pardon, miss?'

'Lah-di-dah, lah-di-dah.' Jenkins pushed her hat back. 'I am too long in the tooth for this caper. I can't support it no more, I can't. I shall have to retire to me sister's in Devon, and that is all there is to it.'

'What, now, miss?'

'No, not now, boy, soon. At the end of this Season. This will be me last. I know it will.'

'Yes, miss.'

Jenkins started to say something else, but a beautiful vision had appeared at the top of the stairs: Miss Hartley Lambert in a pale lemon skirt and jacket with a large bow to her blouse, and hand-made, beautifully buttoned shoes in the same pale lemon. It all toned beautifully and both the maid and the hall boy could appreciate this from where they were both now standing.

'Good morning, Jenkins.' Sarah paused. She felt so well and so happy that not even Jenkins's somewhat pinched face and faded hat could make much difference to how she was feeling. 'It is a beautiful morning, is it not?'

'Yes, Miss.' Jenkins smiled suddenly. Her mind now made up, she could quite see that it was a beautiful morning, and moreover that Miss Hartley Lambert was as beautiful as the morning itself, with her lovely hair and lemon-coloured clothes and matching side-buttoned shoes.

Sarah stared at Jenkins. She would have liked to have said 'Gracious, Jenkins, I have never, ever seen you smile before!' but she could not, so she said instead, whispering, 'Have you heard, Jenkins?'

'No, miss.'

Sarah leaned towards the maid, her voice still a whisper. 'I am practically engaged. Last night I met a certain captain and we danced twice, and he is so handsome, Jenkins. He is as handsome as he is fun. Can you imagine, me meeting an unstuffy Englishman?'

'About as likely as me becoming a duchess, Miss!'

A small intake of breath, and, following up her smile, Jenkins actually laughed.

'Yes, I know, Jenkins,' Sarah continued out loud, 'I know. Such a thing! But there, you will be relieved, doubtless, when I am no longer always on the mind of the Countess?'

They looked at each other, and again the startling thing happened. Jenkins laughed once more.

'Oh, I don't know about that, Miss Hartley Lambert. Her ladyship enjoys keeping an eye on you young gels.'

'Yes, I know, Jenkins, but not into eternity!'

Daisy returned home in the same hansom that she had quickly taken only half an hour before, and seated in the back, with Jenkins opposite, she sighed with the relief of it all. Thank heavens, she had delayed Mrs Hartley Lambert's exit from London and imminent return to America, and had also persuaded her that, when the handsome Captain Barrymore Fortescue proposed, it would have to be a Westminster wedding. His family would expect it.

Of course, the Hartley Lamberts would have their noses put dreadfully out of joint, and as soon as she realised it Mrs Hartley Lambert's eyes had fairly popped with that particular excitement that comes from the knowledge that you are about to cock a snook at a whole lot of people who have been perfectly beastly to you. (Such a vulgar expression, but oh so *apt*!)

So that was all right, Daisy thought, gazing out of the window.

Of course, in some ways, it could not be denied that Lady Emily had unwittingly prepared the way for Daisy to marry off the immensely likeable Miss Hartley Lambert and her millions to the handsome Barrymore. After all, if she had not had her torrid affair with the young captain, he would not have been nearly so malleable. Daisy was a great believer in the power of love-making to prepare people for yet more love. When robbed of love, it always seemed to her, persons in love immediately fell again. It was as if they had the habit of it, like tying the laces on their shoes! And knowing this, last night she had quite consciously stepped down from her throne of the Great Beauty – because goodness he was handsome – and guided Barrymore towards Miss Hartley Lambert. *Et voilà!* They had taken to each other straight away, for the gorgeous young captain was in mourning for love, sighing for it, and Miss Hartley Lambert had stepped in at just the right moment.

Daisy had let slip over dinner that Miss Hartley Lambert was an heiress of considerable proportions, which fact had doubtless added a great deal to her charms for a younger son like Barrymore Fortescue. It had added wit and beauty, it had added an allure he had probably not really noticed before. It had added everything possible. But then, Daisy always thought, it was just as if a person was a bare room, and their wealth the wallpaper and the furniture. It was surely no worse to find a girl more attractive on account of her wealth than it was to find a man more attractive on account of his looks? So, all in all, when she came to think of it, it was a perfect exchange. And the two of them would make a very happy marriage. Daisy was sure of it.

Far better for Miss Hartley Lambert, as an American gel, to marry a younger son. A younger son would not seek to constrain her, would be gayer and more carefree than the heir to a title – as younger sons almost always were, since they were not weighed down by the thought that come what may their lives were already mapped out for them. Barrymore Fortescue would not lock her up in some draughty castle with typhoid-ridden drains and an ageing mother-in-law with a voice like a corncrake.

'My lady?' Jenkins had already addressed her mistress twice without attracting her attention, so deep was Daisy in her own thoughts. 'My lady?' she said again.

'Yes, Jenkins?' Daisy turned her still beautiful and famous eyes on her.

'My lady,' said Jenkins, thankful at last to have her mistress's attention, 'I am afraid this will be our last Season together.'

'Yes, Jenkins.'

The eyes remained cool, the look disinterested. After thirty years, Jenkins might have been telling her that my lady's bath water temperature was now perfect and ready for her.

'I have decided to retire to my sister's, in Devon, my lady.'

'Yes, Jenkins.'

'And so I must hand in my notice for the end of July, my lady.'

'Yes, Jenkins. Thank you, Jenkins. I shall make a

note of it.' Daisy turned her gaze towards the window. 'Such a lovely day, do you not think, Jenkins?'

'Yes, my lady.'

Daisy nodded. Yes, it was a lovely day all round. Pity about Jenkins. But not surprising really. She would have to train someone else up, but there. Always something to think about – the maids, or the fashions, and now Jenkins.

Of course, what she was not saying to Jenkins was that the reason why she would allow the maid to retire to Devon, taking with her the wretched samovar and whatever else Daisy had promised her, was that Daisy too had made up her mind that it would be her last Season. She was too proud to admit as much to Jenkins. It might make Jenkins smile and look *I thought as much* at her. It might make Jenkins happy, and that would never do.

Daisy was going to retire. She was going to find peace. Where she did not know, but find it she must. And what was more, for the first time in her life, she was going to live within her means. No more anxieties about husbands' gambling, or lovers' debts, or milliners' pestering one.

She was going to be free of all that at last. She had never realised, until now, just how tired she had become. After all, now she came to think of it, more people were pleased by her presence than she was, it had to be said, in the least bit pleased by them. More people wanted Daisy at their balls and dinners, their ladies' luncheons than she ever wanted to be *with*. She could hardly think of one person nowadays whom she actually wanted to see, hardly anyone who amused her as her old friends, in the old days, had used to amuse her. Too much had gone between, too much water flowed under the famous bridge. She wanted no more of it. She wanted peace of mind, no debts and a life she could afford. Those three things would be a warm bath of a life to her. A sunshine-filled morning with nothing to do but pick flowers and think of where to put the luncheon table. Not even a handsome lover would give her such pleasure now.

And so the two of them continued on their way, Jenkins staring ahead, Daisy out of the window, thinking *I do hope I remember where I put that samovar for Jenkins, and whatever else was it I promised her? Not the Family Fender, I hope!*

Sir Lampard Tradescant had made it to London. No-one knew how, but he had. Looking at her brother from close to, part of Aunt Tattie now wished heartily that he had not. He was really very dishevelled. Still, he was at least upright, even if his clothes did look and smell like something out of an old trunk – old-fashioned even to his sister's eyes, so goodness knows what they would seem to Richard Ward and this Edwin Vessey fellow to whom young Phyllis had been busy engaging herself.

Yet, in all truth, Lampard was still Lampard; he still had a certain presence. He still had the whiff not just of moth balls but of the true Victorian about him, the feeling that when he was growing up England was truly English, and not yet becoming Foreign, and over-liberal, and goodness knows what else. Indeed, now that Phyllis had found herself a young man, and Portia was happy once more, Aunt Tattie could not wait to hightail it back to Bannerwick and her medieval sewing frame, her sailing boat and her swimming.

'So where are these young men to whom I must address myself, Tatiana?'

Aunt Tattie brushed some dog hairs from Lampard's trouser legs with a small brush that she always kept hidden in her sewing bag for such emergencies.

'Where do you think, Lampard? Waiting to see you, the head of the family, each by turn in the library, where young men always wait. But Portia's young man is to see you first. Do not forget you used to know him, dearest. Richard Ward, in the old days at Bannerwick. You know, the nice young man Portia used to go sailing with, but he had an arrangement with someone else, a Miss Cecil, so nothing came of it. But, alas, there was a tragedy and he is now a widower. And Portia is a widow, as you may remember, and so they have decided to make a go of it, and since they always were such friends, as children, I dare say that they *will* make a go of it, dearest.'

'Got you, Tatiana. As a matter of fact I do remember him. Long time ago that it was. How long since I was in London, by the way?'

'Some time ago.' Aunt Tattie could not bring herself to tell him fifteen years.

'They are all wearing such odd clothes, Tatiana. I dare say you noticed, did you not? Not a Chesterfield or even a topper in sight, that I could see from the carriage window.'

'I know, dearest. Things have changed a little, but there. The old king set the trend, you may remember, a few years back. He made homburgs fashionable, along with much else.'

'His mother was not a fashionable person, and more power to her for that. She was a great woman. Better than fashion, that, you know.'

'Tail coats are not being worn at home in the evening, Lampard. More and more gentlemen are wearing dinner jackets in London for dinner in their own homes, although never away. But I hear tail coats are still *de rigueur* elsewhere, in the houses of others.'

Her brother turned and stared at her. There was a ghastly silence while he digested this news, and finally he said in a broken voice, 'Is nothing sacred any more?'

'Well, I know, Lampard, it is a shock, I do agree.'

'No-one's wearing dinner jackets in front of me in London, I can tell you that.'

Aunt Tattie stared briefly at her brother's worn clothes. Really, it was so strange, everyone wearing clothes that no-one else liked. Yet no-one really cared what the people inside the clothes were like. As if clothes were all. She had always been considered eccentric at home, even at Bannerwick where people did as they wished, but nowadays, she had noticed, she was almost in the vanguard. Very many people they knew now shopped at Liberty's in Regent Street and talked about a return to medieval principles.

'And then there is Edwin Vessey, Phyllis's intended. He will see you next. He is the second son of a second son, but by good luck his god-father is a bachelor and quite likely to leave him a small estate in Herefordshire, which will suit admirably.'

'Never mind. Let them come at me, and then take me back to Sussex by the sea. Dinner jackets for dinner! Have you ever heard of such a thing? Such times we live in!'

He put a hand on his sister's shoulder, and together they walked slowly forward to the library. What a to-do everything was. Always this or that. For himself, he could not wait to get back to the seaside. Somehow so satisfying at his time of life. But first, duty called. He was, after all, head of the Tradescant family.

'Let's get it all over with!' he murmured to Tatiana.

And so he did.

For all that he had never been sober in his life, and had never known what it was to be married, Lampard's questionings of the parties concerned were short but very much to the point. He was not having any young men marrying his womenfolk who did not have the wherewithal to support them! No matter that Portia was already rich from the Childhays' money, the Vice Admiral had to be shown to be capable of supporting Portia in his own right. If not it would lead to heaven only knew what, irresponsibility, a lack of values, gambling, throwing nuts in ladies' handbags, driving teams of horses too fast through gates that were too narrow, that sort of thing. They had to stump up if they wanted to marry a Tradescant, and see to that Sir Lampard would. Even if it did mean that he would miss his daily swim in the briny, and his bottle of port at night.

Portia, meanwhile, as her darling Richard was having to cope with Uncle Lampard in the library, was trying to cope with her feelings towards Childie. Upstairs, quite alone, she wondered what Childie, always so much older than herself, would make of his widow's marrying Richard Ward?

She thought he would take it hard, that he would not find it easy to share her. And then she thought that, being such a very good-natured man, he might put his hand on her shoulder and say, 'No, go ahead. After all, to be lonely is a terrible thing, and he is your old friend, and what's more he sails. You love sailing, he loves sailing. It is more than one can expect to get out of life, two men who love to go sailing.'

A weight was lifted from her mind when she realised that this was doubtless what Childie would have said, but then she was faced with the shutting of the inevitable door on the past. Did she have to shut it? Did she have to say goodbye to everything that had happened before?

She asked this of May the following day, after everything was settled. May, in her usual down-to-earth way, considered the question and then, putting her head on one side, said, quite decisively, 'No, absolutely not. To live the past in the present is wrong, of course, but to go forward with the past as part of the present is perfectly proper. It should not weigh one down; rather it should lift one up. Remembering past happy times, when one has laughed and the sun has shone, and all is not bleak, should be good not just for one, but for everyone else too.'

There was a pause as Portia reflected on this, and then she said quietly, 'Dear May, how I wish I was as good as you.'

'Come, come, now, Lady Childhays, you go too far!'

They both laughed.

'Emily used to say that. No, she used to say, "How I wish that I was as good and as beautiful as May," which is to say, she would have liked to be you, if she had not been Emily.'

'Poor dearest Emily, what a drama she has lived through these last weeks, one way or another.'

They both paused, thinking back, knowing how near their friend had come to losing everything.

'She will grow stronger. She is good-hearted, she is spirited, she is not utterly selfish. She was rather driven, I felt. By events in Ireland, but never more than now, I would say.'

Both nodded at this, and then spoke together. 'So good about the announcement to come' – 'that Edith and your boy,' Portia finished. 'You must be pleased. And it will hearten Emily so much to have Edith married, and to *your* son. We did wonder, at the beginning of the Season, who would catch George's eye, as a matter of fact. We thought it might be an American heiress, but never really one or other of our daughters. It seemed too good to be true.'

They laughed, and May shook her head.

'No, George is not the kind of person to be attracted to an American girl such as Miss Hartley Lambert. Not that she would have been attracted to him in any case, I am sure. George needed to choose someone like himself, someone who will be more than happy to go to the country and stay there. Who will live for country life, love their dogs and their horses and generally be a country bumpkin, I am afraid. American gels *languish* in the English countryside! It is too much for any of them, coming from their bright interiors to our gloomy climate, to tolerate the damp and the cold, not to mention the dogs!'

'We are mighty uncivilised to outsiders.'

'Yes, but with all that, Englishness still stands for something. Englishness still stands for being and doing and coping in a particular way, and *that* all stands for something too. When all is said and done, the whole world knows what we mean by being "very English". But we are being far too serious on such a happy day. Where will Phyllis marry?'

'She has chosen London. St James's I think, and all that. And afterwards they are to live in Scotland, which will be good for Phyllis because it means that she will come and see me and appreciate everything, most of all the difference in the climate. And George and Edith will marry in September, I hear from my maid.'

'One does always hear from one's maid. I have no idea why one needs a telephone. Yes, George and Edith are to marry at Westminster, honeymoon in Italy, we have a house there, and then come back – to Stilley Street.'

'Where?' Portia frowned. 'Is that in London?'

'Not in London, no,' said May, gravely. 'It is in York, and they will be there for quite a few months. As a matter of fact they will be there until they do not wish to be there any more.'

'Is it large?'

'Oh, no, it is tiny. No room for a maid. Edith will have to cook for George, and George will have to light fires and wash dishes and so on.'

Portia stared. Even coming from an Arts and Crafts background, the eccentric relatives and the odd customs of Bannerwick, she could not imagine a duke's son lighting fires and washing up.

'Does, er, George know about this, May dearest?'

'George, no, not yet. But when he does, he will be thrilled. Believe me, there is nothing that a bridegroom likes better than his feet up on a fender and the smell of his young wife burning

:rumpets in the kitchen. It satisfies something ıatural in them.'

'Not too natural, I hope,' Portia asked, just a ittle fearfully.

'No, not too natural,' May agreed, and then she ›urst into laughter. 'Oh, Portia, your face! You ;hould see your expression – such shock! Stilley ›treet is the family bridal suite. I shall not go into t, it would not be proper, but believe me, it is a ›lace that makes everyone young and in love ompletely happy. They are all alone, they can juarrel without being heard, they can – well, you :now, they can be quite alone. It is truly a little ›aradise, and everything they want is delivered. \nd they do not have to wear evening dress in the vening.'

'Do not tell my Uncle Lampard,' said Portia, vith some feeling. 'He is even now recovering :om the shock of hearing that people at home in ondon do not wear tail coats.'

'Will Uncle Lampard take Phyllis up the aisle, o you think?'

'Oh, I dare say, that is if Aunt Tattie can keep im on a straight path. He actually managed to :ay sober for the whole of his London visit. Aunt attie was impressed.'

'And how long was that?'

'Two whole days! Imagine! It must have been a ıost horrible strain for the old gentleman.'

A footman came into the room to replenish the :e that burned winter and summer. Swiftly king advantage of this, May said to him, 'Bring us some refreshments, would you, please? Champagne. I think it has to be champagne. After all, Portia dearest, we have so much to drink to have we not?'

It was Jenkins's turn to be surprised. After their return to the house, Daisy retired to her morning room to think. She often did this when she was making up her mind. Seated at the window she would stare ahead of her and let her thoughts run just as she used to watch the trout running in the streams when she was a little girl. They had looked so dappled and golden and the gardener on the estate had a way of bending down and tickling them, their heads practically touching the water, which made Daisy laugh, and then long for them not to catch them.

She had caught enough trout in her time, social trout that is, to fill a fishing basket, and now, as she had realised on the cab drive home, it was time to hang up her chaperon's shoes.

She would retire to somewhere immensely respectable and learn to be a respectable person. Heavily veiled, she imagined, she would step out every now and then and be driven around the park. She would read, and patronise the arts. She would see old friends, but only occasionally. She would not sew, she hated sewing, but she would improve her mind. Goodness only knew it must need improving. It had thought of nothing but the social life, and marriages, all its poor old life.

'I wonder, should I read Tennyson, when

retire?' she asked Jenkins later that day.

'You are retiring, my lady?'

'Oh, yes, Jenkins, did I not tell you? I am retiring. After all, Jenkins,' she turned to the maid, 'the Season would not be ve same without you, would it?'

Jenkins looked away.

Silly old woman, Daisy thought spitefully, she thinks I cannot do without her. She thinks I am retiring because she is retiring when in fact I am retiring because I am just so – tired.

'I have just had a thought, a tremendous *thought*, Jenkins. Do you not think instead of saying "I am retiring" people should say "I am tired-ing"?'

Jenkins looked at Daisy blankly. 'If you say so, my lady.'

'Oh, I do not say, I do, Jenkins. No, as a matter of fact, I am not at all sure what I do say any more at all, which may surprise you.'

'Yes, my lady.'

'As a matter of fact, Jenkins, I am thinking of retiring next week. And I thought you should too, as a matter of fact. We should both retire, immediately, with effect from next week.'

'Retire next week, my lady? But I have not yet informed my sister.'

'Do so, Jenkins, at once. You can use my new telephone.'

'My sister does not have a telephone, my lady.'

'In that case write to her, Jenkins, and tell you what, you can have one of my stamps. Here. Take a stamp. Oh, no, vat's not a stamp, is it? It is a piece of paper.'

'The stamps are downstairs, my lady. In the hall.'

'Well, wherever they are, you can have one. There. Never say I was not generous with you, will you, Jenkins? When you retire to your sister's house, never say I was not generous to a fault.'

Jenkins shook her head, suddenly miserable. She had hoped to at least finish this last Season.

'I don't know what has got into you, my lady,' she said, murmuring half to herself and half to Daisy, and certainly not caring in the least if my lady heard or did not hear her.

'What has *got into me*, as you put it, is vat I have become very, very tired, and when a person is very, very tired, do you know something? They want to give up! And vat is what I am doing. Miss Hartley Lambert has found someone, everyone has found someone by this time of the Season, or should have done, and vat quite frankly is enough for me, for ever.' Daisy stamped her small elegant foot on the old polished wooden floor. 'I find I do not want to hear about another wedding, or engagement. I had rather read a book. There! I have really shocked you now, have I not, Jenkins? I have shocked the boots off you. I had rather read the poems of Mr Wordsworth, all of them, than ever, ever hear about a person getting married or becoming engaged, or not getting married or not becoming engaged, again. I would rather ride backwards round the Park on my old mare, facing her poor old tail, than arrange another marriage, or another ball, or sit on a gilt chair watching a bunch of graceless gels trying not to trip over their feet! I would! So next week, Jenkins. Next week we shall pull down the blinds. We shall make it known vat we are leaving town, and I shall retire. Officially! Now, good morning. You can go down to the servants' hall until further notice. And do not, please, forget to write your letter to vat sister of yours. It is most important, as you will doubtless have gathered.'

Daisy stood up and swirled, there was no other word for it, she positively swirled with joy, and as she did so a dreadful thought came to Jenkins, a truly awful thought, the kind of thought that she never imagined she might ever have to entertain.

Was it possible that her mistress had never really enjoyed the social life? Had she truly only done what she imagined was her social duty? While Jenkins was imagining herself as a downtrodden person, overworked and unappreciated, had her mistress, all that time, imagined herself in just the same way? Hard worked and in many ways downtrodden too, doing things all day that she had really rather not? Because if this was true, why then there was no such thing as the 'better off'. There was just – life.

Jenkins turned away from the thought. It was almost godless in its implications. She had resented my lady for more years than she cared to remember, and she was not going to stop now. She was being sent away to Devon six weeks earlier than she wished. That at least was something to think about with resentment. By the time she reached the corridor outside the world was back to normal. They were back on either side of whatever it was that divided them, mistress and maid, as they should be, not, as Jenkins had suddenly seen them both for a few dizzying seconds, just ordinary human beings.

May had taken Portia to visit Herbert Forrester's two houses in Kensington.

'Very handsome houses, do you not think?' May asked after their sporty little journey in a hansom cab, a journey that made them both feel like girls again, let off the hook, out for a canter.

'They are handsome,' Portia agreed. 'But will he be happy to be so far out?'

'He will be happy for a while, I think, anyway. It is the change, do you see, Portia, the change from York. Mr Forrester misses Mrs Forrester so dreadfully. It is too awful to think of being on one's own like that—' She stopped, turning. She had forgotten. 'I am sorry. Of course, since you are newly engaged, I keep forgetting you have been widowed.'

'No matter, May. I do too, if the truth be known. I never thought that the sorrow would leave me, but since Richard I feel young again. We know each other so well, d'you see? It is not like getting used to a whole new way of life; we already know each other as well as any two people can.'

She said no more, but May was aware that

Portia possibly knew Richard Ward better than she had even known Lord Childhays. That was how deep youthful friendship ran, after all.

They turned now at the first landing of the first house, and went together into the drawing room.

Portia stopped and her mouth fell open, as May had been expecting that it might.

'May! Goodness, May darling, that must be the first item to go, now you are here in charge. Thank heavens that you were called in to help Mr Forrester. Was it left behind by the previous owners? Well, it must have been, of course.' Portia started to laugh. 'You must have the removal men round straight away, and they must take it away and burn it.'

May was quite quiet before she turned to Portia and put her hand on her arm. 'No, Portia, it is not be removed. It is only newly purchased, and it will be the apple of dear Mr Forrester's eye when he returns from his travels.'

'You cannot! May tell me, please, you will not leave this here, in this room?'

'Portia, shall I tell you something? It gives me great joy to do so. Mr Forrester set his poor old heart on a piece like this, and while it is not to my aste and not to yours, it will give him more joy than any of my taste imposed on the rest of the house.'

'Anything, but not that,' Portia said, shuddering ightly and dramatically, and then, seeing May's most stubborn expression, she started to laugh. 'Oh, very well, you are probably quite correct.'

May smiled. She knew, better than anyone, that her dear old friend needed a new beginning to his life, and somehow, she could not say why, this great silver-decorated cupboard was just that. From it, carrying as it would a vast amount of varying drinks and glasses, would come, she hoped, great rays of happiness and hope. She remembered when she was young and at the convent how she had set her heart upon a prayer book, how she had thought that prayer book would never materialise, and when it did, with its red leather and its gold, with its thin paper and its ribbons to place at special days, how it had seemed to her to be the most beautiful book in the world. Very well, the cupboard was not for church, but it was something upon which her old friend had set his heart, just as she had set her heart on her book of prayer. It was a symbol of a new beginning, and as such it could not be more important.

'Come on, May, let us get started with the swatches of materials.'

Portia dug deep into her old Gladstone bag, hardly able to believe how happy she felt. Everyone was marrying someone, somewhere, it seemed to her suddenly. Outside the window London jogged by in its usual fashion, a positive cornucopia of people and transport, and yet, also positively jolly. Cab drivers, omnibuses, people of all kinds, all busy, delightfully uncaring of each other, as people in London always seemed to be.

As they both went to the window holding up the scraps of material to the light, Portia glanced down to the street below. How strange! She thought she had just seen Daisy Lanford alighting from a hansom below. But that was just not possible. She glanced down again a second or two later, but the lady, whoever it was, had disappeared quickly into the house next door. She must have imagined her.

'Is the house next door for sale too?' she asked May, casually.

'As a matter of fact, it is. Mr Forrester has no need of two houses, after all. Not for a widower, living alone and never likely to be any different now.'

'No, well, that is true.'

'Mr Blundell, the builder, told me they were both built by the same man, for himself and his son, so once upon a time the gardens were linked, but not now, of course – this is pretty, do you not think?' She held up a piece of crewel work.

'Go beautifully with that cupboard.'

'Portia.' May's look told her friend that she must stop being so facetious and start concentrating. 'This house is not for us, it is for Mr Forrester. We must try to think of what he would like.'

Portia nodded, but found it difficult to remember Mr Forrester from the dim and distant past. She could only really think of what Richard would like. She thought of him suddenly now with longing. They would soon go sailing together. They would take dogs out. They would go for walks. They would hold hands in front of the fire. A new start for them both, at a time when she had truly never believed that could have been possible.

A little later, feeling herself to be in a bit of a muddle as to which particular piece of crewel work May was now fancying for Mr Forrester's drawing room curtains, Portia glanced down to the street below once more. This time she was quite sure that the person coming out of the house next door was Daisy Lanford.

She turned to May to point her out, but May had gone, and so Portia shrugged her shoulders, and then smiled to herself. If she was right and the older lady below, so beautifully dressed in fashions of a few years ago, was indeed the famous Daisy Lanford, Herbert Forrester's arch enemy, goodness – what a set-to there would be!

Interlude

Edith lay back on the pillows. Downstairs she could hear George whistling. If they had been in the Dower House on his father's estate, goodness, he would not be whistling, in case the servants heard, and he would not be making tea either, because the servants would not allow him near the stove.

They had made love, and he had spread her hair out behind her on the pillow and left her with a rose beside her face, and now she had to lie there as he had arranged her until he reappeared with the tea.

Divine Circe, the Society writer, had written of their wedding.

The bride in old-fashioned satin, and a train that required twelve attendants, all of whom were in satin too. Satin knee breeches, white satin jackets with gold epaulettes, and all of them carrying satin-covered wands with rosettes and ribbons. A truly tasteful and beautiful sight, and bringing sighs from the waiting crowds as the bride arrived with her father, Mr Rory O'Connor from Ireland, stepping out of the Wokingham family carriage, generously loaned to Mr O'Connor by the bride's future father-in-law, the Duke of Wokingham. The bride's extravagantly long train was attended not just by twelve small boys but by six bridesmaids in pale pink satin with overskirts of muslin. There was too a hint of a royal wedding, many years before, in the bridal flowers. Altogether a most happy and popular occasion, the Wokingham heir marrying an exquisitely beautiful young girl from Ireland. There was not a person there who could not but have wished them all health and happiness all their lives.

Their continental honeymoon had of course been everything a honeymoon should be, but it was when they returned to this little house in which Edith now lay so blissfully awaiting her bridegroom bringing her tea that their married life really began, and they had time to get to know each other in a way that was not possible with servants always around.

'There we are, my dearest,' George whispered.

'Thank you, my darling. May I move now?'

George stood staring down at Edith. He hated her to move. She looked too beautiful. 'You may sit up for your tea,' he agreed, at last.

Edith sat up and took the teacup from him. It was a nice cup with pretty blue flowers decorated on it, and old. She took it, smiling up at George. 'You are clever, dearest. Making tea. I did not know you knew how.'

She stared down into the cup. And stared. There was tea in the cup, that certainly was true, and the tea was floating, dozens of little black leaves all along the top of the cup. Beneath the leaves, as she now saw, was – the water.

'Oh, George!'

'Yes, dearest?'

'Oh, *George*!'

George stared from his bride's laughing face to the cup in his hand and back again.

'I rather thought it did not look quite right,' he agreed with her, finally, and was only too relieved when she sprang out of bed, grabbed her wrap and returned with a tray and a pot all made and laid as it should be.

'Oh dear, what a failure as a husband I am, to be sure.'

'No, dearest, that you are quite definitely not. Tea, after all, can always be arranged. Love cannot.'

After tea George once more reassured himself as to the love.

Old Enemies

Daisy, walking skilfully between all the small tables in her crowded drawing room, reached the window giving out onto the street below. She was expecting this Mr Blundell, this builder fellow, and really it would be a dreadful disappointment if he was held up, for she was quite excited about her plans to turn the garden into an Italian Garden.

She had thought about her little garden from the moment she had moved in. She had really concentrated upon it. She had brought her whole imagination to bear on it, which meant that she had many ideas to tell Mr Blundell, but they were ideas that she wanted put into execution straight away. They could not wait until spring. She must have the ideas acted upon at once or she would forget them, or grow tired of them, or, worse, feel unexcited by them.

Ah! There he was, and – she squinted down at her fob watch rather than peer at her gold engraved eighteenth-century drawing room clock

- exactly to the minute, which was always so :eassuring in a person.

Before moving to Kensington Daisy had never ıad to do with a builder in her life, for the simple eason that on her various estates, or in London, it was always the family agents that dealt with such hings. But now she had cut herself off from the :ountry, let her remaining estate, and must be :ontent with what little she had; namely nine edrooms and a small garden in Kensington.

Mr Blundell had seemed to understand. Moreover, the reverence in his eyes had deepened. As a matter of fact, as the maid announced the lear little man, and Daisy swam towards him in a 'ery fetching deep red velvet skirt and an em-roidered waistcoat of which she was very fond, he realised of a sudden that, since her retirement, Ir Blundell and herself had become really firm iends.

Not that he would take advantage of their little ılks together, that would not be his way, but he ould, she imagined, tell his wife little bits of ttle-tattle, little things that Daisy had let drop, ıd really she did not mind that at all.

It was a privilege for Mr Blundell to deal with aisy, and they both knew it, and because of this was understood between them that he was lowed to go home and tell Mrs Blundell little ems such as King Edward's liking lobster salad r tea, and the Duke of Wokingham's being a very ticent man. In this way Daisy also knew that she ensured that Mr Blundell's account, sent in discreetly to her housekeeper, and never referred to by either of them, was kept well within the bounds of day to day reality.

'Mr Blundell. How good of you to come so quickly.'

Mr Blundell, who had fallen wildly in love with the Countess on the first day of their meeting, touched his moustache lightly as he heard her greeting. She had such a pretty voice, the voice of an angel, he had told his wife, who had not minded in the least, because all women everywhere were fascinated by a woman who had been mistress to a king.

Find out if she has her own hair!

Mrs Blundell had asked him that only the other week. What a thing! Of course she had her own hair, and her own hands and feet.

Now Mr Blundell stared in reverence as the Countess seated herself in the velvet-covered chair, beside which he stood, hat in hand.

'I am ever so glad vat you could come to meet me so very quickly, Mr Blundell. Why, I truly thought you must be dreadfully muddled up with all your spring plans and so on.'

'My lady.' Mr Blundell bowed again. 'You may call upon my services whenever you wish. I should come if it was midnight, or dawn, or on the outbreak of war. I would always come when you summoned me. I am your devoted servant, my lady.'

Daisy smiled and thought *goodness, he goes to*

far, really he does, but I will have to let him. Seconds later she said, 'You know, I really do believe what you say is true, and you are my devoted servant, Mr Blundell.'

Mr Blundell gave another little bow. He could not help his heart beating faster whenever he stood in front of the famous Countess. Just knowing that she had pleased the then Prince of Wales in her youth was excitement enough, but knowing too that she not only paid her bills on time, but required him to be constantly visiting her, to dance attendance on her, was quite wonderful. All other clients had faded from his notice in comparison to her ladyship. Even Mr Herbert Forrester, former owner of the house itself, paled to insignificance beside the glamour of her ladyship, rich though he might be.

'Of course—' Daisy paused. 'Of course,' she started again. 'You do not know who lives next door, who bought the other house from the family that owned them, do you, Mr Blundell? My neighbour, as it were?'

'I do not, my lady.'

It was Mr Blundell's custom to pretend ignorance rather than betray confidences. It made it easier to avoid any awkwardness. Besides, he had only met Mr Forrester just once. The rest of his dealings had been with the Duchess of Wokingham. She was a nice lady, but lacking, in his opinion, the great grandeur of the older generation, lacking the Countess's style, her hauteur, her ability, when he thought about her on his return home, or when he was running through the accounts in his office, to make Mr Blundell shiver with delight.

Being in the presence of the Countess was like being in the presence of old King Edward himself, so much of the grand style did she exude. She was a Victorian, she was a great woman, she was everything that the country now, sadly, lacked, in Mr Blundell's less than humble opinion. Style! The old style! No cutting corners or waiting for someone else to pick up the pieces! No, she was a great, great lady, and still a great beauty, and he would lay down his life for her, he often thought. Not just his expertise, but his life.

'So, Mr Blundell, you can obviously execute my plans for turning my little garden Italianate? You can do what I want?'

'I can do whatever you want, my lady. Of course. We shall have plans drawn up immediately.' He had not heard a word of what she had been saying.

'And another thing, Mr Blundell?'

'Yes, my lady?'

'My little dog here, Tippitty.' She stroked the head of her small King Charles spaniel, who sighed contentedly and stared into the fire as her mistress's beringed hand travelled over the top of her head. 'She must be allowed for. She must be allowed to exercise where she wants. You will not be fidgety about that, will you?'

'No, my lady. Of course not.' Mr Blundell bowed again.

'Oh, and Mr Blundell. One more thing?'

He straightened up. 'Yes, my lady?'

'The gentleman who bought the house next door. Would you by any chance know if he is a bachelor?'

Mr Blundell knew of course that Herbert Forrester was a widower, but his lips, even in front of the Countess, were permanently and professionally sealed.

'I, er – I, er—'

'No matter. It is just that my new maid, Gribben, told me yesterday that there are no female servants employed in the house. So it occurred to me, Mr Blundell, that it might be a bachelor's house.'

Mr Blundell hesitated. He could see that the Countess was a little disturbed by this news of an all-male, all-bachelor household. It seemed to imply wild parties involving punch bowls.

'I do know that Mr Herbert Forrester is a widower, my lady. But that is all I know.'

There was an appalled silence.

'Mr WHO?'

Mr Blundell now felt the full force of the Countess's royal manners as she sprang to her feet, setting aside her little dog and staring into his face as if she was about to order his head to be removed from his neck.

'A Mr Herbert Forrester, my lady.'

In an instant, Daisy knew who had perpetrated this trick on her. Augustine Medlar!

It was she who had so warmly recommended

the house to Daisy, sending her off hotfoot to see it. As soon as she heard that Daisy was retiring she had recommended the house. She must have known that Herbert Forrester, Daisy's sworn enemy, had bought the one next door. How Augustine would be laughing now, fit to bust! Daisy imagined she could hear her horrible cackle coming from beneath her gilded canopy at Medlar House. Oh, the horror of it all. She sank back onto the sofa and plucked up her dog once more. She had been bested by Augustine yet again. It must be her revenge. Not content with not helping Daisy in any way to find Miss Hartley Lambert a suitable husband, Augustine had allowed Daisy, indeed encouraged her, to live next door to the man she hated most in the world.

'You may go, Mr Blundell, and when you set about drawing up my garden plans be sure to make the walls ten foot high!'

Mr Blundell fled. He had no idea why the Countess had reacted as she had. He might never know, and he was heartbroken. He had climbed the ladder to his goddess's feet with such care, and now, at the mere mention of a name, she had thrown him to the bottom again. He would have to make her garden so entrancing that she would forgive him. Quite apart from anything else, if he lost the Countess's custom Mrs Blundell would never, ever forgive him.

No more mention was made of the matter until the Italian Garden had progressed sufficiently for even Daisy to be contented with its elegance, its fountains, its paving, and statuary. It all looked suitably foreign and warming, some of the statues being only partly clothed. The leaves in the road outside were beginning to drift past Daisy's long windows when Herbert Forrester alighted from his motor car, brand new, and bought at Dover, and gazed up at his new London house.

From the outside, anyway, it looked just as it should. Tall, elegant, freshly painted, curtains at the windows, brass knocker shining.

'Good afternoon, Jepson,' he said, handing his nan his hat as his chauffeur drove off to the mews where the car would be garaged. 'First time I have nade a journey in a motor car without having ecourse to the car behind, do you know that, epson?'

'If I may say so, Mr Forrester, sir, you are ooking very well, quite yourself again.'

'Thank you, Jepson. It feels as if I have been way a year, when it is only a few weeks.'

'May I lead the way, sir, while the hall boy takes our portmanteaux to the upper floors?'

'You may, Jepson.'

Jepson led the way up to the first floor, his heart eating a little. Supposing Mr Forrester did not ke the Duchess of Wokingham's choices? He, las, would be the first to hear of it.

Herbert followed his manservant up the stairs ondering what he would feel also. Supposing he id not like May's choices? How would he tell er? He felt so rested, so much more himself, that it seemed much more than a few weeks since they had stood in the first floor drawing room and she had undertaken to furnish the house for him.

They turned together at the top of the stairs, and followed each upon the other into the big double room, Herbert trying to look composed and sophisticated. But as soon as he stepped into his new London drawing room he knew that he need not have worried. The room was perfect. It was everything that he had never before enjoyed. It was quite evident that 'our May' had in every way fulfilled her brief, and interpreted exactly what a chap wanted out of a house. The room appealed at once as being relaxed, charming, masculine, very much a gentleman's drawing room, nothing frothy or flowery about it.

First of all, centre stage and shining with its own novelty, there was the cupboard that he had always longed for. A great dark cupboard with silver side pieces. Magnificent! And – he quickly turned its big key – inside, glasses and bottles filled with all his favourite drinks. He turned to Jepson, his eyes shining with enthusiasm.

'By golly, Her Grace has done us proud, eh Jepson? Just what we both wanted, wouldn't you say?'

Jepson smiled. He had been thrilled to see the cupboard. One day, when he was a rich, retired butler, he would buy a cupboard just like it.

'It is going to save a lot of leg work, one way and another, if I may say so, sir.'

They both laughed.

'Tell you what, Jepson, to celebrate my return, why don't we have a drink together? I know it's not the form, but let us face it, this cupboard is quite something, wouldn't you say?'

'Yes, sir. I would indeed, sir. It is, if I may say so, sir, a gentleman's cupboard.'

Later, as they both stood, a little awkwardly, either side of the fireplace, Herbert lit a cigar, which he could, thank God, now he was alone in his own drawing room, and asked, purely to make conversation, and after a few appreciative puffs of the cigar, 'Oh, by the way, Jepson, who bought the house next door? I know it was sold just after I left, but I never did ask to whom. Too busy enjoying the delights of Europe: Florence, Rome, Paris, Vienna. I never thought I could stop travelling, and then one day it seemed to me that home was beckoning. I suddenly longed for the understatement of England, for its uncertain weather, for its solid decency. Something very reliable about England, you know that, Jepson?'

'Yes, sir.'

Jepson paused for a minute before continuing, because it was all really rather exciting. The former mistress of the previous king living next door, their nearest neighbour, a famous woman, and a most elegant and stylish lady by all accounts.

'Quite an exciting personage bought the house eventually, sir. On her behalf it was sold first, I believe, to a Lady Medlar, who then sold it on to the Countess.' Jepson paused. 'A beautiful lady she is too, the little I have glimpsed of her. The

Countess of Evesham, sir, is still a beautiful woman. I expect you have heard of her, sir? Quite exciting, we all think, that she is living here, in Kensington.'

There was a small choking sound and Jepson looked round at his master, momentarily alarmed. Indeed, judging from Mr Forrester's expression the news of the Countess of Evesham's living next door was, if anything, proving a little bit *too* exciting.

'Is something the matter, sir?'

'I shall have to move, Jepson. There is nothing for it, I shall have to move!'

Herbert looked wildly round his new drawing room. Just when he had found some sort of haven for himself, just when everything was boding well for him, when he had returned from abroad to home and hearth, hopes high for a comfortable future, he had to find his old enemy, the woman who had tried to seduce him, who had humiliated him beyond endurance, living cheek by jowl, breathing the same air, doubtless looking at the same view from her drawing room windows.

'If it's any comfort, sir,' Jepson told him, after some lengthy explanations, 'the Countess has hardly been known to go out. She is, as I understand it, very much an indoor person, so it may be that you will find that you never see each other from one year's end to the next.'

'I will give it three months, Jepson, that's all and at the end of that if we're not all embroiled in some fearful scandal, some dreadful shake-up ur nerves all shot to pieces, then my name is ot, and never was, Herbert Forrester.'

Jepson nodded, not really understanding, but ıen it was given to a gentleman's man to under-tand very little. A gentleman's man reacted, he almed, and he made good, but he did not attempt) understand.

'I tell you what, sir, shall I bring up Mungo, the ttle Griffon dog, to say hello to you? He's fairly ursting his buttons to make your acquaintance.'

'Very well, Jepson, but believe me, stay indoors! ou may bet on it, our neighbour will have made ouble for us within the month.'

'I hardly think so, sir.'

Herbert sighed. 'There goes a man who doesn't ıow the Countess.'

Epilogue

Daisy was visiting Augustine Medlar, althoug only briefly, and then only to make quite sure th Augustine knew, once and for all, that she, Dais could not care less if the devil himself lived ne door to her.

'Enjoying life in the land of the governes Daisy? Enjoying life in Kensington?'

'Enjoyment is far too palid a word for Augustine. I am *worshipping* life in Kensington.'

Augustine looked as she felt, startled. She cou never have imagined, not in a thousand years, th Daisy was capable of enjoying life in Kensingto although it had to be said that Daisy had nev looked better. It was quite provoking, just as t fact that Daisy's protégée had been successfu married off was torture. Following Daisy pleading with her to find a husband for M Hartley Lambert, Augustine had done her best thwart any plans that Daisy might have be harbouring for her protégée. She had spre rumours that she was not as wealthy as h been thought, she had pointed up the mothe vulgarity, she had done everything she could to make sure that Miss Hartley Lambert danced only with the oldest and most infirm of gentlemen, but now the Season had drawn to a close and it had to be said that all Augustine's efforts had come to nothing. Daisy had once more triumphed. The girl was successfully paired off. So irrepressible was her old adversary, the seducer of other people's husbands, the favourite of the Prince of Wales for so long, so undeniably imperturbable, that even Augustine had to feel a grudging admiration for her.

'Why, Daisy, I never thought that you of all people could be happy with the quiet life.'

'No, well, there it is, Augustine. One reads poetry, one walks one's dogs, one studies the designs of Italian Gardens, one plays chatty bridge with one's neighbours, all dear persons like oneself, intent on the quiet life.'

'All of them?'

Augustine felt, of a sudden, as if she had seen several pigs flying past her large, floor length windows.

'Oh yes, all of them. Without any doubt, Augustine, all, to a person, are dear, kind, sweet people. And we are all aware that at our time of life we can enjoy each other's company completely at ease with each other, none of the hurly-burly of Mayfair and its environs. None of the clamour and stridency of the fashionable world. We are, in short, *content*. Why, Mr Herbert Forrester and I have even just shared a litter of puppies. Imagine!'

'A what?'

Now the whole table seemed to swim befor
Augustine's gaze. Was it possible that Augustine
in directing Daisy to Kensington, encouraging he
to retire to a backwater, had actually helped her t
achieve some kind of middle-aged content?

She peered down the long table at her ol
friend. 'You certainly look very well,' she sai
sadly. 'You certainly look very well indeed.'

'Oh, I am blooming, Augustine, perfectl
blooming. And you should see ve puppies. M
Forrester and I are in heaven.'

'You arranged to have puppies together?'

Daisy gave her gay, rippling laugh and flappe
her napkin at Augustine, feeling full of the joys c
late summer.

'Arranged? Good gracious no, Augustine. Yo
are the person who arranges things, not me. Aft
all, you arranged for me to live next door to de
Herbert Forrester. Gracious goodness, no – on
would never arrange a marriage between a Kin
Charles and a tousle-haired Griffon Bruxello
unless one had bats in the belfry.'

What had happened was that naughty Tippe
had, at the appropriately inappropriate mome
burrowed under the hedge that surrounded o
of the more decorative turns of the new Itali
Garden and in a second, in a trice, married hers
to Mr Forrester's small, tufty-headed Griffon.
had been a hideous moment, and no throwing
water, or pulling of tails had made the slight
difference.

However, and this was where the story took a turn for the better, Herbert Forrester had been so remorseful about Mungo's behaviour, and so concerned for Tippett, sending the best vets in the land to attend the birth, besieging Daisy with flowers, and she knew not what else, that Daisy had finally had to ask him to dinner, and to visit the puppies.

It was there, in Daisy's kitchen, that they had discovered their mutual adoration of dogs. It would not be unfair to say that Herbert Forrester loved dogs as much as Queen Victoria herself. Daisy could see that straight away, and there and then she had forgiven her old enemy, just as he had seemed to forgive her.

All so long ago.

They had both agreed on that.

And now, of course, with so many dogs in common they were in and out of each other's houses, *and* the gate that was shared by both their gardens, busy with all the comings and goings.

'All my new neighbours are charming, but Herbert Forrester is more so than *any* of them. He and I are having such a pleasant time of it, Augustine. I knew you would be so happy to hear *vat.*'

Augustine Medlar was not happy to hear it at all, and she was too little the actress to be able to disguise it either.

Maintaining an innocent exterior Daisy smiled to herself, thinking of how Herbert would laugh when she gave a first-hand account of her luncheon with Augustine. Mimicking Augustine's sad face at Daisy's happy news would be hilarious.

She knew just how much Herbert would laugh, and then he would say, 'Mind if I have a cigar, now?'

Which of course Daisy would not, because ever since the Prince of Wales she had *always* enjoyed a man who enjoyed a good cigar.

'But you are both so different!' Augustine looked provoked beyond endurance.

'Quite so,' Daisy replied. And then after a tiny second she raised her glass. 'Here's to everything, Augustine, vat *makes* us all so different, and to everyone who is different from us too. Here's to life, always changing, and yet somehow remaining oddly the same. To life!'

Daisy smiled with such gaiety that even Augustine was forced to raise her glass and drink the toast.

'To life!'

THE END

The author invites you to visit her website at
www.charlottebingham.com

THE BLUE NOTE
by Charlotte Bingham

It is wartime and Miranda, little cockney orphan Ted and Roberta (Bobbie) have been evacuated to an old-fashioned household in the country. Despite the war, the children's time spent with two unmarried sisters at their rectory is idyllic and turns their underprivileged lives into something very near to heaven.

But when the local Committee for Evacuation objects to the spinsters' attempt to adopt all three children, it is Bobbie who is reluctantly sent away to grow up in very different circumstances. And before long, all three children who have come to think of themselves as a family are parted – seemingly forever.

After the war, and purely by chance, the three are united. Miranda, now a beautiful model, wonders whether she is in love with Teddy, who has become an aspiring young photographer. But Teddy can only think of her as his sister, having fallen for Bobbie, who has given her heart to the mysterious Julian during a halcyon summer by the sea. There are many intriguing complications and all hearts are destined to be broken before a dramatic conclusion can be reached.

'This wide-ranging historical love story will satisfy all of Bingham's fans' ***Sunday Mirror***

A Bantam Paperback

0553 81274 2

THE LOVE KNOT
by Charlotte Bingham

Unbeknown to three young women their paths are about to cross, and in such a way that none of their lives will remain unaltered. Beautiful Leonie, brought up in the East End by foster parents, receives a surprise visit from her wealthy godmother and is sent to work at Lady Angela Bentick's private nursing home near Buckingham Palace; Dorinda sails from France without her wastrel husband and becomes a celebrated member of London's *demi-monde;* and Mercy is saved from social ignominy by an older man with whom she falls passionately in love.

That all three determine on making their own way at a time when to be independent was to risk social ostracism, or even tragedy, is partly due to the influence each comes to have on the others' lives. The love knots that they all face in their relationships finally unravel, but not before hearts have been broken, and scandals risked.

'The author perfectly evokes the atmosphere of a bygone era . . . An entertaining Victorian romance'
Woman's Own

A Bantam Paperback

0553 50718 4